DEAD SILENT

Born above a shoe shop in the mid-1960s, Neil spent most of his childhood in Wakefield in West Yorkshire as his father pursued a career in the shoe trade. This took Neil to Bridlington in his teens, where he failed all his exams and discovered that doing nothing soon turns into long-term unemployment. Re-inventing himself, Neil returned to education in his 20s, qualified as a solicitor when he was 30, and now spends his days in the courtroom and his evenings writing crime fiction.

To find out more about Neil go to www.neilwhite.net and visit www.BookArmy.co.uk for exclusive updates.

By the same author:

Fallen Idols
Lost Souls
Last Rites

NEIL WHITE

Dead Silent

AVON

This novel is entirely a work of fiction.
The names, characters and incidents portrayed in it are
the work of the author's imagination. Any resemblance to
actual persons, living or dead, events or localities is
entirely coincidental.

AVON

A division of HarperCollins*Publishers*
77–85 Fulham Palace Road,
London W6 8JB

www.harpercollins.co.uk

A Paperback Original 2010

A catalogue record for this book is
available from the British Library

ISBN 978-1-84756-128-2

Set in Minion by Palimpsest Book Production Limited,
Grangemouth, Stirlingshire

Printed and bound in Great Britain by
Clays Ltd, St Ives plc

Mixed Sources
Product group from well-managed
forests and other controlled sources
www.fsc.org Cert no. SW-COC-001806
© 1996 Forest Stewardship Council

FSC is a non-profit international organisation established
to promote the responsible management of the world's forests.
Products carrying the FSC label are independently certified
to assure consumers that they come from forests that are managed
to meet the social, economic and ecological needs
of present and future generations.

Find out more about HarperCollins and the environment at
www.harpercollins.co.uk/green

Although my name appears on the cover, *Dead Silent* wasn't written in isolation and then sent straight to the printers. My best efforts were scrutinised by my editors at Avon, Maxine Hitchcock and Keshini Naidoo, and I am eternally grateful for the advice they gave throughout the whole process, as well as for the hard work of all those who work at Avon, especially Sammia and Kate. Without them, I wouldn't be writing these acknowledgements in my fourth book. In particular, I would like to thank my agent, Sonia Land, for giving me the opportunity to work with Avon.

My family has to bear the brunt of my writing distractions, with many evenings and weekends lost to my books, with many more lost hours still to come. It may be that they prefer it that way, but just in case they don't, I can only thank them for their patience.

The rest of you, especially the people I meet at library events and by email, thank you for making my job more interesting and for reading my books, and I look forward to meeting more of you in the future.

Neil White

To Thomas, Samuel and Joseph, as always

May 1988

Bill Hunter looked through the wrought-iron gates as he came to a halt outside Claude Gilbert's house. He wiped his forehead with his sleeve, the interior of the police car heavy with the first real promise of summer, and turned to his passenger, Paul Roach, a fresh-faced young officer with scrubbed cheeks and the swagger of youth on his side.

'Do you know why houses like this are on a hill?' Hunter said, and pointed towards the large Edwardian property, a square block of sandstone walls and white corners, roses creeping around the edges, a wide gravel drive leading to the doors at the front.

Roach didn't seem interested, responding with a shrug.

'It kept the professionals out of the smog when the mills were running,' Hunter continued. 'It was peasants like us who had to live in the valley, where the smoke from the chimneys choked us every day.'

Like Rome, Blackley had been built on seven hills, except that Blackley's majesty didn't go much beyond the terraced strips and large stone cotton mills that scarred the once-green slopes.

'The clogs and machinery are long gone, old man,' Roach said, and then he looked back to the house and smiled. 'I wouldn't mind a piece of this though.'

'What about the old-fashioned stuff, like making a differ-ence?' Hunter said.

Roach nodded at the sheen on Hunter's worn-out trousers and the scuffs on his shoes. 'You're not a great career advert,' he said.

Hunter turned off the engine and it seemed suddenly quiet, the bustle of the town centre out of earshot, just the long curve of the street in front of them, the houses bordered by ivy-covered high walls. He reached for his jacket and climbed out of the car.

Roach joined him on the pavement and looked around. 'So where has Gilbert gone?' he said.

'We won't find out standing here,' Hunter said, and he pushed at the gate, the creak from the old hinges the only sound in the street.

'Do you think they'll serve us strawberries on the lawn?' Roach said.

Hunter shook his head, and then, as the gates clanged against the supporting brick pillars, he stepped onto the gravel drive, the confetti of cherry blossom blowing against his shoes.

'What's he like, Claude Gilbert?' Roach asked.

'Depends on which Claude you mean,' Hunter said. 'The television Claude, the morning show legal expert, the media's favourite barrister – he's a real charmer.'

'And the courthouse Claude?' Roach said.

'Like a lot of them, stars in their own universe,' Hunter said. 'When you've been in the job longer, and you've been spat on and punched and uncovered sudden deaths, then maybe you'll look at lawyers' houses and wonder why they get so much when we do all the dirty work.'

'It's a great view though,' Roach replied, looking along the lawns, and when he heard Hunter grunt his disapproval, he added: 'You're a dinosaur, Bill. The miners' strike ended the class war. Do you remember them all marching back? That was the end of the revolution, so let's cut out the working-class hero stuff. Thatcher won.'

Hunter scowled as he watched Roach march towards the double doors at the front of the house.

'When were they last seen?' Roach shouted over his shoulder.

'About a week ago,' Hunter replied.

'So it could be a holiday.'

'Claude's chambers don't think so. He's halfway through an assault trial, and by disappearing they've had to abort it.'

'What, you think they've run away?'

'It depends on why they've gone,' Hunter replied. 'Bit of a gambler is Claude, so the rumours go. Maybe he's had that big loss that always comes along eventually. If Mrs Gilbert is used to all of this, the fancy furniture, the dinner parties, the cash, she's not going to settle for nothing. They could have emptied their accounts and gone somewhere.'

Roach didn't look convinced. 'House prices are rising. There'll be plenty of money tied up in this place.'

Hunter took a step back and looked up at the house. The curtains were drawn in every window. 'Maybe he got too involved in a case? Lawyers think they're immune, but they're not, and they're dealing with some real nasty people. I know judges who have been threatened, just quiet words when they're out with their wives, thinking that no one knows who they are.' He stepped forward and pressed his face against one of the stained glass panels. 'There's a few letters on the floor, so they haven't been here for a while.'

'What do we do?' Roach asked, looking around.

Hunter followed his gaze. There was someone watching them from the other side of the road, a teenager, a newspaper delivery bag on his shoulder. 'Go ask him if he knows anything.'

Roach paused for a moment, and then he shrugged and walked away. Hunter watched him until he was a few yards away, and then he rammed his elbow into the glass in the door. When Roach whirled around at the noise, Hunter shrugged and said, 'Slipped,' before he reached in and turned the Yale lock. Roach pulled a face before heading back to the house.

The pile of letters scraped along the tiled floor as Hunter pushed open the door. He pointed at the envelopes. 'See how far back the postmarks go.'

Hunter squinted as his eyes adjusted to the darkness inside. The hallway stretched ahead of them, with stairs leading upwards, the stained glass around the doors casting red and blue shadows along the wall. They both crinkled their noses. The house smelled stale.

Hunter looked into the living room to his left. Nothing unusual in there. Two sofas and a television hidden away in a wooden cabinet, crystal bowls on a dresser, nothing broken. There was a room on the other side of the hallway dominated by a long mahogany table.

'No sign of a disturbance,' he said. 'What about the letters?'

'These go back a couple of days,' Roach said, flicking through them. 'Bills and credit card statements mostly.'

Hunter went along the hall to the kitchen. It was a long room, with high sash windows looking along the garden. There was a yellow Aga and a battered oak table, and china mugs hung from hooks underneath dusty cupboards.

'They hadn't planned to leave,' Roach said. When Hunter turned around, Roach was bathed in the light of the open fridge door, holding a half-empty milk bottle. 'This is turning into yoghurt. They would have thrown it away.'

Hunter scratched his head. He ambled over to the window and looked out at the two lawns, green and lush, separated by a gravel path. There was an elaborate fountain in one corner of the garden, with a wide stone basin and a Grecian statue of a woman holding an urn, with a steel and glass summer house in the other. Hunter could see the bright fronds of plants.

Hunter looked downwards, at the floor and the walls, and then out at the garden again. He was about to say something when something drew his eye, a detail in the garden that didn't seem quite right. He looked closer, wondering what he'd seen that had grabbed his attention, his eyes working faster than his mind, when he realised that it was the lawn itself. It was flat all the way along, green and even, but there was a patch near the back wall where it looked churned up, as if soil had been newly piled up on it.

'What do you think to that?' Hunter said, before turning around to see Roach kneeling down, examining the skirting and the wall. 'What is it?'

Roach looked up, his brow furrowed, his cockiness gone. 'It looks like dried blood,' he said. 'And there's some more on the wall.'

Hunter followed his gaze; he saw it too. Just specks, and some faint brown smears on the white wall tiles, as if someone had tried to clean it away.

'What do we do?' Roach said.

Hunter pursed his lips, knowing that he was in a lawyer's home, and lawyers can make trouble.

But blood was blood.

'You can forget about your strawberries,' Hunter said, and headed for the garden. As Roach joined him, Hunter lit a cigarette and made for the path that ran between the lawns.

'Where are you going?' Roach shouted.

'Gardening,' was the reply.

Hunter walked quickly down the path, towards the disturbed patch of grass at the end of the garden. He stopped next to the soil beds beside the high garden wall, just before the path wound round towards the summer house. Hunter pointed. 'Can you see that?'

Roach looked and shrugged. 'Can I see what?'

'Soil,' Hunter replied. 'On the grass, and there on the path.' He pointed at some more dark patches. 'Someone's been doing some digging round here.'

'It's a garden,' Roach said. 'It's what people do.'

Hunter ignored him and strode onto the soil beds, dragging his foot along the ground, his face stern with concentration. Then he stopped. He looked at Roach, and then pointed downwards.

'It's looser here,' he said. 'Crumblier, less dense. And there's soil on the lawn and the path. Perhaps they thought it would be rained away, but it's been hot all week.' Hunter pointed to an old wooden shed, painted green, on the other side of the garden. 'Get some spades.'

Roach looked aghast. 'We can't rip up a barrister's house just because we've found some old blood.'

'Is that because he's a barrister?'

'Yes,' Roach answered, exasperated, 'because he can make trouble for us if we get it wrong.'

Hunter drew on his cigarette. 'We can wait for the rest of the squad to arrive, and they can get the excavators in here because you saw spilled gravy.'

Roach looked uncertain.

'Or we could dig a hole and then fill it back in again,' Hunter said.

Roach waved his hand to show that he had relented. 'Just the flower bed,' he said, his voice wary, and then he walked over to the shed. When he returned, he was holding two spades. He rejoined Hunter by the soil bed and said, 'Someone's been ripping that shed apart.'

'What do you mean?'

'Just that,' Roach replied. 'All the slats from the back are gone.'

'We'll dig first before we worry about vandals,' Hunter said, and thrust the spade into the dirt.

It was hot work: after twenty minutes of digging their shirts were soaked and they had wiped dirty sweat trails across their foreheads. They were about two feet down when Roach cried out in disgust, 'What the fuck is all that?'

Hunter looked down. There was movement in the soil. Flies started to appear out of the dirt, their tiny wings making a soft hum around Hunter's head. Roach scraped again at the soil, and then Hunter heard the soft thud of spade on wood. He looked at Roach and saw that he had gone pale, his sleeve over his mouth.

'It stinks,' Roach muttered, and that's when Hunter caught the stench; it was one he recognised, like gone-off meat, beef left on a warm shelf.

Hunter grimaced and started to move the soil from whatever it was that Roach's spade had hit. Another swarm of flies buzzed around Hunter's spade; as the soil was removed, the thudding sounds from his spade became louder, acquiring an echo. They looked at each other, both sensing that they were about to find something they didn't want to see.

When they had finished, Roach climbed out of the hole and looked down. 'It's the same wood as on the shed,' he said.

Hunter took a deep breath. Their digging had exposed wooden planks, painted green, wedged into the hole. The planks had supported the soil, and the hollow sounds that came from beneath told Hunter that there was a cavity.

'Who's going to look first?' Roach asked.

'It might be a dog,' Hunter said.

Roach shook his head. 'That's more than a dog.'

Hunter grimaced and then lay down on his chest so that he could reach into the hole. He moved the remnants of dirt from the end of the planks with his fingers, breathing through his mouth all the time to avoid the stink of whatever was in there and shaking his head to swat away the flies. He managed to ease his fingers under one of the pieces of wood and pulled at it, until he felt it move and was able to shove it to one side. Sunlight streamed into the hole and he heard Roach step away quickly before his lunch splashed onto the path nearby. Hunter clenched his jaw and swallowed hard, the smell making him gag.

The sunlight caught a body, naked, a woman with long dark hair.

Hunter pulled at another plank, and then one more, laying them on the lawn next to the hole, and then he stood up, taking deep breaths.

Roach turned back to the hole. 'Fuck me,' he whispered, wiping his mouth.

In the hole was a woman, crammed into the space, curled up on her side, her face green, her dark hair over her face, with blood on her shoulders and dirt on her bare legs. The hole was small, barely enough space to contain her, not enough room to stretch out.

As Hunter looked, he noticed something else. He lay on the floor again, just to have a closer look, and then he struggled to his feet. He looked at Roach. 'It's worse than that,' he said, his face pale.

'How can it be worse?' Roach said.

'Look at her hands,' Hunter said, his face ashen. 'Can you see her fingers, all bloodied and shredded?'

8

Roach didn't answer, quiet now.

Hunter pulled the boards towards them and turned them over. 'Look at the underside.' Roach looked. 'There are scratchmarks.'

'I see them,' replied Roach.

Hunter turned to Roach. 'Do you know what that means?'

Roach nodded slowly, his face pale too.

'She was buried alive.'

Chapter One – Present Day

Standing at the door, I stretched and gazed at the view outside my cottage. Clear skies and rolling Lancashire fields. I could see the grey of Turners Fold in the valley below me, but the sunlight turned the tired old cotton town into quaint Victoriana, the canal twinkling soft blue, bringing the summer barges from nearby Blackley as it wound its way towards Yorkshire.

Turners Fold was my home, had always been that way – or so it seemed. I'd spent a few years in London as a reporter at one of the nationals, a small-town boy lost in the bright lights, but home kept calling me, and so when the rush of the city wore me down, I headed back north. I used to enjoy walking the London streets, feeling the bump of the crowd, just another anonymous face, but the excitement faded in the end. It didn't take me long to pick up the northern rhythms again, the slower pace, the bluntness of the people, the lack of any real noise. And I liked it that way. It seemed simpler somehow, not as much of a race.

The summers made the move worthwhile. The heat didn't hang between the buildings like it did in London, trapped by exhaust fumes, the only respite being a trip to a park, packed out by tourists.

The tourists don't visit Turners Fold, so it felt like I had the hills to myself, a private view of gentle slopes and snaking ribbons of drystone walls, the town just a blip in the landscape.

But it has character, this tough little town of millstone grit. My mind flashed back to the London rush, the wrestle onto the underground, and I smiled as the breeze ruffled my hair and I felt the first warmth of the day, ready for a perfect June afternoon. I heard a noise behind me, the shuffle of slippers on the stone step. I didn't need to look round. I felt sleepy lips brush my neck as Laura wrapped her arms around my waist.

'I thought you were staying in bed,' I said.

'I want to take Bobby to school,' she replied, her voice hoarse from sleep. 'Early shift next week, so I won't get a chance then, and I need to start revising.'

'Sergeant McGanity. It has a good ring to it,' I said.

'But I need to get through the exams first,' she said. 'What are you doing, Jack?'

'Just enjoying the view.'

Laura rested her head on my shoulder and let her hair fall onto my chest. She had grown it over the winter, dark and sleek, past her shoulders now. I looked down and smiled. Cotton pyjamas and fluffy slippers.

'What about later?' she asked.

'I'm not sure,' I replied. 'I might take a look at the coroner's court, see if there's an inquest.'

'Morbid,' she said, and gave me a playful squeeze.

'Where there's grief, there's news,' I said. 'And the Crawler has been quiet as well, so the paper needs to be filled somehow.'

Laura grimaced at that. Blackley had been plagued for a couple of years by a peeping Tom, loitering outside houses in a balaclava, taking photographs. Some thought that he had even gone into people's homes. There had been no attack yet, but everyone knew it was just a matter of time, and so the local press had attached a tag and criticised the police. The name made for great headlines, and sales went up whenever his name went on display.

'He has lean patches,' Laura said. 'The surveillance must take time.'

'So no suspect yet?'

Laura gave me a jab in the ribs. 'You know I wouldn't tell you anyway.'

I turned around, moved her hair from her face and kissed her, tasting sleep on her lips, stale and warm. 'I hate a discreet copper.'

Laura's green eyes shone up at me, her dimples flickering in her cheeks. 'I've learnt to avoid trouble, because it follows you around,' she said, and then she slipped out from under my arm to go back into the house.

I listened as she grabbed Bobby when he skipped past, his yelp turning to a giggle. He was seven now, getting taller, his face longer, the nursery cheeks gone. It seemed like the morning was just about perfect. We'd settled for drifting along, now the buzz of new love had worn off, and there were more carefree mornings like this: Laura happy, Bobby laughing. He was Laura's son from her now-defunct marriage, but he was starting to feel like my own, and I knew how much he brightened up the house, except for those fortnightly trips to see his father, when the house seemed too quiet.

My thoughts drifted back to work. I'm a freelance reporter, and I write the court stories, because crime keeps the local newspaper happy. People like to know what other people are doing.

But if I was going to get the stories, I knew I had to go

to court. It was enthusiasm I was lacking, not work, because it was harder to get paid these days. The recession had hit the local papers hard, with estate agents and car showrooms no longer paying for the double-page adverts and people increasingly turning to the internet. The paper needed me to fill the pages, but wanted to pay less and less for each story, and so it felt like I had to run faster just to stay in the same place.

I turned to go inside and was about to shut the door, when I heard a noise. I paused and listened. It was the steady *click-click* of high heels.

I was curious. There were no other houses near mine, and the shoes didn't sound like they were made for walking. Unexpected visitors made me wary. Working the crime stories can upset people – names spread through the local rag, reputations ruined. The truth doesn't matter when court hearings are written up. The only thing that matters is whether someone in court said it.

The clicks got closer, and then she appeared in the gateway in front of me.

She was middle aged, bingo-blonde, dressed in a long, black leather coat, too hot for the weather, and high-heeled ankle boots.

'You look like you're a long way from wherever you need to be,' I said.

She took a few deep breaths, the hill climb taking it out of her, her hands on her knees. She stubbed out a cigarette on the floor.

'There are no buses up here,' she said, and then she straightened herself. Her breasts tried to burst out of her jumper, her cleavage ravaged by lines and too much sun, and her thighs were squeezed into a strip of cloth three decades too young for her.

Before I could say anything, she looked at me and asked, 'Are you Jack Garrett?' Her accent was local, but it sounded like she was trying to soften it.

'You've come to my door,' I replied, wary. 'You go first.'

She paused at first, seemed edgy, and then she said, 'My name is Susie Bingham, and I'm looking for Jack Garrett.'

'Why?'

'I've got a story for him.'

I nodded politely, but I wasn't excited yet. The promise of hot news was the line I heard most, but usually it turned out to be some neighbour dispute, or a problem with a boss, someone using the press to win a private fight. Sex, violence and fame sell the nationals, the papers wanting the headline, the grabline, not the story. Local papers are different. Delayed roadworks and court stories fill those pages.

But I had learnt one other thing: it pays to listen first before I turn people away, because just as many people don't realise how good a story can be, who see a rough-cut diamond as cheap quartz.

I opened the door and stepped aside. 'Come in.'

Susie nodded and then clomped past.

Bobby went quiet as Susie entered, suddenly shy. As I followed her in, I nodded towards the stairs. 'Can you tell Mummy I've got a visitor?' As Bobby trotted off on his errand, I gestured for Susie to sit down.

She put her coat onto the back of the sofa. 'I like your house,' she said, looking around. 'I've always wanted a house like this. Cosy and dark.'

I smiled to show that I knew what she meant. The windows to the cottage were small, like jail views, the sunlight not penetrating far into the room, only enough to catch the dust-swirls and light up the table in the corner where I write up my stories.

'We like it,' I said, putting a pad of paper on my knee, a pen in my hand. 'And if we're talking home life, where do you live?'

'Just a small flat in Blackley,' she said. 'Nothing special.' She went to get another cigarette out of her packet, and I noticed a tremble to her fingers. I gave a small shake of my head, and so she put the cigarette away. 'I'm sorry,' she said. 'I didn't mean to be rude, but I'm a bit nervous.'

'That's okay,' I said. 'Just tell me why you're here.'

Susie smiled and looked embarrassed. The powder on her face creased and, as she showed her teeth, I saw a smudge of pink lipstick on the yellowed enamel. I'd guessed Susie's age at over sixty when she'd first arrived, but she seemed younger now that she was out of the sunlight. She sat forward and put her bag on her knee. She looked like she was unsure how to start. I raised my eyebrows. *Just say it*, that was the hint.

'It's about Claude Gilbert,' she blurted out.

I opened my mouth to say something, and then I stopped. I looked at her. She didn't laugh or give any hint that it was a joke.

'I've met Claude Gilbert,' she said.

'*The* Claude Gilbert?' I asked, and I couldn't stop the smile.

Susie nodded, and her hands tightened around the handles on her handbag. 'You don't look like you believe me.'

And I didn't.

Blackley was famous for three things: cotton, football, and for being the home of Claude Gilbert, a barrister and part-time television pundit who murdered his pregnant wife and then disappeared. It was the way he did it that caught the public imagination: a blow to the head and then buried alive.

'Claude Gilbert? I haven't heard that name in a while,' I said, and then I tried to let her down gently. 'There are Claude

Gilbert sightings all the time. And do you know what the tabloids do with them? They store them, that's what, just waiting for the quiet news days, when a false sighting will fill a page, the same old speculation trotted out. Newspaper offices are full of stories like that, guaranteed headlines, most of it padding. Ex-girlfriends of Ian Huntley, old lodgers of Fred West, all just waiting for the newspaper rainy day.'

'But this isn't just a sighting,' she said, frustration creeping into her voice. 'This is a message from him.'

'A message?'

She nodded.

That surprised me. *From* Claude Gilbert? I looked at her, saw the blush to her cheeks. I wasn't sure if it was shame or the walk up the hill. The Claude Gilbert story attracted attention-seekers, those after the front-page spot, but Susie seemed different. Most people thought Claude was dead, but no one really knew for sure. If he was alive, he had to come out eventually or be caught. And anyway, perhaps the truth didn't matter as much with the Claude Gilbert story. A good hoax sighting will still fill half a page somewhere, even if it was only in one of the weekly gossip magazines.

'Wait there,' I said, and shot off to get my voice recorder.

Chapter Two

Mike Dobson peered into the bathroom, the door slightly ajar. The shower had been running for a long time, and he could see Mary through the steam, her head hanging down under the jets, her shoulders slumped, the water running down her body until it streamed from the ends of her fingers.

He looked away quickly, not wanting to be caught, and leant back against the door frame. He closed his eyes and took a deep breath. He glanced towards the bed, too large, cold and empty. Was middle-age meant to be this lonely?

But he fought the feeling, tried not to think about it. He knew it would end like it always did: a drive to the back streets, always looking out for the police, then over in an instant, a grope in his back seat, the crinkle of the condom, then quick release; forty pounds gone and just the shameful churn in his stomach as a reminder.

His wife must have sensed his presence, because she shouted out: 'Close the door.'

He clicked it shut and then returned to the large mirror in the bedroom, a mock-gothic oval. There was a spotlight over it and he stepped back to button his shirt, a white collar over red pinstripe, and put on his tie, not fond of what he saw in the glare. His cheeks were sagging into jowls and the lines around his eyes no longer disappeared when he stopped smiling. He flicked at his hair. It was creeping backwards, showing more forehead than a year ago, and some more colour was needed – the grey roots were showing through.

He looked towards the window as the water stopped and waited for the bathroom door to open. He could see the houses just outside his cul-de-sac, local authority housing, dark red brick and double-glazing, most of the gardens overgrown, with beaten-up cars parked outside and a satellite dish on every house. He had grown up on that estate, but it had been different back then. He wasn't sure when it had changed. Maybe the eighties, when a generation had got left behind and had to watch as everyone else got richer.

Mike enjoyed the view normally. His house was different, a large newbuild, five bedrooms, the showhome of an estate built on the site of a former warehouse, but they'd had no children, and so four of the bedrooms were either empty or used for storage.

The bathroom door opened. Mary appeared, a large towel wrapped around her body, her face flushed, her hair flat and darkened by the water. She looked down as she walked over to the dresser and started to rummage through her drawers, looking for underwear.

'Don't watch me,' she said, not looking at him.

'I'm not watching.'

'You do,' she said, her voice flat, emotionless. 'You do it all the time.'

He felt the burn of his cheeks. She had made him feel dirty again. 'I'm going downstairs,' he said.

She looked at the floor, her hands still, her body tense, and he could tell that she was waiting for him to leave the room.

'I'll make you breakfast,' he said.

20

Mary shook her head. 'I've set the table already. I'll eat when you've gone.'

Mike took a deep breath and left the bedroom.

The house was quiet as he walked downstairs. There was a window open and the curtains fluttered as he walked into the living room. Pristine cream carpets, lilies in vases, pale-coloured potpourri in a white dish. The breakfast table was immaculate, as always, with a jug of juice in the centre of the table, cereal in plastic containers and napkins in silver rings; his dining room looked like a seaside guest house. He heard a noise outside and saw a group of smiling children going to school, their mothers exchanging small talk or pushing small toddlers in prams. His house seemed suddenly quiet and empty.

He checked his watch. His first appointment was getting closer. What would Mary do? Another empty day. It had been easier when they were younger, clinging to the hope of children, a family, but that had faded as each month brought bad news. As they'd got older, all her friends had had children and built lives of their own. But they had remained as they were and every day the house seemed to get a little quieter. How had his life got to this?

But he knew why. It seemed like it all came back to that day, when everything had changed for him.

Don't think about it, he said to himself. He closed his eyes for a moment as the memories filtered back, the familiar kick to the stomach, the reminder. Then he thought he saw her, just for a second, like someone disappearing round a corner. A quick flick of her hair, and that laugh, muffled, her hand over her mouth, like she had been caught out, her delight in her eyes.

He opened his eyes and looked down at his hands. His fingers had bunched up into a fist, just as they always did when he thought of her.

21

He shook his head, angry with himself. He reached for his briefcase; it was by the front door, as always, next to the samples of PVC guttering. Another day of persuasion ahead of him, of sales patter and tricks.

Mike faltered when he saw someone approach his front door. He felt that rush of blood, part fear, part relief, and he thought he heard a giggle, and turned to see the flick of brunette hair disappear just out of sight. He peered through the glass pane and saw a blue shirt. His heartbeat slowed down. Unexpected visitors always made him nervous, never sure if the moment he dreaded had just arrived: the heavy knock of the police, the cold metal of the cuffs around his wrists.

It wasn't that. It was just a parcel, some ornament for the house Mary had ordered. He smiled his thanks and took the parcel, his hand trembling, his sweat leaving fingermarks on the cardboard.

He checked his watch. It was time to go.

Chapter Three

I bolted up the stairs to fetch my voice recorder. I had started to write a novel, a modern-day tale about life and love's lost chances, but I had got only as far as the first two chapters before I realised that I didn't know what to write next. The voice recorder was next to my bed for the inspiration that would come in the middle of the night, but it had been elusive so far.

Laura stopped drying her hair when I went in. 'Who is it?' she asked.

'Someone with a story,' I said.

'We've all got a story.'

'This one's a little different,' I replied.

Laura gave me a suspicious look, and then turned the hairdryer back on. I got the impression that she didn't want to hear any more.

I picked up the voice recorder and went back downstairs. Susie was standing by the oak sideboard underneath one of the windows, looking at our family photographs.

'Your boy is cute,' she said.

I smiled. 'He gets his good looks from his mother,' I replied, skirting the issue. I waved the voice recorder. 'I'm ready for your story.'

Susie sat down again, her bag going on the seat next to her. 'Where do you want me to start?'

'The beginning,' I said. 'Tell me how you know Claude Gilbert.'

Susie blushed slightly. 'I'm an ex-girlfriend of his.'

That surprised me. I knew some of the background to Claude Gilbert's story, most people did. He was local legal aristocracy, with a judge for a father and two lawyers for sisters. He had started to make forays into television, invited onto discussion shows back when there were actual discussions – so different to the American imitations of today, where people with no morals fight about morality. But it was his wife's death and his disappearance that turned him into headline news: the missing top lawyer, the old school cad, dashing good looks and a touch of cut glass about his accent. Susie struck me as too different to Gilbert, too earthy somehow.

'Were you his girlfriend before or after his wedding?' I said.

Susie looked away. 'It wasn't like that.'

That meant after, I thought to myself. And I'd heard about Gilbert, read the rumours, the tabloid gossip.

'Let me guess,' I said. 'You were a law clerk.'

'How did you know?' she asked, gazing back at me in surprise.

'An educated guess,' I said, and gave her a rueful smile. 'What legal experience did you have?'

'Not much. I used to be one of the typists.'

'And don't tell me: you had the best legs.'

'No, that's not fair, I worked hard,' Susie replied, offended.

'I've hung around enough Crown Courts to know how it works,' I said. 'The local law firms employ glamorous young women to carry the file and bill by the hour, just to pat the hands of criminals and soften the blows with a sweet smile.'

'You make it sound dirty.'

I shook my head. 'It's good marketing, that's all, and don't knock it. Do you think your social life would have been what it was if you had stayed in the typing pool? Would you have been wined and dined by the barristers, invited to the chambers parties or taken to the best wine bars, just as a small thank you for the work?'

'It was more than marketing,' she said, blushing. 'We got on, Claude and me.'

'Or maybe he was just touting for work, or flirting, or maybe even a mix of the two?'

Susie looked down, deflated. 'You're not interested, I can tell.'

'Oh, I'm interested all right,' I said, smiling. 'You say you've got a message from Claude Gilbert. Well, that's one out of the blue and so if you want me to write a story about it, I have to prove that it was from him, and not from some chancer hoping for a quick pound. The first question people will ask is why the message comes through you, and so how well you knew him is part of the story. Someone who once shared drunken fumbles at chambers parties is not enough. Were you ever a couple, a proper couple, seen out together, things like that?'

Susie shook her head slowly, and when she looked back up again, she seemed embarrassed. 'You guessed right, it was when he was married. Before, you know, Nancy was found. We saw each other when we could, but it was hard. He was a busy man.'

'And a married one,' I said.

Susie reached into her bag. 'Here,' she said, and thrust an old photograph towards me. 'That's me with Claude.'

The photograph was faded, and a white line ran across one corner where it had been folded over, but it was easy to recognise Susie. The woman in front of me was just a worn-down version of the one in the picture, now with redness to her eyes and the blush of broken veins in her cheeks. The photograph had been taken in a nightclub or wine bar, to judge by the purple neon strips at the top of the picture. The man next to her was unmistakably Claude Gilbert, the handsome face that had adorned a thousand front pages, the eighties-styled thick locks that flowed in dark waves from his parting to his collar. His arm was around Susie's shoulders, his jacket pulled to one side to reveal the bright red braces over the brilliant white shirt. He leered towards the camera, a cigarette wedged into his grin.

'Okay, so you met him once,' I said. 'He was on television. How do I know that this isn't just a shot you took when you were out one night, a souvenir of meeting a star?'

'You don't,' Susie replied. 'All you can do is trust me. I know where Claude Gilbert is, and he wants to come home.'

Wants to come home. My mind saw the front pages for a moment, the bold print under the red banner of whichever national wrote the biggest cheque. I exhaled and tapped the photograph on my knee.

'So, are you interested?' she asked.

I flashed my best smile. 'Of course I'm interested,' I said. 'It's the story of the year, if it's true.'

Susie looked happier with that, and she settled back in the sofa.

'But I need to know more,' I said. 'Where has he been, and where is he now?'

'London.'

'That's not very specific. How long have you been in contact with him?'

'A few months,' Susie said. 'I saw him, purely by chance, and since then, we've sort of rekindled things, and I've persuaded him to come forward.'

26

I watched her, tried to detect whether I was being conned. I let the silence hang, but there was no response from Susie. Liars fill the gaps to persuade the listener of the truth. Susie sat there and looked at me, waiting for my next question.

'But why does he want to use me to come forward?' I asked.

'Because if he turns up at a police station, they'll lock him up.'

'They still will,' I said. 'The paper won't shield him.'

'Claude told me that any jury will have convicted him before he stands trial, because there have been twenty years of lies told about his case. He wants to give his version first, to make people wonder about his guilt. It will go in the paper on the day he surrenders himself, that's the deal. If not, he won't come forward.'

I thought about that and saw how it made sense. If he could have his trial with the doubt already there, he might have a chance. But I wasn't interested in the trial. I wanted the story before his arrest. Someone else could cover the court case.

'So tell me your story then,' I prompted.

Susie nodded and straightened her skirt. 'I saw him in London, like I said. I had been to see an old friend. She lives in Brighton, so we meet up in London. We went to a show, the usual stuff. I went down on the bus and I was waiting to come home, just hanging around Victoria coach station, having a smoke, when I saw him.'

'How could you be sure it was Claude Gilbert?' I said. 'He's been on the run for more than twenty years, and there are a lot of people in London. It takes just one to recognise him and his life is over.'

'One did,' she said. 'Me. But no one else would have recognised him, or at least only someone who really knew him.

It was just the way he walked, sort of upright, as if he thought the whole street should step to one side.' Susie must have seen the doubt in my eyes. 'And it wasn't just his walk,' she added quickly.

'What else?'

'Oh, it was just everything. I knew Claude Gilbert well, and I knew it was him.' Susie thought for a moment. 'He does look a lot different though. He's fat now, has a bushy beard, all grey, with big glasses, and his hair is long and wild, pulled into a ponytail.'

'Not quite the dashing gent he used to be?'

Susie laughed. 'No, not really, but I knew it was him straight away. I shouted "Gilly", because that's what I used to call him. No one else called him Gilly, and when I shouted it, he looked straight at me, recognised me straight off. He looked shocked, even scared, and just as I started walking towards him, he marched off really quickly.'

'Did you think about calling the police?' I said.

Susie looked less comfortable and shifted around on the sofa. 'Why would I do that?'

'So they could catch him. He's a murderer on the run.'

Susie flashed me a thin smile. 'He didn't do it,' she said quietly. 'The murder, I mean.'

'Because he told you? He's had more than twenty years to get his story straight.'

'Because I know him, that's all,' she said. 'I know what people thought of him – that he was a show-off – but in private he was a gentle man, tender, not the person he was in public. He couldn't have murdered his wife.'

'But he lied to her by sleeping with you,' I said, before I could stop myself.

'Being an old flirt doesn't make him a murderer,' she said tersely, her face flushing quickly. 'It wasn't like that anyway.'

'What was it like?'

She sighed, and I saw regret in her eyes.

'He dazzled me, I suppose,' she said. 'He took me to places I couldn't afford, wouldn't think about going to. I was flattered. People like Claude Gilbert didn't go out with people like me. He went to public school and spoke properly. I was just a silly girl from Blackley who went to the local comp and who wanted to be a typist.'

'But he was married.'

'Yes, he was,' she replied, her voice stronger now, 'and so, yes, he lied to his wife. He told me he loved me, and I suppose that was a lie too, back then. But that doesn't make him a killer.'

'Was it going on when his wife was killed?'

Susie shook her head. 'It had ended a few months before.'

'And were you a couple for long?'

'Just a few weeks.'

'Were there others for Claude?'

Susie looked down. 'Yes, a few. I didn't know back then, but he's told me about them now.' She took a deep breath and looked back up again. 'This is why I trust him,' she said. 'He's being honest now, because he wants to get his life back.'

I thought about what she said, how she was so certain. I heard Laura's hairdryer switch off upstairs, Bobby's chatter filling the gap.

I looked back at Susie. 'There's a flaw to your thinking.'

'Why?'

'Because if he didn't do it, why did he run?' I said. 'Some people think he was killed as well, buried somewhere and they just haven't found the body. That's the only scenario that doesn't make him a killer. But if he is alive, then he ran, and he made sure he wasn't found again. That, in most people's eyes, makes him guilty.'

'I can only tell you what I know, Mr Garrett,' Susie said. 'He is alive, I have met him, and he wants to come home.'

I paused to pull at my lip, just a way of hiding my excitement. But I knew not to get excited. This could be a con-trick, or a delusion.

'I'm not asking you anything the papers won't ask,' I said. 'Claude Gilbert gets more sightings than Bigfoot, but he still hasn't been caught. Whoever runs the exclusive will have their rival papers mocking the story.'

'If Claude comes forward, there'll be no mocking,' Susie said.

I couldn't disagree with that.

'So, until I turned up today, what do you think had happened to him?' Susie asked.

I thought back through the stories I'd read, the debunked sightings, the endless speculation. 'The smart money says that he is living in some exotic country, protected by powerful friends, but people always prefer the exciting versions. That's why we get rumours about shadowy men on grassy knolls, or secret agents killing princesses in Parisian road tunnels. He hit his pregnant wife and buried her in the garden, alive. He was a criminal lawyer, and so he knew what he faced if he was caught. He emptied his bank account and he ran.'

'But what if I'm telling the truth, that he didn't kill Nancy?'

I leant forward. 'To be honest with you, it doesn't make a damn jot of difference.' When she looked surprised, I added, 'Whatever Claude says, an editor will shape it into ifs and maybes, just to protect the paper, because that's the editor's job. Mine will simply be to write the story.'

'So you *will* write the story?' she asked, her eyes brightening for a moment.

I felt the smile creep onto my face, couldn't stop it. 'Provided that your story with Claude Gilbert comes out too,' I said. 'Full disclosure. Everything about your relationship.'

'But I thought it would all be about Claude,' she said, suddenly wary. 'Everyone will hate me. I was sleeping with a murdered woman's husband.'

'Full story or no story,' I replied. 'You've told me that Claude Gilbert wants to come out of hiding. But what if he chokes and disappears, or if it turns out that I'm being conned, that this person isn't Claude Gilbert? You're my back-up story, and I'm not going into this without one.'

Susie put her bag back onto her knees and gripped the handles as she thought about it, then she slowly nodded her agreement.

'Good,' I said. 'We'll talk in more detail now.'

'And then what?'

'By the sound of it, we do whatever Claude wants us to do.'

Susie was about to say something when she looked towards the stairs. As I looked around, I saw that Laura had come into the room. Bobby stood behind her, uncertain.

Susie gave Laura a nervous smile. 'Hello,' she said. 'I'm sorry for coming so early.'

Laura smiled back. 'It's okay. Are you here with a story?'

Susie leant forward and was about to say something when she caught my small shake of the head, a warning not to say anything. She looked troubled for a moment, but then she sat back and remained silent.

Laura glanced at me curiously as Bobby ran across the room, pulling on his school coat and grabbing his bag.

'I'm taking him to school, Jack. I won't be long.'

I waved as they went, and when we were alone in the house once more, Susie looked at me and asked, 'Do you keep secrets from her?'

31

'Don't you think I should keep this secret, for your benefit?'

Susie thought about that, and then she nodded her agreement.

My motive wasn't to protect Susie though. It was to protect Laura, because she is a police officer, a damn good one, honourable and honest. If she heard the story, she would see it as her duty to pass it on. And what if Susie was lying? It would make Laura look stupid.

But, as I looked at Susie and took in the determination in her eyes, I was starting to believe her, and I felt a tremble of excitement at the prospect of the story.

Chapter Four

Susie refused my offer of a lift back to Blackley, and so I took her into Turners Fold to catch her bus. As I watched her clatter along the pavement in her heels, a freshly-lit cigarette glowing in her fingers, walking into what counted as rush hour around here – pensioners shuffling to the post office and young mothers meandering home after the school run – I could tell that the big meet-up was going to be on her and Claude Gilbert's terms. I wasn't happy about that, but sometimes you've just got to roll with the early blows, because in the end the story will come out on *my* terms.

Once Susie was out of sight, I dialled the number of an old friend, Tony Davies. He had been my mentor when I was a young reporter on *The Valley Post*, at the start of my career before the bright London lights pulled me in, and was now seeing out his days writing features for the weekend edition.

'I need help on something,' I said when he answered. 'But I need to keep this quiet. Can you come to me? I'm outside. It won't take long.'

'Are you still in that red Stag?'

I looked at the dashboard. A 1973 Triumph Stag in Calypso Red. Nothing special in the history of cars, but it had once been my father's pride and joy, the sports car for the working man. 'For now,' I said.

Tony's phone went dead. I watched the people go by and waited for him to appear.

Turners Fold isn't large, just a collection of terraced streets and old mill buildings, some derelict, some converted into business units, disused chimneys pointing out of the valley. The town is cut in half by a canal and criss-crossed by metal bridges, and the predominant colour of the town is grey, built from millstone grit blocks, the modern shop fronts squeezed into buildings designed for Victorian England, when the town had hummed to the sound of cotton and was smothered in smoke, the air clean only when the mills shut down for a week in summer and the railway took everyone to the coast.

But it was where I grew up, for better or worse, the town that gave me flattened vowels and a dose of northern cynicism. It seemed to me that Turners Fold deserved better than its lot, its life and character crumbling year by year, because it seemed like the only way to succeed was to leave. Just for a moment, I sensed the shadow of my father. He'd been a policeman in Turners Fold before he died, and he had walked these streets, known everybody's name, or so it had seemed. What would he have made of Susie Bingham? Not much, was my guess. He had been absorbed by my mother, who was all curls and dark eyes, a natural beauty – although I have to fight to keep that memory, her final year tainted by the cancer that took her away.

I had been back in Turners Fold a couple of years now, but I didn't feel rooted there. Sometimes I looked for old faces whenever I was in town, old school friends or sweethearts, just to find out where they had gone with their lives, but it seemed like most of the people I saw were just worn down and wondering why their lives had turned out like they had. Then I saw Tony, a shuffle to his walk and a shiny pink scalp heading out of the *Post* building. He saw me and waved. I leant across the passenger seat to let him in.

'You're wearing a jumper, for Christ's sake,' I said to him. 'It's a bloody heatwave.'

'Fashion is all about consistency,' he replied, grinning, showing his buckled front teeth, the result of a bad rugby tackle many years before. 'Like you, in this car. If you're trying to remain incognito, this car isn't the best way.'

'My father cherished this car,' I said.

'I'm sorry, Jack, I didn't mean—'

'Don't worry,' I interrupted, smiling. 'I'm thinking of getting rid of it anyway.'

'Why?'

'I want someone to look after it properly, like he did. A Sunday polish, a regular service. I don't do that.' I tapped the dashboard. 'I keep it because it was my father's car, but then I think what he would say if he could see how I drive it, how I don't wash it enough.'

'So what are you going to do?'

'I'm going to sell it to someone who'll treasure it like my father treasured it. That's what he would have wanted.'

Tony nodded quietly to himself. He had been good friends with my father and I knew that Tony still missed him.

'So, what can I do for you?' he asked eventually.

'Claude Gilbert,' I said simply.

He flashed me a look, part amusement, part curiosity. 'What about him?'

'If I want to find out more about him, who would I speak to?'

'You're two years too late with this,' he said. 'We did a special on the twentieth anniversary a couple of years ago.'

'Maybe it deserves another run out.'

35

He looked at me, surprised. Then his eyes narrowed. 'You've got an angle on this,' he said, his tone suspicious.

'There's always a new angle.'

He shook his head. 'I know you, Jack. I trained you, remember? You don't chase fairy tales.'

'I can't tell you,' I said. 'Not yet anyway. I just want to check it out first.'

He considered me for a moment, ran his finger along his lip. 'All right,' he said eventually. 'If you really are looking into it, there's only one man to speak to: Bill Hunter. He was the plod who found the body, but he's retired now.'

'Still living the case?' I queried.

Tony grinned. 'You can see it in his eyes that it's the one case that still keeps him awake. He follows it like a religion, keeps every piece written about it, from hoax sightings to alternative theories. He's not Claude's biggest fan.'

'The one that got away?'

'Something like that.'

'Where will I find him?'

Tony scribbled down an address. 'But try the allotment plot just behind your old school first. He's always there. We used it for the photoshoot a couple of years ago. You know, retired policeman tending his plot. And of course, the digging reference was subtle too.'

'You reckon?' I said.

'There's nothing new, you know that, don't you?' Tony said. 'We rehashed everything for the anniversary, so I know the *Post* won't be interested.'

I looked towards the *Post* building. 'Is that place still surviving?'

Tony pulled a face. 'Not really. The internet is killing us. There are rumours that we're going to be taken over by one of the big groups, and we'll just turn out the free papers from there.'

'You deserve better than that,' I said. 'You're a proper journalist. You taught me my trade.'

'And I've done everything,' he replied, 'and so it's hard to get excited any more. I'm just looking forward to retirement.'

'How's Eleanor?'

'*Not* looking forward to my retirement,' he answered with a chuckle, and then he reached for the door handle. 'If you need any help, Jack, call me. Maybe there's time for one last crack at being a proper journo, but I won't hold my breath.'

I smiled. 'Will do. Take care.'

I looked down at the piece of paper with Bill Hunter's details on, and then looked up to see Tony disappear into the *Post* building. I smiled to myself. Would the Claude Gilbert case stop me from ending up like Tony, churning out fillers for the local paper?

I was whistling to myself as I turned the engine over and pointed the Stag towards Blackley.

Chapter Five

Mike Dobson faltered as the customer leant towards him to place a cup of coffee on the table. It was the scent of Chanel No. 5, an air of sweet flowers that took him by surprise, rushed him back to more than twenty years earlier, to *her* smell, the faded Chanel, and those moments together, her hair over her face, her eyes closed, her nails dug deep into his chest. Then he grimaced as the images changed, became slashed with red, over her face, in her hair, splashed onto his hand.

He closed his eyes. He could train himself not to think about it, to live a normal life, but then a perfume would suddenly send him back, or the scent of lavender in bloom, heady and filled with summer.

'Excuse me,' said a distant voice, breaking into his thoughts.

Mike opened his eyes quickly and saw his customer. She looked concerned.

'Are you all right?' she asked.

He forced an apologetic smile. 'I'm sorry. Just a spot of toothache, that's all,' and he gestured towards his cheek and laughed nervously.

She winced. 'That's not nice. We can do this another time, if you don't feel right.'

He shook his head. 'No, it's fine,' he said. He took a deep breath. *Switch on*, he told himself. 'Like my manager said, we can go half-price if you sign up today. It's a special offer that ends tonight, so you really need to make a decision today.'

'But I don't know,' she said. 'It seems such a lot of money for something so . . .' She searched for the right word as she nodded towards the sample next to him, a cross-section of white PVC fascia to replace the wooden boards that lined the roof edges.

'Unglamorous?' he offered, and when she smiled, he added, 'There's nothing glamorous about damp getting into your house, about the smell of mould in your bedroom.' He banged the sample with his hand and tried another smile. 'It might be just guttering, but it's like saying that your roof is just tiles.' He leant forward, and she leant in with him. 'And it will stop your house being the one the neighbours talk about, the one that lets the street down, because you've got paint peeling off your wooden boards. You'll never need to paint them again if you've got these.'

She sighed and sat back on the sofa, the movement wafting more perfume towards him. He felt nauseous, wanting to turn away, to get away from the memories, but the customer was nearly at the point of buying, he could sense it. She was falling for the sales tricks, the limited discount, the call to the manager. But something stopped him from forcing it. She distracted him, casually dressed, wearing those low-cut jeans that show off the hipbones, a sea horse tattoo visible just below her beltline.

He closed his eyes again, just for a moment, and filled his nose with the Chanel. The sale was over, he had to get away, before the other images drifted into his head. Blood. Smile. Hair. Still. Dirt.

'Okay,' he said, his voice faint. 'It is a lot to pay.' He passed over his card. 'If you change your mind, call me.'

He felt her fingers brush his as she took the card from him and his cheeks flushed. She tapped it against her chin. 'I will, thank you.'

He collected his samples, his breathing heavier now, and then he rushed for the door. He needed to be outdoors, where the breeze would take her scent away.

He climbed into his car, the samples thrown quickly into the boot, and took some deep breaths. Mike could sense her still watching him as he turned the key in the ignition.

Chapter Six

I followed Tony's hint and headed for the allotments behind my old school, a collection of vegetable patches and ramshackle sheds that brought back memories of bent old men in flat caps. The allotments were mostly empty, but a man leaning on a spade pointed me towards Hunter's plot. It was at the end of a line of bramble bushes and cane supports and, as I walked towards it, I got a close-up of my old school, two large prefabricated blocks, glass and panelling that looked out over sloping football fields, really just scrappy grass and wavy white lines. It was halfway up one of the slopes that surround Turners Fold, and I remembered how the wind used to howl across the fields, making my teenage legs raw during PE lessons.

As I got closer, I heard mumbles of conversation, and then laughter, and as the allotment came into view I saw three men on deckchairs, a bottle of single malt passing between them.

I realised I had been spotted, because the smiles disappeared and the bottle was put on the floor.

'I'm looking for Bill Hunter,' I said.

The three men looked at each other, and then one asked, 'Who are you?' He was a tall man, with a beaky nose and a shiny scalp, grey hair cropped short around the ears.

'My name is Jack Garrett, and I'm a reporter.'

He looked at me, and his eyes narrowed. I thought that I was suddenly unwelcome, but then he asked, 'Bob Garrett's lad?'

'Yes,' I said, my voice quieter now, caught by surprise.

He turned to his companions and winked. 'I'll speak to you boys later,' he said, prompting them to struggle to their feet and make their way towards the rickety mesh gate. I could smell the whisky as they went past. Once they'd gone, he turned to me and said, 'I'm Bill Hunter.' He held out his hand to shake.

His grip was strong and he kept hold of my hand as he said, 'I remember your father,' his voice softer than before, some sadness in his eyes. 'He was a good copper, and he shouldn't have died like that.'

'Did you work with him?' I asked.

'Not much,' he said, 'but I remember when he was killed. How many years ago is it now? Two?'

'Three,' I replied.

He shook his head. 'Time goes too quickly, but I remember it. When I first started out, people didn't carry guns like they do now. They did in the cities, I suppose, but they never brought their trouble this way.'

'They came this way eventually though,' I said, taking a deep breath, the memory bringing a tremble to my voice.

Hunter nodded to himself and patted me on the arm. 'I'm glad I'm out of it. Everything is so different now, much more dangerous.' He leant forward and whispered, 'Ask any of the new ones, and they all say that the job isn't how they thought it would be, that it's all about chasing targets, ticking boxes. And when they get a new problem?' Hunter chuckled. 'They just invent a new target. But those who are in can't get out. They've got kids and mortgages.' He gestured towards one

44

of the deckchairs. 'Sorry. You didn't come here to listen to my moans. Sit down.'

I sank into the low chair as Hunter dried one of the cups with an old cloth. I reached up to collect the whisky he had poured for me, the aroma rich and pungent as it wafted out of the enamel cup.

'So why do you want to know about Claude Gilbert?' he asked.

I was surprised. 'How did you guess?'

'Jack, lad, I've been retired for fifteen years now. I'm almost seventy. All the criminals I've locked up are either dead, retired, or have given birth to the next generation. The only reason reporters ever look me up is Claude Gilbert.' He winked at me. 'I don't talk to many, but seeing as though it's you, I'll tell you what you want to know.'

Chapter Seven

Laura McGanity looked around at the other officers in the room: they were mostly young, the ambitious ones marked out by the earnest way they sifted through their paperwork, the rest happy just to chat as they started their shift. They were in a room lined by glass walls and filled with computer screens, part of the shiny new police station on the edge of town. The windows looked out over the car park, and the glass walls gave her a view into a large atrium, where the officers ate their canteen food and gossiped.

Some of the officers had decided what they were doing that day, advice forms from the Crown Prosecution Service clutched in their hands, directing the collection of evidence to make the cases fit for court. The younger ones bustled around, anxious to get out of the station, the warm weather beckoning them outside, happy to take whatever the radio threw up that day. The older ones went through the motions, stoked up on coffee and walking round the station holding pieces of paper, their eyes already on the clock.

Laura sighed. She had gotten used to being a detective at the bottom of the pile, following the direction of experienced officers. Now she was the director, a room of young and eager faces looking to her for advice, and it felt suddenly hard. She had no stripes yet, but everyone knew why she had chosen the starched white shirts and shiny black trousers: brushing up on her community skills was the quickest route to sergeant. In return, Laura was expected to be a mentor, take on some responsibility, but a few of the old guard were just waiting for her to go wrong, happy to see another prospect fail, to justify their own lack of progress.

Her sergeant came in, a woman in her thirties with dark hair cut close to her head and a square jaw, lines starting to etch themselves around her lips from sucking on too many cigarettes. There was a young officer behind her, his cheeks fresh and flushed, eyes flitting nervously around the room. 'Fresh meat,' someone whispered, and Laura heard a chuckle.

The sergeant clapped her hands and barked out, 'Can I just have everyone's attention?'

The chatter died down.

'Can we all keep an eye out for the Crawler?' she shouted. 'Two more reports last night. They might be false, it seems like any noise gets called in as a peeping Tom, but just be vigilant. He might go on to attack someone, so don't ignore anyone suspicious. Talk to them. Get their name.'

Everyone mumbled to themselves as they went back to their work, and the sergeant made her way over to Laura.

'I want you to do me a favour,' the sergeant said, and she nodded to the young nervous officer in the corner of the room, his shirt hanging off his skinny shoulders. 'Can you take Thomas with you today? It's his first day after training school. Do the town centre circuit with him, introduce him to the store detectives, just have him feeling like a cop.'

'No problem,' Laura replied, knowing exactly why she had been chosen. Thomas looked young and scared. The older ones would fill him with cynicism, and the crewcut brigade would just teach him bad habits.

Laura remembered her own time as a young constable,

how it was often harder for the women, the men attempting to shield her from the fights, expecting her to spend the day patting old ladies' hands. But Laura liked the rucks, the excitement, the chases. It was why she joined, for the dirt, a different life to the one she'd had as a child in Pinner.

'Thomas?' said Laura, and when he looked up, Laura beckoned him over.

He tried to make himself seem big, his thumbs hooked into his belt, but Laura detected a slight quiver to his voice as he said hello.

'I've got a trip into town, and I need some help. I thought you could come with me.'

Thomas smiled and nodded. 'Good. Thanks.'

As they made their way out of the station, threading their way through the atrium that was busy with detectives, all serious and intense, Laura wondered whether making sergeant would be worth missing out on all the fun of CID. What would she do if she never got back in there, if she had to carry on wearing the uniform?

That was something she didn't want to think about.

Chapter Eight

'So, what do you want to know about Claude Gilbert?' Bill Hunter asked.

I took a sip of the whisky and coughed as it went down. Beer was more my thing, wine when I was with Laura, but I didn't want to be rude.

'The answers to the two big questions,' I said. 'Did he do it, and where did he go?'

Hunter scowled. 'Of course he did it.'

'How can you be sure? If I remember it right, not everyone is convinced.'

'Usually just people looking for attention,' Hunter said. He took a sip from his cup. I could smell the whisky on his breath as he started to talk. 'I'll tell you something about Claude Gilbert: he was nothing but a Daddy's boy made good.'

'He was a barrister,' I replied. 'Not many of them are working-class heroes.'

'Yeah, but a lot are decent people too,' he snapped back. 'They just had a better start in life than I did. But I've no chip on my shoulder. If people treat me well, I have no complaints, but Gilbert wasn't like that. He was arrogant, even though he didn't deserve to be. It wasn't talent that put him in that big old house. It was Daddy, His Honour Judge Gilbert. He gave him what he wanted, and maybe a bit more, but I don't think Claude saw it like that. I've been cross-examined by Claude, and he spoke to me like I ought to be cleaning his shoes or something. But let me tell you something: he was a loser, right up until the day he disappeared. He gambled, he played around, and most times he either lost or got caught.'

'But why does that make him a murderer?'

'Because it makes him desperate,' Hunter said. 'He should have been a better person, with his background. Educated at Stonyhurst, and part of some head-boy clique, a group of toffs who played at gangs, just an excuse to bully the new boys. They had all this blood brother nonsense, secret codes, and when they grew up, they carried it on. Gambling parties, and some sex parties, so it was whispered to me, probably drugs too – though the sort of people who were invited aren't the sort who talk to people like me. But Gilbert was lazy, and not that gifted. He was the one who failed in the clique, ended up at one of the universities that he thought was beneath him, but his father bailed him out eventually, got him a place in chambers. Then Claude learnt how to work the system: plead guilty at the last moment, bill the state for preparing the trial, and he made a lot of money out of being average.'

'He wasn't alone in that,' I said. 'My father used to talk about how much the lawyers got paid compared to him, and he was the one made to look guilty when he got in the witness box.'

Hunter leant over to pour me some more whisky, but I put my hand over the cup. I had to drive away from there.

'Your father was right to be cynical,' Hunter said. 'I was one of the good guys and I didn't get too much.'

'If it helps,' I said, 'those days are gone now. Even barristers are feeling the pinch.'

'What's wrong?' Hunter replied. 'No more sports cars, no second homes in France?' He scoffed. 'I'll hold back the tears. And anyway, even all the money Gilbert had wasn't good enough for him.'

'How do you mean?'

'Because he tried to get more by throwing it away in casinos,' Hunter said. 'His old school friends had gone to work in the City. This was the eighties, and they were making big money. Claude was stuck on the northern circuit, but he couldn't say no to the high life when it was there to be had. Claude was richer than most of us, but he was the pauper in his crowd. Even when he started doing television, you know, one of those awful debate programmes, it didn't change things. It just took him away from home more often, gave him another chat-up line, and he had some big debts by the time he disappeared.'

'Didn't everyone live the high life back then?' I asked. 'It was the boom before the bust.'

Hunter smiled ruefully. 'My life didn't change much. The only change I saw around here was the mills closing down. And maybe that's what sucked him in: that all around him he saw people losing their jobs, but he had the house and the sports car, and so he thought he was still the high-roller, the big man. There were rumours around court that Claude had talked about giving up the law to become a professional gambler, that he thought he had the knack of the skill games, had even tried counting cards at the blackjack tables, but he didn't have the brain for it and started to lose money.'

'Maybe he owed money to the wrong people,' I said. 'Lawyers find out things that they shouldn't know, and gambling debts made him liable to be blackmailed. Maybe he had to pass on information that he was supposed to keep secret.'

53

'What, are you saying that Nancy was killed by gangsters?' Hunter said.

'Maybe him too,' I suggested.

Hunter shook his head. 'I've thought about that, but why get rid of the bodies separately? Why be so cruel to Nancy?'

'If Nancy was buried alive, Gilbert knew he was on a timer,' I said. 'Perhaps he had to say what he knew before she died.'

'I've heard that theory, but I don't believe it,' Hunter said. 'They found his car at Newhaven, abandoned. That's the other end of the country. What gangster would dump the car so far away, as some kind of red herring?'

'So why do you think the car was there?' I asked.

'Because he jumped on a ferry,' he replied.

I smiled. 'Maybe that's why a gangster would dump the car all the way down there, to make you think that.'

'That would be good in a detective novel, but real criminals don't work like that,' Hunter said. 'Why go all the way down there? Why not the airport?' He shook his head. 'Gangsters wouldn't set up a false trail. They would get rid of the body and leave no trail.'

'So what about all the sightings?' I said. 'Do you think any might be true?'

Hunter leant in. 'They've either been unconfirmed or proved to be false. Any tall, suave stranger in a foreign land was thought to be Claude Gilbert. There was a sighting a couple of years ago, some hobo in New Zealand living out of his car. Someone hawked a photograph around the papers and the media went crazy. But all the locals knew him; he had been there all his life. And there was a man in Goa. A book was even written about him, naming him as Gilbert, but people from England knew him. He was just some busker from Birmingham who had moved out to Goa to get spiritual.'

'I was told that you never really let go of the case,' I said.

He looked sheepish for a moment. 'He's guilty of a cruel murder, but he was able to just walk away from it,' he said. 'I suppose it got to me.'

'So what do you think happened to him?' I asked.

Hunter smiled, and I could tell that he was enjoying the audience, that his theory was one he had gone over in his head countless times.

'I don't know for sure,' he said. 'He got on the ferry, but he had a head start on us by a few days, and life was different then. You paid by cash and so were harder to track. You didn't have to give up an email address or do it on a computer. All he would have needed was his passport, or any passport, and he would be in Europe straight away. What happened after that is something we'll never know. Perhaps he had friends who helped him out.'

'His old school friends? The head-boy clique?'

'I don't know, and you would be a brave man to print it; those people have got the money to ruin you,' Hunter said. 'But if you want my theory, I'll tell you: Claude Gilbert is dead.'

I raised my eyebrows. 'You sound pretty certain,' I said, and hoped that he wasn't, because that would be the end of my story, apart from some human interest piece on a female hoaxer.

'He boarded a ferry, I'm certain of it, and that's why his car was left behind,' Hunter said. 'Remember that he wouldn't know his wife's body would be found. It's a long voyage from Newhaven to France, plenty of time to think about things. Where was he going? How would he live? How much had he left behind?' Hunter shrugged. 'So he jumped.'

'Killed himself?' I queried.

Hunter nodded. 'Gilbert was a cowardly man. He hid behind his father, and then behind his wig and gown. He buried his wife because he couldn't cope with the killing part, and so he let Mother Nature do the job. But when it came to it, to the thought of life on his own, maybe even some guilt, he couldn't cope.' He raised his cup in salute. 'I think he ended up in the English Channel somewhere, drowned by his own misery.'

But if that was true, I thought to myself, who was in London trying to get me to broker a newspaper exclusive?

Chapter Nine

Frankie Cass was looking out of his window, as always. In winter, the hills that overlooked Blackley glistened like sugar when it was cold, the parallel strips of stone terraces like slashes in the ice, but he preferred it like this, in the summer, when it was warm enough to open his window and let the sounds from outside waft into his room. Birds sometimes rested in the sycamore and horse chestnut trees outside his window, and in spring he watched the gardens around come alive with flowers.

He checked his watch. It would be change of shift soon at the rest home across the road. There had been some new staff members, pretty young girls. Polish, he thought, or Romanian, judging from their accents as they walked past his house, laughing and talking, their speech fast and clipped. Sometimes they didn't bother to close the curtains when they got changed in or out of their white uniforms. If it was hot, they showered.

His tongue flicked to his lips as his binocular lenses crawled along the wall, looking for a glimpse, a flash of skin.

He heard the car before he saw it. It was the way the engine strained that caught his attention as it battled to climb the steep hill. He swung the binoculars to the road and smiled. A convertible, bright red, a seventies relic, the number plate showing white on black. He scribbled down the number and made a note of the time, before watching as the driver climbed out. He saw the camera and notebook and made another note: *reporter*.

He raised the binoculars to his eyes again. He would keep watch. It's what he did.

Claude Gilbert's house wasn't what I expected.

I had always known of the story – most people did around Blackley and Turners Fold – but I'd never had cause to visit the house. It was on a road that climbed a steep crescent away from the town centre, the houses large and imposing, shielded by trees and bushes, just the high slate roofs visible and the occasional bay window.

The Stag didn't enjoy the climb though; I could hear every rattle with the roof down, every scream of the engine. But it made it, and once I'd switched it off, the only thing I could hear was the ticking of the engine as it cooled down. There was no one else around, and as I looked over my shoulder, I realised that Blackley had disappeared behind the high walls and the trees.

I looked over at Claude Gilbert's house. The walls were taller than me, with ivy creeping along the top and only the tips of conifers visible from where I had parked. I took a few pictures and then I walked towards the gates, but I was surprised when I got there. I had expected some closed-off shell of a house, the centre of national notoriety, but from the sign on the gate I saw that time had moved on and the house had a new life: Blackley View Residential Care. I looked around again, and I noticed signs on other gates or fixed between trees. Accountants. Surveyors. A housing association. It seemed like no one lived on the street any more, all the grand old houses of Blackley given up for business use. The good money must have moved out of town, to the rolling fields and old stone hamlets of the Ribble Valley.

I gave the gate a push and it swung open slowly, screeching on its hinges and coming to a halt as it brushed against the gravel on the drive. The Gilbert house was different to the others on the street. Rather than blackened millstone, it was painted in a sandstone colour, the corners picked out in white, just like in the photographs I had seen whenever the story had been reported. The paint looked jaded though, the windows flaky and worn out.

As I got closer to the house, I saw the alterations. There was a ramp to the modern front doors, which swished open as I approached them. As I stepped inside, I saw that a grand old hallway had been transformed into an entrance lobby, laid out with plain chairs and low tables on a thick flower-patterned carpet. Stairs swept imposingly up to the next floor, the balustrade thick and strong with twisted spines, but the elegance was undermined by the stair-lift that ran along the wall and disappeared around the bend at the top.

I heard movement, and when I looked, I saw a woman walking briskly towards me, middle aged, her hair dyed dark brown and her figure trim in a tight white tunic. She smiled and asked if she could help. I checked out her name badge, and I saw that she was the assistant manager.

'Hello, Mrs Kydd. My name is Jack Garrett. I'm a reporter.'

Her smile faded. 'What can I do for you, Mr Garrett?'

'I'm doing a piece on Claude Gilbert,' I said, and gave her an apologetic smile. 'I know you'll get this a lot, but the story starts here.'

'We do get this a lot,' she said, her tone brusque. 'We can't just keep on giving up our time to show reporters around.'

'I know that,' I replied, trying to be conciliatory, 'but I

promise I'll include a picture of the sign. Call it free advertising.'

'They all say that too,' she said, and then she shook her head in resignation. 'C'mon on then. I'm on a break, so let's get rid of you.' She set off towards a room just off the hallway. As I followed her in, I saw that the edges were crowded with high-backed chairs, all centred around a large television against one wall. There were a few old people in them, wrapped up in cardigans despite the stifling heat generated by large radiators. A couple of them watched the television, the volume almost deafening, but the others just looked down at their laps.

I smiled a greeting, and one old lady glanced at me, a twinkle in her eyes, but no one else seemed to notice I was there. Or perhaps they didn't care.

Mrs Kydd led me to a corner of the room that overlooked the garden, visible through a large conservatory that ran the full width of the house. I could see two long lawns outside, a wide path between, and a glass and steel summer house in the corner of the garden.

'This is where Mrs Gilbert was attacked,' Mrs Kydd said, pointing to a spot by an old cast-iron radiator.

'How did they know?'

'There was blood on the skirting boards and walls. There wasn't much, as if he had tried to cover his tracks, but there were a few small spots and streaks that he missed.'

'It sounds like you know the story,' I said.

'I work here, and so I've read about it,' she replied. 'And writers turn up. They all like to talk about it, all of them thinking they've got a new theory.'

I raised my eyebrows at the dig, and she smiled at me, pleased that I'd spotted it. I took some pictures, trying to get the garden in the background, to show the route to her death.

'Does it bother the residents, you know, what happened here?' I asked.

Mrs Kydd shook her head. 'Our residents get well looked after, and it's a nice home. They know about it, but to most of them it is just another news story. They were all middle aged and older when it happened, so maybe it doesn't hold the attention like it does with the younger ones.' She smiled. 'And it's only the fact that he got away that makes the story interesting.'

I didn't disagree, because that was the interest that would sell the story.

I looked back towards the garden. 'Is that where the body was found?'

Mrs Kydd looked over her shoulder. 'You might as well see that as well,' she said.

I followed her outside, through the conservatory and then down another ramp, relieved to be in the natural warmth of summer rather than the suffocating artificial heat inside.

As we walked along the garden path, I looked around, tried to imagine how it must have been back then. Although I could see the chimneys and roofs of the nearby buildings, I saw that the height of the boundary wall just about stopped anyone from seeing into the garden. The road ran along one side, and on the other the land dropped away to a park, so that the house stood proudly on a hill. Claude Gilbert would have been able to drag his wife all the way down here without being spotted.

'What happened to the house after Gilbert disappeared?' I asked.

'I don't know much about that,' she replied, turning towards me. 'Only what I've read in the papers.'

'Like what?'

'That it was repossessed by the bank when the mortgage didn't get paid.'

'Do you get many people coming round to take a look?'

'We did a couple of years ago, for the twentieth anniversary, but it's been quiet since then.'

'What about his family? Are they ever in touch?'

'There was somebody once,' she said. 'He said he was Claude Gilbert's father.'

'The judge?' I said, surprised.

'That's what he said. He was a nice old man, seemed sad about it all, and not just for Claude. He just wanted to pay his respects.'

'How long ago was this?'

Mrs Kydd thought for a few seconds, and then she said, 'Springtime last year. And he brought that.' She pointed to a single rose bush, kept trimmed and neat. 'He asked us if we could plant it there, where Nancy was found, as a tribute.'

I looked at her, and then back at the flower bed. 'It's just a patch of dirt,' I said, and then looked at Mrs Kydd. 'It seems strange that it looks so ordinary.'

'I've thought the same thing a few times, when I've been able to snatch a quiet moment in the garden,' she replied. 'That's why he wanted the rose bush there, as a marker, so we don't forget what happened here.'

I thanked her for her time and strolled through the garden to make my way back to my car. I stopped a few times to take pictures, trying to show how ordinary it looked, but when I got back onto the street, I looked back towards the house, gripped by the sensation that I was being watched. I couldn't see anyone, but I sensed it, from the gentle shiver at the back of my neck to the way the hairs stood up on my arms.

I climbed into my car, wary now.

Chapter Ten

Thomas and Laura walked through the town centre in a slow, rolling police stroll, past the old wooden shop fronts and then the glass windows of the chain stores on the precinct, fast-food wrappers overflowing from rubbish bins. Laura felt self-conscious in her uniform, still getting used to the feel of it again after the years spent in plainclothes. Both of them were in short sleeves, but they were warm in their stab vests, their belts heavy with equipment, the radio squawking constantly on their chests. She could feel her backside straining against her black trousers, the cut doing little to flatter her figure.

Thomas seemed quiet, and his body language defensive, as if he was wary of the first spot of action.

'You okay?' Laura asked.

'Just looking around, observing,' Thomas said, his voice quiet, and then he gave a laugh, the first time Laura had heard it. 'It's easier at the training centre, because you're expected to get it wrong, just so you can be told how to get it right, but this is it, right now,' and he pointed at the floor. 'I'm not here to get it wrong though.'

Laura smiled. 'Don't be hard on yourself before you start. We all make mistakes. Just be courteous to people, be firm with those who deserve it, and don't tell lies. It's better to say sorry than tell a lie. And for the rest of it? Just use common sense and follow your instincts. That's all the job is about.'

Thomas nodded and looked down.

They walked for a few minutes in silence, until Laura asked, 'Are you enjoying the job so far?'

Thomas looked up. 'What, do you mean today?'

'Just generally,' Laura said. 'When you walked into the briefing room, how did you feel?'

Thomas blushed, his cheeks pink behind only a hint of stubble. 'Honestly?' he said, and then he laughed again. 'Scared rigid. Maybe tomorrow will feel different.'

'It will,' Laura said. 'Every day feels different. That's what's great about the job.'

Before either of them could say anything else, they heard a shout. Laura looked up and saw a young man twenty yards away in a green polo shirt, the uniform of one of the music chain stores, trying to hold on to a gaunt man in a scruffy blue puffa coat, his eyes encircled by black shadows, his cheeks pale and sweaty, a games console under one arm.

Laura started running, Thomas a step behind. Then the man pulled away, the sight of the sprinting uniforms giving him the push to make a break. The games console fell to the floor as he ran.

Laura's equipment jangled against her hips, her breaths loud in her ear, the adrenalin of the pursuit pushing her on. She could hear a couple of cheers from some college kids, and then she was panting: her detective years hadn't involved many foot-chases, and motherhood had made her heavier than when she had last worn the uniform. As the thief went around a corner and into one of the open car parks, Laura guessed that it would turn out to be his day. Her chest began to ache, her throat dry, sweat across her forehead, and her legs slowed. She stopped running and reached for her radio, sucking in air as she tried to make her voice fit for broadcast.

Then Thomas ran past her.

Laura took a large breath and jogged after him. As she rounded the corner, Thomas came into view, but Laura saw that he had stopped, and the thief was heading out of the other side of the car park. Laura came to a halt next to Thomas and tried to get her breath back, her chest pumping hard in her shirt.

'What happened?' Laura asked, gasping.

Thomas looked down, and Laura saw that he was taking deep breaths too, fear in his eyes.

'What's wrong?' she said.

'He pulled a needle out of his pocket,' he said, between breaths. 'He shouted he would give me AIDS.' He looked at Laura. 'I'm sorry. I bottled it.' He gave a large heave of his shoulders and then kicked at the gravel. 'My first test and I got scared.'

Laura put her hand on his shoulder, turning him away from the shoppers who were watching them. 'And you'll bottle it again,' she whispered. 'You'll just care less about it. Next time, just keep running and hit him as hard as you can with your baton, but remember that you may struggle to get a second shot in.'

Thomas nodded, and then turned back the way they had just come. 'Let's go back to the shop, see if they've got it on video.'

Laura nodded and smiled. 'Okay, we'll do that,' she said, and decided that she liked Thomas.

Frankie ducked behind the gatepost, just to check that the road was clear, and then he crept out. He wasn't dressed properly, in jogging bottoms and a crumpled old T-shirt, his

slippers making slapping noises on the tarmac as he shuffled across the road. He had to slow down as he reached the
driveway of the rest home, the gravel hurting his feet through
the soft soles.

The doors to the rest home opened automatically, so he
went inside and looked around anxiously, worried about
who he would see, wanting to avoid the big boss. Then he
saw someone he recognised wandering through one of the
rooms. 'Mrs Kydd?' he shouted. He shuffled towards her.
'Mrs Kydd?'

She stopped and then turned slowly towards him. He
noticed her uniform looked tight, stretched across her chest
so that it pushed her breasts into a tired-looking cleavage.

'Hello, Frankie,' she said. 'What do you want?'

'Was he a reporter?' Frankie asked.

'Were you watching again?'

'I heard the car, that's all, and so I watched him,' he said.
'What's the big deal? Why can't you tell me?'

She put her hands on her hips.

'I saw him taking pictures,' Frankie persisted. 'What did
he want? Was it about Claude Gilbert? What did he say?'

'Slow down, Frankie,' she said, her voice raised. 'Yes, he
was a reporter, okay, and he's writing a story about Nancy.'

'Does he think Claude killed her?'

'He didn't tell me what he thought,' she said. 'He just
wanted to see where she died.'

Frankie looked at her chest again until she folded her
arms, aware of his gaze.

'He needs to speak to me,' he said. 'Did you tell him
about me?'

She shook her head. 'No, I didn't. Please go, Frankie.'

'If he calls again, tell him to come to my house,' he said,
but then he flinched when he felt her hand on his arm.

'Are you all right, Frankie?' she asked. 'Are you eating okay? You look poorly again.'

'I'm fine,' he said.

'You need to look after yourself, Frankie. If your mother could see you now, she would be worried about you.'

Frankie looked away.

'Hey, I'm sorry,' she said. 'I didn't mean to upset you. He said he was called Jack Garrett. He sounded local. If you think he might want your help, call him. He might be interested in what you've got to say.'

Frankie didn't respond.

'You've got to look after yourself though, before you go chasing him,' she said. 'Eat properly. Get some sleep.'

'I'm fine,' he said, and he turned and walked out of the rest home, shuffling quickly along the drive, ignoring the pain in his feet from the sharp stones. He could sense Mrs Kydd watching him, even after the automatic doors had swished shut.

Chapter Eleven

I checked my notepad and looked at the scribbles I had made after Susie had gone. I had written down Maybury and Sharpe as Susie's old law firm. If Bill Hunter was right, that Claude Gilbert had ended up as fish food in the English Channel, the story would end up being about Susie and another Claude Gilbert hoax.

The firm's name was well known to me. I had devoured the court reports in the local paper when I was a child, those short paragraphs of shame the only part I found interesting, and the names of the defending solicitors always stayed with me: Harry Parsons, Jon Halpern, Danny Platt – crafty lawyers who managed to find new ways to repackage remorse and excuses for their clients. Maybury and Sharpe had been one of the main players, but Susie Bingham had been talking of a time two decades earlier, and the shrinking of legal aid had seen the firm splinter into its different departments, the ambulance chasers not wanting to be weighed down by the criminal work. The new offshoot was now known simply as Sharpes, staffed by enthusiastic young clerks and a couple of ageing solicitors, who huffed and puffed their way around the Magistrates' Court like relics from a lost era. I just hoped that someone there remembered her.

The office front suited the firm, old-style, with frosted

windows and gold leaf lettering; no neon sign at Sharpes. When I walked in, I saw that the reception area was quiet, just one client waiting, his face bearing the familiar look of heroin addiction: high cheekbones, blackened teeth and prickles of sweat on his lip. The receptionist was a young Pakistani girl, her hair sleek and long, and when she smiled at me, her eyes were bright jewels in the office gloom.

'I want to have a word with Mr Halpern or Mr Platt,' I said.

She reached for the phone. 'Are you due in court?' she asked, her voice quiet, almost a mumble, just the smallest trace of the Peshwar in her Lancashire accent.

'No, I'm the court reporter, Jack Garrett. I need some help with a story, and it involves this firm.'

She considered me for a moment, and then picked up the phone and spoke to someone, her words barely audible. She pointed to the room next to reception. 'Wait in there,' she said.

The waiting client didn't pay me any attention as I went into a small square room, with just enough room for a desk and chairs on either side. I could hear a whispered conversation through the door, and then it was opened briskly as Danny Platt walked in. His hair was long and unkempt, but the grey patches that broke up its darkness gave away his age as over fifty. His face bore the scars of long hours, with lines etched deep around the eyes, and the bulge of his stomach strained against the buttons of his creased blue shirt. He looked unkempt, like legal aid work was getting tougher.

'Mr Garrett,' he boomed, as if he was delighted to see me. He was eating a sandwich though, and it was obvious that I had disturbed him. 'Between sittings, so make it quick,' he said, holding up his lunch. 'What can I do for you? A quote you didn't get?'

As he sat down, he took a bite from his sandwich. Mayonnaise collected at the corners of his mouth.

'Do you remember Susie Bingham?' I asked. He looked quizzically at me as he searched his memory, skimming through all the thieves and prostitutes he had helped over the years. 'She used to work for Maybury and Sharpe, about twenty years ago,' I added, to help him out.

I saw the beginnings of a smile.

'You remember her?' I asked.

He nodded, grinning now. 'Very attractive woman,' he said, and he chuckled. 'Great figure. It was hard to stop the eyes from following her legs upwards, if you know what I mean. Why do you ask?'

'She came to me with a story, and I'm checking her out first, just to see whether I can believe her.'

Danny put his sandwich down and wiped his mouth with his handkerchief. 'Is it about this firm?' he asked, his smile fading.

I shook my head. 'No. You don't even need to be mentioned.'

He relaxed and took another bite of the sandwich. 'She was a real good-time girl,' he said, chuckling again, exposing the food in his mouth. 'Big fan of the chambers parties, so I remember, and the police ones. Always guaranteed to end up with someone.' He leant forward, as if he was worried someone might overhear. 'She was familiar with most of the young bar, if you get my drift,' he said, and gave his nose a theatrical tap. 'She was pretty generous with the police, just for the rough and ready thrill, but she liked the rich boys best, particularly the younger ones. It was the accents, I think.' He gave a small laugh. 'There was a Christmas party once at the court, and some rumour went round that she'd fucked one young barrister in a judge's chair. It got plenty of giggles

71

around the court, and she didn't mind at first, but the judges weren't happy. When it looked like the young man was in trouble, she stuck up for him, told everyone it had never happened.'

'Maybe it didn't.'

'It happened, no worries there,' he said, but his jokey smile came across as sleazy.

I made some notes. It might fit into the story, if there ever was one. 'Did you trust her?' I asked.

'Oh yes, totally,' Danny said. 'A good clerk, so I remember. Left to work in a bigger firm, although I think she regretted it because they only used her for prison visits, just a flash of a leg, and she was better than that. The clients liked her and she took decent trial notes.' Then he drifted away for a moment, enjoying some distant memory, before he said, 'I think we almost, you know, just once, at an office party, but I was married, and so I backed off.' He sighed at the memory. 'She left not long after, but let me tell you something: I regretted it at times – saying no, I mean. She was an attractive woman, and the memory would be nice.' When I raised my eyebrows, he said, 'I don't mean to put the woman down. She was no kid, but she was enjoying herself. What's wrong with that?'

'What about Claude Gilbert?' I asked. 'Do you know if she ever had a relationship with him?'

Danny Platt's eyes widened at the mention of Gilbert's name. 'Why are you asking about Claude Gilbert?'

'I just remembered that he was around at the same time,' I said, trying to hide the reason for my visit. 'He was a good-time boy. It's not inconceivable that they got it together.'

'So it's a Claude Gilbert story,' he grinned, revealing the bread squashed into his teeth. 'I was wondering what story there was in Susie.'

I decided not to deny it as he thought about his answer.

'It's possible,' he said. 'He did a lot of work for us, and so will have known Susie well. Claude lived in Blackley, and so he would come here for conferences, to save us the journey to his chambers. The clients liked that, and he had a way with the clients.'

'I've been told he was arrogant.'

'It depends who you ask,' Danny said. 'There are different types of barristers. There are the diligent ones, those who prepare everything; but most of those wouldn't interest even their wives, let alone a jury. Then there are the charmers, those with the smile, the swagger, can play the jury, get them on their side. Claude had a bit of that but, most of all, he just got on with the punters.'

'So what was his secret?'

Danny laughed. 'The first secret most criminal lawyers learn: cigarettes. He didn't have to read his papers. As long as he threw his fag packet onto the desk, left open, facing the clients, they loved him, made them feel like he was on their side. And he gave the police a hard time. That's why he didn't do prosecution work, just to keep up the illusion. Clients don't expect to get off, not really. All they want is to see someone put up a fight, so that they know they gave it their best shot. Claude did that, and he gave it to them straight. What their chances were, the jail term they would get. Lawyers like Gilbert are well liked.'

'By criminals,' I said.

Danny shook his head slowly. 'By clients,' he responded. 'We all make mistakes from time to time, remember that. It's just that some of us do it more often. My clients are maybe not people you would want as neighbours, but they are human beings, and Claude Gilbert respected that.'

'So Gilbert was a good guy?' I queried.

'There are plenty worse.'

'But not everyone kills their wife.'

'He's not been convicted of that.'

'Do you think that makes a difference?'

'To me, it does,' Danny said. 'Innocent until proven guilty. It's what makes us civilised. Sometimes letting a few bad ones get away is a price worth paying.'

'Do you really believe that?' I said.

'I don't know,' he said, smiling, 'but if you'll print it, trade might just pick up.'

I closed my notebook and thanked him for his time. It seemed like the interview was over.

As I went to leave, Danny put his hand on my arm. 'If you see Susie again, pass on my regards. Maybe there's still time for unfinished business.' He raised his eyebrows and grinned at me.

I looked down and saw the glimmer of his wedding ring, and then I noticed the drip of coleslaw on his shirt, and the chewed bread between his teeth.

'Maybe some dreams are worth letting go,' I said, and then as I left the room I muttered, 'for her sake'.

Chapter Twelve

Frankie grunted as he pulled his Vespa onto its stand outside the *Blackley Telegraph* offices, the sister paper to *The Valley Post*. The building was all seventies glass and steel frames, with painted panels and a brightly-lit sign on the front, although one corner had cracked so that leaves and dust had blown in over time.

Frankie remembered when it was new, when he was a boy, excited at seeing the old tramlines and cobbles exposed like skeletons from underneath the tarmac when they rebuilt the town centre, before the buses that rumbled past it every day dirtied the front.

He looked around nervously though. He didn't like it around the bus station. The gangs of kids used to taunt him, take his money and laugh at him, small groups of trouble dressed all in black. He had bought a scooter when his mother died – she wouldn't let him have one when she was alive – so that he wouldn't have to get the bus any more.

He walked into the *Telegraph* building and then jumped as the entry mat emitted a buzzing sound when he stepped on it. There was a large wooden counter in front of him, with photographs from the paper pinned to the wall behind, showing people in suits holding giant cheques and a display of schoolboy football teams. That day's edition was fanned out on a small round table. A young woman appeared out of a doorway. Her badge said she was called Jackie.

He lifted his goggles onto his crash helmet. She looked surprised, startled almost, although he didn't know why. He always wore them, particularly in summer. They kept the flies and fumes out of his eyes.

He smiled. She was wearing a vest top, and he could see the outline of the lace on her bra-cup. He liked that.

'What can I do for you?' she said.

Frankie thought she sounded nervous. He watched her delicate fingers as they toyed with a pen in her hand. He wondered where she lived.

'I'm Frankie,' he said quietly, 'and I'm looking for a reporter.'

'You've come to the right building, Frankie.'

He shook his head. She didn't understand. 'No, not any reporter. He drives a red sports car. Jack Garrett.'

'Why do you want him?'

'He's writing about Claude Gilbert.'

She raised her eyebrows at that. 'He doesn't work for us. He's freelance, lives somewhere in Turners Fold.'

'Do you have an address?'

Frankie thought she was about to tell him, but she stopped and looked embarrassed. 'I can't give out addresses,' she said.

'But I need it,' he said, and he leant forward onto the counter. It made her step back quickly.

'Just wait there,' she said. 'What's your name again?'

'Frankie.'

'Just Frankie?'

He nodded.

She disappeared into the doorway again, and Frankie could hear her whispering to someone. They were talking about him. He felt tears prickle his eyes. He had blown it again.

He should have found the reporter on the internet, made his own way there.

He turned to leave, his fists clenched with frustration, and as he rushed for the door, his footsteps set off the entry buzzer again.

He took some deep breaths and put his fingers to his cheeks when he reached the street. They felt hot. He slipped his goggles back over his eyes and then sat astride his scooter, fumbling quickly for the keys. He shouldn't have gone there. Now they had a name. His name. He pressed down on the kickstart pedal, and then raced down the bus lane, working quickly through the gears until he was out of sight of the building.

I sat in my car and thought about Bill Hunter. He had remembered my father's death and, as soon as he had mentioned it, I knew I would call at the cemetery. It was quiet, and I drummed my fingers on the steering wheel, wondering whether I should go in.

I hadn't been for a few months; visits had recently become confined to Father's Day and Christmas and I felt bad about that. I looked along the rows of granite slabs, broken up by the occasional splash of colour from flowers left in memoriam. Our house had memories of him dotted around, his Johnny Cash records, old photographs, but I knew I should visit the grave more often, to keep the dirt from the gold-etched words: 'Robert Garrett – Beloved Husband and Father'.

I closed my eyes and swallowed, fought the wetness in my eyes. This was why I didn't come often – because whenever I saw the patch of grass, I imagined him under the ground, in the box, still and cold. I fought the images, tried to see the grave as merely a marker, a focal point, because that wasn't how I wanted to remember him. I wanted to think of the man who had been in my life, strong and quiet and caring, not the police officer who had been shot in the line of duty.

Losing both parents had toughened me up, perhaps too much. When I looked at Laura, saw her smile or heard her laugh, or whenever I caught her in an unguarded moment, vulnerable and soft, unlike the tough cop I knew she could be, I felt a need to hold her, to be the strong man. But most times I stopped myself; something inside of me held me back, as if I was waiting for the rejection.

So maybe losing both parents hadn't toughened me up at all. Maybe it had made me too fragile, so that I was scared of the knockbacks.

I turned the key in the ignition.

'I'm sorry, Dad,' I whispered, 'but I'm going to have to sell the car.' Then I laughed at myself. Not really for talking to myself, but because it was about something as trivial as a car. It wasn't that simple though. My father had owned that car throughout my childhood. It was how I remembered Sunday mornings, my father with a sponge in his hand, washing it down. I had friends at school whose fathers owned better cars than a 1973 Triumph Stag in Calypso Red, but to my father it was a reward for his police work, the drives on sunny days his escape from the humdrum of family life.

I let my words hang there for a minute or so, just giving him a chance to hear them, to know that I wasn't being disrespectful. It was my last real connection with my father and somehow I wanted him to know that I was doing it for the right reason, not because I was trying to dim his memory.

My thoughts were interrupted by my phone ringing. I took a couple of deep breaths before I answered.

'Hello?'

'I've got some material for you.'

I smiled. It was Tony Davies.

'What like?'

'Just the archive stuff we used for the Gilbert anniversary edition. I've done you copies. I'll drop them off later.'

I thanked him and hung up. I gave a quick salute to the lines of headstones. At least I was making progress.

Chapter Thirteen

Mike Dobson closed his eyes as he lay back on the sofa. It was one of those summer evenings when the heat never really disappears and the neighbourhood children seem to play too late, the laughs and shrieks drifting in through the open windows.

The television was on in the corner of the room, but he couldn't concentrate. Why was it that the memories came back to him so strongly? He could go for months when there was nothing, but then it took just a small thing, like the sight of his naked wife, frigid and cold, or the flowery sweetness of the scent of Chanel. He was swept more than two decades back, and the images assaulted him, mixed up the past with the present, as if she was in the room with him.

Summer nights like these were the worst, when the sun took all evening to set over the lavender bushes in the garden, their delicate smell drifting in through the open window. And with the smells came the sounds, the sensations. He felt her touch for a moment, that spark, that excitement, her hand in his, her fingers soft and light, sitting together in the park. Then he remembered those other moments. His mouth on her breast, soft murmurs, loud moans, two bodies together.

But then came the blood, as always. He could feel it on

his hands, and his eyes shot open as he heard the thumps, the knocking, like a desperate drumbeat, the shouts, the muffled cries.

Mary was watching him. He glanced over quickly and he thought he saw a shadow behind her, someone moving through the door. He blinked and it was gone, and all he could see were Mary's cold eyes.

He clambered to his feet to go to the fridge. When he got there, he leant against the door for a moment, his forehead damp, before reaching for a beer.

When he walked back into the room, Mary looked pointedly at the bottle. 'Do you think you should?' she said.

'I feel like I want to,' he replied, taking a long swig. When she shot a stern look at him, he added, 'I've had a long day. No one's buying, and I'm hot.'

He went outside, to wait for the sun to drop lazily behind the houses, catching the duck and dive of evening birds and the buzz of midges over the laurel bush in the corner of his garden.

He closed his eyes for a moment and let the scents creep back in again, and he was taken back to stolen hours, a country drive, the weight of her in his arms, laughing, his mouth on hers, the caress of her fingers in his chest hairs, the summer of innocence.

He heard a sound, like a thump on wood; as he looked up, he saw Mary step away from the window. She had been watching.

He took another pull on his beer. He knew he shouldn't think of it, but then he felt that burn, that familiar need.

He went back into the house and took his car keys from the hook by the door.

'I'm going for a drive,' he said, and he was met by silence as he slammed the door.

Chapter Fourteen

I was sitting in my garden as I flicked through the newspaper articles Tony had dropped through my door. I had views over Turners Fold to distract me, the strips of grey terraced houses and small fingers of chimneys sitting between the slopes, and towards the jagged lines of drystone walls dividing up the hills, black and white dots of cattle sprinkled as far as I could see.

I took a sip from my wine glass and noticed how Claude Gilbert's house looked different in the old black and white photographs, the garden slightly overgrown, less formal. I smiled as I held up a photograph of Claude, the one that had spread to the nationals, his dark hair thick, a superior smirk. Did he really want to come home? I plucked an article from the bottom of the pile and saw that the picture used was the full photograph, with Nancy Gilbert sitting next to him, an austere look on her face. The photographs used later were more relaxed shots, showing her laughing and happy, as if they were meant to prick the general conscience – the public wouldn't warm to the hunt if she was some uptight rich bitch.

As I read the articles, I saw nothing new, just stuff that had been rehashed countless times since. I slipped the cuttings back into the envelope when I heard the hum of car tyres and watched as Laura's charcoal-grey Golf crunched onto the gravel outside our gate. As she stepped out of the car, her white shirt open at the neck, I raised my wine glass. 'It's open,' I said.

'So I see,' she replied, and gave me a weary smile. When she joined me at the table, a glass in one hand, she put her arm around my neck and her head on my shoulder. I could feel the collar of her stiff white shirt, and, as I reached behind and felt her legs, my hands brushed over the coarse regulation black trousers and my fingers crackled with static.

'It still seems strange, seeing you in your uniform,' I said, as I got the waft of her perfume mixed in with the sweat of the cells. I had put Bobby to bed, but from the shouting I could hear drifting through the open window he must have heard the car. 'I'll go say goodnight in a minute,' she said sleepily. 'I just need to slow down for five minutes.'

'Life tough at the top?'

'I'll tell you when I get there,' she said, and stretched out a yawn. 'I'll need to do some revision soon though. It feels like I've forgotten how to study. I wasn't the best at it in university, but I must have done it at some point.'

'I was a crammer,' I said. 'Go out until Easter, and then just rush it through at the end.'

'But you were younger then. So was I. This is a sergeant's exam. I'm supposed to know the stuff already.'

'You'll do it easily,' I said. 'It's just about staying cool enough to remember what you already know.'

She sighed. 'I'm already the old stager.'

'What do you mean?'

'I was holding the hand of a new one today,' Laura said. 'He didn't look old enough to be crossing the road on his own.'

'I'm sure someone said that about you once,' I said.

Laura grimaced. 'That's why I don't like it. It just feels like it's all slipping by too fast.' She squeezed me and then murmured in my ear, 'Will you still love me when I pass my exams?'

'What do you mean?'

'I'll have to stay in this uniform for a while longer,' she said, 'at least until I can go back into CID.'

I turned to face her, and sneaked a soft kiss. 'I like it,' I said, and then I raised my eyebrows mischievously. 'Could we, you know, just once, in the uniform?'

'And the handcuffs?' She tapped my nose playfully. 'I'll try not to make them too tight,' she said, and then she peeled away from me. 'I'm going to say goodnight to Bobby.'

I grabbed her hand. 'Before you go, I've got a scenario for you,' I said. 'Think of it as revision.'

Laura turned and looked at me. 'Go on.'

'Someone is wanted by the police. If there was a sighting of him, would I be obliged to report it?'

'Who is it?'

I shook my head. 'No names.'

She paused at that and tapped her lip with her finger. 'I'm trying to think of what crime it would be if you didn't.' After a few more seconds, she said: 'It would depend on what you did with the information. If you alerted him to help him get away, or gave him shelter, then yes, but if you just failed to report it, I'm not sure we could do much.'

I nodded to myself. 'That's what I thought,' I said quietly, and let go of her hand.

As I took a sip of wine, I realised that Laura was staring at me.

'Is it something to do with the woman who was here this morning?' she said.

'I don't reveal my sources, you know that,' I replied.

85

'I don't need to pass my sergeant's exam to work out that she's connected,' she said. 'But is it anything that will get you into trouble?'

I raised my glass and smiled. 'I'll tell you when I find out more. There is one thing I have to do though.'

'Which is what?'

'Go to London,' I said.

'And what will you do when you get there?'

Laura looked at me strangely when I said, 'Hopefully, make us rich.'

Frankie stared through his binoculars from behind a stone wall, his knees in long grass.

He had ridden into Turners Fold and asked questions about the reporter in the old red sports car. He got lucky, because the third person he asked knew where Jack Garrett lived.

It had been a long time since he had been in Turners Fold. It had once been on his cycle route, the long pull out of Blackley, and then a fast green run into Turners Fold, free-wheeling along a road bordered by straggly grass verges and drystone walls until he hit the fringes of the town, as the country views turned into small-town huddles. He used to like sitting by the canal and eating ice cream as the barges drifted past, and the people on board always waved back at him as he sat by the bridge, dipping his feet into the water as he rested his legs.

But that had been a long time ago, when his mother had been alive. She would run him a bath for when he got back, sweaty and tired, always hungry, and he would tell her what he had seen. He missed that more than anything. It was all part of her being around, more than just someone to clean for him or make his meals. He'd had someone to share his secrets with, the things he could see from his window, who wouldn't laugh at him for thinking like he did.

It was an easier ride now. His Vespa purred up the hills, and so he was able to take in the views as he got higher and the air became fresher.

Frankie had seen the car before he reached the house, the red Triumph parked on a small patch of pink gravel at the front of a grey cottage, its stones large and worn, the old slates on the roof jagged and uneven. He had pulled into a small track by a farm gate and then switched off the scooter's engine and clambered over the gate, binoculars in his hand. He had walked along the wall until he could get a good view of the house, to see who else was there before he spoke to the reporter.

He knelt down so that the lenses just peeked over the wall. He saw the reporter, a glass of wine in his hand, but then Frankie was jolted when he saw who else was there.

He ducked down quickly. She was a police officer – he could tell that from the stiff trousers and the white shirt – and that scared him. He didn't want the police at his house.

But she had looked pretty, and so he got to his knees and looked again towards the house.

He liked the way she smiled as she leant over the reporter and then gave a giggle. She was just back from work and it had been a warm day. She would be taking a shower soon. He scanned the house with his binoculars, looking for the bathroom, and then he found it. There was frosted glass in the window, but the top pane was partly open and he could see the clear glass of a shower cubicle.

His hand scrambled around in his bag as he nudged the notepads and yesterday's newspapers aside, until he found his camera. It felt hot in his hand. He closed his eyes for a moment and apologised. To his mother. To the policewoman at the cottage. And to himself. He knew he shouldn't, that it was wrong to look at naked women, his mother had told him that. But he wanted to see her. As long as she didn't know he was there, where was the harm in that?

He watched as she went inside and then, as the light went on in the bathroom, he trained his camera on the window, waiting.

Chapter Fifteen

Mike Dobson drove slowly around the Mill Bank area of Blackley, an eye on his mirror for the police. The streets ran through mainly open spaces now, from which rows of terraces had long since been cleared, ready for the urban regeneration that had never happened. The grass grew long and wild, nature reclaiming the land, fluttering through those piles of bricks and grit that hadn't been taken away by the diggers, security fences stretching along their edges, protecting the tyre-fitters and builders' merchants with jagged silver spikes.

There were still some rows of houses, but the windows were mostly blocked by steel shutters, awaiting the attention of the bulldozers. Water trickled onto the street from one, the pipes ripped away by scrappers, and the walls hosted the garish scrawls of graffiti artists.

The streets were busy with women though, the balmy weather making it easier to work, but the roads were quiet, traffic still too light. Mike's car bounced into the potholes as he crawled along and the women peered into his car, smiling, their teeth browned by drug use and decay.

But he didn't want them. He was looking for someone else.

He did a couple of circuits before he saw her, standing on a corner, well away from the other girls. He felt a small tremor of anticipation. It had been a couple of months now, but whenever he went looking she was the one he sought out. She was different from the rest – nicely spoken, almost polite, a couple of wrong turns in her life bringing her to this point – but it was her looks that drew him. Her hair was long and dark and she had an easy smile, but it wasn't just that. She looked like Nancy and, whenever Mike saw her, it was like Nancy was back, from the way she tossed her hair as she walked, to the provocative rise of her eyebrows when she smiled.

He slowed down as he reached her. She bent down to peer into his car and he leant across the passenger seat, puffing slightly as his stomach strained against the seatbelt.

'Looking for business?' she drawled, as she pulled her hair back over her ears. Nancy used to do that.

'Don't you remember me?' he said.

She shook her head.

'That's okay,' he said, and then opened the car door. 'Get in.'

She climbed in and put her bag on her knees. It was gaping open and Mike could see the packet of cigarettes squeezed in next to the baby wipes, her tools for the evening.

As he set off towards his usual place, the site of an old factory, now reduced to a concrete patch and dark shadows by the redbrick viaduct that overshadowed the town, he said, 'I just thought you might remember me, that's all.'

'Why would I?'

'Because I treated you nicely,' he said.

She paused for a few seconds, and then she asked, 'How many times?'

'With you?' He blushed. 'Not many.'

She didn't respond to that, and he guessed that she wasn't interested in idle talk. As the car crunched slowly to a halt, just the dark walls ahead of him, she asked, 'What do you want?'

'Something more than this,' he said quietly.

'What do you mean?'

He shook his head. 'Nothing, it doesn't matter.' And then, 'Who are your regulars?'

'Taxi drivers mainly,' she said. 'And men like you, who don't like their wives any more.'

He looked down at that, suddenly ashamed, and picked at his fingers. 'Take off your top,' he said quietly.

'An extra fiver for that.'

He nodded. 'I know.'

'Full sex?'

He nodded again, his cheeks red.

'Thirty quid,' she said.

'It was forty last time.'

'Call it a loyalty discount,' she drawled.

He got out of the car to sit in the back. She clambered in there with him, climbing between the gap in the front seats, and slipped off her T-shirt. She looked thin and pale, her skin mottled, her bones too visible in her shoulders. Her fingers were grubby and her nails bitten short.

The leather car seat was cold on his backside as he pulled down his trousers. He felt ridiculous, exposed, his eyes darting around, watching out for the police. The car was filled with the noise of the condom wrapper being torn open, and then he gasped and closed his eyes as her hands worked it onto him.

She climbed on top of him and tears squeezed out between his eyelids, part shame, part relief. Then she started to move up and down quickly, functional, passionless, getting him from start to finish, her hair brushing against his face, the seat creaking beneath him.

He ran his hands along her back, felt her naked skin under his fingers, the ridge of her spine, the fine hairs in the small of her back, and then he leant forward to kiss her. She moved her mouth out of the way and shook her head, going faster, and then it came at him in a rush . . . just a release, nothing more.

She climbed off him too quickly and stepped out of the car to put her knickers and T-shirt back on. He pulled at his trousers and then tossed the condom and wrapper out of the car window. As he clambered out of the back seat, puffing and wheezing from the exertion, he went towards her, to touch her hair, but she pulled away and smoothed her skirt instead.

'I need to go back,' she said. 'I'll walk if you don't want to take me.'

'No, I'll take you,' he said. 'I'd like to spend more time with you.'

She looked wary. 'What do you mean?'

'It isn't just about this,' he said, and he gestured around him, at the car, at his lap. 'I want something more.'

She looked away and thought for a few seconds. 'I'm not going to your house.'

'No, it's not that,' he said, and then he sighed. 'This will sound stupid, but it's about feeling someone in my arms, someone who will hold me. I can make it better for you, more than this.'

She folded her arms and looked at him. 'That would be expensive.'

He took a deep breath. 'I know, I know. I'll come and find you when I can arrange it.'

She didn't say anything for a few moments, and then she said, 'I'll walk back, it's okay.'

And then he was alone again. His breathing returned to normal, and he climbed back into the driver's seat and started the engine, the noise loud in the shadows around him.

Chapter Sixteen

The early morning train to London was busy, filled with pensioners on cheap advance bookings. The journey was shorter than it used to be, just a couple of hours from Lancashire to the bright lights, and the aisles were busy as people tottered to the buffet car to relieve the monotony. A group of Scottish students swapped boyfriend-talk on the opposite table and the air was filled with the smell of sandwiches. I looked up as I saw Susie making her way towards me, two coffees in her hands, a magazine tucked under her arm.

'I thought we might have gone first class,' she said as she lowered herself into her seat. 'We're going to make some big money from this.'

'You wouldn't like first class,' I said. 'You get free coffee, but you'll also get businessmen trying to impress the rest of the carriage.'

Susie smiled and slid one of the coffees over to me.

'When do I get to meet Claude?' I asked.

Susie didn't answer at first, as she fiddled with the lid on her coffee. 'Whenever he calls,' she replied eventually.

'But you know where he lives. Why can't we just go there?'

'Like I told you, he needs to know that you're on your own, that he can trust you,' Susie said.

'You can vouch for that.'

'How do I know someone hasn't been following us since we met this morning?' When I didn't answer, she said, 'We just go to where I've been told to go and we hang around. Claude will find us, don't worry.'

I thought about the prospect of meeting Claude Gilbert, and it was hard not to smile. I took a drink of coffee, and then said, 'Claude comes second though. I need to see someone first.'

'How do I know you're not speaking to the police?' she said, shocked.

'You don't,' I replied. 'But these stories don't sell themselves. I'm trusting you, and so you've got to trust me.'

Susie considered this before saying, 'But will they let you write it up how Claude wants it?'

I looked out of the window as I thought about that. The truthful answer was that they would go with what they think will sell papers and they wouldn't give a damn about Claude, but maybe it was too early for a lesson in the cold world of journalism. Fugitives don't get copy approval.

'If it is Claude, then yes,' I lied, 'but the story might change if he goes to prison.'

'But he won't,' Susie said. 'He didn't kill Nancy.'

I turned away again and looked at the reflection of my cup in mid-air, a ghost against the backyards of some Midlands town that we were racing through, the landscape getting brighter. I could see Susie in the reflection too, but as London got closer, the cold reality of having to sell her story to a ruthless press started to sink in, and so I began to wonder whether her story really made sense, that Claude Gilbert could have been undiscovered all these years – but I was willing to gamble my reputation on the chance that I was about to write the best story of my career.

*   *   *

94

Mike Dobson lay alone in bed while Mary cleaned the kitchen downstairs. He thought he could still smell the night before on him, the latex on his fingers, her cigarette smoke in his hair. And it seemed like Mary knew. He didn't know how, but she always seemed different after he went for a drive. Maybe it was the way that he no longer pawed her or tried to tease out a response, hoping that their sex life would reignite just once and become something more than it had been for most of their marriage. Or perhaps the flush to his cheeks gave him away.

Mary always cleaned the house afterwards. At least that's how it seemed.

He turned over and looked towards the window. He could see the tops of the sycamore trees in the park nearby, giving the roofs a frame, and birds swirled overhead. It felt like freedom out there. In here, it was stifling.

He closed his eyes. It had once been good with Mary, but they had been younger then. She had been the quiet girl who worked on the tills when he had his first job in a super-market. He had loved her the first moment he saw her, from the nervous way she toyed with her hair to the way she blushed when he tried to make a joke. But their sex life had always been the same, all shy and coy, as if, for Mary, it had only ever been about the closeness afterwards.

They should have had children, and maybe that would have changed things, but they had found it difficult. For a while it became all about producing children, so the fertile days turned into an obligation, and as they failed, as all Mary's friends got families, Mary became colder.

It was just the way it was, he knew that, but Mary hadn't seen it that way.

He hadn't meant to look outside of the marriage, but it had come along when he wasn't expecting it.

He put the pillow around his ears and tried to stop himself thinking of it. It had gone on too long now. He prayed for the day when he could get through a summer and not see her face, red, bloody, or hear her shouts. But the memories hit him like a punch each time.

He heard a car pull up outside, and he wondered again whether it was a police car, that gnawing dread of discovery back again, but then he heard the loud chatter of his neighbour.

He threw back the sheets and sat on the edge of the bed. As he looked around the room he saw a shadow just disappear from view, like someone skipping through the doorway. He ran his hand across his forehead. He had the sweats again. He always got them at this time of year, when the scents brought everything back. He needed to get out of the house. He had to sell things, it was what he did, but the fake smiles were wearing grooves into his cheeks. To make money he had to overprice, but the internet and lack of credit made people shop around.

Maybe it wouldn't matter, he told himself. So what if he lost all of this? He could go abroad, sell cold beers and hot pies to expat Brits in a Spanish seafront bar; for a moment, as he thought of it, his life seemed to have a point. But then his mood darkened again. He knew that he couldn't. He felt tied to Blackley, as if events beyond his control would occur if he went elsewhere and the life he wanted to leave behind would just drag him straight back.

He climbed out of bed and went to the shower. He had to start another day.

Chapter Seventeen

Lancashire felt like another country as I rode the underground to Canary Wharf, squashed into the carriage and making snake-shapes with my body to find a space between the suits. This had once been my life, working at the *London Star*, my first break in the city before I went freelance. I had travelled to London with my head filled with tales of long lunches in Fleet Street, deadlines met through the fog of flat beer; Tony Davies was to blame for all these stories. When I had arrived there, it was the glass and steel of Canary Wharf that had been my playground instead, most of my journalism done on the telephone. That's why I went freelance, just so I could feel the big city more, to try and find its heartbeat. And it had worked for a while, the fun of getting to drug raids first, and cultivating police sources. Laura had been one of those sources, before the move to the North.

The good times in London had waned eventually. I struggled to get to the underbelly because I didn't really know the city. I knew the landmarks, the geography, but the people constantly surprised me. They had a confidence, almost an arrogance, and I realised that I had never stopped being the northern boy, a long way from home.

Canary Wharf looked just as I remembered it when I emerged from the cavernous underground station – flash and fast and all about the money. But the real London was not far away, the ethnic mix of Poplar, from the window boxes of the London pubs to the takeaways and noise of the East India Dock Road. In the Wharf I brushed past dark suits and good skin, the strong jaws of the successful who I guessed would know nothing of the real Docklands, the hard work replaced by flipcharts and bullshit.

But I wasn't there for a tourist trip or to wallow in the memories. I was there to meet my old editor, Harry English, still head of the news desk at the *London Star*. I'd given him a wake-up call before I left Lancashire, promised him the first feel of the story, just to get an idea of its value. He was waiting for me on the marble seats opposite the tube station exit. To reach him I had to weave through the crowds of young professionals enjoying their lunch break and a group of salesgirls trying to persuade people to test-drive a Volvo. Times must be hard. It had been a Porsche the last time I had been down there.

Harry grinned when he saw me and then coughed as he clambered to his feet.

'Jack Garrett,' he said. 'Good to see you again.' He grabbed my hand warmly to give it a firm pump. 'What have you been up to?'

I patted my stomach. 'Enjoying more of the high life than you. You look well, Harry,' I said, and I meant it. He was tall, six feet and more, but he used to be fat, his chest straining his shirts and his face a permanent purple as he cursed his way around the newsroom. He'd shed some of that fat and settled for stocky, and it suited him.

'I had a heart attack last year,' he said, his smile waning.

'I didn't know,' I said, shocked. 'I would have come down.'

'It's not the sort of thing that you send postcards about,' he replied, and then he looked around and curled his lip in disdain. 'And so I have to eat out here now, box salads, sometimes that sushi stuff, but that's just rice as far as I can tell.'

'Beats dying, Harry.'

He grimaced. 'Just about,' he said, and then straightened himself. 'So what hot story have you got? If it's about a footballer, forget it. They can get injunctions quicker than I can type the story. Sell their weddings for thousands and then bleat about privacy when they break the vows.'

'No, it's not about footballers,' I said. 'It's about Claude Gilbert.'

Harry looked surprised for a moment, and then he chuckled. 'Not that old has-been,' he said. 'The internet ruined that story. We could run a hoax sighting for a couple of days a few years ago, but now some distant relative on the other side of the world can wreck the story before lunchtime on the first day, and it gets splashed all over the rival websites. Unless you can dig him up, no one will bite any more.'

My expression didn't change, but he must have seen the amusement in my eyes.

'What have you got on him?' he asked, his face more serious now.

'Someone's told me that she's involved with him, romantically, and that he wants to come forward.'

He laughed. 'Do you believe her?'

I shrugged. I wasn't sure.

'But you've come all the way to London to check it out,' Harry said, his laughter fading. He watched people going past for a few seconds, and then he asked, 'Why now? It's not another Ronnie Biggs, is it, going to jail to die – because I don't think Claude will get out again like Ronnie did?'

I shook my head. 'He wants to tell his story before the police come for him. The press decided he was guilty twenty years ago, and so he wants to give his version before he goes before a jury, just to give himself a fighting chance.'

Harry wasn't laughing any more. 'And what if you decide not to go along with his plan?' he said. 'You could just expose him and be the man who caught Claude Gilbert.'

'I'll see how good his story is first,' I said. 'I'm still not sure it's really him.'

'And if it isn't?'

'The story runs as another hoax,' I said, 'and you get a bit of northern brass for your city readers to snigger at. She's an ex-lover of Gilbert who was seeing him a few months before his wife was buried alive, and she says they've re-kindled the romance.'

I could see Harry's mind race through the sales figures, the syndication rights.

'I can see that there's an angle, but the hoax is page eight at best, not the front,' he said. 'You might just get your train fare back. We need Gilbert himself for the banner headline.'

I smiled. Harry hadn't yet said anything I hadn't expected.

'So, where are you meeting him?' he asked.

I shook my head. 'She hasn't told me yet,' I said, and I patted Harry on the arm. 'I'll keep my movements quiet for now.'

'What, you don't trust me?' he said, feigning a hurt look.

'You're an editor,' I said. 'You would shit in your grand-mother's shoes if you thought it would get you good circulation figures, and Claude isn't going to come forward if there's someone with a big lens hiding behind a tree.'

'Okay,' he said, chuckling again, holding his hands up in submission. 'What do you want?'

'An expression of interest,' I replied. 'Six-figure sum if it's true. Exclusive rights.'

'And picture rights?'

'That depends on the big number.'

Harry nodded. 'If you get Claude Gilbert, I'm sure we can sort something out.'

'Good,' I said. 'We've got a deal.'

'So what next?' Harry asked, and he looked pleased with himself.

'I find Claude Gilbert,' I replied, and started walking back to the arched entrance of the underground station, the excitement of a guaranteed front page putting a smile on my face.

Chapter Eighteen

Frankie parked his scooter in the same place as he had the day before, near the cottage outside Turners Fold, his helmet chained and padlocked to the footboards. He clambered over the gate again and set off along the two-rut track, looking around as he went, checking that no one could see him. When he got close to where he had been the night before, the spot marked by a stick jammed into the ground, he crawled along the floor to make sure that he couldn't be seen, his knees swishing through the long grass that gathered against the wall.

He peeped over the wall and smiled when he saw he had the same view, that he'd got it right. The bathroom window was closed now but the curtains to the bedroom were open, like they had been the night before, when he had caught her as she went in after her shower, a towel around her body.

He wanted to get closer now. He had taken a few pictures the night before. He had trained his camera on her but then turned away as her towel slipped down her body. His camera had carried on clicking though, because he knew it was different that way. He wasn't looking at her body, he knew it was wrong to do that, but his pictures were different. They were just photographs, not really her. Not really any of them. His photographs. Just scrambles of colour.

He reached into his bag and produced his water bottle. He knew he could be there for a long time.

Then he noticed that her car wasn't there. There was the red sports car, but the house looked dark.

It was time to get closer.

I found Susie waiting for me under the vast timetable at Victoria station as we'd arranged, conspicuous in her heels and short skirt among the backpackers and metropols. I weaved through the travellers; when I caught Susie's eye, she rushed towards me and grabbed me by the arm.

'About time,' she said, her voice tetchy.

'What's wrong?' I asked. 'Why the urgency?'

'Because I can't smoke in here,' she said, and she set off towards the exit.

'Slow down,' I said, laughing. 'Don't you want to know how I've got on?'

'Walk and talk,' she said. Once we got outside, she pulled a cigarette packet from her handbag and lit up quickly. She blew smoke past me and sighed. 'Go on, what's the news?' she said, suppressing a cough but seeming calmer now.

'I went to speak to my old editor.'

Susie looked suspicious. 'You told me that much, but why couldn't I come along?'

'Because I didn't want you to be annoyed if he wasn't interested.'

'And is he interested?'

I nodded and smiled. 'Oh yeah, he's buying,' I said, although when a smile broke across her face too, I added quickly, 'but Claude's got to come forward. Without him, *you* are the story, and if it's just you, you won't get much more than a new handbag out of it. And it could ruin your life.'

Susie took another long pull on her cigarette, a determined look in her eyes. 'He'll come forward,' she said. 'Follow me. I know where we need to be.'

She walked off ahead of me, towards the jukebox rumble that drifted onto the street from the Shakespeare, a red-fronted pub opposite the station, though the music couldn't compete with the constant roar of diesel engines from the stream of buses and taxis. It was a busy corner of London and right now it seemed like everyone – suits and shoppers, groups of old ladies – was leaving, heading for the trains or coach station.

Susie pointed ahead, past a double-decker heading to Brixton. 'That's where I first saw him, crossing the road there,' she said. 'He was carrying a Sainsbury's bag, with a newspaper under his arm.'

'So he was living around here, not just passing through,' I said.

Susie smiled. 'You're sharp.'

'So why don't we just go to where he is, if he's not far away?' I said, trying hard to keep the frustration out of my voice.

'Because this is how he wants it.'

'And how long do we wait?'

'Until he feels the time is right,' Susie said.

'Is he watching us now?' I asked, looking around.

Susie shrugged. 'Possibly,' she said. 'Probably, even.' She brandished her phone. 'He'll call me, when the time is right.'

I sighed, impatient. I pointed to a small park nearby, really just a triangle of grass behind black railings. 'We'll go in there and wait.'

We crossed over and stepped up to the gate, but it was locked. Instead, we had to settle on the wall near to a statue of some old soldier. I tried to give myself a good view down the street towards where Susie had said she'd first seen him, but I couldn't help wondering again whether this was some elaborate hoax. And for what purpose? Susie looked ill at ease as she sat on the wall. It was low down, really just a base for the railings, and so she had to position her legs side-saddle to protect her modesty. She kicked away an old sandwich carton and then slipped off her coat. I saw her tattoo, barbed wire wrapped around her arm, the black now faded to grey, the sharp outlines made jagged by time.

'He must have friends down here, someone sheltering him,' I said. 'A person couldn't stay hidden for this long without someone helping him.'

Susie didn't answer. Instead, she blew smoke into the air as she lit another cigarette.

'Do you think it might have worked out for you and Claude if he hadn't been married?' I asked.

Susie looked up at that, and the sunlight caught the make-up on her face, the powder dry in her creases. 'Maybe,' she said, and then she smiled, lost for a moment in some old nostalgic thought. 'They were good times, you know. He was an old romantic really, despite what you might think of him.'

'I don't think anything of him,' I replied. 'I just don't buy that image, that's all, not when he was a married man.'

'You make it sound dirty. It wasn't like that.'

'Whatever it was like, he was betrothed to someone else.'

'You don't strike me as a man high on morals.'

'Neither are many newspaper editors,' I said, 'but their readers might be, and so they'll write it up to suit. Especially the papers that don't get the exclusive. You'll make some money, sure, but the cash will be tarnished, and your life will stop being your own.'

Susie nodded as if she understood, but then she said, 'It's not about the money. It's about Claude getting his life back.

We'll need the money, and that's why we're doing it like this, but people will be interested in him, not me.' Then she sighed, and for the first time I saw a trace of regret flicker into her eyes. 'If Nancy hadn't died, do you think our little fling would have mattered?' she said. 'So he was a bit of a rat. Most men are, but the person I knew was also tender and caring. That was the memory of Claude Gilbert I carried through the years.'

'And now?'

'Just the same. He seems sadder, that's all, worn out, but still a good man.'

I held up my hand in apology. 'Okay, I'm sorry,' I said. 'I just don't like having my time wasted, that's all.'

'I can only tell you it from my side,' she said quietly, and then we both returned to watching the stream of passers-by.

'Will Claude be able to answer the main question people will ask?' I said.

Susie looked up. 'Which is?'

'If he didn't kill Nancy, who did?'

Susie let out a breath at that and scratched the side of her mouth with a varnished nail. 'I'll let him tell you that.'

We stayed there for over two hours, watching the traffic get busier as time crawled towards the evening rush hour. I scanned the pavements, looking for a glimpse of someone that might be Claude Gilbert, but I couldn't spot him. Susie smoked incessantly, and the ground around her feet became a collection of brown dog-ends as we made small talk.

'Why don't you just ring him?' I said eventually.

Susie shook her head. 'That's not how he wants it. It has to be on his terms.' She must have spotted my scowl, because she added, 'I need a drink. I'm sorry it's not worked out yet, so let me make it my round.' When I looked at her, she smiled. 'It's the least I could do.'

I felt a stab of guilt. Susie knew that, for as long as Claude Gilbert didn't appear, the story would become about her, the northern girl who loved her murderer on the run, maybe the last mistress before the murder; I knew how much her life would change.

'No, don't worry,' I said, returning the smile. 'It's on me.'

Susie looked pleased with that, and we moved away from the rush of Victoria to the peace and quiet of Belgravia.

Chapter Nineteen

Back at the police station, Laura was showing Thomas how to watch the CCTV from one of the local supermarkets. It was never a case of click and play, Laura knew that, with every system needing different software. It showed nine different views, like a grainy *Celebrity Squares*, and isolating one camera view seemed more difficult than it needed to be, just to catch the pensioner dropping the bottle of cheap sherry into the tartan trolley.

She turned as she heard a cough from the doorway and saw a face she hadn't seen for a few months, his hair cropped army-short, a folder under his arm. Laura felt her cheeks flush red.

'DC McGanity,' he said, and then he looked down at her uniform. 'Sorry, is it plain old constable now?'

'Joe Kinsella,' she said, laughing, and her eyes followed his glance downwards, to the shine on her black trousers and her stumpy black boots. 'Sometimes you've got to move sideways to find the route up,' she said. 'Enough about me. What are you doing in Blackley?'

'Looking for you,' he said.

Laura raised her eyebrows. 'This sounds ominous,' she said. 'Where's the rest of the squad?'

Joe worked on the Major Incident Team, based at

headquarters a few miles away. Whenever there was a death that seemed too much for the local police, they descended on Blackley and took over the station. But Laura hadn't heard of any recent murders.

'It's just me and Rachel,' Joe said, indicating the woman standing behind him. 'This is Rachel Mason,' and he gestured towards Laura. 'This is Laura McGanity. We worked a case together recently.'

Laura straightened herself as Rachel looked her up and down, just a quick glance and a smile, but the warmth didn't make it to the eyes. Rachel was trim in a smart grey suit, cut closely to her body, with a shirt that gaped open at the breast. Her hair was Abba-blonde, sleek and straight and over her shoulders, her skin pale and smooth. Her ice-cold, blue-eyed stare told Laura that Rachel Mason had little interest in Joe catching up with old friends.

'So the rest of the pressed-shirts have stayed at headquarters,' Laura said.

'For now,' he said, and then he raised his file. 'I'm here for a cold case review, so I'll be hanging around for a while. I want to ask your advice though.'

Laura was surprised. 'Me?'

Joe nodded. 'Especially you.'

Laura turned to Thomas and told him that the footage needed to be on a watchable disk before the prosecution would use it, then followed Joe and Rachel out of the room, heading for the canteen. Joe didn't say much and Laura sensed that he was avoiding her gaze. He bought three coffees and they all sat down.

'I'm not sure what I can advise you on,' Laura said, as she took a drink. 'I'm off the big stuff now.'

Joe stirred his coffee and looked embarrassed for a moment. 'It's about Jack,' he said.

Laura was taken aback. 'Jack?' she said. 'What's he been doing now?'

Joe put his folder on the table and leant forward, speaking in a whisper. 'It's nothing to worry about, Laura, but we need to know what he's doing.'

'You're talking in riddles,' Laura replied. 'Who is *we*? Do you mean you and Rachel, or is there a bigger *we*?'

'There are others who are interested too,' Joe said. 'Tell me about the woman who went to your house yesterday morning.'

Laura had raised her cup to her mouth, but now her hand paused in mid-air. 'Have you been watching us?' she said, her voice indignant.

Rachel smiled, but it was sneering.

'We haven't been watching you,' Joe said solemnly. 'Or Jack.'

'So it's her,' Laura said, almost to herself, and then she sat back and folded her arms. 'Who is she?'

'If she said she was called Susie Bingham, then she is exactly who she said she was,' he replied. 'But why was she at your house?'

'To see Jack.'

'Has he mentioned why?'

Laura paused and closed her eyes for a second. It was the same old story, Jack's reporting career causing problems for her, once more torn between her duties as a police officer and her loyalty to Jack.

'No, he won't tell me,' she said.

'So you asked?' Joe said.

Laura took a sip of her coffee to give her time to think of her answer. 'A woman came to my home,' she said. 'I wanted to know who she was, but he wouldn't say.'

Joe watched her for a moment, and then he nodded. 'Okay,

I understand,' he said. 'But will you call me if you find anything out?'

'Don't make me spy on my boyfriend,' Laura said quietly.

He shook his head. 'No,' he said. 'I want you to spy on Susie Bingham.' He got to his feet. 'And this conversation remains confidential. If no news comes this way, then none goes the other. Is that okay?'

Laura nodded slowly, and then gave a small laugh. 'It will pique his interest more if I tell him.'

Joe smiled at that, but then he added, 'I mean around the station too. We'll pretend we haven't spoken.'

'Why round here?' Laura asked. 'Who the hell is she?'

'I'll tell you one day, but not just yet.'

Laura thought back to the early morning visit. Whatever the woman had said, it had sent Jack to London.

'Is Jack in danger?' Laura asked.

Joe thought for a moment. 'I don't think so,' he said, and then he walked off, his folder back under his arm, Rachel trailing behind him.

When she was alone again, Laura glanced over towards the room she had been in before to see Thomas looking over, a concerned look on his face. As Laura turned away, she took a sip of coffee, just to occupy her mind – but her hand was shaking on the polystyrene cup.

We turned into Lower Belgrave Street, and it seemed to immediately fall quiet, a haven so close to the bustle of Victoria. We found a pub halfway along, the Plumbers Arms, a dimly lit, one-room place with a dog-legged bar and high wooden seats, beer mats pinned up behind the bar and bright purple pansies hanging from baskets outside.

Susie sat at one of the tables as far from the bar as she could, her eyes concealed behind dark glasses. She asked for a vodka and coke, and I settled for a pint of bitter. I watched as the froth disappeared before I had taken my first sip.

I raised my glass. 'To Claude Gilbert.'

Susie nodded, although she seemed uncomfortable.

'He must live around here,' I said.

Susie flashed a thin smile. 'Why do you say that?'

'Because you're hiding, here in the corner, behind those dark glasses,' I replied.

'It's the clientele, that's all,' she said, looking down. 'They make me uncomfortable.'

'What do you mean?' I asked, looking around. There were a couple of suits by the doorway, their shirt collars un-buttoned, their ties pulled down, and the rest looked just like normal drinkers, except better dressed. 'They're just like you and me, relaxing after work.'

'No, they're nothing like you and me,' she said. 'They've had all the chances, and I haven't, and I can tell that they know that when they look at me.'

I patted her hand. 'You've been in the North too long,' I said, and then tapped my shoulder. 'You need to lose the chip.'

Susie shuffled in her seat. 'Yeah, maybe, but I know that you wouldn't see people like that in Blackley, with that confi-dence, that sureness, like an arrogance, because the ones that have it leave Blackley and end up somewhere like this.'

I didn't pursue it. I had come to London on the promise of a long-lost murderer coming out of hiding, and it had come to very little so far, so I wasn't in the mood for Susie's northern neurosis. Self-deprecation was the northern default, I knew that – get the hits in yourself before someone else has a go and hits even harder. I turned the conversation instead to small talk and kept on glancing around the pub as we chatted, watching how the barman worked the bar, always polishing and talking, like he knew the customers. He waved them goodbye and called them by their first name, so he was more than just some Australian working his gap year.

Susie grabbed her cigarette packet. 'I'm going outside,' she said, leaving me alone at the table. The barman walked over to me, collecting glasses on his way.

'Does the lady want another vodka?'

I shook my head. 'Not yet,' I replied. I looked towards the door and saw a small plume of smoke drifting away from her; she had her phone clamped to her ear. 'Does she come in here much?' I asked the barman.

He shrugged. 'Ask her.'

'She might lie to me,' I said.

'And I'm not going to get between you both,' he said, before walking back to the bar, glasses in his hand.

Susie came back into the bar, pocketing her phone as she came to the table. She glanced at the barman walking away. 'What were you talking about?' she said.

'Nothing, just taproom chit-chat,' I said. 'He asked me where I was from, that's all.' It was a lie, but Claude was in control at the moment, and I didn't like that. 'So where is he?' I asked.

'He's not ready,' she said.

'What do you mean, *he's not ready*?' I said, slamming my glass down on the table, making everyone in the pub turn round. 'He better get ready, because I've come a long way for this. I've set it up with an editor. If he pisses me around, I write what I've got, which is you.'

'This is a big deal for him,' she said, her voice barely audible. 'He's scared. He's giving up his freedom on a gamble that people will believe him. Just be patient. He's booked us into a hotel. You'll meet him tomorrow.'

I closed my eyes for a moment to keep my temper in check, and I thought of Victoria station, just around the corner. I could hop on the Victoria Line and be at Euston within fifteen minutes. I could catch the next train north and cuddle in behind Laura instead of spending the night in whatever fleapit London hotel Claude had found for us. But then the headline came back to me, front-page exclusive.

'If there's no sign of Claude before lunchtime tomorrow,' I said, 'I go home and the story dies.'

Susie nodded. She understood.

'And I tell the police all you've told me.'

Susie didn't reply to that.

Chapter Twenty

Frankie left the cover of the wall and headed towards the house. He had been watching through his binoculars and had seen no sign of life inside. He crossed the field in front of the cottage, and then checked up and down the road to make sure he hadn't been spotted.

He went to the front door first. It was solid wood, painted red, with a brass knocker. He always had a cover story. Looking for a relative, unsure of the house number. This time he could use the journalist as cover. He banged loudly on the door, but the sound came back as echo. He waited a few more seconds, until he was certain that the house was empty.

He checked up and down the road once more, and then went to the side of the house, slipping on his gloves, his camera in his pocket, small screwdrivers in a pouch in the small rucksack on his back. He pulled on a ski mask, and he felt his excitement rise at the familiar itch of the fabric on his face. The path around the house was blocked by a waist-high gate and so he hopped over that and went into the back garden, not much more than a paved courtyard overlooked by a field that rose in front of him. Frankie smiled. No one could see the back of the house.

Frankie looked up. People took care on the ground floor,

but he knew that it was higher up that people got sloppy. Then he saw it, a window slightly ajar, with superhero curtains and stickers on the glass. A child's bedroom. The window must have been left open to let out some of the warmth and then not closed properly.

He took a deep breath and climbed onto the ground-floor window sill, using the wall for grip. Once there, he was able to reach up to the window sill above, and then, by scrambling, he was able to work his way upwards until he had one foot on the upper sill, his gloved fingers feeling through the gap in the window. When the window lock popped off its latch, Frankie clambered inside.

He looked around. It was a child's bedroom. He didn't want that. He took a drink from the water bottle that he always carried in his bag. He was used to waiting, and so he came prepared.

He went onto the landing and saw that there were only two other rooms upstairs, one of them a bathroom.

He went there first. It was where he got to know someone best, where they hid all their secrets.

The bathroom was small, with a bath under the window and a shower cubicle opposite. He sneaked a look into the glass-fronted cabinet over the sink but there was nothing of interest. Some painkillers, a spare tube of toothpaste.

Frankie looked into the shower and saw a pink plastic razor, and he held the blade up to the light to get a view of the stubble under the blade. He smiled as he thought of her under the water, running the blade up her leg, naked.

He was aroused, his breaths shallow as he put the razor back.

He moved into the bedroom. He had been saving it. No, more than that. He had been savouring it, his favourite part. He knew how to be silent, how not to leave traces, how to make his footsteps silent as he crept upstairs. Sometimes he would stand at the end of the bed, just watching them sleep, and if they slept naked, he found it hard to control himself, knowing that all that prevented him from touching was a thin sheet.

He had almost been caught a few times, but he always knew his exit, moving swiftly and quietly, so they were never really sure in their half-sleep whether he had been there.

If it was too hard at night, then he would visit during the day, when he knew they would be out. He tracked their movements, made notes, so that he knew their work patterns. He knew how to open windows or doors, he practised at his own house, and the ones at the back were always the least secure. He was never in there long, but he liked to lie on their beds and take deep breaths into their pillows, so that he got closer to them than he could get with a camera lens. If they weren't there, they wouldn't know, and so it didn't matter.

He went through their drawers if he was alone. A bra or freshly washed underwear, the cloth between his fingers, rubbing gently. Sometimes, he found sex toys. He liked that. Once he was finished, he was gone. Just a quick check that he had put everything back, so that they would never know when they climbed into bed that he had been there, his head on their pillow.

Her bedroom was dominated by the double bed, with an old wooden wardrobe in one corner and a dresser in the other. He tutted when he saw that a hairdryer had been left plugged in. That could be dangerous. More than that, she would bend down to unplug it and see him, because he knew where he was going to be when she came home: under the bed.

He pulled his camera out of his pocket and took some

pictures. There was no shutter sound – he had chosen one he could disable, and with a slow shutter speed, so that he could take pictures without a flash. He had learnt to hold the camera steady so that there was no shake.

But all that was for later.

He checked his shoes for dirt and, when he was sure that they were clean, he climbed onto the bed. He lifted the ski mask and buried his face into each of the pillows. He could tell which was hers from the traces of perfume.

Frankie reached across to a small set of drawers by the bed. The top drawer was as he thought it would be, filled with her underwear.

His cheeks burned up. He rummaged in the drawer and came out with some knickers, silky and blue. He took off his glove and felt the cloth between his bare fingers, shiny and cold. As he settled into her side of the bed, he tugged at his belt with his other hand.

This wouldn't take him long.

Chapter Twenty-One

Susie grimaced as she went into her room.

'People pay to stay here?' she asked, looking around, her nose crinkled. 'I don't know why they made it non-smoking. At least it would disguise the smell.'

I couldn't argue with that. She had the room next to mine, both identical small spaces decorated in woodchip paper, with a single bed against a window and a narrow track of worn-out carpet leading to the door. It smelled musty, like too many sweaty feet.

'It doesn't look like he's treating you that well,' I said.

Susie sat down and started to lift up the blanket.

'Don't,' I said quickly. When she looked up, I smiled an apology. 'You'll get a better night's sleep if you don't see what's under there,' I said. I pointed towards a door. 'At least there's a bathroom,' and I stepped into her room to click on the light. An extractor fan roared into action and a yellow bulb cast a dusty light over a toilet and a small shower, the curtain stained with mould at the bottom. I conceded defeat. 'If he sticks to his promise, maybe I'll treat you to a night in the Savoy.'

Susie looked around, unimpressed, and then said, 'I'm sorry, Jack. I didn't think he'd make you wait. Perhaps he's getting scared. It's a big change to his life.' When I didn't respond, she tried to sound more cheery. 'So, what do we do for the rest of the evening?'

'We separate,' I said. 'Claude's made me wait, and so I'm going to look round a few old haunts, find a few old friends. What about you?'

Susie looked hurt for a moment as she got the hint that I was planning an evening alone. 'An early night, I suppose,' she said, looking down at her pillow.

'Good,' I replied, and then I turned to go.

I felt a twinge of guilt, but this was a business arrangement anyway, not a date. More than that, the plans I had for the evening couldn't involve Susie. Or, at least not with her knowledge.

As I went into my own room, I felt my phone buzz in my pocket. I pulled it out quickly, hoping it would be Laura, but saw a London number on the screen. I took a guess, and got it right.

'Hello, Harry.'

'Any joy?' came the reply, his voice gravelly, interspersed with wheezes.

'Not yet,' I said. 'I've got to wait for Claude to show himself, and he seems shy at the moment. We'll see what tomorrow brings.' I clicked off the phone.

The room seemed suddenly quiet, though the noise of London still drifted in through the window I had opened: the sound of engines and car horns, shouts and bangs, a city always on the move.

I took a deep breath. I needed another drink, but I had something else to do first.

Frankie heard the rumble of the diesel engine as it came up the hill. He went to the window and looked out, and then jumped back when he saw the Golf. He remembered it from the day before.

He moved quickly to the floor, under the bed, his ski mask pulled back down. He looked up at the bed springs, and then across the room. There was nothing on the floor to make her bend down. He had unlocked the window and checked out the drop. He would have to jump out onto a small patch of grass or wait until she was asleep and then creep out.

He didn't mind waiting. He was patient, and he had learnt to control his breathing so that no one would know he was there.

He went still as the engine turned off, his legs curled up so that his feet couldn't be seen. Then he heard voices come into the house. A woman and a child. Frankie smiled to himself. She would come up the stairs soon, as she must have been at work. She was called Laura. He had found some bills in one of the drawers and some love letters in a small shoebox in the wardrobe. He had tucked some of those into his pocket. They would make for good reading later on.

He became aroused again. Would she be in her uniform, her shirt buttoned tightly? He waited for a few minutes, listening intently, before he heard soft footsteps on the stairs that turned into firm footfalls as she came into the bedroom. She was wearing ankle-high black boots, and the bed sank under her as she sat down to take them off. His breathing had slowed down so that it was impossible to hear. He knew he would be discovered only if he was sloppy or if she looked under the bed. But who ever looked under their own bed?

The boots were thrown to the floor and then he watched as she peeled off her socks. She went to the curtains to close them. She hadn't noticed that the window was unlocked.

It was harder to control his breathing as her trousers dropped to the floor, and then her underwear. He extended

123

his arm as she stood up, as he could tell she was facing the other way. He guessed she was unclipping her bra. He took a couple of quick photographs, the shutter silent, and then pulled his arm back in again.

She rummaged around for a towel and then went into the bathroom.

He clicked on the camera screen and reviewed the pictures he had taken. He had got her, naked, distracted; the private Laura McGanity. He liked her. From the photographs he had stolen from a drawer, she reminded him of his mother, from the way she brightened when she smiled, the dimples in her cheeks, her teeth bright. He remembered how protective his mother had been of him, and for him. She had told him that it was a bad world out there, with people who would laugh at him, or hurt him. Try to keep away from the outside world, she had told him. At home, no one would hurt him. His mother was gone, and he missed the way she would hold him, his head to her breast, whispering his name into his ear. *My Frankie, my Frankie.*

That's why he loved his camera. He could look at the outside world but still stay hidden, still stay unhurt. He would try and get more pictures before he left, but he had no need to take any more risks now. He looked at the bed springs again. It was all about the wait now, for that moment when he could creep out undetected.

The shower stopped, and he realised that she would be coming back into the bedroom shortly. Frankie closed his eyes and concentrated on slowing his breathing so that she would never know he was there.

Chapter Twenty-Two

I closed my room door quietly, the lock making not much more than a soft click, and crept along the hallway. I paused outside Susie's door and listened. I could hear the television, so I kept going and walked slowly down the stairs, hoping that a creak wouldn't give me away.

The hotel lobby was just a corridor with a small counter, rows of key rings behind, and then a glass door to the street outside. But there were also rooms at the back of the hotel, and a green plastic sign pointed that way as a fire exit. Susie's room overlooked the front, and so I knew she wouldn't see me if I went out the back way.

I couldn't see any staff, and so I followed the green arrow, past clusters of doors, to a wooden fire door. It was unlocked and opened into a small yard, and once through that, I was in the alleyway that ran along the back of the line of hotels.

I walked slowly along the alley before taking up a position at the end of the street, so that I could see who went in and who went out of the hotel. The street was busy with a mix of dossers and young travellers, most heading for Victoria station, and the midsummer lightness made it hard to conceal myself. I just had to hope that Susie didn't spot me if she went out. She didn't want to spend the night alone, I could tell that, and she had been in touch with Claude throughout the day. I guessed that she would risk a trip to meet him. I looked around to see if I was being watched – wondering whether Claude was watching me somewhere nearby – but I couldn't see anyone loitering. It was just the usual London bustle.

My hunch proved right, and I was there for only thirty minutes before Susie emerged from the hotel. She looked left and right and then walked swiftly away from me, bustling along in her heels, the clicks loud in the street. I set off after her, fifty yards behind, my eyes fixed on her hair. She turned down a side street, making it more difficult to follow, and so I hung back and waited for her to go onto the next street before rushing down to see which way she went. By the time I got down there, I saw that she was just disappearing around another corner, and so I raced once more to keep up with her.

I stopped at the next corner and peered around it, getting ready to begin the pursuit again, when I saw that she had stopped and was speaking on her phone. Susie was listening, not talking, and she was looking around anxiously. I cursed under my breath and felt the hairs rise up on my arms. Claude was watching, had been all along. I looked around quickly, tried to look out for someone ducking behind a corner, or the flash of a binocular lens as it caught the fading sun. Then I saw it, a camera lens on the other side of a bus shelter.

I looked behind me, just in time to see the yellow roof-light of a black cab switch off as Susie climbed in. As it drove away, I stepped out from behind the corner and cursed to myself.

I'd lost her, and maybe lost Claude too.

Laura looked around the living room. Something wasn't right. The feeling had been there ever since she came home, a sensation that she wasn't alone that made her skin prickle under the soft cloth of her T-shirt. Her eyes shot to the ceiling. She thought she'd heard a creak. Was it just Bobby getting out of bed? No, it wasn't that, she knew it.

She reached for the remote control and silenced the television. It was suddenly too quiet. Her eyes drifted to the window; the night was drawing in, so that the view outside had turned purple.

She looked over her shoulder, to the table at the other end of the room where Jack did his writing, past the front door, her gaze drifting to the other windows. She thought she could see movement outside, but maybe it was just the shifting of the branches in the breeze.

Laura rose slowly to her feet, her ears keen, the creaks of the sofa like loud cracks now. She was being stupid, she told herself, there was nothing to make her think she wasn't alone. Except that receptor in her brain that detected the presence of a person, like human radar, a certainty that someone was watching her.

She cursed the location of the cottage, so isolated and vulnerable, just a rickety wooden door protecting her from whoever was outside. Why did this have to happen when Jack was a few hundred miles away? But then she was angry with herself. Why did that matter? She thought back to her training all those years ago, and the self-defence refresher courses she had been on, those afternoons being hurled onto a mat by a police instructor. If someone was outside, she would have to deal with it on her own. She remembered what she had told Thomas the day before: get the first strike in and make it a good one, leave no room for a second assault.

As she moved through the room, her eyes flicked between the windows and looked for movement. All she could hear was the shuffle of her bare feet on the rug that turned into quiet slaps as she stepped onto the stone floor that ran to the end of the room. The kitchen was nearby, and she thought about getting a knife. But what if she was disarmed? It would be used against her. Then again, what if whoever was out there was *already* armed? Laura could feel the tension in her muscles as she crept forward, her eyes scanning the windows all the time.

Then her eyes shot to the front door. Had she locked it when she came in? *Think, think.* Bobby had been in the car, and she had shopping bags with her. She had come in and put the bags on the table, and then she had got changed. So, no, she hadn't. She wasn't in the habit of locking the door. She had moved to the North so she could stop doing that. The keys were on the table, attached to her car keys. She grabbed them and moved slowly forward, keeping an eye on the latch. Was it moving?

Laura rushed at the door and threw her weight against it, panting, scared now. She thrust the key into the lock and turned it quickly, taking deep gasps when she heard the lock click into place. Then her eyes flicked around the room. Were the windows locked?

Then she thought of Bobby and ran for the stairs.

Chapter Twenty-Three

I walked quickly towards the camera lens, angry at the intrusion. A figure stepped out from behind the bus shelter, the camera pointed downwards.

'Sorry, Jack,' a voice said, and when I got closer, I saw that it was Dave, one of the staff reporters at the *Star*, a public schoolboy turned mockney, his take on East End fashion a flat cap and tight jeans.

'Did Harry send you?' I asked, although I knew the answer even before he shrugged and looked sheepish. 'How did you find me?'

'Harry thought you were being too cloak and dagger, and so he had me watching you when he met you. As soon as you went back on the tube, I followed.'

I shook my head. His accent had got worse, all mangled vowels. 'But I was looking around,' I said. 'I would have recognised you.'

Dave reached into the canvas bag hanging from his shoulder and pulled out a grey scarf. 'I just kept my head down with this around my face,' he said. 'I was on the next carriage, watching you. You've been out of the game too long, Jack, and you're getting sloppy.' He put the scarf away and patted me on the shoulder. 'I'm sorry, Jack. I hope I haven't blown your story.'

'Doesn't Harry trust me?' I frowned.

Dave slumped slightly. 'It's not that,' he said. 'We're struggling, Jack, all the papers are, and Harry was worried that someone else would hear of the story, whatever it is, and offer more. We wanted something in the bag so we could go first. Harry knows you're good for your word, but everyone has their price, and what if you got an offer you couldn't refuse?'

'I know I'm a journo, but I've got honour too,' I said, angrily. 'I gave Harry first refusal. He's still got it, but he's pushing it.'

Dave said nothing. He was just doing his job.

I blew out, frustrated. 'C'mon,' I said. 'You've spoiled my story. The least you could do is buy me a drink.'

As I set off back towards the hotel, Dave ambled alongside, his legs gangly and awkward. I wasn't in the mood for talking just yet, and we walked past the hotel and on towards Victoria, where the traffic fumes assaulted my nostrils and a hundred different languages made no sense around me.

'Where are we going?' Dave asked.

'To feel the city,' I said.

I had realised when I first moved to the capital that the way to appreciate the city is not to go with its rhythms, but to stop and watch it rush by. The underground used to excite me, the echo of the trains as they rumbled out of the tunnels, and then the hum as they set off. They reminded me of my success, of how journalism had taken me a long way from home, but once that wore off, I took to walking, so that I could *feel* the city, not simply rush underneath it.

'Is this another northern way, Jack?' he said. 'No public transport?'

'I'm building up a thirst.'

The route took us towards Westminster, and most of it

wasn't pretty, just lines of office blocks, the drabness broken only by the occasional theatre or church. If it wasn't for the stream of red buses, I could have been pretty much anywhere.

'So, cards on the table,' Dave said, 'why are you here?'

I realised then that his brief had been just to follow me and get pictures. Harry hadn't trusted Dave to know much about the story.

'Just following a tip,' I said.

He pulled a face and then asked, 'How is it up north?'

We had reached Parliament Square and, as we threaded through the tourists outside the splendour of Westminster Abbey, the London Eye turning slowly behind the Parliament silhouette, I thought of Laura, alone in our Lancashire cottage. I had a sudden yearning to be there, away from all this noise and hostility. I wanted to hear nothing but the crackle of branches outside our window and the rustle of the sheets as Laura nestled into the crook of my arm. I wanted to smell her perfume, feel her hair wind around my fingers.

'It's good,' I said.

'You're not being very talkative.'

'You're here to find out what I know,' I said. 'That makes me go quiet.'

Dave sighed at that and kept on walking.

We made small talk as we headed to the South Bank, and for a while we caught the remnants of street theatre, young African men in ragged T-shirts scratching a living by doing football tricks, or mime artists standing motionless in Tudor costumes. We stopped for a few minutes to watch them and take in the view, the murky Thames as the backdrop.

'I miss this sometimes,' I said.

Dave looked at me, surprised. 'You said you liked it in the North.'

'I do, but it's so familiar,' I said. 'Maybe I never stopped being the northern boy, dazzled by the bright lights. Should I have asked Laura to leave all this behind? She's from Pinner, and I know that's got a small-town feel, but it's nothing like where I'm from.'

'Laura?'

'I met her down here, a detective, and she moved to Lancashire with me.'

'She must be special,' Dave said.

'She is,' I said.

'You weren't like this in the old days,' Dave said. 'You've gone soft.'

I smiled. 'Maybe.' I pointed towards a footbridge that would take us over the river. 'Let's go for that drink.'

We sauntered towards Molly Moggs, a small bar on Charing Cross Road, intimate and quaint. Although I didn't fit into its normal clientele – it was on the edge of the Soho gay scene – it was quiet and good for a drink. Inside the pub, the inevitable drag act hadn't got going yet; only a skin-and-bones old man in short skirt and lipstick gave a hint of how the pub would finish the night.

I lifted my phone out of my pocket to let Dave know that I was making a call and then pointed him towards the bar. When Laura answered, I thought she sounded distracted.

I told her that my story wasn't panning out like I had hoped and tried to keep the rest of the bar out of our conversation, but Laura didn't seem talkative.

'Are you all right?' I asked.

'I'm fine,' she said. 'It's good to hear your voice though.'

'You just don't seem like you're talking much.'

'No, Jack, everything's fine. I'm just tired, that's all.'

We exchanged our goodbyes, and a promise that we would have some time together the next day, and then the line went dead.

The city seemed lonely at that point. People rushed past the pub windows, and in the bar young men in suits smooched or gossiped. An old man with wild hair and a long beard came in, and squeezed past me as he made his way to the bar.

Dave headed back with the drinks. 'Do you fancy hitting a club afterwards?' he asked, his eyes alive with the thought of a boozy late night.

I thought again of Laura alone in our cottage, just the television for company, the papers for her sergeant's exam spread across the table.

I shook my head. 'I need to get back to the hotel,' I said. 'I'm tired.'

Dave looked disappointed. 'You really have changed, Jack,' he said.

I raised my glass. 'I know, and I'm happy.'

Laura clicked off the phone. She was convinced she had heard something upstairs. She had checked that the windows were closed and so it must be Bobby.

The noise became louder, something heavy moving along the floor.

She ran upstairs, two steps at a time, and she heard a bang.

'Bobby!' she shouted as she rushed into his room, clicking on the light. He was sitting up in bed, rubbing his eyes against the light. Then it sounded like someone was in her room, the rumble of feet loud.

Laura bolted towards her room and threw open her bedroom door. Her window was open, the curtains blowing. She had checked it was closed not long before.

She went to the window and tried to see outside. She had no torch and so all she could do was peer into the shadows.

She reached for her phone and dialled 999, a quiver in her voice as she gave out her address. The cottage was isolated and they might catch him on the way down the hill.

Laura ended her call and listened out for movement outside. There was nothing. She looked into the darkness for a few moments, stared at the lights from the small huddle of cottages on the opposite hill, dots of yellow against the purple of the night, the light pollution from Turners Fold in the valley below not reaching them. It was the silence that struck her. For the first time since they had moved north, Jack was a long way from home.

She closed the window, making sure it was locked, and then went back downstairs to wait until the police arrived. She hoped it was someone she knew. She looked at her hands. They were trembling.

Bobby appeared on the landing. 'What is it, Mummy?'

Laura tried to smile. 'Nothing,' she said. 'Go back to bed.'

Chapter Twenty-Four

The morning came around too quickly. The sun was just blinking through the trees as I waited outside the hotel for Susie. I heard the fast click of her heels before I saw her, and then my face was shrouded in her smoke as she took a long pull on her first cigarette of the day. The coughing that followed rattled her body, her cheeks a mottled purple.

'Do you always get up at this time?' I asked, once she had recovered, my voice filled with morning bleariness.

She shook her head. 'Not since Maisy was a child. It was Gilly's idea.'

I was surprised. 'I didn't know you had a child.'

'Any reason why you should?'

'I just thought you might have mentioned her. Most parents do.'

Susie anticipated my next question. 'No, she's not Gilly's child,' she said. 'I got married not long after Gilly disappeared, but it didn't work out.' She raised an eyebrow at me. 'I bet that would have added a zero onto the price, Claude Gilbert's child.'

'It would have added something,' I said. 'So, where do we wait?'

'Same place as yesterday,' she replied.

'I'm patient for a story,' I said, 'but this is wearing thin. If he's not here soon, I go home.'

Susie nodded. 'Okay, I understand. We'll go for breakfast later. That might help.'

We went to the same park as the previous day, but it was still locked, and so we settled on a wooden bench that looked towards the entrance to Lower Belgrave Street.

As we waited, Susie asked, 'Why did you follow me last night?'

I looked at her. I knew there was no point in lying. 'To see if you led me to Claude.'

'But that isn't what we agreed,' she said. 'Claude will make himself known.'

'Yeah, and I'm not sure this was in the agreement either, nursing a hangover with no sign of Claude.'

Susie fell quiet, but I wasn't in the mood for apologising, and so I had only the passing crowd to entertain me. It seemed different in the morning; quieter, more earnest, everyone with the day ahead, teeming out of the station, heading for work or onward travel. The lights began to flicker into life as the shops began another working day, and I stared into the crowds, looking for a face that didn't fit. Everyone seemed passive, passionless, concentrating on whatever was streaming through their headphones. I expected Gilbert to stand out, his eyes flitting around him, furtive, alert, always waiting for the recognition.

But there was no one who caught my attention. Just a stream of suits and anonymity.

I checked my watch. Eight thirty. 'C'mon, let's go for that breakfast,' I said. 'He's running out of time.'

Laura let the steam from her coffee bathe her face as she held the cup to her chest. She was scouring the fields, looking for some hint of whoever had been in her house, but it was hard to concentrate.

It had been a long night. She'd had no real sleep, just snatches in the chair, too scared to go to bed. She had tried to do some revision for the sergeant's exam, but the words just swam before her eyes whenever she looked at a page and her head dipped and jerked as she tried to stay awake.

Coffee had kept her going, but now her eyes felt heavy, the skin sore under her eyes, and her legs twitched if she stayed still.

Who had been in the house, and why?

She checked her watch. She had to go to work soon, Bobby to drop off on the way, and then the house would be vulnerable again. Would someone be waiting for her when she got back? If Jack wasn't home, she would take Bobby and stay away.

Laura cursed herself. She was supposed to be stronger than this, and now she had a whole day to get through on hardly any sleep.

She took a gulp of coffee. She would wait until the caffeine kicked in, and then she would set off.

She turned away from the window and looked at the papers strewn by her chair, revision books and specimen questions scattered over the floor. It would be a long day, and she knew that this wasn't the best preparation. She jolted when she heard a noise from upstairs, and then cursed as hot coffee spilled over her knuckles. She knew that it was only Bobby, but she was jumpy, unnerved.

Laura sucked at her fingers to cool the heat from the spilled coffee and then headed towards the stairs. She had to start the day, somehow make everything seem normal again.

Mike Dobson joined the rush-hour queue into Blackley.

He worked out of one of the office complexes by the motorway, and so he knew he would be late, but he was nonetheless drawn to check out the streets he had driven around the other night, just to see if she was there. He'd thought about her ever since the other night, of her promise that they would do more than just pull up by the old viaduct.

The cars that streamed into Blackley snaked their way to work through twisting back streets, around some convoluted one-way system designed to get traffic in and out of the narrow Victorian streets without snarling up, and so for the last part of his journey Mike was taken through the streets he sometimes crawled at night.

Tears formed in his eyes. He should leave Mary, he knew that, but he couldn't. Fear kept him there, scared of how much Mary might know of his secret, and how much she would strike back if he left her.

He heard a horn behind him, and as he looked up he saw that the queue had moved forward. He raised his hand in apology and set off to rejoin the back of the queue twenty feet further on.

As the car in front sent up small flumes of blue smoke, he looked out of the car window again, glancing up and down the streets, hoping for a glimpse of the girl, maybe on her way to the shops or something, doing something ordinary that would make her more real, not how she was when he saw her last, short skirt and vacant grin.

He sighed. He couldn't see her. There was always tonight though. As he thought about that, he felt the excitement begin to flutter in his stomach.

Chapter Twenty-Five

We settled into a café at a crossroads on Lower Belgrave Street. It fancied itself as upmarket, real food having been replaced by cakes and small Italian biscuits. Oil paintings of Tuscan views lined the walls and the air hung heavy with the smell of strong coffee. I saw the relief in the owner's eyes as we settled at the back, at a table in the shadows. I felt bleary-eyed and smelled of stale beer, and Susie was wearing the same clothes as the day before, so we hardly fitted in with the well-groomed businessmen sitting at a table by the door, their shoes so polished that they reflected the sun streaming through the large windows.

We didn't talk. I didn't want to miss Gilbert if he showed up, and so I concentrated on the door, my camera in my hand under the table. Susie had sent a text to let Claude know where we were, her hand shielding the screen from me.

The Italian coffee did a good job of waking me up and when the businessmen moved on we had the café to ourselves. I drank the coffee slowly, not sure when Gilbert would arrive, if he ever would. Over an hour passed as we watched the streets grow gradually quieter, until the morning rush was done and the tables outside were empty.

Then Susie grabbed my hand.

'He's here,' she said in a whisper. I saw the excitement in her eyes and looked quickly towards the doorway.

There was a man at a table outside, the waiter taking out a large coffee to him. I felt my hand tense around my camera and found it hard to suppress a smile. If this was Gilbert, it was obvious that his roguish charm had long since left him. He was tall, I could tell that from the way his legs stretched out under the table, but his once-handsome face was now concealed behind a long beard, mainly grey, and above it I could see the spider's web of broken veins. His eyebrows were bushy, with grey fingers of hair pointing to the side, but it was the hair on his head that drew the eye. In the pictures from the newspapers, his hair had been dark, thick and lush. Now, it was bushy and wild, straggling down to his shoulders.

It could be Claude. He looked familiar. I pulled my camera out from under the table. Susie started to look round, and then shook her head. 'No,' she hissed at me. 'No pictures, that's the deal. If you take one, he'll run.'

'But his picture will be everywhere once he comes forward,' I said.

'Except that he still has an escape route if he changes his mind,' Susie countered.

I paused for a moment, and then relented and put it back into my pocket. The man outside had picked up *The Times* and was holding it in front of his face, which must have been the signal, because Susie put her hand on mine. 'You can go speak to him now.'

I rose quickly to my feet and threaded my way through the tables. My mouth was dry with nerves as I drew closer, wondering whether the most infamous fugitive in recent history was really on the other side of the window. I heard the scrape of Susie's chair as she followed me.

The man looked up at me as I strode to his table and, for a second, I saw doubt in his eyes, mixed with some fear, but then he recovered his composure and folded the newspaper back onto the table. I sat down opposite, Susie behind me.

'Hello, Claude,' I said.

His cheeks flushed and his tongue flicked through his beard as he licked at his lips. Then he tutted and wagged his finger. 'A lot of people make that mistake,' he said, his voice deep and rich. I had a moment of doubt as I heard traces of Eastern Europe in his accent.

Then Susie leant towards him. 'Gilly,' she said. 'It's okay.'

He swallowed and then whispered, 'Not here.' He put his folded newspaper under his arm. 'Follow me.'

He stood quickly and brushed past my shoulder as he started to walk along Lower Belgrave Street, past the lines of black railings and porches supported by bright white pillars, with black and white chessboard floor tiles, and pinks and violets and purples trailing from window boxes. I rushed to keep up with him, the fast clicks of Susie's shoes just behind me. His head was down, his steps quick.

I wondered if he was heading for the town park I could see ahead, some trees breaking the building line, but then he ducked quickly through a gate and then down some steps. I looked at the number – forty-six – and made a mental note for the story as I stopped to let Susie catch up. I heard the lock of the door below turn, and spun around to look at her.

'Is he backing out?' I said.

'He won't,' she said, her face determined. 'It's a big moment for him, that's all. It's been a long time.'

I looked down the steps, into the shadows of the small concrete yard. But I hesitated. The person didn't look much like Claude Gilbert, and all I had were the promises of a chain-smoking long-lost lover.

I walked down the stairs slowly, ready for him to rush out, and then gave a firm rap on the door. There was no answer, so I knelt down to the letterbox.

'Mr Gilbert, please open the door.'

There was silence for a moment, and then I heard Susie clomp down the steps behind me. She pushed me to one side.

'Gilly,' she shouted, her face pressed against the glass panel in the door. 'Please open up.'

There was silence for a few seconds, and then I heard footsteps and the low rumble of a key being turned. There was another moment of silence and so I turned the handle. The door swung open slowly and I entered the flat.

Chapter Twenty-Six

Laura was distracted as she wrote her statement.

She was in the report-writing room, another glass box, designed to be a quiet space for officers to work, away from the briefings and the CCTV and the chatter. But what should have been a simple write-up of an arrest she had made a couple of days earlier was turning into a patchwork of mistakes and corrections, the page filling up with crossings-out and initials.

She put down her pen and reached into her pocket for a mint; she could taste her tiredness on her breath. Laura knew what the problem was: the visitor from the night before. Laura knew about the pervert who had been watching people's houses, but she also remembered Joe Kinsella's warning about Jack's story. Was Jack getting involved in something that he needed to keep away from?

She leant back in her chair and looked through the glass walls, into the atrium, at the case-builders heading for the morning canteen run, and the police drivers exchanging moans about their lot, the files delivered to court, taking a break before they began the forensic runs, taking samples to the lab.

Laura knew who she was looking for: Joe Kinsella. He had planted the seed, hinted that Jack might be getting in too deep again. Laura tried to fight the urge to find out more; she suspected that Joe was just drawing her in so that he could find out what Jack knew, but she couldn't fight the doubts. What was it about Jack's story that was making Joe so secretive?

She leant back and looked at the ceiling. Who was the woman who had been at the house the day before yesterday, who was now sharing a hotel with Jack? And why were the police watching her?

Laura thought more about what Joe had said, and remembered that there were some spare rooms on the top floor, furthest from the lift.

She closed her file and went to find Joe.

The basement flat smelled musty when I went inside. It was small, with a dark corridor that went past a box of a kitchen and into a living room furnished with a threadbare sofa and a television on a chipped mahogany table, the wallpaper flowered and old.

My quarry was sitting in a chair in the corner of the room, its filling spewing out through the ragged cloth on the arms. His fingers were steepled under his nose.

'Why did you follow Susie last night?' Claude said quietly, the Balkan accent gone now. 'I said that I would contact you.'

'You had already,' I said, trying to stay calm. 'You were in the pub last night. You came in just after me.'

He tilted his head. 'You have a good memory,' he said, 'and now you see how easy it has been to stay hidden.' He gestured towards a chair by the window.

The springs creaked loudly as I sat down. 'I need to record this interview,' I said, as I rummaged in my pocket for my voice recorder.

'No,' he said, his voice stern. 'That's not what we agreed.'

'And neither was the cat and mouse game around London,' I said. 'I know you wanted everything your way, but now I've found you, I reckon my rules apply.'

'Then there is no interview,' he said.

I pulled my phone out of my pocket. 'Okay,' I said. 'I'll be able to report your arrest at least.'

I pressed nine, and hovered with my thumb over the button, holding his gaze and ready to jab it twice more, but his nerve held steady. I remembered that he was a gambler, poker being one of his vices. Was this a bluff?

'That's not what you want though, is it?' he said. 'You haven't come to my home just so that you can report what will be all over the internet within the hour.' He crossed his legs and tapped his lip with his finger, and then he shrugged. 'If you want to record it, do it your way.'

I turned off my phone and reached for my voice recorder again. I placed it on the arm of the chair. 'Tell me your story,' I said.

He smiled at me. 'I am Josif Petrovic. I lecture in human quantum energy.' The Balkan accent had returned. 'I am from a small village in Serbia called Kovaci, near Kraljevo. I grew up in the mountains nearby, and so I learnt about herbs and flowers, and then I went to university in Belgrade. I am an expert in my field.'

I sighed and looked at the ceiling. My attempt to gain control of the situation hadn't lasted long. I reached out and clicked off the recorder. I let the silence linger for a few seconds before I said, 'Well played, Claude.'

He acknowledged the compliment with a nod.

I pulled out my notebook and a pen. 'So let me ask the one big question, Claude: why now?'

He flashed a look at Susie, and then he looked at his lap, at his clasped hands, and I saw his shoulders slump. When he looked up again, he looked less confident, some of the bravado gone.

'I'm getting old,' he said. 'I'm tired of running and I want to make things right.'

I held out my hands to appease him. 'Tell me your story.'

Claude sighed and looked at the ceiling. I thought I saw tears in his eyes, and then he looked down to smile at Susie. He took hold of her hand. 'I knew this day would come,' he said, his voice soft and quiet. 'I had a speech prepared, but I can't remember it now.'

'I don't need a speech,' I said. 'Just the story.'

He swallowed, and then said, 'It might not be the story you are expecting to write.'

'What do you mean?'

'You want to ask me why I killed my wife, and where I went.'

'Susie told me that it wasn't like that.'

He gave a small laugh. 'It would be easier if it was. For me, anyway.'

'Easier?' I said, confused.

'Yes, easier,' he said. 'If I had killed Nancy, I would just have my guilt to deal with, but through all of these years, I've had to watch as my name was maligned, and Nancy's killer stayed free. That made it harder, so much harder.' He waved his hand at me. 'And the story wouldn't be as good for you if I was guilty.'

'Why is that?'

'Because the story would be about my capture, nothing more,' he said. 'For you, there would be some television interviews, but they won't pay, and the exclusive in one of the Sundays would sort out some bills, but it would become someone else's story, book deals done with people who knew me. You would just sink into a bit-part role, a postscript.

146

No, the real headline is not who found Claude, but who killed Nancy.'

'All I've heard so far is Susie's gut feeling,' I said. 'And if you didn't kill Nancy, why did you go on the run?'

He looked at me and pulled at his beard. 'Because no one would have believed me,' he said eventually. He leant forward in his chair. 'I've got a much better story for you, and it will be all your story if you write it.'

I held out my hands. I was listening. But my fingers were trembling.

'Clear my name,' he said.

I looked at Susie, who was staring at Claude. 'People have tried in the past,' I said. 'There have been theories, and some wild ones. I'll be just another crackpot.'

He nodded. He understood. 'But none have had my story,' he said, his voice firmer now. 'Help me prove my innocence, and I'll go north with you. Press conference, exclusive rights, the whole lot. That's why you're here.' He nodded towards Susie. 'That's why she brought you down.'

'But what if you run out on me?'

He held out his hands and smiled. 'Then you have this, our meeting. But I'm done running.'

Chapter Twenty-Seven

As Laura walked along the landing on the top floor of the station, with views down into the atrium three floors below, she saw that it wasn't Joe in the office on the other side of the glass wall, but Rachel Mason, the icy blonde. She was hunched over some papers on her desk and speaking quietly into her phone. Laura hovered in the doorway to listen in to what she was saying, but could catch only murmurs.

Rachel must have sensed her presence, because she turned round and looked at Laura. Her eyes were cold, and Laura noticed that she closed her file with the other hand, the one that had been open on the desk. Laura knew she ought to move away from the door, but she knew that Joe had played her the day before, dropping hints about Jack being in danger, knowing that she would come back. And so she was there, just as he wanted.

Except that he wasn't there.

Rachel ended her call and swivelled round in her chair.

'Morning, Laura,' she said, the smile that flashed onto her lips not reaching her eyes. 'What can I do for you?'

Laura walked into the room and saw the boxes in the corner, filled with paperwork. Some of it looked old, the edges yellowed and dusty.

'I just came for a chat,' Laura said. 'Yesterday was the first time in a while that I've seen Joe, and it's good to catch up.'

Rachel sat up and smoothed back her hair so that it streamed over her grey suit jacket, her shirt bright blue, the front gaping open at the breast, revealing just the start of her cleavage. Laura felt dowdy in her polyester uniform and pulled herself straight, thrusting her fingers into her equipment belt; then, realising that she just looked awkward, she leaned against the door jamb.

'What, like in a let's-go-for-coffee-and-make-idle-talk kind of way?' Rachel said.

Laura shrugged. 'Maybe.'

Rachel shook her head. 'No, you don't mean that,' she said, and then gestured towards a chair surrounded by boxes. 'If you can find a space, sit down.'

Laura had to move some papers and when she looked again at Rachel, Laura saw that she was smiling at her.

'What's wrong?' Laura asked.

'I can read you,' Rachel said.

'I thought I was more enigmatic than that,' Laura said, sarcasm in her voice.

'Less than you think,' Rachel replied.

'So what do I want?'

Rachel's eyes narrowed for a moment. 'You want to find out what I know about whatever Jack's doing,' she said. 'Jack's visitor was just some woman until yesterday, but now you're worried.'

'You don't have to be a genius to work that out,' Laura said, her irritation showing. 'You set up some vague threat to Jack and then wonder why I'm here.'

'So just come out and ask me what we're investigating.'

Laura folded her arms. 'Okay,' she said, rolling her eyes,

frustrated at having to play the game. 'What are you investigating?'

'The same as Jack.'

'But I don't know what Jack is up to.'

Rachel sat back. 'Then if you want to know what I'm looking into, ask Jack. If you know nothing, you can't help me.'

'And you won't tell, even though you think Jack might be in danger?'

Rachel just smiled.

Laura sighed, trying not to let Rachel's smugness wind her up.

'You need to drop the stand-by-your-man stuff,' Rachel said. 'Your first duty is to the job.'

Laura ground her teeth. 'I know where my duties lie,' she said.

Rachel stared at her. 'We are still police officers, PC McGanity. Be as loyal to Jack as you want, and I admire you for it, but as soon as you buzz your way in through those secure doors, you lock the rest of the world out. Sometimes we have to sacrifice things. It's hard, I know that, but if we don't do the job properly, it just makes it harder for everyone. You can't expect to get involved with a reporter and then keep his secrets for him.'

'I don't need a career lesson from someone who was still flashing her knickers behind the bike sheds when I joined the job,' Laura snapped.

Rachel's smile was cold. 'Be angry with Jack, not me,' she said. 'He shouldn't have told you.'

'He *hasn't* told me.'

Rachel shook her head. 'I don't believe you, because I can see your struggle, in here,' and she tapped the side of her head. 'Between your uniform and your love life. Not everyone makes the right choice.'

'And which is the right choice?'

'The one that makes you happiest,' Rachel said.

Laura nodded slowly and then stood to go. Just before she got to the door, she turned and said, 'I don't know anything about you, and I can see the confidence in your eyes, but I've been doing the job longer than you, and there's more to being a good copper than a sharp suit and good hair. You need to be able to read people, tell when they are lying, and when they are speaking the truth, and you do it badly.' Laura walked away, feeling angry with herself for losing her temper, but at least she had let Rachel know that she wasn't to be cowed.

She took a deep breath and looked down as she heard the jangle of her equipment on her belt, saw how her thighs pressed against the cloth. Rachel had used Laura's uniform against her, made her feel less of a police officer. Laura's cheeks were burning with rage as she reached the stairs, determined that Rachel wouldn't get away with that a second time.

Chapter Twenty-Eight

'So tell me your story,' I said, my hand poised over my notebook.

Claude Gilbert looked at me, and then at my pen, and for a few moments he just stared at it, as if he knew that there was no going back once he started talking. Then he sat back in his chair and turned the stare towards me again, his eyes bright against the dull grey of his beard, which he stroked with his stubby fingers, the nails chewed down, feathers of loose skin alongside them. When he spoke, his voice was strong.

'I am the victim of an unbelievable coincidence,' he said slowly, clearly, and then added, 'and my wife was not the woman you think she was.'

'What do you mean by that?' I asked, sceptical, surprised.

'Just that,' he said. 'I've always been the villain, the rogue, the womaniser. That's what the papers said, that Nancy was the devoted wife, pregnant and loyal. And that picture they sometimes use, you know, the one taken at some garden party, where she's laughing as she tries to hold on to a straw hat, caught by the wind,' he scoffed. 'A real English rose, don't you think?'

'There's a problem,' I countered, and I nodded towards Susie, who looked at the floor, embarrassed. 'You *were* a womaniser.'

He took a deep breath and sat up in his chair. He pointed his finger at me, the tip crooked. 'That does not make me a murderer,' he said, stressing every word. Then he sat back with a slump and exhaled loudly. He looked at the ceiling as he spoke, his voice quieter now. 'I've had plenty of time to reflect, Mr Garrett. Twenty-two years, so I know how I behaved, and I don't care what you think. Yes, I was selfish, a drunk and a flirt, had affairs, but, despite what you think of me, I loved my wife dearly.'

'And Susie?' I asked. 'Did she mean so little to you?'

He looked towards her and smiled, his beard creasing. 'It's not about Susie, any of this,' he said. 'Back then, Susie was just a good time I once had. I know that sounds cruel, but it wasn't meant to turn out like this. We've talked about it, and things are different now.'

As he turned back to me, I raised my eyebrows.

'Don't judge me,' he said, shaking his head. 'It is possible to hurt someone you love. And I know I was hurting Nancy, because when I went home and looked into her eyes, I saw a woman I still loved dearly, who was beautiful and who was fun, and who still loved me back.'

'And what do you think she saw in your eyes?' I said. 'Betrayal?'

He slammed his hand on the chair, sending up a small dust cloud and making me jump, a deeper flush to his cheeks now. I didn't say anything. I let the silence hang there, wanting to hear things his way. He took a few deep breaths, and then he held up his hand in apology. 'Nothing you can say will change anything. I was in the wrong and so I don't blame Nancy. I was never there. I was either working or drinking, and when I was at home, I was always too tired to be a proper husband, if you know what I mean.'

'And gambling?'

He nodded. 'That too,' he said, and then he broke into a smile. 'I was in a lean spell, and so I had to keep on working to earn the stake money.'

'And while you were watching the cards turn at the casino, Nancy was home alone, in that big house?'

Gilbert nodded, his eyes filled with regret. 'She was a passionate woman, and she had needs, I realise that now. And because I wasn't around to fulfil them, she went looking elsewhere.'

That surprised me. 'What do you mean?' I asked.

'What do you think I mean?' he said, and he leant forward again, his arm resting on his knee, his eyes boring into mine. 'Nancy was pregnant when she died, everyone knows that,' he said. 'It's what has kept me in the papers, that I buried my pregnant wife alive. But I am going to tell you something that has not appeared in any newspaper I've read, so listen well, because *this* will make your story unique.'

I looked over at Susie, who was watching intently, her bag perched on her knees. I nodded to let him know that I was ready.

He spoke clearly, slowly, just to make sure that I understood. 'The baby was not mine.'

I opened my mouth to speak, but nothing came out.

Gilbert nodded, a look of triumph on his face. 'You heard me right,' and he pointed at my notepad. 'Write it down: she was pregnant with another man's child.' He became more animated. 'You haven't seen that in the papers, have you?' he said, his finger jabbing at me.

I shook my head slowly. 'How can you be sure?'

He laughed, but it was bitter and short. 'Shall we just say, Mr Garrett, that we weren't straining the bedsprings too often back then? Oh, there were moments, when Nancy felt needy, or after too much wine, but they were weeks apart.

I remember that I was surprised that we could have conceived, but still, it was life-changing, or so I thought. My child, my heir. Why would I think that it was another man's child?' He shook his head. 'It was the scan that made me suspicious, that the expected date of the birth didn't seem right, didn't fit in with when we had last been in bed together. And then Nancy changed. She became more withdrawn, cold. I don't know what her plan had been, whether she had always known that it wasn't mine, or whether she was just unsure, but then one day she sat me down and told me the news, that the baby couldn't be mine, that she was carrying another man's child.' He licked his lips again. 'Can you imagine how I felt?'

'Angry,' I said, before I had the sense to stop the words. His eyes narrowed and he scowled at me. 'So whose baby was it?' I asked.

He sat back, a sour expression in his eyes. 'A cheap little man, an insurance broker of all things. He did the neighbourhood rounds in his nasty double-breasted suit. This was before internet payments, when the insurance man would call at the house. He must have caught Nancy in a weak moment.'

'Or a lonely one,' I said. 'Or do you prefer your competitors to be as well educated as you?'

'She was no Lady Chatterley,' he quipped back. 'Mike Dobson was his name.'

I scribbled it down and then asked, 'So what did you do when you found out?'

He stroked his beard again, some of his anger dissipating. 'I did what all weak men do,' he said. 'I ran away. I knew someone with a small lodge in the Lake District, and so I spent a few days there. I did some walking, the clear air did me good, and I drained a few whisky bottles, which didn't. I just didn't know what to do. People are different now. Men are different. They weep at everything, from football matches to princesses they have never met, and we have become a nation that pins flowers to road signs.' He grimaced. 'Back then, I felt like I had lost everything. I couldn't face my friends, didn't know what to do. I was angry and, yes, I wanted to hurt Nancy, but not physically, you understand, just emotionally. So I struck at her in a way that made sense to me.'

'You made her poor?' I guessed.

He nodded and smiled. 'You have me worked out already, don't you, Mr Garrett? I went to my bank, withdrew all my money and headed for France.'

Susie took hold of his hand, cradling it gently in her palm.

'I almost jumped, you know, when I was on the ferry,' he said quietly, looking at Susie. 'France was getting nearer and I didn't know what I was going to do when I got there. So I stepped onto a railing, and I was ready to go, but I was even too cowardly for that. I climbed down and slunk off into France. I caught the train south and rented a small house just outside Carcassonne.'

'What were your plans?' I asked.

He looked back to me and dropped Susie's hand. 'I didn't have any. For a week, I drank wine and took long walks, and after a while things didn't look so bad. It's a beautiful part of the world, and it seemed a long way from Blackley. Our careers suck us in, make us feel that nothing else matters, but I felt like I had stepped away from it, and it was glorious. I had cash, I had sunshine, and I thought I had got some sweet revenge on Nancy – she couldn't pay the mortgage without me. I thought about roaming Europe for a while, maybe even going to Monte Carlo and blowing all I had in the casino, and then I could drink wine as her life fell apart. Let her bring up her little bastard in some rented hovel somewhere.' His eyes looked distant again. 'Then, one day, I caught sight of a newspaper, and my face was on the front. My French wasn't brilliant, but I knew enough to get the gist, that Nancy was dead, and that I was the chief suspect. That's when my life changed.'

'So why didn't you hand yourself in?' I said.

'Because I was in a mess,' he said. 'I had to deal with the shock of Nancy's death and how she died, and then when I thought about it, I knew how it looked. Wife found buried in the garden, a husband who emptied the accounts and ran? I knew the system, and anyone that does wouldn't trust it to save them. I would go to prison, I knew that, and I knew what sort of men were in there. A good advocate can convince a jury of almost anything, and I would have been a high-profile catch.' He gave a rueful smile. 'At the time, it made sense to keep on running.'

I glanced at Susie, and saw that she was staring at him, as if his story caused her personal pain. Perhaps she felt some guilt that she had encouraged his lifestyle, as if she were complicit in some way.

'Where did you go next?' I asked. 'Where does all of this Josif Petrovic stuff come from, this human quantum energy thing?'

'Serbia,' he replied. 'It was 1988 when Nancy died. The Iron Curtain wasn't even ruffled back then, and so I headed east and hid behind it. It was the perfect place for a runaway Englishman, because the authorities weren't too keen on helping out the Brits. I had some Yugoslavian contacts from university and so I was able to build a life over there. I was working in a tyre factory until the Berlin Wall came down, and when the Balkan Wars started, I had to go running again. I came back to England and reinvented myself as an expert in alternative therapies. There's always someone willing to buy a crystal or self-help tape, provided you package it correctly.'

'And human quantum energy?'

He looked at me carefully, as if he knew I was testing him.

'We all have a quantum energy field, like an electric field in our bodies,' he said. 'It is what drives the electrons around our bodies, makes us feel good or bad. If you feel bad, you can overcome it by correcting the human quantum energy, taking it to a higher orbit. It fights stress and disease.'

I nodded, impressed. 'That doesn't sound like a northern lawyer, all that mystic nonsense, but then lawyers are used to arguing a position they don't believe in. Paid bullshitters. Isn't that what most lawyers are?' He didn't respond, and so I asked, 'When you look back, do you regret running?'

His eyes twinkled. 'At first I did, but then I got a different life, even started to enjoy it. And do you know what, Mr Garrett, I had even started to think that I would never be discovered.' He rubbed his stomach and chuckled. 'Getting out of shape gave me a disguise.'

'But what about your wife?' I asked. 'You staying on the run meant that Nancy's killer stayed free.'

His laughter subsided, and then he sighed. 'And me being in prison would have changed that?'

I made a note and then tapped my pen against my lip. I needed some more of the emotional angle.

'Do you ever think about her?' I asked. 'About what Nancy went through?'

He folded his legs and pursed his lips so firmly that his mouth disappeared behind the bush of his beard. 'Of course I do, Mr Garrett, every single day. Can you imagine it, being stuck in that hole, unable to get out, knowing you are going to die? You can only imagine how you would deal with it, but I *knew* Nancy, still loved her, and so in my head I hear her screams, her cries, her panic.' He tapped his head. 'So you can see why I don't like to think of her too much.'

He watched me and stroked his beard. He seemed wary.

'You don't like me,' he said eventually.

'Am I obliged to?'

'I would feel better if you did.'

'I don't have to like you to write the story,' I said. 'I should call the police, for Christ's sake, but I don't want to, because I'm curious, and because I'm a good reporter. I want to write the best story I can, but walking out of here and not calling the police puts me at risk of prison. Like you, I don't like the thought of someone's hairy hands holding me down in the middle of the night to whisper sweet nothings, and so excuse me if I don't join your fan club.'

He nodded. 'I understand.'

'So where do I start?' I said. 'If I'm going to prove your innocence, where shall I look first?'

'When I conducted a trial,' he replied, 'putting another suspect before a jury helped, because jurors like playing detective.'

'I'm not risking prison to set up red herrings,' I said. 'Call me pompous, but I'm not a lawyer, so I don't think purely of what can be proven in court. I am only interested in the facts, and in your case, innocence. I am not interested in whether someone can be fooled into finding you not guilty.'

His cheeks flushed again. 'I'm not talking just about my innocence,' he said. 'I'm talking about finding Nancy's murderer, and so to find the real killer you should look to the only other person who had something to lose by Nancy being pregnant.' He held out his hands. 'Mike Dobson.'

160

Chapter Twenty-Nine

I didn't feel like talking much on the train heading north. I just wanted to watch the English countryside fly past through grubby windows and reflect on how I might have just walked out on the scoop of the decade, all on the promise that Claude Gilbert would wait around while I looked into Mike Dobson.

Susie seemed to have different ideas though, and she recounted her days with Gilbert all those years ago, her voice low and her head dipped towards the voice recorder on the table in front of her, her face animated as she talked of their casino evenings and trips out of town whenever a trial took him away for a few nights. I had stopped responding though, just giving the occasional nod when I sensed a pause, her voice barely a distraction. Then a pause turned into silence.

I looked at Susie and realised that she had stopped talking. She was looking at me.

'What's wrong, Jack?'

I looked across, eyes wide with innocence. 'Nothing.'

'There is,' she said, and reached across to pat my hand. 'Tell me.'

'Like I said,' my voice sterner, 'there's nothing wrong.'

Susie sat back in her seat and turned towards the window, although I could sense her eyes still watching me. I tried to

161

look at the trackside golf courses and stretches of fields as we raced northwards, but I couldn't ignore Susie's gaze.

'What?' I said, trying to keep the irritation from my voice.

She smiled at me, a knowing look on her face. 'Men like you end up killing themselves,' she said.

I scowled. 'What are you talking about?'

'You know what I mean. Men like you, northern men, you just keep it all in, hold everything back until it turns into a poison and eats away at you. No one would laugh if you told them what was wrong.'

'Maybe Claude was right,' I said. When she looked confused, I added, 'That we have turned into a nation of mourners, of emotional wrecks. What's wrong with keeping things to ourselves? And anyway, there's nothing to tell.'

'No, no,' she said softly. 'I've met a lot of men like you.' She wagged her finger at me, playfully. 'It seems like I've spent most of my life trying to change them, to open them up.'

'To like you?' I asked, cruelly.

Susie went red at that. 'Yes, and to like me,' she said, traces of hurt in her voice. 'You should try it, liking people.'

'I do like people,' I said. 'That's why I'm a reporter, so I can meet people and tell their stories.'

'No, it's so you can observe people and comment on them,' she said, shaking her head. 'It's nothing to do with liking them. And now you're taking it out on me because you're worried about losing your story, because you met Claude Gilbert and you let him go. Or is it just because you lash out when people get too close?'

I looked at her and thought that I didn't need Susie to tell me what had been going through my mind ever since we walked out of the flat. Then I felt guilty, because Susie hadn't gone all the way to London and back just for me to take it out on her. And because I knew she was right.

'I'm sorry,' I said. 'I was just thinking about the story.'

'You need to think about your girlfriend too, and that little boy,' she said. When I frowned, she added, 'Every time I mention them, you hunch up or put your hands in your pockets, all defensive.'

'Do I?'

Susie nodded. 'You just need to tell her that you love her.'

I turned to look out of the window.

'Look, you're doing it again.'

'I'm not.'

'You are. The minute I said the word "love", you turned away to avoid the subject. Have you been hurt in the past?'

'What do you mean?'

'Are your parents divorced?'

I shook my head. 'Both of my parents are dead.'

Susie nodded slowly and reached out to take hold of my hand. 'Don't think that everyone will walk out on you. You won't get hurt every time.'

I looked at the veins standing up on the back of her hands, her fingers stained nicotine-brown, before I was rescued by the ring of my phone. I pulled my hand away and checked the number. It was Harry English.

I slipped out of the seat and headed for the vestibule between the carriages before answering. It was noisier, and I knew I would be interrupted by people walking along the train, but at least I was out of Susie's earshot.

'Hello, Harry.'

'How did you get on?' he said.

I looked out of the window and saw that the view had become more northern, the brickwork darker, the horizons spoiled by industrial units, away from the greenery of the Home Counties.

'I met him,' I said.

Harry fell silent, and I could sense the publication figures turning over in his head.

'So when do we meet?' he said, eventually, his voice quieter than normal. 'We need a big splash, a press conference.'

'Not yet.'

'What do you mean, not yet?'

'I've got to prove his innocence,' I said. 'If I can, he'll come forward.'

'But you know where he lives. Why wait?'

'Because I promised, Harry,' I replied.

Harry sighed down the phone. 'That's why you couldn't cut it at a desk. Too much damn honour.'

'Yeah, and I remember yours from last night, with Dave following me.'

'It's called control, Jack.'

'Whatever you say,' I said, my voice weary. 'If you print anything, Harry, I'll deny it and you'll lose the exclusive. Just be patient and it will work out.'

'I'm just glad it wasn't on our expense sheet,' he growled, and then hung up.

I smiled as I looked at my phone. I knew that Harry would forget about it soon. Journalists don't have grudges, just deadlines, and Harry would listen again when the time was right.

I glanced through the door into the carriage and I saw that Susie was on the phone as well. I realised that there was only one escape route out of this: to follow the trail set by Claude Gilbert.

Chapter Thirty

The parting at Blackley station had been brief, just a promise to call Susie when I found out more. She was suspicious, obviously worried that I would sell the story and keep her share, but I wasn't like that. Journalists can be unscrupulous, but they have to be loyal to sources or else the sources dry up. Now I was heading back to my house, the taxi meter ticking over as I had made a detour to collect Bobby. Laura was still at work and so he had been picked up from school by old friends of my father, Jake and Martha, who lived on a quiet estate at the edge of Turners Fold.

Bobby was quiet in the back of the car, almost as if he resented me for going away, but I knew he had been hurt badly by his real father, who chose to sleep around rather than look after his child. He made do with contact visits every fortnight, two nights in the capital, but his vowels were getting flatter and London was becoming just a memory for him now. I ruffled his hair to extract a smile, but he just looked at me, his brown eyes wide, his hair across his forehead in wisps. I noticed that it was getting darker.

'Are the flowers for Mummy?' he asked, and pointed to the bunch of pink roses that I'd picked up outside the station, the petals emerging from the buds.

I smiled. 'Yes, they are.' I lifted them to his nose so he could smell them.

He screwed up his nose as he sniffed at the flowers, and then he asked, 'Is that man coming again tonight?'

My smile faltered. 'What man?'

'There was a man in the house last night. I heard him. Mummy was scared, I could tell.'

My stomach rolled as Bobby said the words and I felt the flowers shake in my hand. Someone in the house, when I was away? I caught sight of the taxi driver watching me in the rearview mirror.

'No, I know who that was,' I said, but my voice was hoarse. I tried to smile, just so that Bobby wouldn't be scared, but I knew that I didn't sound convincing.

Bobby was silent the rest of the way home, and as the taxi made the long climb to the cottage, I saw my red car parked up ahead, bright against the grey stone walls. Then I noticed a car further along, and a man knocking on my door. As he turned towards the taxi and stepped out of the shadows, I saw that it was Tony Davies, and that he had a bag in his hand.

As I climbed out of the taxi, he said, 'It's not booze in here. Sorry, Jack. Just long forgotten secrets.'

His smile died when I didn't offer much of a response. 'Everything okay?'

I nodded towards Bobby and raised a finger to my lips. Tony winked that he understood; once Bobby had darted upstairs to get changed, he asked, 'What's wrong?'

'It's Laura,' I said. 'Bobby told me that someone was here last night, and that she was scared.'

Tony cocked his head, concerned. 'What, you think it might be something to do with your Claude Gilbert story?'

'I don't know,' I said. 'Maybe Laura can tell me more, but it doesn't sound good.'

166

I went through to the kitchen and grabbed a bottle of white that had been in the fridge for a few days. I asked Tony what he had brought while I poured us both a drink.

Tony put the bag onto the table, and then he looked up at me, his teeth crooked in his smile. 'Did you find Claude?'

I faltered for a moment, unsure whether I should be truthful.

He banged the table and laughed. 'You did!' he exclaimed. I raised my finger to my lips again and pointed upstairs, from where I could hear Bobby making banging noises. Tony leant forward and whispered, 'You found Claude Gilbert, didn't you?'

I felt a smirk tug at the corners of my mouth.

His eyes widened, and then he pointed at his bag. 'Jesus Christ, Jack. This is all too late now.'

'What do you mean?'

'You've got the front page of the nationals now. You've made it.'

I grimaced. 'It's not quite as simple as that.'

'Why not?'

I put my hands on top of my head and sighed.

'Jack?'

'You know how it is when you have a great story, but you think it can become fantastic?' I said.

'Yes, I do,' Tony replied. 'And I know what to do: you write the good one and put the fantastic one to the back of your mind – because a deadline has to be met, a page has to be filled.'

I put my hands down and shrugged in apology. 'I know that, you taught me it when I first started out, and it was good advice. But Claude has a different plan.'

'Oh Jack, what have you done?'

I took a deep breath. There was no other way to put it. 'Claude Gilbert wants me to prove his innocence,' I said.

Tony's mouth opened, and then closed again.

I nodded. 'I did that too.'

'But he's not innocent,' Tony said. 'His wife was buried alive. He emptied his account and ran. Cut and dried.'

'That's not what he says.'

Tony shook his head. 'I cannot believe we're having this conversation. You sat in a room with Claude Gilbert, you knew it was him, and you left him there?' He scratched his head, leaving red trails on his bald pate. 'What kind of story have you got now?'

'I've still got one. I found Claude Gilbert. I have his address.'

'A picture?'

'That was one of the conditions of the interview: no pictures,' I said.

'How do you know it was Claude Gilbert? Because he told you?' Tony laughed. 'Did he look anything like Claude Gilbert?'

'No longer slim and stylish,' I said. 'Just a worn-out old man, scruffy and fat.' When I spotted Tony's sceptical look, I said, 'He's a man in disguise. He could hardly step out of the history books. He'd be spotted immediately.'

'Come on, Jack. You don't really believe him, do you?'

'I've met him, and he convinced me.'

'So what name is he using?' Tony asked.

'Josif Petrovic.'

'What kind of name is that?'

'A Serbian name,' I replied. 'He was disguised as some kind of Serbian mystic. He said that he fled there first because the authorities were less inclined to help the West in checking out the truth of his past. When the Balkan Wars started, things got a little trickier, so he came back to England.'

Tony sighed. 'You've been taken in by a Serbian conman.'

'But Susie knows him from back then in the eighties.'

'So she tells you.'

'She checks out.'

'So it's the perfect con,' Tony said. 'She gets her Serbian boyfriend to pretend to be Claude Gilbert, and she knows enough about the case to make it realistic. The papers buy the story, pay you, and she gets her cut. Then somebody comes up with proof that he really is Josif Petrovic, and the story dies. The paper won't care too much about Petrovic because they sold papers that day, but every time you try and pitch another big story to the nationals, they'll laugh down the phone at you, just before they slam it down.'

'But if that's what he was doing, why did he send me away on some pointless search?'

'To increase the price. There'll be leaks, anticipation, the cheque books start to appear. They cash in as your story goes around the world, and then disappear when the debunking starts.'

I blew out. 'You think I've been twirled?'

'Definitely,' he said. When I looked disappointed, he added, 'Don't worry. I know someone who wants to fill in some of the gaps.'

'Who?'

'Frankie Says.'

I was puzzled. 'What kind of name is that?'

'Not his real one, but I got a call from Jackie at the *Telegraph*. He was in their office the other day, looking for you, talking about Claude Gilbert.'

'How did he know, and who is he?'

'He lives across the road from the Gilbert house. He must have seen you snooping around, because he did the same with us when we did that nostalgia piece. Reckoned he knew some big secret, but he would only pass it on if we wrote him a hefty cheque. We told him that it wasn't that sort of piece and so he slunk back across the road.'

'And do you think he had a big secret?' I said.

'If he has, he's sat on it for more than twenty years,' he said. 'No, he's just some oddball who fancied a moment in the spotlight.'

'Why the name, Frankie Says?'

'It was an eighties piece,' Tony said, 'and you remember those T-shirts, with the big lettering? "Frankie Says Relax", and all that? Joking around in the office ended up with him getting that name.'

I tugged on my lip as I thought about him, and I remembered what Bobby said, that someone had been in the house. 'It means he tracked me down,' I said. 'Is he dangerous?'

Tony shook his head. 'He's harmless.'

'Okay,' I said nodding, unconvinced. 'I'll check him out tomorrow. Just to add some interest to the story.' Then I looked towards the bag on the table. 'Is that all the major parts of the story?'

'Most of what I could find that was useful,' he said, pushing it towards me.

'Plenty about her unborn child?'

He grimaced again. 'That's the final tragedy of the case.'

'Does it say anywhere that the baby wasn't Gilbert's?'

Tony paused and then looked at me. 'I don't think so,' he said slowly, and then, 'Should it?'

I smiled. 'You know it doesn't, because it's the first I've heard of it too. And if I was faking it as Gilbert, I wouldn't start with that revelation. It's too easy to disprove.'

'But it certainly gets a headline,' Tony said, still sounding sceptical, but then he stroked his chin. 'So Petrovic is saying that Nancy Gilbert was having an affair?'

'With a man called Mike Dobson.'

Tony gasped. 'You've got a name?' he said, incredulous.

'Straight from the mouth of our Serbian conman,' I said. 'Now, do you still think he's fake?'

Tony shook his head slowly. 'Unless it's a distraction. You'll now look at that and not him.'

'But he's making me put off his payday. If it was a con, he'd just want the quick exposé, the cheque in the bank.' I patted Tony's bag. 'So show me what you've got.'

Tony reached in and pulled out a bundle of clippings, fanning them out over the table, just photocopies, something we could write on.

'This is the report the day after the body was found,' he said.

I picked it up and read. *Barrister's wife found dead*. A simple headline, giving the facts that had since spawned hundreds of pages of newsprint.

'What have you got that hints at Gilbert being innocent?' I said.

'Nothing,' he said, and then he paused, before delving into the pile of papers. 'This is a different angle though.' He pulled out a piece of paper with a bold headline: *Lake trial collapses after Gilbert disappearance*.

'Alan Lake?' I queried.

'The one and the same.'

I whistled. That made it more interesting.

Alan Lake was a well-known figure on the northern arts circuit, a beloved sculpture artist, famed for being a reformed criminal who discovered his talent for art while in prison. It rescued him, gave him an outlet for his aggression, and his work sold well, his name now the cachet.

But he was like a pet to the air-kissing classes. I had seen some of his sculptures: a reclining woman portrayed by sweeping lines of smooth white stone, or a kissing couple, the stone carved so that thin columns curved around each other. Although they were pretty in their own way, they were nothing special, but the social glitterati liked the danger of the work of a violent criminal in their homes. So now he did the dinner party circuit, where he fine-dined on hints of gangland, tough talk from the back streets of Manchester, but no specifics. I wasn't sure whether it was because there were bad things he couldn't confess, or whether the hint of it, genuine or not, just made his prices higher.

'So what had he done?' I asked, skim-reading the article.

'Glassed a girl during a pub fight.'

'Hardly the stuff of gangsters,' I said. 'How did Lake get implicated?'

'Eye witnesses. The victim seemed keen on her day in court, and one of the barmen was giving evidence.'

I winced. 'Did he have a death wish?'

Tony could only shrug. 'The trial was going okay, by all accounts. People had shown up in court, given their evidence well. It was looking bad for Alan Lake.'

'And Gilbert was his defence lawyer,' I said, looking at the paper.

'That's right, but when Gilbert went missing, the trial had to start again a couple of months later. New counsel, new jury, but the same old witnesses. But the witnesses weren't so keen second time around. Some changed their stories, and the main man, the barman from the club, he said the police had threatened him and put words into his mouth, that he had been told what to say. Remember, this was the eighties. The years before had been filled with tales of the police beating confessions out of people. Remember the campaigns for the Birmingham Six, the Guildford Four? They were still in prison then, but it was in the public consciousness, and so the jurors lapped it up. The barman did a runner to Spain afterwards, with rumours of a cash windfall, if you get my drift. So the case collapsed.'

'And Alan Lake walked free.'

Tony nodded. 'And it seemed like Alan Lake got his artistic conversion when he was inside, waiting for his trial.'

'So Gilbert's disappearance was very convenient for Alan Lake,' I said.

'Yes, it was, but putting pressure on a barman is in a different league to burying alive the wife of your barrister, if that's what you're thinking.'

'Maybe he wasn't in control?' I said. 'He was facing a few years in prison, and then suddenly his barrister goes missing. Perhaps he just got some of his heavies to put some pressure on Mrs Gilbert to find out where he'd gone and they went too far. Perhaps it was Mrs Gilbert's death that led to Lake's conversion into one of the good guys.'

'But if you are going to run an exposé on Alan Lake and accuse him of murder, you'll need good evidence,' he said. 'Stick to the adulterer for now, Mike Dobson.'

I started to shuffle through the papers, glancing at the headlines, looking for something I hadn't heard of before.

'How much did you tell Laura?' Tony asked.

I looked up. 'Nothing,' I said. 'I didn't think it was fair on her.'

'Why?'

'Because she's a policewoman. How will it look if it comes out that she had access to the location of the most wanted man in Lancashire?'

'Whether she knows or not,' Tony said, his eyebrows raised, 'it will look like that anyway.'

'I know, but there's nothing I can do about it. For now, it's a press secret, and part of my story will have to be that I didn't even tell my police sergeant girlfriend.'

'Sergeant?'

'That's what she's going for.'

Tony nodded. 'Good on her,' he said. 'So what now?'

'It's getting complicated,' I said. 'Alan Lake is something new into the mix. I'll look into that, and then I'll try and find out about this Mike Dobson. But there's one other thing first: I need to find out who was in my house last night, and whether it's got anything to do with me going after Claude Gilbert.'

Chapter Thirty-One

Tony had gone and Bobby was in bed by the time Laura walked through the door, her dark hair pulled into a clasp at the back of her head, showing her pale skin, the pallor of the Irish, Laura's lineage. Her crisp white shirt and stiff black trousers gave her a stern appearance that didn't fit the gleam in her eyes.

She came behind me and wrapped her arms around my neck. When I turned round to kiss her, she pulled away, her smile filled with tease and her cheeks creased into dimples.

'I'm beat,' she said, and slipped off her coat and threw it over the sofa, before walking through to the kitchen. Then I heard her stop. She put her head around the door.

'Thank you,' she said, her voice softer now, holding the flowers I'd bought at the station. 'I'm glad you're back.'

'It's good to be back,' I said.

'No, not just because of these,' she said, holding up the flowers before going back into the kitchen to make herself a drink. I followed her.

'Bobby told me about the man who was here last night,' I said, concerned.

Laura was leaning against the worktop and her smile had gone. She took a deep breath and her hand went to her eyes to wipe them. When she looked at me again, I thought she looked tired.

'I was scared, Jack,' she said. 'It's too quiet up here.'

'Who was it?'

'I don't know. I just heard something upstairs, and then the window was open. By the time I got there, he'd gone.'

'Are you sure there was someone there?'

Laura nodded. 'You've been making waves, Jack.'

I didn't like the sound of that. Late-night visits to the house just when we had been talking about Alan Lake.

'What do you mean, waves?'

'Joe Kinsella wants to know what you're doing. He knew about that woman's visit to the house the other morning, although I'm not supposed to tell you this.'

Then I remembered what Tony had told me, about the man who was looking for me. Frankie Says.

'I'll be careful,' I said. 'People being interested tells me that there is a story to tell, but I won't put you in danger, or Bobby.'

'So what *is* the story?' she said. 'You have to remember us in all of this. That should mean more than a story. I know it's important to you, but someone was in my home last night, and it makes me scared.'

I put my arms around her and pulled her into me. Her shirt collar jabbed me in the neck, stiff and starched. 'It does mean more,' I said.

Laura looked up and her lips brushed mine. 'I hope so,' she said softly. 'Don't go away again.'

'Do you really want to know about the story?' I said.

'Yes, I do.'

'Have you heard of Claude Gilbert?' I said.

Laura looked surprised. 'Everyone has heard of Claude Gilbert,' she said. 'What about him?'

'He wants to come home.'

176

She looked confused for a moment. 'What do you mean, home?'

'To Blackley. That's why Susie was here the other morning. She's in contact with him.'

'Claude Gilbert?' she said, bewildered, and then she laughed. 'That would be one hell of a story, if he did. Are you sure it's not a hoax?'

'I don't think so,' I said.

Laura looked at the papers on the table. 'Claude Gilbert?' she said, still disbelieving.

I started to smile. 'Good, isn't it?'

'And that's why you asked me, the other night, about knowing about a wanted criminal?' she said.

I nodded. There was no point in denying it.

'If you've got access to Claude Gilbert, you've got to write the story,' she said, grinning now. She walked towards the stairs.

I went back to the table as Laura went to get changed and began to sift through the papers again. I had hardly made a dent in them since Tony had gone, though it was mostly just recaps of what I already knew anyway. I saw a younger Bill Hunter staring out from one of the pages, the bitter ex-policeman who discovered the body.

I was still reading the article when Laura came back down the stairs.

'You can tell me all about Claude Gilbert after,' she said.

'After what?' I said, and then I looked up. 'Oh,' I said. 'After that.'

Laura was on the bottom step, dressed in her police shirt, her checked black and white tie done neatly to her neck. But her legs were bare, and from what else I could see as the shirt flapped open, I could tell that she wasn't thinking about work.

She smiled and held up her handcuffs. 'Like I said the other day, I promise I won't make them too tight.'

I put my papers down. Claude Gilbert could wait for a bit longer.

Mike Dobson was frustrated now. He had done three circuits of his usual drive around Blackley's darkest corners, but where was she? He had slowed down at every corner, at every cluster of women underneath the streetlights, but she wasn't there. Just old prossers who had spent their lives on the streets, hard women with ruined lives, or single mothers in tracksuits, trading handjobs for a ten-pound bag, fully signed up for the H-plan diet, hoping one day to get away from the street.

He didn't want that any more. A few months ago, he would have settled for what he could find, a release in the shadows, a business transaction, nothing more, with no details exchanged, no promise to call back. Things were different now. He had met *her* now, and she felt like a thousand great memories rediscovered. Her smile, her laugh, her looks. Just like Nancy.

He closed his eyes as his thoughts went back to Nancy. He thought he heard someone, a whisper in his ear, but there was no one there. And then there was something else. A soft thump, fist on wood, frantic and fast.

He gripped his wheel. That was the sound that haunted him. He set off quickly, away from there, back to Mary. He needed some normality, angry with himself that he had thought he had seen something more in some ragged young street girl.

Laura lay next to me, her arm across my chest. I ran my fingers down her back and then further, her skin still warm from our lovemaking, her back slick with sweat. She murmured and put her leg across me.

'We've got a problem, Jack.'

I ran my fingers through her hair. 'It doesn't seem that way.'

She lifted her head to look at me. 'We have, and it's about your story.'

I raised my eyebrows. 'What's wrong? Is it about the person in here last night? I know I should have been here, but . . .'

'No, it's not about that,' Laura interrupted, holding up her hand, and then she sighed. 'Okay, it is partly about that, because this thing is growing, and it's going to drag me down.'

'What do you mean?'

She put her head back onto my chest and I continued stroking her hair. I knew she was going to tell me, because she had started the conversation, and as soon as someone does that, they're just waiting for the nudge. I decided that silence was the best way.

After a few moments of thought, Laura looked up again and said, 'It's Joe Kinsella.'

I put my hands over my head as I lay back and stared at the ceiling. 'What did Joe want?' I asked.

'To know all about you,' Laura replied. 'He knew that Susie had been here, and I had told no one.'

'How would he know that?' I said.

'He must be watching her.'

'Is he working from Blackley now?'

Laura nodded. 'It sounds a bit hush-hush, but it must be about Claude Gilbert. He didn't say as much, just said that it was the same thing you were looking into.'

'Why the hell has Claude Gilbert become so interesting all of a sudden, after all this time?' I asked.

'I don't know,' Laura replied, 'but he told me that I have to pass on what you know.'

179

I looked at her. 'Why did he say that?'

'Because I'm a copper, and it's what I'm supposed to do.'

'But you've told me now. The confidence has gone the other way.'

Laura took a deep breath. 'I know.'

Then I realised what the problem was. 'You're going to tell him, aren't you?'

Laura nodded slowly, and I thought I could see tears brimming onto her eyelashes.

'I'm sorry, Jack,' she said, a quiver to her voice. 'I can guess how much this story means to you, but I've got to do what's right for me as well. It might feel as if I'm putting my job before you, but it's not like that, I promise.'

I put my arms around her and pulled her into my body. I felt her tears on my chest.

'Do I tell you I love you enough?' I said.

Her hand ran across my chest. She sniffled. 'You can never say it enough,' she said quietly. 'Why do you ask?'

'Just something Susie said,' I replied. 'She reckons I hold back because my parents died. If I do, I'm sorry.' I kissed her on the top of her head, took a deep breath of the scent of her hair. 'Don't worry about Joe Kinsella. You're a policewoman. You are what you are. I don't want you to stop being that.' I pulled away and cupped her face in my hands, and then kissed away the tear that was running down her cheek. 'Do what you need to do, but first I've got to tell you something.'

'Don't, Jack,' she warned me. 'If you tell me, I'll have to tell Joe.'

'I know that, but do you think you'll be believed if you say you didn't know?' When Laura looked down again, I said, 'There's your answer. You tell Joe, and then no one can say you held it back.'

Laura nodded slowly.

'I met him,' I said.

Laura looked up at me, confused at first, and then her mouth started to open, her eyes wide. 'Claude Gilbert?'

I nodded, and then started to smile.

'You met Claude Gilbert?' she repeated, and then she began to laugh. 'Jesus Christ, Jack, what are you doing here? Why aren't you writing the story? And where is he, if you found him?'

I grimaced, not looking forward to saying again what I had said to Tony. 'I walked away,' I said.

'What!'

'Claude wants to prove his innocence before he comes out of hiding.'

Laura looked sceptical. 'That will be a tough one.'

'He's given me a name, and a story that would help him,' I said, and so I told her all about Mike Dobson and the affair, and the escape to France, and the baby.

'So where do you start?' Laura asked.

'With anyone who wants to speak to me. There's already someone who seems pretty keen.'

'You be careful, Jack,' she whispered. 'I'm not sure all is what it seems.'

And with that, she kissed me, a soft, moist, tear-dampened kiss, and we slid slowly down the sheets again.

Chapter Thirty-Two

Morning found me outside Frankie's house, a three-storey block of blackened millstone, with large bay windows at the front and side, and double wooden front doors. The path from the gate curved between the two low walls that held back the flower beds. Except that there were no flowers. Brambles blocked the tarmac path and grass sprouted through in places. The gate creaked as I opened it, the latch stiff. My footsteps echoed between the walls and the over-hanging rhododendron bushes, and I had to duck in places to make my way to the house.

As I got nearer, the garden opened out, and I saw that the lawns were long and sweeping, like those at the Gilbert house; but these were unkempt and overgrown, the green broken by the yellow speckles of buttercups. Rose bushes filled the beds in front of the windows, but the petals lay fallen on the soil, the heads brown.

I looked up at the house. There were no signs of life, the windows gloomy, grubby net curtains hanging in each one. I went to the doors and knocked but the sound came back as deadened thuds.

I stepped back and looked up at the windows again. I couldn't see anyone, not so much as the twitch of a net curtain. I stepped forward to bang on the door again and then turned to look around me. As I looked back towards the road, I saw that Frankie's house was more elevated than the Gilbert house; I reckoned I would be able to see into the garden if the bushes were trimmed back.

There was still no answer, so I scribbled 'Call me' onto the back of a business card and posted it through the letterbox.

I hadn't gone too far down the path before I heard something behind me. When I turned around, I saw a man in the doorway, staring at me. He was tall, late thirties, with unkempt dark hair and bright rosy cheeks, as if he had been sitting in front of the fire all morning.

I started to walk back towards him. 'Frankie?' I asked.

He nodded, but looked nervous.

'I'm Jack Garrett,' I said, as I got to the door. 'You were looking for me the other day.'

He nodded again.

'So why didn't you answer the door?'

He was still not saying anything.

I peered past him, along a dark hallway.

'Shall we talk inside?' I suggested. When he didn't answer, I added, 'It's about Claude Gilbert,' trying to nudge him into a conversation. 'You can tell me about Claude Gilbert.'

He started to say something but stammered, and then he moved out of the way so I could go into the house.

As I walked past him, I put my sleeve to my nose as the smell from the house hit me, like old rotting rubbish. I heard the door close behind me.

As Laura walked into the briefing room, she saw Thomas in the corner, looking at some incident logs that related to an arrest she had been involved in the day before, where a husband had beaten his wife until she was left cowering in a corner, blood streaming from a nose that hadn't looked straight. There had been numerous incidents before, but the victim had always refused to make a statement. Now she finally had, but the prisoner hadn't got past the interview stage before his wife had arrived at the front desk to make a new one that exonerated him.

'Hello, Laura,' Thomas said, brighter than he had been earlier in the week. Maybe that nervousness was starting to fade. Laura remembered that transition from the early part of her career.

Laura smiled her greeting, but she knew that she appeared distracted, her conversation with Jack the night before still preying on her mind.

She went to a spare computer and logged on. Her fingers hovered nervously over the keys, scared to type in the name of Mike Dobson. Misusing a police computer would get Laura the sack, and maybe even a court appearance, and she knew it would look as if she was helping Jack with information. But she didn't want to go to Joe Kinsella with half a story. If she was going to give up Jack's findings, she wanted it to be with something reliable, and not the ramblings of some imposter whose address or pseudonym Jack wouldn't disclose.

She closed her eyes. Everything told her not to get involved, to just pass on the name to Joe Kinsella, let him do the running, but Laura still wanted to stay loyal to Jack. There was no prospect of the London Met kicking in the door of a Belgravia apartment on the word of a reporter. Different force, different targets, with nothing to gain except more paperwork.

Laura let her fingers drift across the keys to find something on Mike Dobson. She wasn't hopeful – he would be a middle-aged insurance salesman and probably led a blameless life.

The list was small, just three. One was a teenager, another one a serial burglar in his forties. The first was too young to be Nancy Gilbert's lover, and the second maybe a rough edge too far – though people find love in strange places. The mistake Laura had made with her husband told her that, all muscles and bright smile, and too happy to share it around. He had given her Bobby and also a mistrust of men. Laura looked at the burglar again, but when she brought up his record she saw that he received two years for robbery in March 1988, a couple of months before Nancy died. That was back in the good old days, when prison was tough and people didn't walk out of jail after just a few weeks just because there was no room at the inn. A bunch of crooks climbed onto the roof of Strangeways the year after and changed all that, but back then, in early 1988, Mike Dobson the burglar had the best alibi of all. He was behind bars.

But as Laura looked at the remaining Mike Dobson, she realised that he was about the right age, early fifties, and his life wasn't blameless. He didn't have a record, but the force monitored kerb-crawlers, just so that they could send out a few letters when the local residents complained, and his name came up as the owner of a vehicle that had been spotted patrolling the red light zone. He had avoided the warning letter so far, but by good fortune alone.

Laura smiled at that. If he was married, he would soon forget about the purpose of Laura's visit once the door clicked closed and he was left alone to explain himself to his wife.

Laura looked over at Thomas. 'Do you fancy a home visit to offer some community advice?'

Thomas nodded and then reached for his jacket and hat, both still pristine. It was too nice to stay indoors.

As they left the room and walked into the atrium, she glanced upwards and saw a figure on the top-floor balcony.

It was Rachel Mason, the sunlight streaming in through the high windows, catching her hair and making it gleam. Laura looked away, but she could feel the woman's eyes tracking her as she made her way to the station exit.

Chapter Thirty-Three

Frankie loomed large over me. He was dressed in black, saggy jogging bottoms and a ragged T-shirt. The hallway was dark, and his hair stuck up at odd angles, as if he had just spent a few minutes rubbing his fingers through it. He was caught in silhouette by the light that crept in through the stained glass panels over the doors.

'Go in there,' he said, pointing towards the room at the front of the house that looked towards the Gilbert house. His voice was deep, too deep, so that it sounded distorted, like an old 45 played on 33.

As I entered the living room, the smell became stronger.

'Bloody hell, Frankie, what the hell have you been doing in here?' I said, before I could stop myself.

Although the windows were dirty, and the net curtains old and grey, there was enough light to illuminate the scene. Old newspapers and magazines were piled up against one wall, stacked into uneven towers reaching almost to the ceiling, like newsprint Jenga, and they looked like they could topple over at any moment. And then there was the kitchen rubbish – old cereal boxes and carrier bags overflowing with pieces of paper and rotting food. Against the other wall were black binbags, knotted together. I kicked one, just to gauge what might be inside.

It was heavy, dense, and when I peered inside, I could see dirty rags.

'I don't have a washing machine,' Frankie said.

I looked around, and then looked down at his clothes. There were sweat rings under his arms and food stains on his pants. I guessed he didn't have a table either.

'I just buy more clothes when I need them,' he said, by way of explanation.

'But this is a health hazard,' I said.

Frankie's shrug was his only reply.

I tried to work him out. Tony was right, there was something not quite right about him, although I couldn't pin it down to something I could recognise. He looked alert, but his eyes seemed to stare, his brow permanently furrowed, and his movements seemed slow and deliberate.

'Do you collect these things?' I asked. 'The newspapers, the boxes?'

'I might need them someday,' he said. 'I keep them so I have them when I need them.'

'But what about the rubbish?'

'I don't mind it,' he said, nonplussed.

'This is a big house, Frankie. Do you live here on your own?' I left the living room and walked down the hall, curious to know what else was in the house.

'Where are you going?' I heard him say, as he followed me.

'You went looking for me,' I said, 'which tells me that you want me to write about you. If I do that, I need to see what sort of person you are, whether I can believe anything you want to tell me.'

I went through a door at the end of the hall and found myself in the kitchen. I stepped back and exhaled. The air was sharp with the crisp smell of mould, dishes piled up in the large porcelain sink, the food on them dried-on and old.

There were paper plates on the workspace, alongside a collection of crumbs and smeared butter.

'Come out of there, please,' he said.

I turned round to face him. 'How can you live like this?'

'This is my house,' he said, his voice indignant.

I thought I saw some pain in his eyes, embarrassment, and I took the hint. 'I'm sorry, Frankie,' I said. 'But if you've got information for my story, I need to see whether I can trust you.'

Frankie recoiled. 'It's not about me,' he said, and he started to back away down the hall.

'Hey, hey,' I said, my hands outstretched, my voice filled with apology. 'Just tell me why you were looking for me.'

He looked down and thought for a few seconds, and when he looked up, he said, 'I want paying.'

'For what?'

'For what I know about Claude Gilbert.'

'I know everything about Claude Gilbert,' I said, watching him.

'Not everything,' he said.

'I can't give you a price if you don't tell me,' I said.

'I want half.'

'Half of what?'

'Half of what you get.'

I frowned. 'No can do, Frankie. It's going to have to be good to get that, and the story is too old for there to be anything new.'

He turned away from me, and I could hear him muttering to himself as he thought about what to say. I said nothing. If people have a story they want to tell, patience is usually all that is needed to bring it out.

'Come upstairs,' he said.

'Why?'

'I've got lots of things about Claude Gilbert up there.'

'Why don't you bring it down?' I said.

He shook his head. 'I can't.'

I sighed. He had gone quiet again, staring at me, his brow furrowed, waiting for me to decide.

'What's your surname, Frankie?'

'Cass,' he said.

'Okay, Frankie Cass,' I said eventually. 'Show me.'

I followed him out of the kitchen, and it seemed as if night had fallen when I walked behind him on the stairs, with what little light there was on the landing blotted out by his frame. The steps creaked as we walked, the carpet covering just the central section. Looking down, I noticed that the wooden edges looked scuffed, in need of more varnish. I could sense that the house had hardly changed in years. The banister felt pitted and the dust made my nose itch.

As we walked along the landing, heading for the next flight of stairs, I asked, 'Isn't the house too big for you on your own?'

'She loved this house.'

'Your mother?'

Frankie didn't answer, and so I said, 'It doesn't mean you have to be a prisoner here.'

He stepped onto the next set of stairs. 'I'm not a prisoner,' he said, and started to climb.

I thought about going back, we were going higher in the house, to the top floor, but instead I did what I always did: I let the story take me. As I followed, his breaths grew shallower with the effort of climbing.

We ended up on a small landing, with three doors leading from it. Frankie went towards the furthest door and opened it. It creaked loudly, and the sunlight that streamed in through the windows made me blink and squint.

Frankie turned to me and tilted his head, a sign that I should go through. I walked past him slowly but once I reached the doorway I stopped and gasped.

'Jesus Christ, Frankie.'

Chapter Thirty-Four

Laura brought the police car to a halt outside Mike Dobson's house. It was at the head of a cul-de-sac of new houses, and she smiled to herself when she thought how the battenburg markings on the car would be making the curtains twitch all along the street.

'What car does he drive?' Thomas asked, trying to see past Laura and along the drive.

'Mercedes,' Laura replied. The only car on the drive was an Audi TT, dark blue, soft-top. 'Maybe Mrs Dobson will be in,' she said, as she stepped onto the pavement, squaring her hat as she headed onto the drive.

Laura heard the other car door slam, and then Thomas joined her at her shoulder.

'What are you going to say?' Thomas said.

'You should never let preparation get in the way of spontaneity,' she said.

'You're going to make it up as you go along,' Thomas said, smiling.

'Something like that,' Laura said, and then she gave three short raps on the glass door of the porch. There was a solid wooden door just behind it, and Laura exchanged glances with Thomas as it opened. The woman in front of them was tall, with hair lightened by streaks and curled by tongs.

She wore make-up and had long black eyelashes and a hint of rouge to her cheeks. Her clothes looked too smart to be worn just around the house. Laura spent her spare time in jeans and T-shirts, but Mrs Dobson was turned out in a navy blue silk blouse with gold trim around the buttons and sleek matching trousers, the crease down the leg sharp and bold.

'Hello, officers,' she said. 'Can I help you?'

Although her tone was polite, Laura sensed the curtness, that she wanted the police off the drive. Laura got a sense of why Mr Dobson might be buying his affection elsewhere.

'Is it Mrs Dobson?' Laura asked. When the smile slipped, just for a fraction, a look of panic in the woman's eyes, Laura said, 'We need to speak with your husband.'

The politeness returned, but so did the frost.

'He's at work,' she said.

'Where's that?'

'Why do you want to speak to him?'

'I can't discuss that,' Laura said.

Mrs Dobson paused for a moment, and then said, 'I do think it would be better if I got him to call you.'

'When?'

'I'll do it straight away, officer,' she said.

Laura dug into her pocket and handed her one of her business cards. 'If he could do it today, we'd be most grateful,' Laura said.

Mrs Dobson looked down at the card, and then back at Laura. For a few seconds, her face remained passive. Then she smiled, although Laura could tell that it was forced.

'Will do,' she said, just a touch too jauntily, and then went to close the door.

As they went back down the drive, Thomas glanced back and then said, 'Why would a man go with a heroin addict on a back street when someone like her waits for him at home?'

'If a man is the straying type, having Miss World waiting for him won't stop it,' Laura said.

I turned around in Frankie's room, amazed at the walls.

The room was small, maybe ten feet square, with a single bed against one wall, the covers dishevelled, and a dresser against another. There was a computer on a desk, wires coming out of the back in a tangled mess, but it was the walls that drew the eye. They were covered in pictures and clippings, some of the headlines I'd seen myself, brought over by Tony the day before, screaming out the search for Gilbert in bold, black letters. There were photographs pinned on top of them, hundreds of them, the scene the same in most – a view from Frankie's room towards the Gilbert house.

I looked back at Frankie, who was looking at the pictures himself now, and I detected a greater focus, his eyes more alive now, a soft smile on his lips.

'Do you save everything connected to the Gilbert case?' I asked him.

When he turned to me and nodded, he looked proud, and for the first time I saw his teeth as he smiled, bright white against the flush of his cheeks.

'I saw what happened,' he said, his gaze earnest, waiting on my response.

'So why didn't you tell the police?' I asked.

He shrank back at that, thrust his hands into the pockets of his jogging bottoms. 'I couldn't,' he said, shaking his head.

'Why not?'

He stepped away from me and looked at the wall. I could see his shoulders moving as he took some deep breaths.

'Frankie?'

When he turned back, I saw that his excitement had been

replaced by something else. Wariness? No, it was something more than that. Fear. Frankie was scared.

'Why are you frightened?' I said.

He dropped his eyes to the floor before he spoke. 'Mother told me to keep it quiet,' he said. 'She said it would just make trouble for me.'

'But if it was the truth, why worry?'

I thought Frankie had tears in his eyes. 'Mother said they would accuse me,' he said.

'Why would they accuse you?' I said, but I knew as soon as he said it that he was right. I remembered Colin Stagg, the London man wrongly accused of a brutal murder based on not much more than being the local misfit, and here was Frankie, with a view of the Gilbert house and his walls turned into a montage of the Nancy Gilbert murder.

I stepped towards the walls and I looked through the stories. I was able to read some, Frankie breathing over my shoulder, his breath stale on my cheek. At first, they were the usual collection of theories, about Gilbert's gambling, his whereabouts, but then I noticed something for the first time – that the stories were never about Mrs Gilbert, the murder victim. Claude was the story, the celebrity lawyer, the dashing murderer who disappeared into history. The poor woman buried under a collection of planks and half a ton of soil barely got a mention.

And then I looked closer at the photographs pinned to the wall. The clippings were about Claude, but the pictures were different. They were mainly of a woman, her raven hair tied onto her head, stepping out of a car. As I looked along the wall, there were more pictures of her. Cleaning the car. Bending down in the garden, tending to a flower bed. Carrying bags. Walking with a dog. Hanging out washing.

I recognised her. Nancy Gilbert, the forgotten victim.

I turned to Frankie, who was no longer focused on me, but was staring at the photographs, the intensity back in his gaze.

'You liked her, didn't you, Frankie?' I said softly.

He looked at me and then shook his head, stepping away from the wall.

'I thought you wanted to know about the murder,' he said, his voice an angry rumble.

'I do, but I want to know about you and her,' and I tapped one of the photographs. 'You were spying on her.'

'I take a lot of photographs,' he said, his voice getting defensive.

'But mainly of Mrs Gilbert,' I stressed. Then I tried to be more conciliatory. 'C'mon, Frankie, don't be shy, we've all liked someone, maybe just from afar. It's nothing to be ashamed of.'

'I'm not ashamed.'

'You seem it.'

He put the heel of his palms to his forehead, as if he had been struck by a pain in his head, his eyes closed.

'Are you going to pay me for the story or not?' he said quietly, his eyes still shut.

'Just tell me what you know.'

He turned quickly away and sat down on his bed with a slump. 'I knew I shouldn't have looked for you. It's starting again.'

'What's starting again?'

'This!' he shouted, making me jump, and he waved his hand at the wall. 'All of this. Claude Gilbert. Nancy Gilbert. I know what happened but no one wants to listen to me.' He banged his chest with his hand.

I bent down to try and meet his gaze. 'Tell me, Frankie, and I'll print it.'

He looked down, his chin in his chest, and I could sense

199

him thinking it through, his need to tell the story weighed against what he saw as the risk. I left him alone for those moments, allowing him to come to his own decision, then I saw him nod to himself.

'There were two of them,' Frankie said.

That surprised me. 'When?'

'In the garden,' he said. 'I saw them.'

'Who was in the garden?'

'The murderers.'

'Did you tell the police?'

He gave a noncommittal shrug.

'You can't remember telling them?' I asked.

He shook his head. 'They wouldn't have believed me.'

'So why should I?'

'Because it's true.'

I watched him as he stared hard at me, his glare intense, his brow furrowed. I pulled my voice recorder out of my pocket and showed it to him. 'If you tell me about it, I'll record what you say. Is that all right?'

He nodded.

'Can I sit down?' I asked, and went to sit down on the end of the bed. There was something about him that troubled me, an edginess that made him unpredictable. He didn't answer, but I settled down anyway.

'Tell me what you saw,' I said.

He looked at me. 'In the garden. I saw them. There were two of them.'

'Two people?'

Frankie nodded solemnly. I got the feeling I always had when I sensed some life was being breathed into a story. It was like a tingle in my cheeks, a flutter in my stomach; I was feeling it right now. I nodded at him to continue, my teeth just lightly chewing at my lip.

'I like looking out of my window,' he said. 'I could see into their garden, Claude's garden, and I can remember that night. I had my window open and I heard voices, but they were too far away. When I looked, I saw two people digging.'

'Did you take any photographs?' I asked, my words coming out in rapid fire, excited now.

Frankie shook his head. 'It was too dark, and they wouldn't have come out. But I saw them. Two people digging, right where they found her.'

Frankie's gaze flicked towards the photographs again, and I realised then why he hadn't told the police anything.

'You'd been warned off, hadn't you?' I said. I stood up and crossed to the wall and tapped one of the photographs. 'Nancy had complained about you, about your camera looking at her from your window. Is that right?'

Frankie looked down and nodded. I saw a tear appear on his eyelash.

'I didn't mean to upset her,' he said, his voice breaking. 'But when they found her, I knew they wouldn't believe me, and so Mother told me to stay quiet, not to say anything.'

I went to the window and looked out. The view into the Gilbert garden was good. There were some trees in the way now, but they didn't look as well grown on the photographs on the wall. As I looked at the photographs of Nancy Gilbert, something occurred to me.

I looked down to my car in the street and then back to Frankie. I pulled my car keys out of my pocket. 'I just need to think about this,' I said. 'It's pretty big stuff.' I sat down on the bed next to Frankie and held up the keys. 'Will you get my notebook out of my car? It's in the glove compartment.'

He looked up at me and wiped his eyes. 'Are you in the red one?'

I nodded.

A smile spread on his lips. 'I like that car. Can I sit in it?'

I smiled back. 'Of course you can. Take as long as you want. Just don't drive it.'

Frankie grabbed my keys and went out of the room.

I listened for the rumble of his feet down the stairs and then I stood quickly and went to the drawers on the dresser. It was the windows in the photographs that made me think of something, because it seemed like Frankie tracked Nancy with his camera, and so he might have taken some that he kept just for himself, for those lonely nights in.

The dresser was scuffed mahogany, dusty on top, with a mirror and five wide drawers underneath. There was a keyhole in each drawer but they opened easily as I pulled. I whistled when I saw the contents. More newspapers, some going back twenty years or more, the front pages yellow, the print faded to grey. The next drawers down were just the same. I lifted some of the papers up, just to check underneath, but there were no photographs.

I went to the window and saw that Frankie was still outside.

I looked around the room. There wasn't really anywhere else. Then I noticed the gap under his bed. I smiled to myself. Where else?

I went to the floor and looked under. It was all in shadow, and so I swept my hand underneath, almost at full stretch, and then my fingers brushed something, pushed to the back.

I jumped up and pulled the bed away from the wall. There was a red hatbox. It was dusty, but I could see trails in the dust, as if someone had lifted the lid a few times. I lifted the box up and shoved the bed back against the wall. My nose itched from the dust as I removed the lid carefully, but then I gasped when I saw what was inside.

It was filled with photographs, just like the ones pinned

to the wall, but the colours were fresher. I lifted one out. It was the Gilbert house, but I could only tell that from the angle of the picture. The photograph of someone in a window was zoomed in, a young woman changing into a white tunic, but it wasn't anyone I recognised. I glanced out of the window and towards the rest home. Frankie had been spying on the nurses. I flicked through and it showed the same woman in her underwear, and then in her normal clothes before leaving the room.

I shook my head. These were too recent. Frankie had spied on Nancy Gilbert more than twenty years ago, and it looked like the habit had continued, but I was looking for older photographs, from before she died. The box was filled with photograph envelopes, and so I pushed the newer-looking ones to one side and looked for the faded ones, the ones in dated styling. I found one and grinned as I pulled out the photographs. I had them. It was Nancy Gilbert, but in these she was naked, getting changed, drying herself with a towel, and then putting on her clothes, knickers first, then the bra.

I felt grubby, like I was part of the voyeurism, but it was compelling just the same, staring into the secret life of the story's forgotten character – Nancy Gilbert in her own home, perhaps not long before she was murdered. I was engrossed in shuffling through that set, and then I reached in for another envelope. The photos were the same, Nancy Gilbert getting undressed this time. I turned one over, and I saw that there was a date written on the back. Twentieth of February 1988. Three months before she died. I reached for another envelope. It was just the same. Nancy Gilbert through her bedroom window, naked.

I flicked through, embarrassed now, but then I saw something in one of the photographs. I stopped and looked closer.

It was hard to see so I lifted it towards the window, trying to cast some light onto it. It was a head, a patch of red hair.

I put it down for a moment. Claude Gilbert had dark hair and so it couldn't be him. I went to the next photograph. Nancy Gilbert still naked, but there was the hair again. Someone was in the room with her. The next photograph was similar, but they were closer.

My hands flicked through the photographs until I got to the last few, and I felt a tremble in my hand when I saw two naked bodies on the bed, making love.

Tabloid gold.

Then I heard the door click shut. When I looked up, Frankie was looking down at me, his eyes screwed up with rage, his fists clenched tightly.

Chapter Thirty-Five

'Those are private,' Frankie growled, his voice angry, moving towards me.

I stood up and stepped away, making sure that I didn't turn my back to him.

'You need to come forward with these,' I said, holding up the pictures.

'They're not for sale.'

'Come on, Frankie, everyone has a price.'

Frankie shook his head. 'Not those, Mr Garrett.' He moved closer to me, but I backed away again, so that we were both moving around the room, me walking backwards. 'Why were you looking under my bed?' he asked.

I gestured to the walls. 'Don't be offended, Frankie, but to an impartial observer, you look a little fucking obsessed with Mrs Gilbert. I figured that you must have had more than pictures of Mrs Gilbert climbing out of her car.' I held up the pictures again. 'Is this your wank stash?'

Frankie shook his head, his face purple with embarrassment. 'It's not like that.'

'It is exactly like that, Frankie,' I said, and I sensed him becoming defensive. 'Do the nurses know that you spy on them?'

Frankie took some deep breaths, and I could see that

he looked frightened. He turned away, his hands over his face.

'You've been warned, haven't you, Frankie?' I said, stepping closer to him. 'They caught you with your camera, and you're not supposed to have these any more, are you, Frankie?'

'Please go, Mr Garrett,' he said, his voice muffled through his hands.

'Frankie, you need to show these,' I pleaded, changing tack. 'They could prove that Claude Gilbert didn't kill his wife.'

He didn't move. I put my hand on his shoulder, but he shrugged it off.

'Okay,' I said, 'if that's how you want it,' and I threw some of the photograph envelopes onto the bed and headed for the door. I didn't want to look at him as I left, because I felt the churn of guilt; I had tucked a bundle of photographs into the back of my jeans when I didn't think he could see me. But a man's liberty was at stake, and that was more important than a man's private porn collection. As I left the room, I heard the rustle of paper as Frankie picked up the photographs I had left behind.

I walked down the stairs quickly, wanting to get to my car before Frankie noticed that the photographs were missing. The landing on the next floor down was dark, and I was hoping for a quick getaway, but then I noticed a soft pink glow from underneath one of the doors. I hadn't noticed it on the way up, and it didn't fit with the grime and scuffed old wood of the rest of the house.

I glanced back towards the stairs to make sure that Frankie hadn't followed me, but I could still hear him upstairs, banging about under the bed. I put my hand on the door-knob and turned it slowly, hoping that it wouldn't squeak, and when I saw the room, I felt a shiver.

It was feminine and pristine, with a high double bed and a crocheted pink quilt dominating the space. There was a white dresser against one wall with small jewellery boxes and a mirror on top. In a corner of the room was a rocking chair with a pink satin cushion. On the wall was a large framed picture of a man in a seaman's outfit, his chin strong, his smile stiff and formal, and photographs on a small table next to the bed, of a small child, and the same man as before. There was a faint look of Frankie in his eyes, in the way he frowned, the bold eyebrows making his eyes seem shadowy and sinister. I looked down. The carpet was pink and spotless, the bed immaculately made up. The soft glow under the door had been from the sunlight trying to break through the pink curtains in the window. It was Frankie's mother's room, I could tell that, and it looked like it hadn't been disturbed or used in years.

Or maybe it had been used, but it was the one room that Frankie looked after, a shrine to his long-dead mother.

I heard a noise above me and realised that Frankie was leaving his room. I backed out of the room, making sure that the door closed quietly, and then trotted back down the stairs, squinting as I got back into the sunshine.

Laura and Thomas were sitting in the squad car when they got the call from Mike Dobson. They were just down the hill from Claude Gilbert's house, underneath a stone archway at the entrance to a park, flowers and lawns and a duck pond visible on the other side. Laura realised that this all looked like too much effort for a kerb-crawler's warning, but Thomas hadn't commented. Maybe he thought it was an excuse to avoid doing the paperwork on a bright summer morning.

Then Laura saw Mike Dobson arrive from a distance, the gold Mercedes bright against the grey background. There was something purposeful about the way he drove. As he pulled up behind them, Laura got out of the car, Thomas just behind her.

Laura wasn't surprised by Mike Dobson's appearance. His house was pristine and showy, and the car seemed all about image, so she expected him to look like success. Grey double-breasted suit, shiny black shoes, and a pink tie that contrasted vividly with his white shirt. He was in his early fifties, his neck starting to take over his chin and the crown of his head slowly emerging through the hair. It was dyed, Laura could tell that from the caramel colour, trying to reclaim the hair he'd once had. As he approached her, he gave her a flash of the salesman's smile. Laura smiled back, but it was as insincere as Dobson's. She wanted to catch him off-guard.

'What can I do for you?' he asked.

'Let's walk in the park,' she said. 'More discreet that way.'

Dobson nodded and shrugged. 'Okay,' he said, and strolled alongside Laura as they went under the stone arch, Thomas just behind them, listening.

'I'm sorry about this, Mr Dobson,' she said, 'but we're doing some chase-ups on cars that have been spotted driving around the red light areas.'

His smile twitched, and his cheeks flushed. He stopped walking. 'Red light areas? I didn't know Blackley had them.'

Laura smiled again, trying not to alienate him. 'It's okay, you're not going to court, but we're trying to advise people away from their homes, you know, to make it less embarrassing.'

'But you went to my home,' he said. 'What did you say to my wife?'

Laura shook her head. 'Nothing. Just that we wanted to speak to you.'

'She'll ask me what you wanted. What am I supposed to say?'

'You'll think of something, Mr Dobson,' Laura said.

Dobson nodded, looking down, chewing on his lip.

'Your wife seemed very nice,' Laura said. 'Why would you want to go to a prostitute?'

Dobson looked horrified, and there was a tremble to his lip. 'I do not use prostitutes,' he said, stressing every word, staring into Laura's eyes.

Laura looked away and towards the road that ran alongside the park. She let her gaze climb steadily towards the houses further up, the towering grey blocks of stone. Laura could see the chimneys of Claude Gilbert's house through the trees. Dobson didn't follow her gaze.

'I thought it would be nicer around here,' she said, 'where no one would hear us.' She fixed him with a stern look. 'Just call it a warning, Mr Dobson.'

Dobson stayed silent, not wanting to admit anything.

'Although it's a funny area around here,' Laura added, with a half-laugh. 'Maybe it's not so nice.'

'What do you mean?'

'The red light areas are at the crappy end of town,' Laura said, 'where people survive by stealing and dealing. But around here, someone was buried alive, just up that hill.' And Laura pointed in the direction of Gilbert's house.

Dobson paled and pursed his lips, then the grin came back, just a little more forced than before.

'That was a long time ago,' he said.

Laura raised her eyebrows. 'Oh, so you know which murder I'm talking about?'

Dobson's grin widened but his cheeks paled even more. 'Everyone in Blackley knows about that,' he said. 'Are we finished now? I've got an appointment.'

Laura nodded and smiled. 'Okay, Mr Dobson,' she said. 'Just be careful where you drive, or else next time we have this conversation in front of your wife.'

He turned and walked back to his car. Laura watched him as he opened the door and climbed in. As he gripped the wheel and took a couple of deep breaths, Laura knew she had the answer she needed.

'Do you think he was going to prostitutes?' Thomas asked.

Laura turned to him. 'Without a doubt,' she said. 'Although I wonder whether he's got a lot on his mind right now.'

With that, Laura turned to go, Thomas walking fast to keep up. Now was the time to speak to Joe Kinsella.

Chapter Thirty-Six

I sat in my car and looked at Bill Hunter's house, a redbrick bungalow with rose bushes overgrowing the path and clematis blossoming out from the walls. I had something new with Frankie's photographs – the internet would have made them resurface if they'd been found before – but the story was over twenty years old. How many other times had Frankie told people about the other man, the one he had seen? Tony knew about Frankie, so his obsession was well known to the local press. And I knew that there was only one person who could tell me: Bill Hunter. So I was outside his house, having guessed that he would be at home when I found his allotment plot empty.

I climbed out of my car and bent down to open the small metal gate in the middle of the low brick wall. Hunter must have seen me because as I approached the door his face appeared at the window. He opened the door quickly, took a quick furtive look along the road, and then ushered me inside.

'You seem twitchy,' I said, surprised by his mood. He had seemed relaxed, even jovial, when I had spoken to him at his plot. Now, he seemed jumpy.

'I told you before, you have to be careful when you get involved with the Gilbert case,' he replied, leading me down the hall and into a small conservatory at the back of the house, filled with green wicker furniture and plants.

'What do you mean?'

He moved the newspaper he had been reading before I arrived and sat down. 'People watch what you do,' he said.

'Who?'

'I don't know. Just people,' he said. 'This has been my mystery for a long time, even after I retired. I've asked some awkward questions, and there've been cars outside my house, and people who I thought were helping suddenly lose interest.'

'Are you saying that there's some kind of conspiracy, a cover-up?'

'Not officially,' he said. 'I was a police officer, and I know that official conspiracies don't exist, because there's always a risk that someone will break ranks. But I know something else too: that the people at the top know how to protect themselves. If mistakes were made at the start that let Gilbert get away, no one will be in a rush to uncover them. Leave it like it is, and the secrets die with Gilbert.'

'First rule of public service, so I was told,' I said. 'Look after number one, because everyone else is, and they'll give you up to the mob faster than you can clear your desk.'

He flashed me a cynical look. 'The problem is that the mob don't come with flaming torches these days. They come with Dictaphones and pens.' He looked pointedly towards the voice recorder I had placed on my knee, the red light blinking.

I smiled in apology. 'I'm just looking after number one, like you said.'

'Just be careful,' he replied.

I wasn't sure what to make of him; paranoia is the first option for the deluded. But then I thought of Frankie, and of the two people he saw in the garden.

212

'Have you heard of Frankie Cass?' I said.

Hunter cracked into a smile, but there was concern in his eyes. 'He's tracked you down then.'

'He's got some interesting theories.'

'Frankie is an attention-seeker. He came to the allotment last year and said that he knew something about Mrs Gilbert, and that if I was ever going to write a book about it, he would tell me, for a price. But why wait so long if it was worth hearing?'

'He told me that he kept quiet because his mother told him not to get involved.'

'He told me that too,' he said. 'She smothered him, was my guess, turned him into a social cripple, but I reckon she also told him about right and wrong, and letting someone get away with murder is wrong.'

'Have you ever thought about writing a book?' I asked.

Hunter shook his head. 'Paul Roach beat me to that one,' he said, and when I looked confused for a moment, he explained, 'The other cop who dug up Nancy. It came out around ten years ago. It had been sitting on a publisher's desk for a long time, but then a fake sighting reawakened interest, and so they rushed it out. It's garbage, of course, but it got him a nest egg.'

'There's been talk of Alan Lake,' I said. 'Was he ever a contender?'

Hunter sighed. 'He was, but he was shitting into a bucket at Preston prison at the time, before he was acquitted.'

'But people like Alan Lake don't get their hands dirty, do they?' I said. 'They get their thugs to do their work for them.'

Hunter nodded, conceding the point. 'But we don't know which thugs, and with nothing to tie him down, Lake was never in the picture.'

'Proof and truth are different things,' I said.

'You're right, but think of this: Claude Gilbert wasn't some baby barrister, running hopeless cases for losers. He was a big-hitter, attracting good work. So if it hadn't been Lake's trial that collapsed, it would have been some other big-time lowlife. Lake is just a coincidence, something else that makes the story better.'

'But the cavity,' I said. 'Nancy Gilbert was found in a constructed cavity. If it had been Claude Gilbert and a crime of passion, he would have just buried her and dumped the soil on top. Making a cavity sounds like she was being given a chance. Maybe it was an ultimatum to Claude from Lake's rival dealers, hoping to keep Alan Lake out of circulation for a while – that Claude must lose the case or Nancy dies.'

Hunter smiled and said, 'Wait there.' His knees cracked as he pulled himself to his feet and shuffled slowly out of the conservatory. I watched him go and then glanced around the room. Hunter was married – he played with his wedding ring when he talked about Gilbert, and his house seemed floral, from the rose-coloured swirls of the carpet to the glossy stripes in the wallpaper. But there was something not quite right. I saw a photograph frame on a shelf near the kitchen door, a grey-haired woman beaming from it.

'That's my wife,' said a voice behind me. It was Hunter, holding a file of papers.

'Is she working today?' I asked.

His face darkened for a moment. 'No,' he said flatly. 'She died last year.' He handed me a bundle of documents.

As I took them, I noticed then what was out of place. His gardening boots were in the corner of the room, mud on the edges, and there were some tools on the dining-room table. I guessed that she wouldn't have allowed that.

'I'm sorry,' I said. 'I didn't mean to be insensitive.'

214

'You weren't,' he replied, and then nodded towards the papers he had just handed me. 'Read that.'

As I looked at the title page, I made a poor show of hiding my delight.

'The autopsy report,' I said, grinning. 'Can I use this? I mean, it's not secret or anything like that?'

'Just don't say where you got it,' he said. 'I copied it when I was still in the job, but you can read it and see if you can spot why Gilbert might have created the cavity.'

I flicked through the opening paragraphs, just the usual stuff about the pathologist's qualifications and the time and date of the examination. Then I got to the guts of the report and it made me take a deep breath.

The cavity in which Nancy Gilbert was found was described as five feet long. I turned back to her description, and saw that her height was listed as five feet nine. Then the description of her fingers made me wince. The nails were bent back on five of the eight fingers, with splinters and jagged flakes of paint embedded into the wounds where she had scraped and clawed at the green boards placed over her. Her hair was matted to her head by blood, and there was a fracture to her skull. The cause of death was listed as blunt trauma, not suffocation.

Then I went to the section that dealt with the time of death. I turned a page and grimaced.

There were photographs of the body in situ, reprinted in colour. The green boards were in place on one photograph, put back just to recreate the scene as it had been, and then photographs of the hole with the boards removed. Mrs Gilbert was squeezed into the hole, on her side, naked, the pregnancy bump showing. I could see blood on her finger-tips and over her face, and there was mud there too, but it wasn't the injuries that made me think that I wished I had skipped breakfast, but the colour of the body.

The parts of Nancy Gilbert's body against the floor were purple in colour. I knew that was gravity doing its work, the blood draining downwards, forming and clotting in the lower parts of the body. The rest of her skin had a green tinge, apart from the deep purple of her earlobes and fingertips. Her face was swollen, her distorted features nothing like the pictures I had in my bag, of the attractive young woman with long dark hair. There was blood around her nose and around her mouth, along with much more pooled around her head.

'That's not what you think,' Hunter said, judging where I was in the report from the look on my face. 'It's not all blood, I mean.'

'I don't understand,' I said.

'It's what gets to all new police officers,' Hunter said. 'Your first autopsy is bad, or your first sudden death, but finding a body that's been hanging around for a few days, well, that's bloody awful. The stench is foul, sulphurous and fetid, like your worst ever chemistry lesson. That's the gases forming inside the body, in the intestines, making less room for whatever was in there. It squashes the insides, so that when you move them, and sometimes even before that, it's like stamping on a toothpaste tube. It forces shit out of the mouth.' He pointed towards the photographs. 'That's what is in the photograph, not dried blood.'

I put the report down and took a deep breath. My palms had gone slick.

'You need a bacon sandwich,' he said, smiling, enjoying my discomfort. 'It's what we always did after a fatal. We went to one of those cheap roadside places and got a large bacon sandwich.'

'Not a job for the vegetarians then,' I said.

Hunter shook his head and then pointed towards the

216

report. 'The pathologist couldn't be certain when she died, because bodies will reach the temperature of the immediate environment within around a day and a half, but it would have been quicker in this case, because she was naked and in a cool space.'

'Her immediate environment being a small pit a couple of feet underground.'

'Precisely, and then it becomes just guesswork after that. She had been underground for a few days, we know that, because the body had entered the putrefaction stage.'

'What the hell is that?' I asked.

'The stage when the body starts to stink,' Hunter said, grimacing. 'When putrefaction kicks in, the body is slowly turning to mush, helped on by insects and animals on the outside, and gases on the inside. But it was slowed down because she was underground. Above ground, it's easier to work out, and it all goes a lot quicker, but if you bury a body in soil, it takes longer. There is less air, and it is colder, and so it's like putting the body in a fridge; it becomes all about the insects and animals and dampness.'

'So if the availability of air is a factor,' I said, trying to keep up with Hunter's explanation, 'by putting her in a cavity, she would have decayed faster than if just placed in the soil.'

'You've got it,' Hunter said, seeming pleased that I understood. 'Buried corpses can take eight times longer to get down to bare bones, but the circulation of air around the body would speed things up.'

'So why do you think Claude Gilbert left her like that?' I asked.

'Because he knew the science,' Hunter replied. 'He will have done enough murder cases to know that, and so I reckon he was going to leave her for a year and then dig her up and get rid of the bones. Maybe he could do it sooner if she decomposed more quickly, but then I spoiled his plan.'

'Would he really think in such a composed way?'

'Who else would? He was a barrister, used to quickly working out the angles, the defences. Why would Alan Lake or his rivals bother?'

'To give him the ultimatum. Pull out or his wife dies.'

'She was already dead when she went in,' Hunter said.

I was confused at that. 'But she scratched the wood and ended up with jags of paint under her nails.'

Hunter smiled at me, like a proud father might do at the awful picture his six-year-old had drawn. 'She was as good as dead,' he said. 'She didn't suffocate down there. She died of her head injury, maybe only a couple of hours after she was buried.'

'But she scratched at the boards. Can a person really be aware enough to do that if they've got a life-threatening head injury?'

Hunter nodded. 'It's possible, when someone is whacked with some kind of cosh. It's not unheard of that someone who died of a head injury had a few lucid hours before the injury kicked in.'

I sat back and sighed. 'So, as far as you're concerned, it is Claude Gilbert alone.'

Hunter nodded in reply.

'But why?'

'I don't know, to be truthful,' he said. 'Perhaps one day we'll get to ask him.'

I tried not to give anything away as I asked, 'Did you hear any rumours that she was having an affair?'

'No, I haven't,' he said, 'and so they can't be true.'

'Why not?'

'Because there's money in this story, and so someone would have come forward with an affair, just to cash in.'

'Maybe Frankie was trying?' I said.

Hunter's eyes narrowed. 'Is that what he said?'

I decided not to tell Hunter what I knew. He was useful but, like most policemen I'd met, he had one unshakeable theory, and if a fact didn't fit it was thrown out. My father once told me, in a moment of candour that hadn't come along too often, that too many people had confessions beaten out of them in the seventies for that reason, and that any police officer who said it didn't go on was a liar.

'He didn't say much,' I said, and then I turned back to the autopsy report. 'If the day of death was uncertain, why has it always been quoted as the fifteenth of May?'

'Because that's when Mrs Gilbert was last seen, and Claude Gilbert emptied his bank account on the sixteenth. Just straight logic, and it fitted with the guesswork.' He smiled at me, a little patronisingly, I thought. 'Keep trying, young man,' he said, 'because I hope someone does solve the mystery in the end, but Claude Gilbert killed her, and for as long as that stays the likeliest truth, you've nothing new.'

I suppressed my smile and nodded in agreement. I wondered what Hunter would say when I walked into a press conference with Claude Gilbert behind me.

Then I received a call. It was Tony Davies. I apologised to Hunter and answered.

'Jack, are you still interested in Claude Gilbert?'

'Yes, I am.'

'Well, just be careful, because I've had my boss on the phone. He's heard that I've been digging up the Claude Gilbert stories, and he's told me not to do it any more.'

'But your paper ran a story not so long ago.'

'It was nothing controversial though, more of a recap and update really. For some reason, you're making people notice you.'

219

'Okay, thanks, Tony.' I hung up.

When I looked at Hunter, he raised his eyebrows. 'People closing ranks?'

I nodded. 'Looks that way.'

'I told you, Mr Garrett, for your own good, be careful.'

Chapter Thirty-Seven

I had grown up surrounded by police officers, and I knew how they risked their lives and the modesty of the rewards. So Chief Inspector Roach's house came as a surprise.

It was a detached house set in a large plot, pillars on either side of the front door and a wide brickwork driveway with two cars on the drive, a red Jaguar and a small Mercedes sports car. The wall was low, the black metal gate only around five feet high, I could have vaulted it with a pretty short run-up, but still Roach felt the need for an intercom. I pressed and said who I was, that I wanted to write an article on Claude Gilbert, and so I needed to speak to one of the cops who found Nancy. There was a buzz, followed by the slow creep of the gates opening.

The door opened before I got to the front step, and a tall man in cream trousers and a ghastly yellow V-neck stood in the doorway, looking like he was on his way to the golf course.

'Chief Inspector?'

He nodded and held out his hand to shake. 'Jack Garrett, did you say?'

'Thank you for seeing me at short notice,' I gushed, pumping his hand. 'I know you're a busy man.' Like most people like him, I knew he wouldn't spot the bullshit if it was wrapped up as flattery.

'What are you writing about again?' he asked, as he led me into his house.

He knew what I was writing about, it had got me admitted to his house, but I guessed he wanted fluffing up again.

'Claude Gilbert, and the people behind the story,' I said. 'It isn't complete without a quote from you, Chief Inspector.' I glanced around as I went in. The house was bright, with glossy floral wallpaper and polished oak floors that ran throughout the ground floor. 'How long have you been Chief Inspector?'

'Five years now,' he said, showing me into his living room, an open space dominated by a cream leather sofa that filled a corner of the room, opposite a huge television screen and a large white fireplace.

'What do you find most rewarding about the job?' I asked, knowing that he would talk for as long as he thought the interview was about him.

'It's a joy just to serve the community,' he said, checking that I was writing it down. 'To work with Blackley's diverse communities, to deliver change and go forward. Those are the challenges of the day and I relish the opportunity to tackle them.'

I almost groaned. It was corporate spiel and I realised then how he had got so high in the ranks. Good cops don't get promoted any more. Good cops just do the job and catch criminals. To get on now, you've got to learn the jargon. It seemed like Roach had memorised it.

'Have you read my book?' he said.

I skirted around the issue, not having been aware of it until Hunter had mentioned it earlier. I saw a framed book cover on a wall: *Claude Gilbert – The Untold Story*.

'A man of many talents,' I said. 'That's next on my reading list.'

'Most of what I have to say is in that book. Buy a copy,' he said.

'Most?' I asked. 'What did you miss out?'

He smiled. 'Which paper do you work for?'

'Freelance.'

'I have a good relationship with the local papers,' he said. 'I like to think that it wouldn't be disturbed by the story you are writing. What's your angle?'

It was my turn to smile.

'Buy a copy,' I said. 'It's going in one of the nationals.'

He pursed his lips and flicked at something on his knee as he crossed one leg over the other.

'What's your theory?' I said, trying to retrieve the conversation.

'There isn't a theory,' he said. 'Just the inescapable facts: Nancy was buried alive, and Claude ran away with the money. There aren't too many conclusions you can reach.'

'Is there any way that Claude could be innocent?' I asked.

Roach shook his head. 'There were no other suspects.'

'Alan Lake's name has cropped up,' I said. 'Did anyone look into him?'

Roach took a deep breath at the mention of Lake's name. 'Why Alan Lake?' he asked, his fingers tapping on his nose now.

'Just a theory I've heard.'

He shook his head. 'Forget it,' he said. 'Alan Lake is a respectable member of society now.'

'I didn't know you exchanged postcards,' I said.

He scratched his cheek with his forefinger, a nervous reaction. 'Mr Lake has been a big supporter of the police since he turned his life around.' He sat up and leant forward, his eyes trying to look into mine, but I just examined my notes again, ignoring the close quarters. 'Is this article about me, or Alan Lake?' he said.

'It's like the direction of the river,' I said. When he looked confused, I continued, 'When it sets out, it doesn't have a destination in mind. It works it out, finds its own route.'

Roach got to his feet. 'Time to go, Mr Garrett.'

He towered over me now, looking down at me, a hint that my time in his house was done.

'Okay, thank you for your time,' I said, putting my notepad back into my pocket. 'It's been useful,' and then I smiled my most insincere smile, just to show that I wasn't to be cowed. I liked cops, my father was one, but I didn't think my father would have liked Roach. What people don't realise is that any response is worth adding to the story. Roach had just given himself a part, particularly if the story drifted towards Alan Lake.

He followed me to the door, but when I emerged back into the sunshine, the door slammed loudly behind me. I returned to my car, happy that his response was worth writing up; as I glanced back through his latticed windows, the thin lead strips ill-matched against the white PVC, I saw that he was talking animatedly into the phone.

I climbed into my car and set off quickly, just to make sure that he didn't get my registration number. I could do without one of those random police stops that always seem to happen in a less than random way, although I guessed that my 1973 Triumph Stag in Calypso Red didn't provide much of a disguise.

I knew I had just one more stop to make: Alan Lake.

Chapter Thirty-Eight

When Laura arrived back at the station, she heard someone call her name. The atrium was quiet, the canteen staff long gone, just a few officers taking a break with a drink from one of the vending machines. Laura looked up and saw Rachel leaning over the railing outside her temporary office, gesturing with a twitch of the head that she wanted to talk. Laura told Thomas to wait in the briefing room and headed for the stairs.

The climb to the second floor was a long one, and Laura ran her hand along the rail as if it would slow her down gradually before she reached the room. As she had expected, Joe wasn't there.

Laura composed herself. The meeting with Mike Dobson was still fresh in her mind, and she wondered whether Joe and Rachel knew more than they were letting on.

'Hello, Laura,' Rachel Mason said, her smile quick and perfunctory. 'Take a seat.'

Laura shook her head and leant against the door jamb. 'I'm okay here, thanks.'

Rachel shrugged. 'Please yourself.'

There was silence for a few seconds as the two women looked at each other, until Laura broke it by saying, 'You called me up here?'

'Okay,' Rachel said, testily. 'I'll start with the same question as before: are you going to tell me what your boyfriend is doing?'

'You'll have to ask him that,' Laura replied.

Rachel sat back in her chair. 'I can tell you don't think much of me.'

'When did this become about you?'

'When I ended up sitting closer to Joe Kinsella than you,' Rachel said.

Laura felt herself blush. 'You don't know what you're talking about.'

'Oh no?' Rachel said, her eyebrows raised. 'Maybe my hunches aren't that good, but I saw the look in your eyes when you saw him again. It put a real bounce in your step for a few seconds.' She tapped a pen on the edge of the desk. 'I'm not competition, Laura. He's not my type.'

'Too intellectual?' Laura asked caustically.

'Too old,' came the reply. 'But I do want to meet your other love, Jack Garrett.'

'What if he doesn't want to meet you?'

Rachel smiled. 'That will be between me and him, because you wouldn't get in our way, would you?' When Laura took a deep breath, Rachel added, 'I'll be in that coffee house by the cathedral in an hour. If you ask him to meet me, he might just get an exclusive.'

Laura folded her arms.

'Thank you, PC McGanity,' Rachel said, and then returned to her paperwork, an unsubtle hint that the meeting was over.

The Alan Lake house was as I expected it. I had made some calls and it had been described as a glass and steel newbuild. I could have drawn it before I'd even seen it, large windows built into the slope of a hill and a turf roof, doing its best

226

to disguise itself. I could guess the brief to the architect: they wanted something different, a statement of their individuality, without intruding on the landscape. Except that they ended up with the same glass and steel box built by everyone else who tried to be different. And maybe I'm being a little *too* green, but if you don't want your house to spoil the landscape, try not building it in the first place.

The Triumph rattled on towards the house until I drew it to a halt next to the raised decking at the front. I looked back and admired the view, the rooftops of Blackley just visible, although I still couldn't help but think that the spot would have been considerably more blissful before Alan Lake poured tons of concrete into the ground.

I tried to call Claude Gilbert, but he wasn't answering his phone; I was starting to question the wisdom of walking away from him.

As I stepped out of the car, Alan Lake came out of the house and waved a greeting, although the way he walked towards me told me that it was more of a warning that I'd been spotted than a welcome to the house. He held his shoulders back and walked with that Manchester swagger – like a waddle – and his fringe was long and trailed into his eyes. Its grey hue as it caught the sunshine told me that the dye was in need of a top-up.

'I don't think we've met before,' he said, his voice nasal. 'What can I do for you?'

'I'm a reporter,' I said. 'I hope you don't mind me cold-calling, but I didn't have your number.'

As I climbed the deck steps to greet him, he seemed to diminish in front of me. He was small, around five six, but wiry with it, his cheekbones pressing against his skin. When we shook hands, his grip was firm and the veins bulged on his hands.

He nodded graciously and smiled. 'No, it's fine. Good to see you.' He gestured towards the house. 'Come on in.'

I'd read up on Alan Lake after Tony's visit the night before. He'd made his name as a hoodlum during the Manchester buzz of the late eighties, piggy-backing on the music scene, the long fringes and the drugs at a time when all the college kids from the northern suburbs claimed to be 'mad for it' and replaced their rounded tones with a Mancunian whine. In reality, Lake had been nothing more than a street-level drug dealer who was handy with his fists, but because he preferred the bright lights of the local clubs to hanging around in alleyways, he became a face, some celebrity clients adding to his status. He got some hardman kudos when he went to prison and drifted back to his native Blackley when his status made bad men jealous.

As I went into the house, the green of the countryside turned into the pristine white of an art gallery, with large monochrome pictures on the wall, nude portraits of a reclining woman, and pieces of sculpture mounted on plinths. I sat down on a large sofa in the middle of the living room, and glanced up to see a large wooden balcony over-looking the space I was in.

'Who do you work for?'

'I'm freelance.'

He cast his hand towards the pieces of sculpture in the room. One was a hand that reached for the sky, but a chain came up with it and pulled it back, the tendons stretched out on the wrist as the hand strained upwards. 'Do you like them?'

I considered it for a few seconds, just to be polite, and then I said, 'I'm a reporter, not a critic.'

'Do you understand them?' he said, his eyes watching me carefully.

'That's the first refuge for those seeking to avoid real opinion,' I said. 'It casts the weakness onto the other side.'

Or maybe he was making sure that I knew about his dangerous past.

'It doesn't sound like I'll get a good write-up,' he said dryly, and I spotted some annoyance in the way he pursed his lips. He was more used to the fawning – people telling him how he had captured pain, laid bare the tortured soul of the captive man.

'Don't worry about your art,' I said. 'I'm here for a different story.'

'Go on,' he said, and I saw that his smile had become strained, his eyes a little darker.

'Claude Gilbert,' I said. 'He was one of your former barristers, so I hear.'

His eyelids flickered for a few seconds and then he took a deep breath, impatience clouding his expression. 'I've nothing to say about Claude Gilbert.'

'I'm surprised at that, because his disappearance delayed your trial and kept you locked up,' I said. 'Although it helped you out in the end, I suppose, when the retrial went your way.'

'You need to be careful what you say,' he said. 'Because if you know that, you know that I was in prison when his wife was buried alive. It was nothing to do with me.'

I heard a noise and looked up. There was a woman looking down from the balcony, elegant and dark, much taller than Lake, her figure clad in tight black leggings and matching polo neck, her hair straight and cascading onto her shoulders.

'Don't worry about Adrianne,' he said, flicking his hand towards her. 'We've no secrets. You see, it's all been written before.' As if that were a stage cue, Adrianne started to glide down the stairs that swept down in a wide curve and then strode haughtily towards Lake. It was obvious that she was a former model – I could tell that from the poised way she walked – and when she sat next to him, he smiled at me, his hand on her leg. It looked like Adrianne was his greatest prize. 'And don't you think I've had this conversation too many times now?' he said. 'You won't catch me out with an ambiguous quote. And I sue people. Remember that.'

'I just want your side of things, how you felt when Gilbert went missing,' I said.

He looked at me with his eyes narrowed. 'I told you that I've got nothing to say about it. It was a long time ago, and I had a different life then.'

'It must have been a relief for you though, in the end. What were you looking at? Three years in prison? Someone was scarred for life, and your empire could crumble. It all worked out for you though.'

He lit a cigarette and leant towards me, smoke curling in the air around him, making the clean light hazy. I saw the brown stains between his teeth as his lips curled into a snarl. 'Don't you think you can cast any blame towards me for Gilbert's wife turning up in a pit,' he said, his voice rising higher, his fingers jabbing towards me, small embers jumping from the cigarette. 'And don't think you can get the better of me. I've been in interviews with some clever detectives, and had more than twenty years of innuendo from hack wankers like you, so don't think I'm going to crumble and confess.'

I shifted in my seat, just as an excuse to avoid his gaze for a second.

He laughed, sharp and angry, his brow creased, his eyes bulging at me. 'And that's what annoys me, that you think I'm such easy meat.' He sat back and slammed the sofa with his hand. 'Well, have some fucking respect. And you coming here? How the fuck dare you?'

Adrianne just smiled at me, superior, haughty.

'That's a "no comment" then,' I said, confident that Lake wouldn't hit me.

He took a couple of deep breaths, and then said, 'I'll tell you what, hotshot, yeah, Claude Gilbert offing his wife helped me out, and I'll tell you why: because he wasn't good that week. He seemed distracted, wasn't really fighting the good fight, if you know what I mean, and so I was glad when he went. But I could have done that by sacking him. He had something on his mind that week, and it wasn't me.'

I smiled. 'That's all you had to say, Mr Lake. You didn't have to turn on the aggression.'

'I'm not a criminal any more,' he said, 'and I don't like it when people come to my home and try to drag me into something that was nothing to do with me.'

'Why do you think I'm trying to drag you into anything? Maybe I'm just getting the quotes from all the affected parties.'

'Don't be smart, Garrett.'

'I don't remember giving my name.'

His eyes narrowed. 'Is the interview done?'

I shrugged. It was his call, not mine.

He stood up and walked to the door. I followed, flashed Adrianne a smile, who just looked away; it seemed that I wasn't even worthy of a word.

When I got outside, Lake said, 'Don't come here again, and be careful what you print.'

'I would have thought it would send your prices higher, a bit more criminal credibility for your clients,' I said, his attitude irritating me.

'I've shaken off my past, Mr Garrett,' he said. 'It's about time everyone else did.'

231

I nodded towards Adrianne, who was watching us through the glass. 'You live off your past, Mr Lake,' I said, and then I headed down to my car.

It didn't start straight away, and Alan Lake smirked at me while I turned the engine over and the car misfired; but it caught on the third turn. The plume of dark smoke I was able to send towards him made it seem worth it.

He didn't move as I drove away, and I knew that he was watching me, had noted my number. But I couldn't help wondering why someone who thrived on his past was so reluctant to talk about the most famous figure in it: Claude Gilbert.

Chapter Thirty-Nine

Mike Dobson looked out of the window at the children playing in the cul-de-sac, screaming and laughing as they cycled on their bikes, the local schools just finished for the day.

'Why were the police looking for you?' Mary said, her voice quiet.

He remembered the conversation with the officer, how she had turned it round to Claude Gilbert and watched how he responded. He was a salesman, and so his job depended on reading people, on working out when they were interested or just playing at it.

'There's been someone hanging around work,' he said. 'They're worried about a break-in, someone casing the place.'

'But the officer didn't know where you worked,' Mary said.

'I gave them my home address by mistake,' he said, looking back at her. Just leave it alone, he thought, but he saw a glare in her eye.

'When?'

'When what?'

'When did you tell them?'

'A few days ago. I thought they would have got back to me before now.'

'Why didn't you tell me about it?'

'Because it wasn't important.'

'It was important enough for them to come here.'

'It's not important, Mary,' he said, and closed his eyes. Their conversations were like this, short little jabs, like apologies for breaking the silence.

But the police visit *was* important, he knew that. They were watching him. But why now, after all these years? It would make it harder for him to see her again. His stomach tightened.

The room was silent as he kept his eyes closed. He heard the rustle of clothes, the soft creak as Mary moved about in her chair. The screams from outside died down as his mind raced back through the years. His nose filled again with the scent, and he felt her hair across his face, her lips wanting, urgent, the grab of a stolen moment. Mary tapped on something, the drum of her fingers loud in the quiet room, flesh on wood, and his eyes flew open. As always, there was movement, just at the edge of his vision, someone moving quickly out of view. When he looked at Mary, she hadn't moved, her hands still wrapped around her cup.

But she was watching him, her mouth set, her eyes cold.

He stood up. 'I'm going out,' he said.

'Where?'

'Just out,' and he slammed the door as he left the room.

Rachel Mason surprised me. She was smart and attractive in her dark blue trouser suit, with blonde hair and a pale complexion; she stood out from the shopping crowd as she walked across Blackley's new cobbled market square. A group of young men in hoodies tracked her as she walked, but they turned away as she sat down opposite me outside the coffee house.

'Pleased to meet you, Mr Garrett,' she said, although there was a frost to her tone.

'Laura must have described me well.'

She shook her head and gave me a condescending smile that told me that it hadn't been Laura's description that had given me away. 'Have you been watching me?' I said.

'We're here to talk about you, not me,' she said.

I was wary of her straight away. There was a bluntness about her that I liked, but I sensed that it was a front, perhaps to hide a lack of confidence. In my experience, people like that tend to go at everything with their claws out.

'Tell me about me then,' I said, and sat back to take a drink of my coffee.

'There's not much to know. You're a reporter living with a police officer. You write up court stories and get the occasional scoop that puts you in the nationals. Beyond that, you're a man, a pretty simple species. Sex and sport fill your head most of the time.'

I smiled back. 'I've never been spoken down to by someone with so little life experience. What are you, mid-twenties?' When she blushed, I said, 'I'm not going to give anything up unless you do. Remember, we don't want the same thing. You want the man. I just want the story.'

'So why do you think I'm interested in you?' she said, her voice more hostile now.

'Claude Gilbert,' I said, and when she raised her eyebrows, I added, 'And I know I'm not giving away too much there.' I swirled the coffee in my cup for a few seconds as I thought. 'It's not the why that interests me though,' I said. 'It's the *why now*.'

'What do you mean?'

'Come on, Rachel, I'm no fool. Claude Gilbert went missing twenty-two years ago. I was a teenager when he went on the run, and you'll have been younger than that. I start writing about him and then all of a sudden it turns out that you're after him too, some smart policewoman from headquarters. That's too much of a coincidence. Except that in police work, there's no such thing as coincidence.'

Rachel looked into the coffee shop and waved at someone behind the counter to indicate that she wanted a coffee. For most people it was counter service, but something about her manner meant that she got what she wanted. As she waited for her drink to arrive, she said, 'You're right, it isn't by chance. It's because we started the same way.'

I was confused. 'How do you mean?'

'Susie Bingham,' she said. 'She got you involved in all of this.' I must have looked surprised, because she continued, 'I'm sorry to disappoint you, Mr Garrett, but you are not the first journalist she spoke to about Claude Gilbert.'

'Who else?'

Rachel shook her head. 'I can't tell you that, but *he* contacted the police, not his editor, and so she moved on to you.'

I detected a barb to the conversation, that I hadn't done the right thing. I wasn't concerned by that. I was a journalist. My first duty was to the story. My popularity came a poor second.

'So why didn't you speak to her?'

'How do you know we didn't?'

That surprised me, because I thought Susie would have told me if she had been questioned by the police.

'Did she tell you anything?' I asked.

Rachel paused as her coffee arrived, and then took a sip before answering. 'Maybe, like you, she saw the pound signs, not the handcuffs.'

I sighed. 'Are you going to be judgemental all day, because I've got a story to write? Okay, let's get the apology out of the way. I'm sorry about my low morals. There, done, but you ought to know that I'm not here to do your job.'

'Have you found him?' she asked.

'What makes you think I'm looking? How do you know I'm not doing a conspiracy write-up?'

'Because the story is up here, in Blackley, not in London.' She studied me for a few seconds. 'Where did you go, Jack?'

I shook my head slowly. 'Wait for the front page.'

Rachel took a sip of coffee and watched me over the brim of the cup.

'How well do you know Susie Bingham?' she asked.

'I met her for the first time a couple of days ago.'

'She told the last reporter that she had seen Claude Gilbert. Did she say the same thing to you?'

'That's between me and Susie.'

'What about the booze?' Rachel said. 'Did you notice that?'

'What do you mean?'

'Susie's just some past-it party girl who never noticed that the party had ended,' she said. 'I asked around the station, and some of the older ones remember her, a couple of them a bit too fondly. She had a good career, but she blew it because it became more about the booze than the clients.'

When I didn't have an answer, Rachel went on, 'She doesn't seem quite the compelling witness any more, does she?'

'I've met him,' I blurted out.

Rachel's cup paused on the way to her mouth, and then she lowered it slowly.

'Gilbert?' she asked, her voice quiet, her gaze steady.

'Who else?' I replied. 'And if I can meet Claude Gilbert within a day of meeting Susie, when you haven't done it in twenty-two years, maybe you should be a little slower to have a go at me.'

'You've met him?' she said, her voice almost a gasp.

I nodded slowly, enjoying her reaction.

'When? Where?'

'A couple of days ago. In London.'

'Are you going to tell me anything more?' she said.

'I will, on one condition.'

'Go on.'

'Laura. None of this backfires on her. She knew nothing about Claude Gilbert. I didn't tell her why I went to London, because I know she's loyal to the job. If anything of this is going to backfire on her, I walk away from here, and you never find out where I met him until he comes forward on my terms.'

'You're assisting an offender,' she said.

I laughed. 'To prove that, you have to prove that it was Claude Gilbert.' I held out my hands. 'Your call, officer, but it won't get you any nearer to Claude.'

Rachel thought about that for a few seconds, and then she nodded. 'Laura gets no fallout from this. But I can't promise anything in relation to you.'

I smiled. 'I wouldn't expect anything more.'

She reached into her pocket and produced a notepad. 'So, go on, talk.'

I shook my head. 'Not yet. I want to know what you've got on him, whether there are any other suspects for Nancy's murder. This is not a one-way conversation. If you're open with me, it goes down as nothing more than an inside source, and I give you what I know.'

'Everything?'

I nodded. 'Everything.'

Rachel exhaled and looked around the square as she thought about what she could say. 'I know I've nothing else to tell you about Nancy's murder, because you've spoken to Bill Hunter,' she said eventually.

'How do you know?'

She raised her eyebrows. 'Bill Hunter might be retired,

but he never stopped being a cop. He gave you what he knew, and then he told me that you were looking.'

'Why you?'

'Because I've been given the job.'

'But he told me that people get interested in Gilbert,' I said, 'that he thinks Gilbert might have friends in high places.'

Rachel nodded. 'I think he does too. That's why they asked me to do it.' She flashed me a sheepish smile, a chink in the ice. 'Maybe I come across as cold, but I don't spend my life looking after the club, the old canteen set. Gilbert knew a lot of the old guard. His wife was killed at the end of the eighties, when it was still all right for detectives to accept hospitality from defence lawyers, like meals and football tickets. It wasn't corruption, no special favours were done, but it was a way of getting the recommendation when the scared punter turned up at the custody desk, not sure if they wanted a lawyer.'

'So what's that got to do with Claude Gilbert?'

'Join the dots, Mr Garrett,' she said, the frost returning. 'Claude didn't get away on his own, and he didn't stay free on his own. No one can be that resourceful. So he had some help, and it will have come from friends in high places. Maybe tip-offs when they were getting close, or help with accommodation, that kind of thing.'

'If you know that,' I said, 'then why hasn't something been done?'

'There's no proof – just guesswork, and rumours from retired coppers who've had too many drinks at the golf club, telling tall tales of the old days,' Rachel said. 'So Joe and I were brought in quietly, once we got the report that Susie Bingham was touting the Claude Gilbert angle. No one was to know.'

'It's different this time,' I said.

'Why is it?'

'Because he wants to come home.'

Rachel gasped, and I saw her cup waver in her hands. I could see the press conference in her eyes, Rachel Mason announcing the arrest in her best new suit.

'It's on his terms,' I added.

'He's a wanted man. He doesn't have terms.'

'He does, because he's not in a cell,' I said. 'He can just disappear again. And his terms must be better than no terms.'

Rachel played with her spoon for a few seconds while she looked into her coffee; then she said, 'What terms are they?'

'That I prove his innocence first.'

Rachel laughed, but it was sharp and shrill. 'Did you believe him?'

I chewed on my lip as I tried to give a truthful answer. 'I don't know,' was the best one I could come up with. 'Were there any other suspects?'

Rachel shook her head. 'The only credible one was some gangland thing, and so Alan Lake was an obvious one. You know, the sculptor?'

My face remained impassive. Rachel had spoken as if I wouldn't know about Alan Lake, which told me that I wasn't being followed any more.

'How far did you get with him?' I asked.

'Not very,' she said. 'He was in prison, and it's hard to work out what he would gain, because the retrial could have gone even worse.' She folded her arms. 'You mentioned an affair to Bill Hunter?'

'Did I?'

'You know you did.'

I shrugged. 'Just something Claude said.'

'Do you have a name?'

I tried not to give anything away as I looked at her. 'No,' I

240

said. 'Just the ramblings of an old man trying to work out why it happened. You would know about it if it was true, right?'

Rachel nodded slowly, not willing to concede a weakness.

'Did Bill Hunter also mention Frankie Cass?' I said. 'He lives across the road.'

Rachel's eyes narrowed as she thought back through the boxes of paper she had waded through. 'I don't know anything about a Frankie,' she said eventually.

'I'm not surprised. I think he will talk to anyone but the police,' I said.

'And so he's spoken to you.'

I nodded. 'He lives on his own in a big house opposite the murder scene, in an attic room mainly, with a view into Gilbert's garden. His room is covered in newspaper articles about the Gilbert case, and to judge by the photographs on the wall, it seems he spent his life taking pictures of Mrs Gilbert when she was alive. Now he lives alone in that big, dark house, which is either rat-bait or pristine, depending on which part of the house you are in.'

'Which is the pristine part?' Rachel asked, her eyes keen now.

'His mother's bedroom,' I replied. 'Or, at least, his long departed mother's. Her old bedroom is preserved like a pink shrine.'

Rachel looked thoughtful. 'I didn't know about Frankie.'

'Maybe he's just some local nutcase,' I said.

Rachel didn't respond.

I leant forward. 'Are you interested in Frankie now?' I asked. 'Because if you are, you're wondering whether Claude is telling the truth – that he didn't kill Nancy.'

That seemed to bring Rachel round.

'Claude Gilbert killed his wife,' she said. 'It's obvious to anyone who looked at the case carefully. She dies, he flies.'

'He gives a different version,' I said.

'I bet he does.'

'He makes sense.'

'He was a lawyer,' Rachel countered. 'His job was to look jurors in the eye and convince them of the truth of his story. The real truth didn't matter.'

'You sound so cynical for someone so young.'

Rachel shook her head. 'I just see it how it is.' She put her head back and flicked her hair, so that it flowed loosely over her shoulders. 'So tell me,' she said. 'What *is* Claude's story?'

'He left his wife, went abroad for a holiday and, while he was away, he read about his wife's murder.'

'So why didn't he give himself up? He could prove when he left the country.'

'Because he's a coward,' I said. 'He stayed away, hoping the real killer would be found, and then, when he realised that he was the one they were looking for, he kept on running.'

Rachel thought about that for a few seconds. 'Why would he leave his wife in the middle of a court case?'

I thought about Mike Dobson, and how I wasn't ready to give him up yet. I might be talking to the police, but my story was still the top of my list, for as long as I could keep Laura out of trouble.

'Because he was a bad husband whose marriage was falling apart,' I said. 'Gilbert was just a coward with bad timing.'

'I don't believe that,' she said, shaking her head, 'and I still think you're holding out on me. You've given me nothing, except that you think you've met him. Give me something real, something we don't know.'

I took a deep breath and wondered how much else I should say. I thought about Claude's address, but the police would be able to prove that he had been there if I did. And if they could prove it was Claude Gilbert, then they could come after me. It was turning into a glorious summer and I wasn't ready to go to jail.

I shook my head. 'You've got everything.'

'I haven't got Claude Gilbert,' Rachel replied.

'You will have soon, and for that, Laura stays out of it. She doesn't know anything else, and if you give her a hard time, maybe I'll tell Claude to stay away, because if you have just one agenda – to catch him and put him in a cell – then he might as well keep on running.'

I put a ten pound note on the table. 'Put that towards the coffee.' The chair clattered on the cobbles as I stood up to walk away. I heard Rachel talk into her telephone as I went. Now I knew that the police would be watching me, I had to find out more about Mike Dobson, before anyone else did.

Chapter Forty

Mike Dobson's hands were tight around the steering wheel and he could feel the tension in his jaw as he ground his teeth.

He glanced towards the glove box and felt a rush of excitement. It made his foot press a little harder on the pedal and so he had to slow down, worried about the speed cameras.

It wasn't rush hour, and the streets of Blackley weren't busy with cars. He wondered whether he should wait until later, but the tightness of his chest and the warmth in his cheeks told him that it had to be now. The police were looking out for punters, it was true, but they would be looking for the late-night crawlers, the ones who were easy to spot. It was early for the girls to be working, but the warm weather made it easier for them to hang around.

The brightness of the town centre petered out into the grubby fronts of tyre-fitters and plumbers' merchants, and then he slowed down as he swung his car into the circuit of derelict terraces. He opened both windows and crawled along, checking in every direction for her, looking for that flick of dark hair and those skinny legs, his eyes flitting around constantly, checking the rearview mirror, always alert for the black uniforms hiding behind the unmarked car windscreen.

He did two circuits and he couldn't see her. He knew he

was attracting attention, the car always did that, and so he pulled into the side of the road and kept watch instead. He was in a street that was dimly lit in winter, located near to an old scout hut surrounded by razor wire and an old basketball court that formed a magnet for young men doing street-level drug deals in the dark. But this was summer time, and so the days were long. The dealers operated indoors in summer, where indiscreet handovers would be less obvious.

He stayed there for over an hour, just watching the street trade. There was a steady flow of taxi drivers talking to pale-faced young women in miniskirts, but still there was no sign of her.

He was about to head back to his empty house, feeling like she was never going to show, when finally he saw her, emerging from a doorway along a street filled with boarded-up buildings, wiping her hand. There was a taxi parked on the road, a green Nissan Bluebird, and the driver drove off quickly; Mike guessed that the ride hadn't cost her hard cash.

He closed his eyes and tried not to think of that. He wanted the afternoon to be special, he had waited a long time for it, and didn't want the remnants of another man with them.

He started his engine and moved his car slowly towards her. As he got closer, she looked at him and he saw a spark of recognition, although her vision looked unfocused. He leant across the passenger seat and she bent down to the open window. The smell of cheap booze drifted into the car.

'You again,' she drawled.

He looked down at her fingers. They were gripping the car door, as if she was trying to stop herself from falling over. There were beads of sweat on her chest.

'I told you I would come and see you again,' he said, his cheeks red with embarrassment.

She shrugged and opened the car door, stumbling slightly as she climbed in. 'Why?'

'To spend some time with you,' he replied.

She gave a little laugh, although it came with a slur. 'This isn't normal boy-girl stuff, you know,' she said, mocking him.

He nodded. 'I'll pay for it, like always.' He reached into his pocket and showed her the notes in his wallet. 'I'll give you two hundred pounds if you'll spend a few hours with me.'

She looked at it and took a deep breath. 'It's a lot of money,' she said. She looked away and opened her bag to produce her cigarettes.

'Not yet,' he said.

As she looked at him, he saw how glazed her eyes were. He fought to hold back his anger. He had sought her out, had even brought her something, and she was like this, so early in the day.

'I don't want the car to smell,' he said. And Nancy didn't smoke, he thought to himself.

She shrugged and closed her bag, and then looked straight ahead. 'No funny stuff, you know that,' she said.

He nodded.

'So where do we go?'

'Just for a drive.'

She glanced along the street and licked her lips. 'Can I trust you?'

'You have up to now.'

She paused as she thought about it, and then smiled. 'You seem like a nice guy. Okay.'

Dobson nodded and then pulled slowly away from the kerb.

Chapter Forty-One

I decided to take a detour and go back to Frankie's house.

For all Rachel Mason's certainty that Claude Gilbert was a killer, I had spotted her interest when I mentioned Frankie Cass. And, if nothing else, she would want to know what he had been keen to tell everyone else. If he was going to be arrested, I wanted to get the arrest picture, and maybe a quote.

But I felt no pleasure in being right as I drove up the hill to his house. There were two police cars outside and a silver Mondeo in front of them. I parked behind the squad cars and looked up his drive, letting out a groan when I saw Frankie being led out of the house. Rachel was holding on to one arm, his hands cuffed in front of him, a uniformed officer on the other side of him. I jumped out of my car and walked quickly towards them.

Rachel noticed me as I got closer. 'Am I going to start seeing you wherever I go?' she said, a look of irritation flashing across her eyes.

'It's my story.'

'It's more than a story,' she said, and continued taking Frankie down the drive. As he passed me, he shot me a look that was both confused and hurt. I had betrayed him.

'But why are you arresting him?'

Rachel stopped for a moment. 'You saw his bedroom.'

'You know I did.'

Rachel smiled. 'If you'd looked closer, you would have seen that not all the photos were of Nancy Gilbert.' She rattled his cuffs, making Frankie wince. 'It looks like we've found the person creeping around people's houses. You know, the Crawler, or whatever the papers call him.' She led Frankie away towards a waiting car.

Oh great, I thought. That was Frankie, and I missed it, a guaranteed quick story, just to keep my byline out there.

As I turned to watch them go, Rachel shouted over her shoulder, 'It's not always about you, Mr Garrett.'

I put my hands on my hips, watching as Frankie was pushed into the police car, and then I turned and headed towards the front door. It creaked open slowly as I pushed it. I could hear people talking inside, just soft mutters, but the sound stopped as I went into the house. A shadow entered the hallway ahead of me. I let my eyes adjust to the dim lighting, and then I saw a face I hadn't seen for a few months: Joe Kinsella.

I nodded a greeting. 'I heard you were around, Joe. It's been a while. How are things?'

He didn't look surprised to see me. In fact, I couldn't work out what he was thinking, as he gave me that usual enigmatic look of his, all dreamy eyes and soft-focus smile.

'You keep popping up in the wrong places,' he said.

'So are you thinking he's a suspect in the Claude Gilbert story too?' I said. 'Bit of a cliché, isn't it? Lone oddball with a mother-fixation as the murderer?'

He took my arm to lead me further along the hallway. 'Is this an interview, or off the record?' he asked, his voice quiet.

'Off the record,' I said. 'I'll tell you if that changes.'

He seemed happy with that. 'Keep the Claude Gilbert connection quiet for now,' he said.

'Why is that?'

'Because I'm asking,' he replied. 'And you call them clichés. We call them patterns.'

'Frankie just misses his mother,' I said.

'Maybe, and so did Ed Gein,' Joe said. 'The voyeurism stuff will keep him busy for a day, and we can have a proper look around.'

'Are you sure it's him?'

'We suspect it,' he said, a half-smile on his face. 'We received information that he's been taking secret photographs of women.'

I closed my eyes for a moment and offered Frankie a silent apology. 'And so you get to have a look around his house, just to see what he's got on the Gilbert case?'

'It's a fringe benefit.'

I laughed at that, but I noticed that Joe seemed serious. We'd met before, and so I knew how he worked, that he was as interested in the criminal mind as he was in the forensic evidence, those almost invisible trails that killers leave behind. He was embedded into the murder squad to look behind the forensics and work out the thought processes, to second-guess the killer. A killer can wash away blood, but behaviour is harder to conceal, because it is behaviour that guides killers. So he studied psychopathy. It kept Joe up to date with the theories, and for the police it was like having a consultant on a cheap salary. So, was Joe right – that clichés are just worn-out truths, but true just the same?

'How far have you been into the house?' I asked.

'I've just arrived,' he said. 'Rachel had the first look, and so she made the arrest.'

I sighed. 'You need to go to the top floor, to the furthest door.'

He nodded, and then turned towards the stairs, inclining

his head to indicate that I should follow him. As I walked behind him, I wondered whether I had just caught a murderer, or whether I had ruined the life of a local man just so that I could add a shine to a story that would be lining cat litter trays the day after it went out.

But that was the game, and so I trudged slowly behind Joe Kinsella as he climbed higher.

Mike Dobson crunched his car to a halt on a patch of shale by an old farm gate. They'd driven into the countryside, away from the shadows of the viaduct and into the honeysuckle and sunshine of the Ribble Valley.

She looked across at him. 'Are we here?'

She was reaching into her bag for the condom, putting the package of baby wipes on her knee as she rummaged. He reached out and put his hand on hers.

'Let's go for a walk,' he said. He smiled and patted her hand, and then pointed at the wipes. 'Leave those behind.'

She looked around, uncertain for a moment, and so he said, 'It's okay. It will make a change from some patch of concrete in Blackley.' He reached past her and opened his glove compartment. 'Spray this on.' He was holding a bottle of perfume. Chanel No. 5.

She looked uncertain but took it anyway. She sprayed it into the air, and then, once she was sure that it was perfume, and not some spray that would hurt her, she put some on her neck. 'It's nice,' she said.

He moved in towards her and inhaled deeply. He closed his eyes. The perfume took him back to a different time, and he felt soft fingers on his face and heard a giggle. He opened his eyes. She hadn't moved. He reached out and traced along her breastbone with his finger, just a feather touch, and then brought it to his nose and took a deep breath. He looked at her. She was young, just like Nancy was all those years ago, with a sprinkle of freckles across her nose, and lips that were full and seductive.

He stepped out of the car and went to the boot. When she stepped out, he passed her a plastic bag.

'What's this?' she asked, swaying slightly, her hand reaching out to the car roof to steady herself.

'Put it on,' he said. When she looked doubtful, he added a 'please' and then turned away, not wanting her to refuse. He heard a rustle as she looked in the bag, and then there was a pause. He smiled as he heard her unclip her skirt, and he continued to look the other way as she stepped out of her own clothes. He could feel his excitement rising and he took some deep breaths to calm himself.

'Like this?' she asked eventually, and when he looked round, he gasped.

She was just how he remembered Nancy. The sun behind her shone through her hair, the light breeze blowing stray ones so that they caught the sunlight, and her legs were visible through the flowered dress, the one that he had bought for Nancy all those years ago but never had the chance to give to her. The pattern was faded now, but his memory wasn't, and it seemed like the last twenty-two years had hardly happened.

'Follow me,' he said, and he stepped away from the car, another bag in his hand.

Chapter Forty-Two

Joe went into Frankie's attic room ahead of me. He turned around, tried to take in all the photographs pasted across the four walls. A uniformed officer came in behind me and whistled. Joe looked at me, and I saw an excitement in his eyes that I hadn't seen in him before. Joe was always the quiet man, the thinker, but Frankie's room seemed to make him agitated.

'What is it?' I asked.

He didn't say anything. He moved close to the walls to examine the pictures, and soon spotted the Nancy Gilbert ones. The window was open, and so the old newspaper clippings fluttered in the light breeze over the computer screen, the screensaver a slideshow of photographs. Joe moved over to the window and looked down towards the care home, at Claude Gilbert's old house. He thrust his hands into his pockets and chewed on his lip. When I joined him at the window, he turned to me.

'Something isn't right here,' he said quietly.

'Frankie?' I said. 'As a witness, or a suspect?'

Joe took a deep breath. He stepped away from the window and returned to his scrutiny of the pictures, taking them in methodically, a couple of seconds with each one before moving on to the next.

I turned round when I heard someone else come into the room. It was Rachel.

'Frankie safely locked up?' I said pointedly.

'For now,' she said, and she pointed at the photographs. 'Those will keep him in a cell for a while.'

'It will be worth all the effort then,' I said. I didn't feel like sharing in Rachel's victorious mood.

'We need to know about his mother,' Joe said, interrupting us.

'What do you mean?' I asked.

He turned to look at me. 'Obsessive loners don't function well in the wider world because their upbringings are too strict, too restrictive,' Joe said, and pointed at the pictures. 'Look at those. Frankie is an obsessive, and he's sexually repressed. He takes pictures of pretty women because he wants to get close to them but can't; he captures them artificially, pastes them on the wall, so that it feels like he's with them, that he's surrounded by them.'

'And you think that it is his mother's fault?'

Joe nodded. 'Nearly always. Fathers affect behaviour with cruelty or brutality, give their children warped ideas about how to treat people, but mothers can do it by suffocation, by too much love, so that the son finds it impossible to love other women.'

'So, if that's applied to Frankie, how would he think of his mother?' I asked.

Joe sighed. 'It's a real paradox. Some part of him will feel hatred or resentment over the fact that she has harmed him psychologically, but at the same time it will become impossible to break out of his mother's hold. He will worship her, and no woman he ever meets will live up to her, and so he hates his mother even more. That hatred can be transferred to other women.'

I took a deep breath and wished a silent apology to Frankie. 'Follow me,' I said, and started to walk out of the door.

'Where are we going?'

'You said you had only got as far as the ground floor,' I said, leading Joe down the stairs to the floor below, until we arrived at the door to Frankie's mother's room.

I put my hand on the door handle. 'You'll want to see this then,' I said, and gave the door a push.

As it swung open, casting Joe's face in a pink light, his mouth moved but no sounds came out. When he looked at me, I saw shock in his eyes.

Then I heard a shout from above.

'Joe, you might want to come up here. And you, Mr Garrett.' It was Rachel.

I went back up the stairs behind Joe and, when I went into the attic room, I saw that Rachel was pointing at the computer, a smile on her face. It was still running the slideshow screensaver, but now it was showing pictures that I recognised. It was my house, I could see my car at the front, and it was showing views of a window. Then some zoomed-in shots came up, and I felt my stomach turn over as I saw Laura, getting undressed.

I looked at Joe, who looked embarrassed, and then Rachel smirked and said, 'She really needs to learn to close the curtains.'

I slammed the door on the way out.

Mike Dobson jumped over the farm gate and held out his hand to help her over. Her touch was light, and he had to reach out to stop her from falling.

As they walked, he kept hold of her hand. Her fingers were soft and warm, and her dress brushed against his leg, the breeze wafting the perfume past his nose. He looked down at his own clothes and wished he'd got changed out of his shirt and tie, but it felt more real like this, because it was how it was back then, stolen moments between appointments, or escapist afternoons when they knew no one was around. He kept his gaze down towards the floor, so that it still felt like Nancy, her fingers warm in his hand.

'Where are we going?' she asked.

'Towards the river,' he said, pointing ahead.

'You're not going to hurt me, are you?' she said. 'You seem like a nice man, but we're a long way from anywhere.'

He stopped and looked at her. She seemed embarrassed, reluctant, and he worried that she was going to bolt back towards the car.

'I told you, I just want to spend some time with you.'

She looked down as if considering her options, but then she looked up and nodded her agreement.

The track followed the line of a low wall, sloping downwards, with long grass in the field that shifted in the breeze like the swell of the tide. Ahead, the long valley stretched away, the view broken by hedgerows and the occasional car roof as it travelled along the lanes that snaked between the farm tracks.

When they got to the edge of the field, Mike jumped down over a gnarled tree root and then put his bag on the floor. He grabbed her by the waist to lift her down, noticing how light she was.

She looked around. They were at a bend in the river, the level so low that the water shimmered over the stones in the middle, and the grass on the other bank trailed lazily over its surface.

'It's nice down here,' she said.

'It is. We used to come here,' he said, pointing towards an old stone folly a little further along the river bank. As her

258

gaze followed the line of his finger, he said, 'We used to go in there when the weather was bad and watch the lightning flash over the cottages.' He smiled, reflective and sad. 'She used to like it in there. Nancy, that was her name. It was a special place for her.'

'Nancy?'

He nodded. 'Just someone I used to know.'

She walked along the river bank, towards the folly. 'I used to go riding around here,' she said.

'Riding? You?'

'Why are you surprised?' she said. Then she looked down at herself, a hint of shame in her eyes. 'I wasn't born into my life. It just sort of turned out this way.'

'I'm sorry, I didn't mean anything by it,' Mike said, and he joined her in front of the folly.

It looked different to how it had been the last time he had been here. It was just a stone shelter, three-sided, and had become somewhere for ramblers to seek refuge from bad weather, built when the land formed part of a country estate that had long since been divided up and sold off to settle death duties. Now it stood derelict. The windows had been smashed and the back wall was supported now by a large metal plate, riveted in the middle, so that the interior was dark, allowing no view of the countryside behind it. Not like it had been back when it had been special to Nancy. There were empty bottles of vodka in one corner and a couple of damp cigarette packets littered the other.

'Come back to the river,' he said, and he turned away. He reached into his bag and pulled out a rug. He spread it on the ground, in the shadow of the tree whose root they had climbed over before. 'Lie down with me.'

'How long are we going to be here?'

He sighed, tried to bite back the irritation. He wanted her to enjoy it, but the moment was being spoiled.

'I'll pay you more, if you want.'

She thought about that, and then lay down on the rug next to him, her hair spreading out against the red tartan. Her arms were rigid, by her side, nervous. As Mike lay next to her, he put his face to her neck and took another deep breath of the perfume before reaching into the bag once more. He pulled out two plastic wine glasses and a bottle of merlot. Her eyes went hungrily to the bottle and, when he poured her a glass, her first mouthful seemed like it had broken a drought.

He lay back and looked up at the blue sky. Small white clouds threatened to spoil the view. He heard a bird rustle the leaves above him, and he could feel the warmth of the sun on his face.

'Kiss me,' he said.

'I don't do that,' she replied.

He closed his eyes, felt his eyelashes get damp.

'Please,' he whispered. 'That's what I wanted from this.'

There was a moment's pause, and he heard her put her glass on the floor. He opened his eyes and saw that the blue of the sky was blotted out by the silhouette of her hair, her face hardly visible, cast into shadow. When she leant down to kiss him, his nose was filled with the perfume. He ran his hand up her back as he felt her lips on his. He tasted cigarettes and stale booze. Her kiss was soft and nervy; his was needing. The ridges in her spine were sharp against his fingers and her ribs felt brittle against his chest. His fingers found the zip on her dress, and he pulled it down slowly before lifting it over her head. Her body was outlined against the sun, her arms skinny, the bones jagged in her shoulders.

He closed his eyes. He wanted to remember the woman

she was, not the stick-thin version in front of him. Nancy's figure had been fuller, her hips rounder.

He gasped as he felt her hands on his belt. She seemed eager, excited, but then, as he opened his eyes, he saw only impatience. She pulled his trousers down and straddled him. He put his hands behind her back, and then ran his hands down to the sharpness of her hip bones. It wasn't right, not quite the same.

'No, you're going too fast,' he said, trying to pull away, but she found him, made him gasp as she started to move on him, backwards and forwards. There was no sound from her. She was efficient, passionless.

'Please stop,' he said. He could feel stones under his buttocks. They were distracting him. But he could smell the perfume and, as he looked at her, with her hair forward over her face, it could have been Nancy.

He pulled her face towards him so he could kiss her. He tasted the decay, old cigarettes and poor hygiene, but the perfume drifted towards him and so he carried on. As she moved, his excitement grew. He tried to stop himself, didn't want it to end so soon, but his hands went up her back, and then to her breasts, before they moved to her neck. His hands were gentle around her throat as she rocked on him. He opened his mouth and moaned. He couldn't hold on much longer, and he felt his grip get tighter.

Chapter Forty-Three

My mood didn't improve as I drove up the hill to our home. I was angry with Rachel Mason, with Frankie, even with Alan Lake, but I was angry mostly with myself. Frankie had been to my house. Was he the man who had been in the house when I was in London, drinking with Dave, and Laura was there alone? From what I had seen on Frankie's screensaver, he had spent some time watching Laura before he was caught. What if Laura had seen him? How far would he have gone?

I cursed myself for going to London. I could have done it a different way, and now I could only imagine the smirks Laura would have to endure around the police station.

I wasn't really concentrating as I swung my car towards the parking space in front of the living-room window and I had to slam on the brakes when, just in time, I saw Tony Davies's car parked there. At least Tony was a friendly face, and I felt like I needed to see one of them.

Before I went into the house though, I looked at the windows. They needed locks, and the curtains were open. We didn't hide ourselves away – there was nothing over-looking the cottage, and it was a joy in spring to wake up to the sun streaming in through the window. After seeing

Frankie's photographs, all that would have to change, and some of our routines would be lost forever.

I tried to ring Claude; I had been trying all day, but he wasn't answering. I scowled. I was furious with Frankie, and now I could feel my big story slipping away from me.

As I walked in, Tony and Laura were around the table, talking, but they stopped when they saw me.

'Jack, how are you doing?' Tony said, and I sensed that he was trying to lift the mood that had been in the house before I arrived.

'I'm doing okay,' I said, although my voice didn't reflect that. My laptop made a clunk as I put my bag on the table next to them.

Laura jumped up and came to me, planting a kiss on my cheek.

'I'll leave you boys to talk,' she said, and then headed for the stairs. I could hear Bobby upstairs in his bedroom.

'How have you got on?' Tony said, when we were alone.

'Good, in some respects, but it's all too much of a jumble to make it into a story,' I said.

Tony nodded towards the stairs. 'How much have you told Laura?'

'Maybe more than I should have.'

Tony nodded as he thought this over. 'It's not good to have secrets,' he said eventually. 'And she might be able to help. You're going to bring a murder suspect out of hiding, and she might know who to speak to first.'

I grimaced.

Tony raised his eyebrows. 'What's wrong?'

'I've been calling Claude all day,' I said, 'and he doesn't seem keen on answering.'

Tony let out a long breath but didn't say anything else as Laura came skipping back down the stairs. She smiled and blew me a kiss as she went towards the kitchen, before emerging with a bottle of wine and an empty glass. 'I'm going for a hot soak,' she said. 'I may be some time.'

I let her footsteps fade upstairs, and then I went to the fridge to pop the top from a cold beer. Tony declined; he was driving. The first sip took away some of my frustrations, but I was still feeling discouraged when I joined him at the table and slumped onto a chair.

'So, where have you been?' Tony said.

'I got my fingerprints all over the case today. Bill Hunter again. Frankie Cass. I even managed a meet with the police and had a visit to Alan Lake's glass box.'

'How did it go with Alan Lake?' Tony asked.

'Let's just say that he isn't the most willing of inter-viewees,' I replied, and I recounted my visit to his house.

'Still on your suspect list?'

'I don't know,' was my answer, and it was the truth, I wasn't sure. The guilt of a hoodlum-turned-artist would be hard to pin down.

'And it turns out that Frankie Cass isn't the greatest neigh-bour either,' I said, and I threw the envelope of photographs onto the table.

Tony looked at me, surprised, and then he reached forward for the envelope. As he pulled out the photo-graphs and started to thumb through them, his mouth opened, and then his eyes widened in surprise. He looked up at me.

'Is that Nancy Gilbert?' he asked, holding up one of the nude shots taken from Frankie's bedroom.

I nodded. 'Frankie was her stalker, but keep going. You haven't got to the good stuff yet.'

I watched Tony's face, waiting for the moment when he got beyond the peep show and on to the important shots.

It didn't take long. He looked up at me, a grin spreading across his face.

'That's not Claude, is it?' he said, chuckling.

'Not unless he changed his hair colour now and again.'

'Does Frankie mind that you've got them?'

'Right now, I don't care what Frankie thinks,' I said. When Tony looked confused, I added, 'He's been here, in the house, taking secret pictures of Laura. So even if Frankie feels angry with me, we're nowhere near even.'

Tony's eyes widened in surprise. 'In *here*?'

I nodded. 'When I was in London.'

He shook his head in disbelief, and then pointed at the pictures. 'So you pinched them?'

'And they stay that way,' I said.

'For how long?'

'For as long as I need them.'

Tony smiled. 'This is how journalism used to be, when we got out there and muscled our way into stories. You're better staying freelance now. In the newsroom we do everything on the phone or the computer these days. So, did Frankie say who it was?'

I shook my head. 'He was too busy throwing me out when he saw that I'd found them. But Claude told me that his wife was sleeping with Mike Dobson. It might be that she entertained the neighbourhood when he was at work, and who would blame her, but it's a start. He's on my go-see list for tomorrow – if I can find him.'

'You need to be careful, Jack. In case he's the killer. People can react differently when they're cornered.'

'Frankie said that he saw two people in the garden, digging late at night,' I said. 'That must rule out lover-boy; crimes of passion don't generally come as a double act.'

'So why are you going?'

'He's part of the story.'

'And Alan Lake?' Tony asked.

'I don't know,' I said. 'He fits in best with the two-person theory, but we've only got Frankie's word for it, and I'm not sure that's worth a great deal. I'll keep an eye on Lake, because he's pissed me off, and so now he's part of the story, even if it is just to remind people what a thug he was.'

'You'll send his prices up,' Tony said.

'Maybe.' I drained my drink. 'I need another one of those.' I wandered back into the kitchen. When I returned, another cold beer in my hand, I asked, 'What brings you here?'

'What do you mean?'

'I thought you'd been warned off, but you're shuffling around like you've caught crabs or something.'

Tony smiled. 'I've been asking around for you. Do you want the big news or the small news?'

'Start with the small,' I said. 'Build up the excitement.'

'It's about Claude's family.'

'His Honour Judge Gilbert?' I asked.

'And Claude's sisters,' Tony replied.

'Go on.'

'It seems that the old judge isn't going to enjoy too much of his judicial pension,' Tony said. 'Quite frail, so the reports say, and Claude's sisters are not too keen on the idea of a third of the estate sitting in a bank just waiting for Claude to turn up.'

'Why doesn't Daddy just rewrite his will?' I said.

'Because he's a believer in the legal process, that you are only guilty of what can be proven against you. Claude has been convicted in the eyes of the public, but never from the wrong side of a brass rail. Until that happens, or Claude turns up dead, the old fool is going to hang on to the presumption of Claude's innocence and leave him a third of his estate.'

'And is it a large estate?'

Tony nodded. 'The judge used to be a QC, and so he made big money. Becoming a judge was semi-retirement for him, because it came with a pay cut, but respect from his peers was a non-taxable benefit.'

'When was all this?'

'A few months ago.'

I tapped my lip with my finger.

'What is it?' Tony said.

'Timing,' I said. 'I wondered why Claude was coming forward now. He looked down on his luck, and if he's in line for a windfall, maybe that would be enough to persuade him out of hiding. But he's got to win his case first.'

'That's quite a risk.'

'He's a gambler,' I said. 'So what about the big news?'

Tony's smile got broader. 'This is where it gets really good,' he said. He leant over to an old leather briefcase, brown and tatty at the corners, and pulled out a bundle of papers. 'I looked into Josif Petrovic. I thought he might just be some Serbian conman hoping to make some quick money out of a gullible young reporter.' When I raised my eyebrows, he said, 'I still see myself as your mentor, Jack, and I know it would ruin your career, peddling a fraudster. So I asked an old friend who works in the tax office to put Petrovic's name through the computer, just to look at his history. He did that, and nothing came back. As far as the government is concerned, Petrovic isn't earning any money. So if he is Mr Invisible as far as money is concerned, how is he paying for his flat? Did he say who owned it when you spoke to him?'

I shook my head. 'I never thought to ask.'

'It's a good job that I did, then,' Tony replied, grinning now. 'Northern Works Limited is the name of the company. The people at Companies House were very helpful. According to the company Articles of Association, they're not a prop-erty company, but they do own a flat in Belgravia.'

'Let me guess,' I said.

'No need,' Tony said. 'It's Petrovic's basement flat. The company is solvent – only ever breaks even – and it's never paid any corporation tax.' He raised his eyebrows, and I thought I saw excitement in his eyes. 'But that's not the really surprising thing.'

'Go on,' I said, leaning forward, eager to know what Tony had found out.

'I'll let you do your own research,' he said, smiling, and patted the bundle of papers. 'I don't want to spoil the surprise.' Then he stood to go, and pointed upwards. 'But don't forget Laura. I don't think she was planning on drinking all that wine on her own.'

I grinned and thanked him. The shadow from the day seemed to have lifted as Tony shuffled to the door, but the room was eerily silent once he'd gone. I put my hand on the papers, ready to go through them. But I was tired and the beer was relaxing me. I knew I had to get the story down quickly, because I knew that Harry English would lose interest pretty soon, the need for an immediate front page more important than a passing interest in one of my scoops, but the thought of a few more beers and of Laura upstairs made Claude Gilbert slide away just for a few moments.

I went to the stereo and slipped on some Johnny Cash. It was the first *American Recordings* album, all about regret and redemption, the singer's low rumble filling the silence, and I knew that none of those emotions had touched Claude Gilbert. It was all about self-pity, and I knew that I had to act soon or else he would be gone.

I took another swig of beer and let out a long sigh. Any late-night writing I did was often court write-ups, or human interest tales I'd picked up on as I listened to the court gossip, usually victims angry at soft sentences, and it was easy to capture that outrage. The readers bought into it, that all their efforts to lead a good life were in vain, even though that was rarely true. Most criminals lead wretched lives – but when did the truth ever matter?

But the Claude Gilbert story *had* to be about truth. I just didn't know what the truth was. That made me think further about Frankie. His mother's room was too different from the rest of the house, which was cluttered and dirty. What did that tell me about Frankie? He was obsessive and furtive – his photographs of the nursing home and of Laura told me that much. Did that make him a killer? How much of a leap is it from taking photographs to wanting to get a little closer? Had Frankie seen Claude walk out on his marriage all those years ago and then gone to offer a little comfort to the abandoned wife? Did it all go wrong when he got to the door?

I sighed. I was getting tired. As productive as the night can be – my best pieces have been written to the sound of the clock ticking its way past midnight – I knew also that the mind has to be bright and active to make the words spin on the page. Perhaps it was time to take some hours out and go back to it in the morning.

There was a photograph on top of Tony's file. It was the Gilbert family picture, a minor private moment now made famous by the headlines. There was the judge at the back, laughing, his head back, skinny and tall, with a hawk-like nose, his two daughters in front of him, one giggling, her hand over her mouth, the other smiling, both pretty brunettes, young, with bright futures ahead. Claude was on the edge of the picture, smirking, a cigarette in his hand, standing casually, almost as if he wasn't part of the joke, distant from his sisters.

I wondered how they would feel if they knew that I had spoken to their long-lost brother? Happy that he was still alive, or maybe angry that a portion of their inheritance was to be denied them? Perhaps they had known all along.

I pushed the papers away as the last of the beer slipped out of the bottle. Tony's big surprise could wait until I was alert enough to enjoy it. I left the table and headed for the stairs, collecting a wine glass on the way.

I couldn't see Laura at first for the steam, and so I perched on the side of the bath and found the wine bottle instead. As I poured, she asked, 'How has your day been?'

I wondered what I should tell her. How would it make her feel if she knew about Frankie's pictures – perhaps Joe would make sure they stayed private?

'The story isn't finished yet,' was my reply.

'How did it go with Rachel Mason?' Laura asked.

'She gave a little, and I gave a little,' I replied. 'I think we have an understanding.'

I heard the movement of water and Laura reared up out of the mist. Her hair was slicked back and wet, her body pink and glistening.

I reached out my hand to her face, but I was interrupted by a loud banging on the front door.

'Who the hell is that?' she asked.

I stood up. 'I don't know, but I'll be pissed off with them when I get down there.'

I marched out of the bathroom, hearing Laura slide back into the water as I skipped down the stairs.

Chapter Forty-Four

Mike Dobson slowly clicked the door closed as he crept into his house, anxious not to wake Mary.

He went to the washing machine first and stripped off, his eyes darting to the ceiling, worried that Mary would hear him. He could still smell her on him. The perfume, the cigarettes, the sweat. He let out a sigh of relief when he heard the motor start and the first gushes of water started to fill the machine. As he looked, he could see his shirt and suit against the glass. She was gone.

He crept upstairs to the bathroom and took a shower, the hot water sluicing away what was left of her, and he tried to bring himself back to normality. But as his head hung down, he imagined he could hear the knocking again. He opened his eyes quickly and stepped out of the shower. He stared at himself in the mirror, at his stomach, his hairline. He looked haunted, his eyes surrounded by sagging skin and dark rings, and that's how he felt – twenty-two years of guilt etched into every line on his face. Those years had gone so quickly, and he had turned into this fat middle-aged man, lonely in his own home, his nights spent patrolling the back streets of his home town, always waiting for the knock on the door.

The memories came back stronger each summer, as the days grew long and the sun stuck the shirt to his back. It was how he remembered it back then. A balmy summer in the late eighties, the rest of the country worried about new-agers and getting on the housing ladder, but he was just wrapped up in a few blissful summer months. Long after-noons by the stream, her head in his lap, her warm smile, twirling daisies between his fingers. It had faded in winter, but spring had brought them together again. He could feel the lazy trail of her fingers down his cheek.

He stepped away from the mirror and dried himself. As he stepped out of the bathroom, he got a sense anew of his home's perfection, the vanilla scent of candles that had been burning earlier in the evening catching his nostrils, and he imagined the flowers on the table, the curtains tied back so that they hung just right, the folds even and tidy. Everything was smart and ordered.

Mike thought of the homes he visited when he was doing his sales visits. Young families with children, brightly coloured plastic around the house, crumbs and debris, the scars of a busy home ground into the carpet. But he saw the happi-ness, heard the noise of the family.

He walked slowly along the landing and a passing car swept its headlight beam over the curtains as he entered the bedroom, lighting up the room for a few seconds so that he could make out Mary, her hair fanned over the pillow.

He climbed into bed and turned away from her. He was desperate for sleep, his legs twitching with fatigue, but he knew he wouldn't get any that night. Mike tried closing his eyes, but every time he did, he was jolted by the steady knock-knock, the noise of her fist against the wood, that frantic drumbeat.

He focused on a knot in the wood in the frame around the bathroom door. That would be his view until the morning.

* * *

When I opened the door, I was surprised to see Joe Kinsella there, Rachel Mason just behind him.

'It's time for a talk,' Rachel said, stepping forward to join Joe, her smile brief.

'I thought we'd had one,' I replied. When Rachel cocked her head, I opened the door wider. 'All right then. I'm writing the story soon, and I could do with some quotes.'

I went over to the table and moved aside the papers Tony had brought along. They'd need to read the newspaper to get the exclusive.

'No need to be coy, Mr Garrett,' Rachel said, as she sat down on the sofa.

'Make yourself at home,' I muttered, and then slunk off to the kitchen, returning with two extra glasses and another bottle of wine. 'You look like you're staying some time, and so we might as well be civil,' I said wearily. I poured wine into the glasses and passed one each to Joe and Rachel.

Rachel raised her glass and took a large gulp of wine. Joe took a sip and put his down on the table next to my laptop.

'So, what do you want?' I asked.

'Frankie,' Rachel said bluntly.

'You've got him,' I replied.

'Only for now,' she said. 'But we'll lose him if we don't find out more.'

'And you think I've got more to help you.'

'Why, do you know something we don't know?' Rachel said, watching me carefully and taking another drink of wine.

I raised my eyebrows. 'I understand the game now,' I said. 'I'm supposed to tell you everything I know but the exchange is only one way.' I shook my head. 'I think we'll play it the other way. You tell me what you know about Frankie and, if I've got extra information, I'll think about passing it on.'

For a second Rachel looked angry, those blue eyes blazing,

but Joe spoke first. 'We'll tell you what we've got if you promise it won't go to print.'

'I can't promise that,' I replied. I wanted them to tell me, but as they'd sought me out it felt like I had the stronger bargaining chip.

Joe looked at the floor for a moment, and when he looked up, he was smiling ruefully. 'We need some help on this one,' he said. 'Everything tells me that Frankie might have killed Nancy Gilbert, but we need more than my instinct.'

That surprised me. 'I thought Claude was your only suspect,' I said. 'So you think he might be innocent after all?'

Joe sighed. 'I just don't know.'

We were disturbed for a second as Laura bounded down the stairs. She stopped abruptly when she saw Rachel and Joe in the room.

'Oh hello,' Laura said, embarrassed as she looked down at herself. She had thrown on some old leggings and a T-shirt with a rhinestone logo across the chest; Rachel was still in her best suit and shirt.

Rachel didn't respond, but Joe smiled. 'Hello,' he said. 'We're sorry for intruding.'

'They're here about Frankie,' I said to Laura.

Rachel raised her eyebrows. 'But you don't know anything about the case, do you, PC McGanity?'

Laura took a deep breath. 'Don't try and outrank me because you've wormed your way into headquarters,' she said. 'You're in my house now, and so if you don't want to speak to me, the door is that way.'

'We want your opinion,' Joe said quickly. 'It was Jack we came to see, but we value your view, so please, pull up a wine glass and let's talk.'

Laura took some deep breaths to calm herself down, and then she went to get an extra glass from the kitchen. When she returned, she filled her glass from the bottle on the table. Rachel held up her wine glass for a refill, and Laura drained the bottle into it.

'So let's talk about Frankie,' I said, as Laura sat down in a chair opposite Rachel. 'Why do you think he killed Nancy?'

'Jealousy is one reason,' Joe said. 'Frankie was obsessed with Mrs Gilbert. You mentioned an affair today. How did that make Frankie feel? It's one thing to come second place to someone's husband, but what happens when she takes on a new lover? It makes him insignificant, and so he gets angry. Does he try it on with her? If her love is being spread around, why not him? He can't cope with rejection, because he's never suffered it. His mother spent her life indulging him, giving him what he wanted. And what happens when someone who doesn't know how to deal with rejection is denied the one thing he wants?' Joe raised his eyebrows. 'He becomes jealous.'

'That's a bit simplistic, isn't it?' I said.

'It's usually the way,' Joe replied. 'When people kill, they're normally operating on some very primeval instinct. It could be blind rage, when the person is no longer in control and is just a passenger to their anger, or it could be the defence instinct, the old cornered rat. For someone like Frankie, rejection and jealousy could hit him hard, because he's not used to it.'

'I'm not sure I buy that,' I said. 'Frankie was someone who wanted to say something, not hide something.'

'Maybe he's scared,' Rachel responded, taking another big swig. She was going at the wine like it was fruit juice. 'He's had more than twenty years to think of his excuses.'

'Frankie didn't have to come forward at all,' I said. 'But you think this might have something to do with Frankie's mother?'

Joe smiled. 'It's always to do with the parents,' he said. 'If Frankie killed Nancy Gilbert, then he did it as an act of retaliation. People who do that follow a pattern, and Frankie fits some of the criteria.'

'Sounds interesting,' Laura said, who was on her way to the kitchen to fetch another bottle of wine. When Rachel flashed her a look, Laura turned back to Joe. 'What do you mean?'

'Killers who murder strangers as an act of anger do it for one of two reasons: either because the anger excites them or because the anger is aimed at someone else, so it's actually an act of retaliation, usually against a parental figure,' Joe explained. 'In this case, it will have been aimed at Frankie's mother.'

'Why do you say that?' I asked.

'Because if Frankie killed Nancy Gilbert, he chose a woman older than himself.'

'No,' I protested. 'You're making him fit a theory, not looking at the facts. You said that he did it because he felt rejected by Nancy. So, if you're right, Nancy has nothing to do with his mother. It is just what it is, a crime of passion.'

'But why do you think he liked Nancy Gilbert, a woman older than himself?'

'Because he could see into her bedroom,' I said, exasperated now. 'He looks at the nurses now. A local voyeur, yes. A murderer? No.'

'Sex always comes into it somewhere,' Joe said, 'but some of the other facts make it sound like it was an act of retaliation aimed at his mother.'

'What like?' I said, holding my glass out so Laura could fill it. Joe put his hand over his, but Rachel's arm shot out quickly, the now empty glass wavering slightly.

'Murderers who kill as an act of retaliation are usually

stalkers on the quiet,' Joe replied. 'They are familiar with their victim in some way, and it could be something as simple as a hello on the street, or a brief exchange when putting out the rubbish. The more extreme ones go further and seek out targets, posing as roofers or builders, pretending to look for work, but really they're looking for victims, for vulnerable lone women.'

'But Frankie didn't do that,' I pointed out.

'Do we know that?' Joe said. 'What do we know about Frankie, except that he obsessed about Nancy Gilbert, and that now he obsesses about the care assistants at the care home in the same house, all the pretty young women that he can't speak to because his mother smothered him?'

'That's a real leap, Joe,' I said.

'But there are other things too,' he said. 'Revenge killers like this tend to act quickly, usually with a blow to the back of the head, with the weapon found nearby. They're not motivated by the use of the weapons, only by the need to express their anger.'

I remembered how Nancy had died when he said that – a quick blow to the back of the head. But then I saw the doubt in Joe's eyes. 'You said that *some* of the criteria fitted,' I said. 'You're not convinced, are you?'

'These things are not an exact science, you know that,' he replied. 'With each killer, there is a variant.'

'So what are the variants for Frankie?'

Joe sighed. 'The blow on the back of the head is a usual sign, but I would expect more of a frenzied attack afterwards.'

'She was buried alive,' Laura said.

'That's controlled though, not a frenzy,' I said.

Joe nodded. 'That's a problem,' he said. 'Most of the wounds in retaliation cases are committed after death, like overkill, as if the attacker just keeps on going until the anger is spent.'

'So it's less like Frankie,' I said.

'Some of it isn't like Frankie,' Joe said, 'but then again we don't know much about Frankie.'

'He keeps pictures of his targets pinned to his wall,' Rachel said. 'If you stumbled across that normally, the loner across the road keeping photographs of the victim as his private porn collection, you would suspect him.'

I looked at Laura, and wondered whether I had done the right thing by not telling her about Frankie's pictures of her.

'So we've got a problem,' Joe said, sighing. 'The motive in a retaliation case is anger, not sex, and so if Nancy was Frankie's victim, she was not an object of desire, but an object of hate. I wouldn't expect the killer to have her all over the wall as a pin-up. And the way the scene was cleaned up? Again, that doesn't fit. Most people's actions after a murder are to do with getting away with it, hiding the traces, aware that what they have done is wrong. An anger-killer thinks differently. He just feels satisfied afterwards, like it's smile and cigarette time. There's no concept of wrongdoing.'

'It doesn't sound like much of it fits Frankie,' I said, shaking my head.

'It doesn't,' Joe said. 'But for as long as some of it does, we have to look at him.'

'Where is he now?' Laura asked.

'Cell number six,' Rachel said, before standing up to go to the bathroom. She had to put her hand out to steady herself.

As she left the room, I asked, 'So, what do you want to know?'

'Just about Frankie,' Joe said. 'Has he told you anything about his childhood? It seems that his mother was very private, because no one seems to know much about the family, except that Frankie's father died when he was a young child, and so it was just her and Frankie in that house. Apart from the complaints about the snooping from across the road, he hasn't really come up on our radar. Until we can find out something about his past, we don't know how much of a suspect he is.'

'Is he talking?' I asked.

Joe shook his head and looked down. 'He's curled up in the corner of his cell, not speaking to anyone. We haven't arrested him for Nancy's murder, just the snooping.'

'So are you looking for evidence that his mother was a tyrant?' I asked. 'Or what about a religious maniac, suppressing his desires? That would be convenient.'

'Don't be like that, Jack,' Joe said. 'I just want to find out what I can. If he's innocent, then good, but I don't want to be the one who overlooks him and then has to dig another young woman out of a grave.'

I nodded and held up my hand in apology. Maybe I was wrong to be giving Joe a hard time. He was honest, I knew that, but I was starting to feel sorry for Frankie, despite what he had done; he was being fitted into Nancy's story just because he was the neighbourhood weirdo, and I felt a certain amount of guilt for having brought up his name when I spoke with Rachel.

'Frankie didn't mention his mother in any negative way,' I said. 'I just got the feeling that he was lonely.'

Joe nodded, and then his phone rang. He pulled it from his pocket and listened to the caller for a few seconds before mumbling a response and hanging up.

He looked at me first, and then at Rachel, who had just wandered back into the room, her hand again reaching for her glass.

'A body's been found,' Joe said to her, his face grim. 'A young girl, a prostitute they think, found bludgeoned in the town centre, near the viaduct.'

'I thought we were only dealing with Claude Gilbert,' Rachel complained. Her voice had acquired a slur.

'We are, but they want me to supervise the scene before the rest of the squad arrive later on,' he replied. He pointed at the wine bottle, and then at Rachel's glass. 'You can't go to a crime scene stinking of booze. Stay here. I'll come back for you.'

'I'll follow you down,' I said. I was still willing to chase a story, even if I was wrapped up in Claude Gilbert.

'It's police business,' Joe said firmly.

I shook my head in response and added on a smile. 'I was telling you, not asking you.'

Joe sighed as he looked at me, but he must have seen the determination in my eyes, because he nodded towards the door. 'We might as well save the planet on the way,' he said. 'We'll travel in the same car.'

I was smiling as I left the house, my camera and voice recorder stuffed into my pocket. Laura raised her eyebrows at the thought of being locked in with Rachel but, from the way Rachel was going through the wine, I guessed that her conversation would dry up pretty quickly.

Chapter Forty-Five

Joe was quiet on the way into Blackley.

'What's wrong?' I said.

He didn't answer at first, and I watched the streetlights paint his face in moving stripes of orange as we drove through the town centre.

'I'm always like this when I get near a murder scene,' he said.

I laughed. 'I don't believe that. You've been in the job too long.'

He sighed. 'Okay, it's Frankie.'

'What, you think you've locked up an innocent man?'

Joe smiled at that. 'He's the town's peeping Tom, and that's what he's been held on. So he's not innocent.'

'That's not why you were at his house though. What happens tomorrow, when you've still got nothing more than your theory, where some bits fit, and some bits don't?'

'He goes home,' he said. 'Where he's been for the twenty-two years since Nancy Gilbert died. Except this time we'll watch him.'

I nodded and then looked back through the window at the neon of takeaways and late-night booze shops that lined the route.

'Will this murder affect your hunt for Claude Gilbert?' I said.

Joe looked surprised at that. 'Why should it?'

'A young woman has been killed. It will affect resources.'

He thought about it. 'Maybe,' he said. 'But when people are killed, the money gets found, and Nancy Gilbert is just as much a murder victim. Tonight is more urgent, I suppose.'

'Why do you say that?'

'I was told that this girl was a prostitute.'

'Does that make a difference?' I asked. 'She's still a human being.'

'I didn't say it was any less tragic,' he replied, a hint of rebuke in his voice. 'Prostitutes make easy prey, that's all, because they put themselves into dangerous situations, and the way they make a living attracts the wrong kind of man. A prostitute murder is often the start of a spree – history has told us that much. We need to catch whoever killed her as quickly as we can, because there might be another dead woman once the sun goes down tomorrow.'

I let out a long breath. I was getting worn down by murder. I had spent most of my reporting life chasing down deaths, accidental or otherwise and, as the tiredness from the day set in, I dreamt for a moment of covering summer fêtes and town councillors cutting ribbons, where a working day meant a happy picture and a few words.

Then that familiar feeling kicked in as we got nearer the scene, that sense of intrigue tainted by tragedy. I was surprised by the inactivity though. There were no flashing lights, nothing to alert any curious onlookers, just two cars parked on a piece of waste concrete, acting as a makeshift cordon, a uniformed officer by each. Joe jumped out and showed his identification, and the two uniformed officers stepped to one side. I went to follow him but he told me to stay by the car, not wanting me to contaminate the scene. I looked around instead. There were CCTV cameras on the top of large poles, but they were pointing away from the small buzz of police activity. All I could see were the backyards of buildings, some derelict, and some small businesses still clinging to existence – a back-street garage or car alarm centre – and the scene was shrouded in the dark shadows created by the viaduct that overlooked the scene.

I saw that one of the police cars was parked so that head-lights faced the body. I caught a glimpse of pale legs and dirty shoes, a flowery dress. No one deserved to die there, not in such an anonymous place. I didn't know her, but I guessed that life had already dealt her some tough blows – it had to be that way for her to be working on the street. To snatch away any chance of a better life seemed a cruel shot too far.

I turned away and looked back along the road. I could see a small cluster of people in the distance, huddled together, watching, but not wanting to get any closer, just the occa-sional burst of orange from a cigarette marking them out. I glanced back towards Joe and saw that he was busy, and so I decided to walk over to the bystanders, to seek out a quote. But as I set off walking, they seemed to disappear into the shadows, like inhabitants of a different world not wanting to get caught up in mine. I turned back to the car. In that moment, I sensed how hard it must be for people like Joe to solve murders like this.

I sat back in the car with a slump, overwhelmed by sadness for a moment, at the loss of a young life just on the other side of the police cars. Someone's daughter, someone's sister, brought to an end on a patch of overgrown concrete under-neath the arches of a worn-out brick viaduct.

Then I saw Joe straighten and look down at the body. He scratched his head and I thought I saw some confusion in his gaze.

Chapter Forty-Six

It was my turn to be quiet as we headed back. The rest of the murder squad had arrived eventually, the crime scene investigators dragged from their beds, and so Joe could leave the rest of them to it. He kept on looking at me, as if he was waiting for the questions to come. It didn't seem like a good time to intrude into the young woman's death, but my reluctance made me worry that I was losing my edge.

'It was nothing unusual,' Joe said eventually.

I looked at him. 'It didn't seem like that from the way you were looking at the body.'

'It looked like a bang on the head and strangulation,' he said.

'That doesn't sound normal.'

'It depends on how you live your life,' he said. 'Prostitutes attract predators, and so I expected some sexual element to her body, or some kind of mutilation. There wasn't any, as far as I could tell. This could have been anything, an unpaid drug debt, or maybe revenge for helping us out over something.'

'Do you think that's a possible?'

'Criminals don't grass, right, the unwritten law?' he said. He gave a small laugh and shook his head. 'That's the biggest myth going. Sometimes those at the shitty end of life just want to talk to someone, and so things get said. That's what most defence lawyers don't realise when they think they're keeping big secrets by advising no comment. Their clients have usually told us more in the car on the way in, or in the fingerprint room on the way out.' Joe smiled. 'They like spilling the news on the lawyers most of all. Who's taking drugs, who's seeing the hookers for the freebies they won't put through the books. Maybe the dead woman said too much about the wrong person.'

'Are you sure she's a prostitute? Maybe she's been dumped down there to throw you off the scent.'

Joe shook his head. 'One of the other street girls found her. They knew her, had seen her working, although we don't know much about her. They think she was called Hazel.'

I didn't say anything because it seemed like no words could properly explain the sadness of her death, a young woman just discarded in the shadow of the viaduct.

Eventually the lights of my cottage came into view, like small fires against the darkness of the hills around, and I felt some relief that I could surround myself with ordinary life again.

We walked into the house, expecting to be met by the sounds of conversation, but instead there was silence. I looked into the living room and saw Laura nursing a hot drink. I was about to say something when she raised her finger to her lips to hush me quiet. Then she smiled.

I walked over to her, curious, and I saw Rachel Mason sprawled on her back, one arm lolling onto the floor, her head cocked to one side, fast asleep.

I raised my eyebrows and grinned. 'Did the wine take its toll?' I whispered.

Laura nodded, not wanting to wake her.

I looked down at Rachel. She looked peaceful, almost

contented, her face losing some of that clench it had when she was awake.

I heard Joe give out a small groan as he came up behind me.

'Have you got a bucket for my car?' he said quietly.

'She can stay here,' Laura whispered. 'I'll just throw a blanket over her.'

'Are you sure?' Joe asked, although I could tell that he wasn't prepared to force the issue.

Laura smiled. 'Maybe it will make her more human.'

Joe nodded and returned the smile. He waved his car keys as a goodbye and headed for the door, before anyone had time to change their mind.

Once we were alone and things had gone quiet again, apart from the sound of Rachel's light snores, Laura went to the kitchen so that we could talk, me following behind.

'How long has she been like that?' I asked.

'An hour, maybe more. She just went, like that.' Laura snapped her fingers. 'She started to slur and tell me how she was jealous of me, that I had a perfect life, and then she just slumped. So I lifted her legs onto the sofa and let her sleep. How was the murder scene?'

'Just the usual,' I said, and as soon as the words came out, I realised what it was that made it such a tragedy: that few people would care much about the dead girl.

I shook away the thought and reached for the almost empty wine bottle. 'You go up,' I said. 'I'll just look over Claude's story first.'

Laura gave me a kiss and then went upstairs as I turned on my laptop. I navigated to the file in which I had stored Claude's story but, when I opened it up, I couldn't bring myself to touch a key. I still had the image of the dead girl's legs in my mind, and the quick-money tale of a long-lost barrister just didn't seem important any more.

I closed the lid and went upstairs. As I walked into the bedroom, I expected to see Laura in bed, perhaps reading a glossy magazine or a book, but instead she was standing naked in front of the mirror.

'What are you doing?' I asked, surprised. When Laura looked at me, I held up my hands in apology and added, 'I'm not complaining.'

Laura looked down at herself.

'I was just thinking about my age,' she said, and she peered closer to the mirror. 'I'll be forty in a couple of years, and I can just feel myself changing.' She pulled at her cheeks to smooth out the skin on her face, but then she dropped her hands and scowled. 'When I stop smiling, the lines don't drop away, and it's feeling a little slacker around here,' she said, running her hands around her stomach and hips.

'What's brought this on? Rachel downstairs?'

'I suppose so,' she said, and then she sighed. 'I just see something of myself in her, from ten years ago maybe, young and arrogant, dressing well.' She blushed. 'Maybe even turning heads.'

I put my arms around her shoulders and pulled her head into my chest. 'We're both getting older,' I whispered into her hair. I cupped her face in my hands and made her look up at me. 'We'll fall apart together,' I said softly, 'and we'll love every minute of it.'

Laura nodded softly, a tender smile on her lips.

'Take me to bed, Jack,' she said.

Chapter Forty-Seven

I knew something was wrong as soon as I heard her.

I had been lying in bed, thinking about how I would get Claude's story moving, when Laura gave a shout. I jumped out of bed and rushed downstairs. When she turned to look at me, I saw anger in her eyes.

'What's wrong?' I asked, and then I followed her gaze as she turned towards the front door. It was open. 'Why is it like that?'

'We've been burgled,' she snapped at me.

I heard a noise behind me and turned to see Rachel stumbling to her feet from the sofa, her shirt and suit creased, her hair crumpled into a frizz.

'What's wrong?' she croaked, and then she groaned and clutched her forehead.

'We've been burgled,' Laura repeated. 'And you were here all along. Why didn't you hear anything?'

Rachel looked down at herself and then her clothes, before her eyes hit on the empty glass.

'I must have been tired,' Rachel said. 'I just drifted off.'

'You were drunk,' I barked at her, and then I looked over to the table. The laptop was still there, but the lid was open. I was sure I had closed it before I went upstairs. Then I noticed that the papers brought by Tony were missing.

'A burglar doesn't take papers and leave a laptop behind,' I said. 'Whoever was in here was after information.'

'Assuming that someone *has* been in,' Laura said, looking at Rachel.

Rachel understood the dig. 'Are you saying I've got something to do with it?'

'Why not?' I said, my voice angry. 'You want the information, you sleep on the sofa, and then the information disappears. Very convenient.'

Rachel winced and held her head as she swayed. 'I've been asleep all night,' Rachel said, and stumbled towards the stairs, heading for the bathroom.

Laura waited for her to go and then she picked up her phone and called the police. I listened as she gave her details, mentioned that she was a police officer, and then she turned to me. 'Is there anything else missing?'

I looked around the rest of the room, expecting to see a gap under the television, where the games console was, but it was still there.

I shook my head. 'Just my papers,' I said. 'Everything I had been working on.'

Laura looked at me, and then ended her call. 'Are you sure you didn't put them away somewhere?'

I shook my head.

'What's going on with this story, Jack?'

'I don't know,' was my only reply. I was starting to wonder whether I was making enemies I couldn't fight.

Then Laura looked past me, and I saw her face soften. I turned around. It was Bobby.

'What's happened, Mummy?' he asked, his voice still sleepy. 'Why are you shouting?'

I saw Laura's face lose some of its anger. 'Nothing,' she

said brightly. 'It's nothing,' and then she went to him and took him back upstairs.

I sat at the table, where I had been sitting the night before, and realised that I hadn't closed the curtains. There had been a clear view from the outside. Although our position at the top of the hill didn't make us immune from the usual urban problems, an opportunistic burglar wouldn't waste time with copies of old newspaper articles. No, it was for some other reason, and that reason had to be connected with the Gilbert case.

And then I realised something else: if it wasn't Rachel, then whoever had done it must have been watching me all along.

Chapter Forty-Eight

Laura could tell how busy the station would be from the state of the car park. Cars were parked along the grass verges on the road that ran past the building and so Laura had to leave hers in the car park of a nearby DIY store. As she walked in, she could hear the buzz of conversation coming from the atrium. There were clusters of officers in dark blue jump suits eating and talking – the search teams who would spend the morning on their hands and knees, combing the scene for leftovers from the murder. A cigarette butt, a broken piece of jewellery, maybe a dropped receipt. The women in the canteen bustled around as the queue for the breakfast sandwiches snaked along a wall.

As Laura walked into the briefing room, it was quieter than normal, most people having been recruited into the grunt work on the murder case. Her sergeant saw her and beckoned her over. When Laura got close, the sergeant pointed at Thomas, who was watching the hubbub through the glass wall. 'It's his first murder and so he's getting twitchy,' the sergeant whispered. 'I've spoken to the crime scene manager, and she's okay for you two to preserve the scene and keep the local interest away. You know what it'll be like, well-wishers with flowers. Keep them back and let the search team deal with everything, but let Thomas see how a murder scene works.'

Laura nodded. 'No problems, but can you give me ten minutes?' she said. 'I just need to speak to someone.'

Her sergeant checked her watch and then said, 'Frankie Cass?'

'Why do you say that?' Laura said.

'He was asking to see you before. If you go down to the cells, make it quick.'

Laura was confused as she left the briefing room. Why would Frankie Cass ask for her? How did he know anything about her? Frankie would have to wait a few minutes though. She had somewhere else to go first.

Laura weaved her way through the atrium to get to the floor above. When she arrived at the burglary team's office, no one looked up. She was just another woman in a uniform, so she rapped hard on the door frame, in no mood to be ignored.

They were all men, young and cocky, dressed in jeans and polo shirts. The one nearest to her, small and thin, with a dark crewcut and a neck ravaged by a shaving rash, raised his eyebrows. 'What can I do for you?'

'I was burgled this morning,' she said. 'Crime Scenes are coming out later, but I want to know whether you know of anyone targeting rural properties.'

He looked around the room, just to check if anyone had any ideas, then he shook his head. 'Forget Crime Scenes today. They'll be with the murder all day.' When Laura turned away, frustrated, he shouted after her, 'And we haven't heard of anyone targeting rural houses. Not small-fry anyway.' When Laura turned back, he added, 'No offence. The rural houses that get done over tend to be the big ones, targeted by the big guns from Manchester or Liverpool, looking for the safe stuffed with jewels. You know how it is with the rest. They live near the burglar, just because it means they don't have to walk as far with the stuff. Did they take your car?'

Laura shook her head.

'Was anything taken?'

'Just some papers my partner was working on.'

He held his hands out in apology. 'Then it doesn't sound like you were burgled. Most houses that get burgled now get done for the car keys. Everything else is either too cheap for the risk or too heavy to carry – but your car?' And he laughed. 'Even gets them home.'

'Okay, thanks for your help,' Laura said sarcastically.

As she walked along the landing, she realised why there was the lack of interest. An unsolved crime looks bad, and so it's easier to say that it isn't a crime at all.

Laura checked her watch. She had time to see Frankie Cass, to find out what he wanted.

She made her way to the stairs and down to the cell complex, two corridors of windowless box rooms that stretched away from the custody desk.

The custody suite was accessed through two sets of large locked doors, like an air lock, usually occupied by bored-looking solicitors' clerks waiting for their turn in the interview room. Her swipe card took her through, and she saw that the custody area was quiet. It was centred around a high desk made from polished wood, two custody sergeants behind it, responsible for a corridor of cells each. When it was busy, it seemed like it needed to be bigger, with sullen prisoners jostling the desk as their solicitors did their best to get their paperwork completed, flanked by the investigating officers, and with a holding cell next to the entrance overflowing with new arrivals. But when it was quiet, it was somewhere for the sergeants and civilian jailers to talk away the day, their eyes on the clock to make sure they didn't miss a review or spot-check.

Laura's eyes went straight to the custody list on the wall behind the desk, seven names written in green on a whiteboard, bold and clear so that any officer could check the board to see whether any of their own suspects were in easy reach. Most criminals either stop completely or keep getting caught. Not many got better at it.

As Laura looked at the board, she saw that Frankie was still in a cell, his name top of the list, writ large. One of the custody sergeants glanced up from his screen and then folded his arms.

Custody sergeants were a strange breed, responsible for the prisoners in the cells, not catching criminals, and so they acted more like border guards, paying close attention to who came through. Laura sensed that she was trespassing.

'He's asking for me,' she said, jabbing her finger towards Frankie's name.

'Not for much longer,' he said. 'Frankie Cass is going home in a few minutes.'

'But why?'

'Because Kinsella didn't pull his finger out soon enough, or pass it on.'

'Joe got dragged into the murder last night,' Laura said.

The sergeant pointed at the clock behind him. 'It doesn't stop that from ticking. Cass has stewed in there all night, and so he's going home.'

'Just let me see what he wants.'

The sergeant pursed his lips and seemed to think for a few seconds, though Laura sensed that he was just exercising his power, that he had already made his decision. 'Through the hatch, and make it quick.' He pointed. 'Number six.'

Laura peeled away from the desk and walked down the corridor. She felt the air become oppressive as the people within sweated out the drugs and the booze, the stink of dirty humanity seeping out from under the solid metal doors. As she got to cell number six, she lifted the metal bar that kept the hatch in place and let it drop down so that she could put her face through.

She took a deep breath as the smell of the cell hit her. It was too warm – it was always that way, to stop prisoners needing blankets, so they had one less thing to wrap around their necks – and so she got the full strength of Frankie's smell: warm feet and dirty clothes. He was curled up on a plastic mattress on a raised platform, the wall tiled white, with an aluminium toilet in the corner. There was no seat or paper.

'Frankie, I'm Laura McGanity,' she said. 'You asked for me.'

He didn't move or give any hint that he knew she was there. He just stared at the wall opposite, his hands clamped between his legs, as if he was trying to knot himself up.

'Is it about the night Mrs Gilbert died?' she said.

He stirred slightly at that.

'Who was there?' she asked.

Laura thought he was going to stay silent, but he turned his head slowly towards her.

'I'm sorry,' he said.

'For what?'

'For taking pictures.'

Laura was surprised at that. 'Pictures?'

He nodded. 'I took some pictures of you. I'm sorry.'

Laura was shocked. Then she remembered the noise in the house, the sensation of being watched, the noises outside, and tried to control her anger.

'That was you that night, wasn't it, Frankie?' she said. 'You came to my home.'

His gaze dropped. 'I'm sorry.'

Laura thought about slamming the hatch closed, trying

not to think about what pictures might have been taken. Or, more importantly, who might have seen them.

'Just tell me about the night Nancy Gilbert died,' she said, cajoling, trying to keep a lid on her temper.

'She told me not to tell the police.'

'Your mother?'

Frankie nodded.

'But time has passed now,' Laura said, 'and the man who killed Nancy still hasn't been caught. You liked her, didn't you, Frankie?'

He nodded and blushed.

'So help us find out who killed her.'

'I don't know who killed her.'

'But you told Jack that two people were there.'

He thought for a few seconds, and then he said, 'She told me not to tell the police.' He turned over to face the wall.

Laura sighed with frustration and closed the hatch, the clang echoing in the corridor. Someone in the cell next door began to kick at the door and shout for their solicitor. Laura thumped it back and walked back to the custody desk.

The sergeant barely looked at her as she left. Back in the atrium, she glanced upwards to the top floor. Joe Kinsella was there again, leaning against the rail and watching the growing crowd downstairs. Then Laura saw the stream of blonde hair behind him. Rachel had done well to make it in so early. Frankie couldn't have been the person to break in, which made the list of suspects very short. The burglary team might be right, that no one had broken in. Maybe the thief had been in the house all along. And if that was Rachel's game, Laura knew that she would have to play by her own rules.

Then she heard a voice behind her.

'PC McGanity?'

Laura turned around and saw a tall man with a broad chest and deep tan, his shirt crisp and white, his decorated pips marking out his rank. Chief Inspector.

'Sir?'

'We need to talk,' he said, and he directed Laura towards one of the rooms on the first floor.

Chapter Forty-Nine

Mike Dobson smiled as he lay back in his bed and looked out of his window, the curtains open, the sky blue, broken only by the occasional wisp of cloud. It felt like it had been a long time coming, this feeling of contentment, of belonging. It was another sunny day, but he hadn't heard the knocking, or been disturbed by the feeling of someone watching him, just at the edge of his vision. Mary was cleaning downstairs, as always.

He checked his watch. He had an hour before his first appointment. He could take some time to enjoy the morning.

He looked at the ceiling, noticing that the paint looked faded, perhaps in need of a touch-up. He thought of how often he had looked at the ceiling with Mary alongside him. Years, he knew that. He knew that Mary was proud of their house, from the way that she cleaned it constantly. It was tidy, contemporary, her imprint on the world.

No, it was more than that. It was their home. He should do more to make it feel that way.

His thoughts were interrupted by the roar of the vacuum cleaner. He would make it right by Mary.

Laura was shown into the Chief Inspector's office. It had the same view as most of the rooms in the station, a balcony and then a drop into the atrium below, but his office had been lined with oak panelling along one wall, with watercolours of Pendle Hill hung on it, and a red leather chair dominated one corner. There seemed to be a hush here that wasn't present anywhere else, and Laura's stomach fluttered with nerves as she sat down.

He smiled, his teeth bright white against the depth of his summer tan. Capped, would be Laura's guess.

'I'm Chief Inspector Roach,' he said, his voice calm, reassuring.

Laura's mind raced as she tried to recall where she had heard the name before, and then it came to her. Paul Roach. He had found Nancy Gilbert. She reddened. She knew what the talk was going to be about: Claude Gilbert. Or, more likely, Jack's story about Claude.

She smiled and said nothing.

'Has your boyfriend mentioned me?' he said.

'Jack?'

'Have you got more than one boyfriend, McGanity?' he said, a growl to his voice. When Laura flushed, he said, 'Defendants who lie in court do that, meet a direct question with one of their own. Gives them thinking time. Don't try it with me.'

'I'm sorry, sir,' she said, flustered. 'I'm just confused, that's all.' Laura looked the Chief Inspector in the eye. 'We have an understanding. I tell him nothing. He tells me nothing.' When he raised his eyebrows, she elaborated. 'It can't be any other way, not in this job.'

He nodded for a few seconds, and then said, 'He's looking for Claude Gilbert. He came to see me the other day.'

Laura thought about Joe Kinsella and his admonishment that no one else was to know why he was in Blackley, that there were leaks higher up. So she said nothing.

'If he thinks he's found Claude, you must come to see me,' Roach said.

'Why is that?' she asked, her eyes filled with innocence.

'I found Nancy Gilbert,' he said. 'I'd like to complete the story.'

Laura thought that there ought to be a 'we' in the story, that he hadn't been alone, but it wasn't the time to pick fault.

'I will, sir.'

He watched her for a few seconds, and then he nodded his head, as if that was enough to dismiss her.

As she stood to go, he said, 'Don't let me find out that you've been holding out on me. You didn't look surprised when I said Claude Gilbert's name.'

Laura gave a respectful nod and then left the office. Back on the balcony, the hush of Roach's office replaced by the hubbub of the atrium below, she closed her eyes. She could hear laughter and, as she opened her eyes and looked down, she saw something being handed round, sheets of paper, a picture on them. Thomas was trying to take them from people, but they were being passed between tables faster than he could keep up.

He must have sensed that she was there because he looked up and stopped what he was doing. The people around him looked up in turn and then went quiet, the laughter in the atrium dying down into an embarrassed hush.

Laura turned and went quickly down the stairs. Rushing into the atrium, she grabbed one of the pictures and felt her cheeks flush: it was her, getting changed in her house, naked.

Laura looked around, her jaw set, tears of anger in her eyes, but no one met her gaze.

'I tried to get them all,' Thomas said.

Laura looked up and saw Rachel Mason looking down

at her, a smile on her face. Rachel gave Laura a nod and then stepped back out of sight.

'We need to get down to the murder scene,' she said to Thomas. But as she turned and walked away, aware of the murmurs growing behind her, Laura knew there was somewhere else she had to go first.

Chapter Fifty

Laura looked angry as she walked towards me. I'd received her text message just a few minutes before, saying that she had some information for me. She had parked in the town centre, just down the road from the court, where her police car wouldn't look out of place.

But there was someone else in the police car.

Laura saw me looking. 'That's Thomas. Don't worry about him. He's too busy enjoying the buzz of a murder.'

'What's wrong?' I said.

She stared straight ahead, but I could see the tension in the way her jaw clenched.

'I've always kept my work from you, you know that,' she said. 'I've been your source when it helped me, but I've never given up a secret.'

'And I've never given up a source,' I replied.

Laura laughed, but it was a bitter sound. 'You wouldn't need to,' she said. 'All the signs will point back to me.'

'So don't say what you're about to say.'

Laura shook her head, and then I saw her wipe her eye. I reached forward, put my hand on her shoulder tenderly, but she shrugged me off.

'I don't do this,' she snapped at me. 'I'm a police officer, and I've promised to uphold the law, to keep the secrets that shouldn't get out, but whatever you're involved with keeps coming into my house, where I was asleep. Where Bobby was asleep. That changes things.'

'My story brought that on, not anything you did,' I said. 'I love what you do. It makes me proud. No, *you* make me proud. Don't compromise yourself.'

Laura shook her head and looked back at the car. 'It changes me,' she said. 'It makes me fight back.'

I said nothing until Laura turned to me again, and part of me was willing her to stay quiet, but I needed to know what she was going to say. Perhaps I needed to know it so much that I didn't think enough of how it might affect her.

'You want Mike Dobson,' she said. 'Here are his details.' She handed me a Post-it note with an address written on it in her neat script.

'How did you get this?'

'Detective work,' Laura said. 'It's what I do.'

'So why are you giving it to me?'

'Because that uptight bitch who camped on our sofa last night went through your things. She's laughing at us. And now she's sent pictures of me around the station, taken by that little pervert.'

I didn't need to ask what sort of pictures they were; I wished I had told Laura about them.

I looked at the piece of paper, and then at Laura. 'Can you prove Rachel took my papers?'

She scoffed. 'Of course I can't, but I know. So I've swapped sides for today.'

I held up the piece of paper. 'You could get in trouble for this.'

'I thought you said you don't reveal your sources.'

'I don't.'

'So who will know?'

I gripped her arm. 'You will know, Laura, that's the point. You're crossing a line here, leaking information to me.'

'It's a one-off. Just do your best to keep me out of it.' She looked at the piece of paper between my fingers. 'Are you going to do anything with it?'

'I've no choice. I'll go speak with him.'

'Be careful, Jack.'

I leant forward and kissed her on the cheek. 'I will.'

Mike Dobson's house wasn't difficult to find, just a short cruise around the town centre and then into an estate of typical new housing, with open-plan lawns and raised brick planters. It was the sort of place my father would have aspired to, with the bricks standing out brightly against the worn-out fronts of the terraced houses that lined the hills behind.

Dobson's house stood proudly at the entrance to the cul-de-sac, with the curtains in the window neatly pulled back and tied up, the vase of flowers on the sill perfectly centred.

I rang the doorbell and waited.

There was a long pause before anyone answered, but there was a car on the driveway, and so I was determined to wait. Eventually a face appeared on the other side of the glass and the door opened.

My mind moved fast as I looked at the man in front of me, trying to compare him to what little I had seen in Frankie's photographs, but it was impossible. Twenty-two years had passed and most of those hung around his cheeks and jawline, with the colour in his hair now coming from a bottle.

'Mr Dobson?'

He nodded slowly.

'I'm a reporter,' I said. 'I want to talk to you about your job.'

He looked surprised. 'My job? I sell guttering and plastic fascias.' He looked down the drive. 'Is this some kind of consumer special?'

'It's not about the job you've got now,' I said. 'It's a job you used to have. Twenty years ago, maybe a little more.'

I saw him stiffen. 'I can't talk about my customers,' he said, his voice wary.

'Why do you think it's to do with a customer?'

He cocked his head and his eyes narrowed. 'Tell me what you want.'

'Claude Gilbert was one of your clients, wasn't he, Mr Dobson?' I said.

I knew I'd hit the mark. His hand gripped the door frame and he paled and swayed.

'Mr Dobson?'

He turned to go inside. I regarded the open door as an invitation. Dobson walked down a short hallway and then into his living room. I followed him in to see that he had slumped onto a long brown sofa that took over the room, opposite a mock-Victorian fireplace. He glanced at the view outside, towards the other houses that crowded around the turning circle at the end of the cul-de-sac.

'What do you mean?' he asked, although his voice sounded faint, as if he wouldn't be able to listen to my answer.

'I'm writing a story on Claude Gilbert, just checking that the official version is the right one – that it *was* Claude who killed his wife. I came across some photographs.'

He turned to me when I said that. 'Photographs?'

I nodded.

'Of what?'

'Of someone with Mrs Gilbert, in her bedroom,' I said. His jaw clenched as he looked at me. 'It seemed that there was a local voyeur who had taken a shine to her, and in the photographs it wasn't Claude having sex with Mrs Gilbert.'

Dobson looked down and ran his hands over his face. 'So what do you want with me?' he said, his voice muffled through his fingers.

'I want to speak to the other person in the photograph,' I said, and watched for the reaction.

He looked at me and swallowed, as if his mouth had gone dry. 'Do you still have the photographs?'

I nodded. Luckily, they hadn't been with the laptop when the papers were taken.

He sat back and exhaled loudly.

'This is going to print, Mr Dobson, and so this is your one chance to give your side of things,' I said. It was the usual newspaper blackmail – that the story was already there and was going to be published, and so an exclusive inter-view was damage limitation. I leant forward and spoke quietly, unsure who else was in the house. 'It was going on when she died, I know that, and that it was your little secret.' I paused. 'And hers.'

He didn't move for a few seconds, but then he looked at me and said, 'What does it matter now?'

'You can tell your side,' I said. 'Something's going on with the Claude Gilbert story and unless you want to get sucked into it, you need to come out now. It's the only way you can control it.'

He shook his head. 'I can't.'

'You must.'

'I mustn't,' he said, angrier now. He put his head back and took some deep breaths. Then he said, 'Thank you for your concern, but I'm going to have to ask you to leave.'

I took out one of my business cards and put it down on the arm of the sofa next to him.

311

'This is going to print, Mr Dobson,' I said firmly. 'Call me if you want your version to go in there with it.'

He didn't respond. As I clicked the door closed, I could sense him still watching me as I went back to my car.

Chapter Fifty-One

Laura and Thomas stood some distance from the spot where the woman's body had been found, by the edge of the police tape that had been strung around the streetlights. Laura had taken bunches of flowers from three sets of well-wishers who had approached the scene and placed them against a lamp post but, apart from that, they were well out of the action. Thomas's attention kept on drifting back to the crime scene.

'I'm sorry about the photographs,' he said, not looking at Laura.

'Why are *you* sorry?'

'I tried to get them all back, but I couldn't, and it upset you.'

Laura sighed. 'I needed to know,' she said. When Thomas blushed she added, 'You're itching to go down there,' and pointed towards the officers in jump suits who were assembled in a line fifty yards beyond the tape, ready to bend to their knees for the fingertip search.

'No, it's okay,' he said, although he didn't sound convincing.

'Don't worry,' Laura said. 'That's how it should be. What did you have yesterday? Petty thefts and drunkenness. There's a dead body now, and so you're bound to be interested.'

Thomas nodded and gazed back towards the crime scene,

more openly than before. 'They seem to know what they're doing.'

Laura followed his gaze. 'Murder cases bring out the best in us. The money and manpower gets found.'

And that's how it should be, she thought to herself. Crime priorities might get shifted around by the prevailing political wind, but taking another person's life should always get top billing. Laura knew that murder cases were handled well in Blackley, that the officers on the Major Incident Team were methodical and thorough, always ready to do whatever it took to find the killer.

'Before we came out, the sergeant said that our job today was to be seen,' Thomas said. 'What did she mean?'

'Hazel was a prostitute, and so most of her friends will be,' Laura said, 'but the other street girls will tell you nothing if you go knocking on their door, or if you interrupt them when they're working. But they will be angry about what's happened and, if we hang around, make ourselves visible and approachable, we might hear whispers that would never make it as far as the police station.'

'What do you mean, angry?'

'Last night they will have been upset about Hazel, but it will have been mixed with relief, that it isn't them on the mortuary slab,' Laura said. 'The relief will have slipped now, and they will be angry that someone just like them, whose life was probably one long kick in the teeth, has been dumped like old rubbish.'

'Would we want them as witnesses, these prostitutes?' Thomas said.

Laura raised her eyebrows. 'In a murder case, you take any witness you've got, and prostitutes tend to be good ones.' When Thomas looked confused, Laura explained. 'The court-room doesn't frighten them. If the defence barrister is a woman, any attempt to browbeat them makes the lawyer look like a bully picking on someone who's had fewer life chances. The jurors start to see them as people, not just prostitutes, so they get an easy ride from the female barristers, just to keep them from losing the jury.'

'And the male barristers?'

'The street girls just treat them with contempt. Remember that they've usually spent years grubbing around in the front passenger seats of other people's cars, and so the pompous arsehole in the wig is just another pervert to them, upstanding one minute, panting dirty the next. No, there's nothing wrong with people like that as witnesses, because they'll tell their stories in blunt and simple terms, and juries like that.'

Thomas shook his head. 'I thought I knew about stuff,' he said, 'but there's so much more to all this.'

'You'll pick it up, don't worry.'

'So, what do you think?' Thomas asked.

'It's a sad case,' Laura replied. 'Beyond that, I have no idea.'

'But she was a prostitute,' Thomas said. 'She was always going to be a magnet for weirdos, and then one day, boom, she meets the biggest one of all.'

Laura looked at Thomas and saw his naivety and prejudice.

'So we write it off, do we, just a bad day at the office?' she said, her eyes wide, questioning. 'You'll meet some lowlifes doing this job, but never stop seeing them as people. That's not a popular view, but it will save you, if you remember it.'

Thomas blushed an apology. 'What do you mean, save me?'

'Police marriages fail,' Laura said, 'but you can forget all that crap about the bad hours. We're not the only job with shift patterns. No, it's because too many coppers stop being human and become rigid in how they see people, where

315

everything is either right or wrong, and only one side is acceptable, so life becomes one big judgement. That's why marriages fail, because not everyone can be perfect, no one can do the right thing all the time – and who wants to live their lives being judged?' Laura shook her head. 'Not me.'

'What's that got to do with a dead prostitute?'

'Because you're judging her, that's why, and if you do that you won't catch her killer, because you won't care enough.' She pointed towards the crime scene. 'Someone's daughter died on that patch of concrete. Remember that.'

Thomas looked down and said eventually, 'I'm sorry.'

Laura sighed as she looked at him, saw how young he was. 'Don't be sorry,' she said. 'Just remember it.'

Laura looked back to the murder scene. She didn't like this, the hanging around, her legs too warm in uncomfortable black trousers and her shirt sticking to her back, the jangle of her equipment belt acting as a soundtrack to her day. She had seen the excitement in the station that morning as she had crossed the atrium, new murders always brought it, the canteen buzzing with chatter at the sight of the out-of-town detectives in their crisp pastel shirts and bright ties.

Laura knew that she should be feeling better about the day, the memory of Rachel's slump into drunkenness bringing the crinkle of a smile to her lips, but her lack of involvement was hurting her. She couldn't understand why she had to do less of the work she was best at – detecting serious crimes – in order to move higher in the ranks. Instead, Laura was having to mentor blushing young constables and wander the streets of Blackley, waiting to be approached. She wanted to be a part of the investigation, and that's why she was frustrated.

But then she saw something out of the corner of her eye, just a hint that someone wanted to speak to her.

There was a young woman on the other side of the road in a dirty old tracksuit, her cheeks flushed and bloated by booze, her stomach drooping over her waistband. She was edgy – Laura had seen that look before, as if the woman wanted to catch Laura's attention but didn't want to be seen to be talking to the police. She kept on turning towards Laura, her arms folded across her chest, glancing around.

Laura nodded towards her and then said to Thomas, 'Keep an eye on her.'

Chapter Fifty-Two

As I drove over to Frankie's house, I thought back to the meeting with Mike Dobson. I knew I had spooked him. Whether something went in a story, true or not, often depended on whether someone could afford to challenge it. Headlines sell papers, not the retractions and apologies tucked away on the inside pages. On the other hand, having an affair didn't make him guilty of murder, so I had decided to leave him for now and see if Frankie had been released by the police.

As I parked the car and walked towards the house, I could hear banging and shouting, like someone breaking furniture, and there was a noise like high-pitched screaming.

I ran for the front door and saw that it was ajar. The noise stopped as I drew near. I knocked hard but there was no answer. I pushed at the door and it opened slowly, creaking, the only sound in the house.

'Frankie?' I shouted.

No response.

I stepped into the hall, again screwing up my nose at the smell. I glanced into the front room, at the bags piled high against the wall, but there was no one else there. So where had the shrieks come from?

I backed out of the room and looked up the stairs.

'Frankie?' I shouted again, but still nothing.

The first step creaked as I stepped onto it, and the sound seemed loud in the hallway. I looked upwards. It was dark, and I thought about turning back, but I already knew what I would do: I would go after the story.

I began to walk upwards, stepping slowly, listening out for any quick movements. There was nothing, just the noise of my shoes on the carpet and the occasional groan of the stairs beneath my feet. When I turned onto the landing and saw the next set of stairs ahead, I wondered how far I should go up. There was no one downstairs and so if Frankie appeared now, I could still make an escape if things turned nasty.

I began to walk slowly along the landing. The light from the open door at the front of the house faded, and I started to see movement in the shadows, just shades of black shifting in the half-light. Something was wrong. I could sense it in my shallow breaths and the clamminess of my hands, leaving sweat marks on the landing rail.

I walked past the door to Frankie's mother's room, and again I saw the pink glow coming from underneath, the immaculate memorial to the most important woman in his life. The door was closed.

I had reached the bottom of the second flight of stairs, and was about to step onto them, when I heard something.

I turned around quickly, trying to pin down the source of the noise. It was a low mutter, like someone talking to themselves. It wasn't coming from the top floor.

I moved along the landing, trying to work out the source of the murmurs, my feet soft on the carpet, my hearing keen. I had taken just two steps before I reached the door to Frankie's mother's room again. I listened intently. The noises were coming from the room.

I turned the door handle slowly and gave the door a light push. As it swung open, it bathed the gloom of the landing in soft pink light. As I looked in, I gasped.

The room had been trashed. The pictures on the dresser had been thrown onto the floor and there were glass fragments where the frames had broken. The sheets had been ripped from the bed and were strewn on the floor. The framed pictures on the wall were askew, the glass shattered in the frames, and old clothes had been scattered around the room.

And right in the middle of it all sat Frankie, his arms wrapped round a photograph frame. He was looking at the floor, and I could see tears streaming down his face.

'Frankie, what's wrong?' I said. 'Who did this?'

He looked up slowly, and as he saw me he glowered.

'What do you want?' he shouted.

'I wanted to make sure you were all right,' I said.

'You took my pictures,' he said, and he sounded angry, the words snapping at me.

I closed my eyes for a moment, and then I nodded. 'Yes, I did. I'm sorry.' I knelt down so that my gaze was level with his. 'I meant to bring them back. I was only borrowing them.' I looked around the room. 'Tell me, Frankie, who did this?'

Frankie shook his head, and then I saw where the skin had been scraped from his knuckles.

'*You* did it?' I said, surprised.

Frankie looked down and then got slowly to his feet. He looked around the room. The picture he was holding tumbled slowly from his grasp and hit the floor. I could see the blood on his hand, the small slashes where he had caught his skin on the broken picture frames. He didn't seem to notice. Instead, he began to turn around, his hand over his mouth, his eyes wide, taking in the damage to the room, his special place.

'They're coming back,' he whispered to himself, tears running down his cheeks again.

I reached out and put my hand on his arm. 'Who's coming back?'

He shook his head. 'She was right. I shouldn't have spoken to you.'

'Frankie, stop this. Who do you mean?'

He shook his head, and then he looked at me, his gaze direct now, his face betraying his anger. 'Go now!'

'Tell me first,' I said, backing towards the door.

He kept on coming towards me. 'Out. Please go.'

I held out my hands, to appease him. 'Just speak to me.'

He shook his head again, but more wildly this time, his anger replaced by distress. 'They're coming again.'

Chapter Fifty-Three

Laura's instinct was right – the young woman who had been watching them before was more than just curious. After an hour of loitering and then walking away before coming back to the same spot, she eventually made her way across the road to where Laura was standing. She glanced around as she walked, her arms folded, a cigarette squeezed between her fingers, her nails dirty and brown.

'Did she suffer much?' she began, her voice hesitant.

'Who?' Laura asked, checking to see whether she was being more than merely ghoulish.

'Hazel,' she said. 'I knew her.'

'She was a street girl,' Laura said, watching her carefully. 'How about you?'

The woman looked away and took a pull on her cigarette. 'Sometimes,' she said.

Laura smiled and wished that she could convince her that she had no need to be ashamed, that just because Laura didn't sell her body meant that there were no desperate circumstances in which she wouldn't consider it.

'Were you working last night?' Laura asked.

The woman looked back at Laura and chewed on her index finger. The smoke trails from her cigarette made Laura instinctively want to step back, but she had to stay close, not give the woman the chance to walk away.

'This is just between me and you, right? I mean, if they find out I was working, they'll take my kids off me. I had to leave them in, but I had no money. If this doesn't stay secret, I'm not talking.'

'I can't promise that,' Laura said. 'But if we don't catch him, you might be next, and your kids might end up without a mother. Which would be worse?'

The woman's face hardened as she thought this over, and then she took a deep breath. 'Yes, I was working,' she said. 'I saw her go off with someone.'

'Who?'

The woman shrugged. 'I don't know his name, but he drives round here a lot and sometimes takes Hazel. He must have had something for her.'

'What did he look like?' Laura asked, her hand going to her radio, so that she could call it in straight away.

'Like they all do,' she said. 'A bit ashamed, making out like they ended up here by accident, but really hungry too, desperate for anything.'

'Age?'

'Fifties.'

'White, black, Asian?'

'White, going bald up top, a bit fat around the face.'

'Car?'

'Merc, gold.'

Laura flashed a look at Thomas; he had heard the description and was just about to blurt something out when Laura gave him a small shake of the head. No name, not yet.

'Would you recognise him again?' Laura asked.

The woman shrugged and then nodded. 'Yeah, I reckon so.'

Laura pulled her radio towards her mouth and pressed the call button.

Chapter Fifty-Four

Mike Dobson couldn't concentrate on the sale. The reporter's visit was too fresh in his mind. It had been his secret for more than twenty-two years. Why now, so soon after the cop's visit? Things were starting to pull together, and the panic clawed at him.

He looked at the old woman. She had called him to her house, some free quote promotion they were running, but he knew she had stopped listening. Or maybe he had stopped talking? He had been there for thirty minutes, tried some of the tricks on autopilot – the charm, the fake discount that took it to the real price – but his mind kept on drifting. He heard a bang, a fist on wood, and he thought someone else must have entered the room. He looked around. There was no one there. The old woman was ignoring him now, watching the television that had been playing constantly in the corner of the room.

She was flicking through the channels, then she hit the local news, and settled in her chair.

Mike had started to load his bag with his samples when he heard Blackley mentioned. He looked up and saw a scene that he recognised, a scrap of concrete punctured by grass in the shadow of the old viaduct. Blue and white crime scene tape was stretched across the pavement, and two police officers stood nearby, on guard. There was a shot of a young woman putting some flowers by a lamp post, the blooms bright and incongruous against the drab concrete and brick.

His stomach took a roll. He had been there the night before. He looked down at his hands and saw the sample of plastic guttering quiver in his hand. His tongue felt large and dry in his mouth.

Then her photograph came up on the screen. It was the girl from the night before. She looked happy in the photograph, which must have been taken before the drugs had scarred her, but he recognised her all the same.

He let out a moan and dropped the plastic in his hand. When it clattered onto the polished wooden floor, the old lady looked round.

'Are you still here?' she snapped.

He looked at the floor, his hand clasped to his forehead, damp and clammy; it seemed to sway underneath him, the grooves and grain moving together, the memories rushing through his head. But they were all vague. He remembered her smell, the Chanel perfume. He remembered the feel of the blanket under him, her bony pelvis on him, the way her hair felt soft in his fingers, but it all seemed blurred now.

He heard a name. Hazel. He hadn't known her name. Had never asked for it.

He looked at the television again. She had gone now. Was he sure he had seen it?

The old lady was looking at him strangely. 'Are you all right?' she asked, more concerned now.

He nodded and scooped up the rest of his things under his arm. He had to get out.

He thought he was going to vomit as he rushed along to the front door, and sucked in the fresh air when he got outside. He looked at his car. A gold Mercedes. Distinctive, bold. Then he remembered the policewoman from the other day. She said he was on a database. Kerb-crawlers. She would remember the car.

He looked along the street and checked for the police. He couldn't see anything. He walked quickly to his car and threw his samples into the back before he clambered into the driver's seat. He checked his rearview mirror. No one there, as far as he could tell. He tried shallow breathing to get his pulse down, but he could feel his heart still drumming fast in his chest, his fingers tight around the wheel.

What had happened the night before? She had been alive when he left her, he was sure of that, but then he thought of Nancy and squeezed his eyes shut and clamped his hands over his ears as the bangs and shouts came back to him again, muffled, desperate.

He had to stay calm. Maybe no one had seen him with her. She wasn't in her usual place when he'd met her. She had been walking along the street, no other girls nearby.

He drove away slowly, not wanting to attract any attention. The journey home seemed too long, every red light against him, all the time sitting exposed at the wheel, expecting to see the flicker of blue lights behind him.

His estate loomed ahead, and he started to think of what he would say to Mary. The police would come to his house, he knew that now, and then what would he say? How could he tell Mary that he was on a database for kerb-crawlers, that the girl had been alive when he'd left her?

Had she been alive when he'd left her? Last night had been exhilarating, confusing. Could he remember actually leaving her?

Then he slammed on his brakes, causing a horn to sound loudly behind him. An angry face shouted at him as the car drove slowly past, but something had occurred to him: DNA.

There would be traces of his all over her, and his car might still have some of hers inside. A stray hair, or the sweat from her hands on the dashboard.

He needed some thinking time. He thought about taking the car to be cleaned, but then he realised that the valets might have heard about it on the radio, and then it would look suspicious.

He reversed quickly into a nearby street, parked his car and jumped out. He was on a dead-end street not far from his own. He looked around again to check that he hadn't been seen, and walked quickly away.

As the entrance to his street came into view, he slowed down. His house was the first one on the cul-de-sac, and so he needed to be careful. As he got closer, he saw a car on his drive, one he hadn't seen before. Someone was there, an unexpected visitor. It was happening already. The police. They were there, looking for him.

He tried to think about where to go. Who else knew? He looked around, panicking, checking for the twitch of a curtain. He didn't know where to go, what to do. He had lived with the gut-tearing fear of this moment for more than twenty years, that he would hear the clang of the cell door every day until his life ended, instead of the early summer birdsong that brought Nancy back to him vividly every year.

He closed his eyes as he thought of her again, but this made him sway and he felt clammy. He opened his eyes, took some deep breaths. He could hear children laughing and playing in the distance, as always. Normal life. Why couldn't he have some of that?

But he knew why.

He started walking quickly, needing to get away.

Then he remembered the reporter. Mike Dobson knew he couldn't go to the police, but the reporter was interested in his story. He was a crime reporter. He might know what was going on with the murder, whether or not he was a suspect. And he could tell his side of the story. That was the deal, he remembered it now.

He drew out his wallet, rummaging among the petrol receipts and business cards, and then he found it: Jack Garrett's card. There were phone numbers. He could make a call, get some help.

He pulled out his phone, about to make the call, but then he hesitated. What if he was overreacting? Maybe he shouldn't rush it. He needed some thinking time.

Chapter Fifty-Five

Susie Bingham's flat wasn't what I expected.

Laura had called, checking whether I was with Mike Dobson. I wasn't, but she let slip that he was wanted for Hazel's murder. It was all coming together for Claude, and so now was the time. The story was going in, and Claude had to come out.

Susie's flat was on the ground floor of a three-storey Victorian building on the edge of the town centre, the windows covered in dust, the white paint flaking off the rotting window frames. Telephone wires cross-crossed the street and a blue trainer hung from one, marking out some teenage territory. The cars along the street looked beaten up, old Rovers and Toyotas, and I guessed that most of the houses were owned by private landlords, charging rents as high as the state would subsidise.

Susie's name was stuck to a doorbell but the front door opened as I pushed it. It gave into a dark hallway, and when I knocked on the first door, Susie's face appeared behind the security chain.

'Jack?' she said, surprised.

'I've got some news.'

Susie unhooked the security chain and opened the door. Walking in, I was taken aback by what I saw.

The flat was small and tired looking, really just two rooms, with a living room at the front containing little more than a sagging pink sofa and a small silver television perched on a rickety round table. The kitchen was in the corner of the room, just a fridge, cooker and a sink. I caught a glimpse of her bedroom through an archway, no door separating the two rooms, only an old blue curtain that hovered beside an old gas meter rooted to the floor.

'How long have you lived here?' I asked.

'A few years,' she said defensively.

As I looked around, she pulled a cigarette from her packet and lit it, as if to emphasise that I was in her home now. The ashtray on the corner of the sofa was half-filled with screwed-up cigarette butts and, gazing up, I saw the ceiling was yellowed by smoke. Then I saw something in the kitchen area that explained why her legal career had taken a dive, confirming the truth of what Rachel had said: that Susie was just a small-town boozer.

I walked over to the fridge and lifted two vodka miniatures from the small collection that Susie had there; when I glanced in the rubbish bin, I saw more of them, empty.

'Developing a problem?' I queried.

'What do you mean?' she said, coughing out smoke as she did so. 'And what business is it of yours anyway?'

My laugh was caustic. 'I've been dragged down to London to meet your boyfriend, who you just happened to see in a chance meeting, and you've got me selling his story, the big-money scoop. And all the time I've had this doubt, tapping away in the back of my head, that maybe I've been wrong all along – that you and your beau were going to take your share and run, once everyone realises that he isn't Claude Gilbert and I'll be the one left behind with a ruined reputation, all because some old soak tried to con me.'

334

Susie looked close to tears. 'What do you mean, old soak?'

'A drunk, an alcoholic.'

'I'm not an alcoholic,' she protested.

'The miniature bottles,' I said, my voice rising, waving them in the air. 'The first refuge for the alcoholic in denial. What game do you play, Susie? Buy them as an afterthought just as you're about to leave the shop, so that no one suspects how much you need them? After all, it's just a small bottle or two. Just a nip here, or a nip there. Except that you do it every time, and now you're the joke of the shop. I bet they're already reaching for the miniatures as you turn around, waiting for you to turn back and say, *oh, and just a couple of those.*'

Susie looked down and said nothing.

'What happened to your legal career, Susie?'

She didn't reply.

'Did it become more about the chambers parties than the courtroom? Did you wobble your way in, one too many times?'

'Go, please.'

'No.'

'Please,' she said, and when she raised her head, I could see tears running down her cheeks.

I shook my head. 'I want to know whether I've been wasting my time,' I said, 'and if I'm not satisfied with your answer, I walk away.'

Susie took a long draw on her cigarette, the orange tip quivering, and stared at me through the smoke.

'Yeah, maybe I like a drink a bit too much,' she said quietly. 'But I'm not dishonest. Not now, not ever. The man I love is Claude Gilbert. If you don't believe me and won't write the story, he'll keep on running, because he knows what will happen if he comes forward without his story being told first.'

I looked at her, trying to find the truth in her eyes but seeing only desperation. I had no idea whether or not it was just the need to get away from that flat, to have a new start with some money in her pocket, even though it would all go on vodka, or whether she truly believed that she could start a new life with a man she professed to love. I could tell one thing though: she didn't have the look of a calculating con-artist, and that was good enough for me.

'Okay,' I said. 'I'm sorry.'

She nodded a teary smile, and wiped her eyes. 'You told me you had some news?'

I remembered then why I had sought her out. 'It's about Mike Dobson.'

Susie looked up.

'He's a suspect in a murder that took place last night.'

She looked surprised at that. 'A murder?'

I nodded. 'A young woman found with her head bashed in. A prostitute. Dobson might have been her last client.'

Susie brightened up at the news. 'That'll help Claude, won't it?' She stubbed out the cigarette and stood, some animation in her eyes now. 'It'll show that he wasn't just making it up.'

'Maybe,' I replied.

'So what now?'

'I'm writing the story tonight. It's going on the front page tomorrow.'

Susie looked surprised at that. 'Already? I mean, does Claude know? What if he's not ready?'

'He's got to be ready. It's affecting my family now, and so I can't wait any longer. Tell Claude he needs to come in tonight. Get him to call me.'

Susie nodded and then sat down again, biting the nail on her middle finger. 'I need a night with him,' she said. 'Our lives will never be the same again. He'll be in the spotlight, people will want to talk to him.'

'He might not get much further than a cell,' I countered. 'This isn't just one news conference and then you both live happily ever after. The police might not believe him. Dobson might have an alibi.'

'But it's his best chance,' she said. 'I want one last night. Tomorrow, everything changes.'

'I don't care,' I said, my voice firm, softened only by my guilt for the rant from a few moments before. 'Get him to call me later, to make the arrangements. We meet tonight, and he goes public first thing. If he doesn't call, I expose him, and I leave out everything about Mike Dobson.'

'He'll do it,' she said eventually.

Although, as I left her, I couldn't help but worry that I had just frightened away the best story of my career.

Chapter Fifty-Six

So this was it, I thought, as I looked at the blank screen in front of me. The story had to be written. I'd given Susie the ultimatum, that it was tonight or never, and I was just waiting for the phone call from Claude so I would know where to go.

It wasn't a hard story to write. I knew how Harry would want it, blunt and sensationalist, claiming that Claude was out of hiding and protesting his innocence. That would be the hook-line for the front page, most of the story on a double-spread on the inside pages. I would write the story in the order that it unfolded: Susie's visit and then the trip to London. Claude's account would come next, and then Frankie's photos would back up his story about Nancy's affair and the child not being his.

Bobby was watching the television at the other end of the room and I was able to work without much interruption. I felt a twinge of guilt that I wasn't paying more attention to him, that I had opted for the flat-screen babysitter, but I had to get the story in and I was feeling that buzz of writing to a major deadline.

My phone went off, the vibrations making it spin on the table. When I looked at the home screen, it showed a number I didn't recognise. I answered and heard a slurred voice asking, 'Is this Jack Garrett?' When I asked who was speaking, the voice said, 'Mike Dobson.'

I tried to sound nonchalant, but I knew the police were looking for him, and so I reached for my notepad and pen.

'Mr Dobson, thanks for calling. I'm putting the story together now. Have you got anything you wish to say?'

There was a pause, and for a moment I thought that I'd lost the connection, but then he said, 'I want to tell you what happened.'

'With what?'

'With Nancy Gilbert.'

'Talk away.'

'I can't, not here,' he replied. 'You need to come and get me. I'm in the park next to Nancy Gilbert's house.'

My mouth went dry and I pressed the pen harder into the paper.

'Just wait where you are,' I said. 'It'll take me about twenty minutes to get there.'

'Okay,' he said, and then his phone clicked off.

I looked over at Bobby and wondered for a moment what I should do. I couldn't take him with me, and the story had to go in. Then I realised that shielding Mike Dobson was very different to meeting someone who claimed to be Claude Gilbert. I remembered the girl from last night, her lifeless legs caught in the glare of the headlights, and I knew that there was only one thing I could do. The story wasn't about Mike Dobson. It was about Claude Gilbert, it had always been about Claude Gilbert. I could write Mike Dobson's story another day. I had promised Harry a front page, and I was going to give him one.

I dialled Laura's number. When she answered, I faltered for a moment. Then I remembered how difficult I had made things for Laura by keeping information from her, but she

340

had still given up Mike Dobson to me. I could repay her with the arrest. I quickly told her where she could find Dobson and then I hung up.

I went back to my story, but it was to find that some of the polish had gone. I had betrayed Mike Dobson. I just hoped that Claude Gilbert was right about him.

Laura clicked off her phone and looked back at the crime scene. She had been there all day with Thomas, manning the blue and white tape while the scene was examined and the fingertip searches completed. The forensic team had gone, and the tape had been left stretched across the street, just to keep out the curious. It bounced in the wind as a television crew packed up its equipment – if you counted a cameraman and a young redhead who had spent most of her time checking herself in a mirror as a crew.

Laura tapped her chin with her phone, working out her next move. Thomas asked, 'Do you think the guy with her last night might be the one we spoke to? Dobson?'

She didn't want to answer the question. How would it look when it came out that she had spoken with Dobson the day before, just before Hazel was killed? She should have given his name to Joe the day before, but Rachel had got in the way of that.

But it *hadn't* been Rachel. It had been her, Laura, who had got in the way, because of her stupid pride; she was jealous because Rachel was in the hot seat and she was confined to wearing the bloody uniform until she got through her sergeant's exam.

Laura looked at Thomas and realised that he was still waiting for her answer. 'Yes, maybe it was Mike Dobson,' she said, and she knew that Thomas was thinking the same thing as her – that they could have stopped him.

She had to make it right.

'I want you to stay here,' Laura said. 'I'll collect you before the end of the shift. You know what to do. Just keep people away.'

Laura headed to the squad car she had been using. It was hardly the car to sneak up on anyone, with its fluorescent markings, but she could get to the park before anyone else, and she didn't trust some of the more excitable cops not to do it with lights flashing and two-tones blaring.

As she pulled away, ready to drive around the piece of wasteland in front of her, she thought she saw something – a red flash, like a blink of light. The windows of the houses facing them across a patch of dust and grass had been like mirrors all day, reflecting back the bright sunshine. Now the afternoon sun had gone, they were turning into dark shadows, and Laura could see into the windows.

She drove slowly towards them, and then she saw it again, a definite red light.

Laura checked her watch. Jack had told Mike Dobson to wait there for twenty minutes, but she knew that Dobson was going to get twitchy; she didn't have much time. She drove past the source of the light, the first-floor window of a redbrick terrace, and was about to put her foot down to get to Dobson when she saw that the light was next to the black wink of a camera lens.

Laura slammed on her brakes and looked up at the house. The camera was on the window sill, pointing into the street. She turned to see what it was pointing at. The detectives had been round to all the local businesses to look at their CCTV tapes, and she had heard the mutters that most were dummy boxes. She had watched them do the door-to-doors and had heard nothing about any footage from any of the houses.

What was the camera looking at? There was nothing there

except wasteland and derelict streets populated by prostitutes and their clients.

Then she got it, and she started to smile. It was the prostitutes that the camera was watching.

Laura jumped out of the car and banged on the front door of the house. There was no reply and so she banged again, louder this time, and heard footsteps shuffle along the hallway. When the door opened, Laura saw a short man with flaking skin peering at her through thick glasses, a small piece of tape holding the frames together. He was wearing a faded checked shirt and baggy stonewashed jeans that looked like they had jumped right out of the eighties.

'I spoke to your people before,' he said.

Laura noticed the wariness in his voice. 'Did you mention the camera?' she asked.

He faltered at that and his eyes flickered upwards, as if he could see it through the ceiling.

'That's right, up there,' she said, pointing. 'I can see it in your window, right now.'

His tongue did a little dance between his lips and then he said, 'It wasn't turned on last night. There's nothing to see.'

'I want to look, just to check,' she said, stepping forward, bluffing him.

He shook his head and barred her way.

Laura stepped back. 'Okay, it's like this,' she said, her hands on her belt. 'You get off on watching men having sex with drug addicts. If that's your thing, fine, we all have needs, but I'm going to pass this on to the team working the murder. You can delete all your stuff if you want, but the experts will still be able to recover it. You can take a hammer to your hard drive, I suppose, but if another girl out there dies, I hope you can live with that.'

Laura saw that he had gone pale.

'I'm going somewhere now, and I'll be going off duty soon, but expect a knock on your door.'

He swallowed, and still seemed incapable of speech.

Laura smiled politely. 'If it turns out that you did leave your camera on last night, try and find a gold Mercedes. Put it on a disk and bring it to the station. Ask for Joe Kinsella. It might stop someone from crawling over your computer, looking at all the stuff you're not supposed to have.'

He nodded. 'Thank you,' he said, and Laura thought his mouth sounded dry as she turned to walk back to the car.

Now she had to get to the park before Mike Dobson decided that he wasn't in a waiting mood.

Chapter Fifty-Seven

Mike Dobson clutched his phone to his chest. He'd made the call, but where was the reporter? What if Garrett didn't come?

His thoughts spun around, as if they were trying to work their way out of his head. He had been in the park all afternoon, looking at the chimneys of Nancy's house. It was never Claude's house to him, but Nancy's, the place where they had passed all those hours. Where he had spent Nancy's last hours. He moaned and clutched his head. It was his last taste of freedom, he knew that, and so he had spent it with a bottle of vodka. The first mouthful had been sour and made his chest burn, but he had persisted with it. He had drunk less than half of it, but that didn't mean that he could avoid squinting as the daylight assaulted him too quickly, his pupils sluggish. He should have drunk less; he realised now that he wanted to remember the day, the sun on his face in an open park, to feel it, not numb it.

His phone buzzed again. It would be his boss, wanting to know why he had missed three sales appointments, worried that some lucky punter had missed out on the chance to buy overpriced plastic guttering. He almost laughed. Is that what his life had amounted to, paying the bills by bullying people in their own homes to buy things they didn't want? Fuck him. None of it mattered any more. It never really had. He could tell his boss exactly where he was. He was at the end.

He closed his eyes and listened to the sound of wings fluttering in a bush behind him, and then the sound of engines from outside the park. He expected the wail of sirens, but there was just the noise of ordinary lives and the high-pitched laughter of college kids on the patch of grass a few yards away. Were they laughing about him, a middle-aged man on a park bench, a bottle of vodka next to him?

He opened his eyes quickly, sensing someone watching him. He looked around, but there was no one there. He tried to peer into the bushes – was someone there? But he couldn't see anything.

He knew he had to keep moving, he had to keep his mind clear so that he could decide what best to do. He would tell the reporter his story, so that everyone would understand, but it wasn't safe to sit in one place in the meantime. If he kept on walking round the park, he would still be able to see the reporter as he came through the gates. He creaked to his feet and set off walking along the tarmac path that would take him around a large pond, where the houses higher up the hill looked down over the park. He stole another glance at the chimneys of the Gilbert house. His head was filled with the clip of his leather soles on the tarmac.

He tried to think about the night before as he walked. Hazel, that was her name, he knew that now, but why had he never asked her? Was she only ever Nancy to him? He had kept quiet for more than twenty years now, and he saw how his life had meant nothing in the end – just one long memory of one awful night. And why would Hazel be dead? He could remember things now, like driving into Blackley, Hazel in the passenger seat, it was coming back to him. And she was Hazel to him now. Why not before?

But Nancy was dead, and he still heard her noises, the soft thumps, sometimes cries.

What would he do next? The police were looking for him, and they would take samples from him. Blood, hair, fingerprints, DNA. What else would they find out when they ran him through the computers? What else would it match up with?

He rubbed the sweat out of his eyes and looked down. He watched his feet walk onwards, one shoe forward at a time, just the constant movement towards . . . what? His arrest? The end of his life? Every step was one step closer. And what about Mary? What would she do now?

He looked up at that thought. He couldn't think about Mary. He had to think about himself now. He hadn't killed Hazel, he was certain of that. But would it matter if he had? He had taken one life. Would one more make him worse, or just the same?

He blinked as the sunlight bounced off the pond and saw someone in the distance. A woman. She looked familiar, but she was just in silhouette. He thought back through his clients. Maybe she looked like one of them. Brunette hair over her shoulders, tall and shapely.

He looked down at his shirt as she came closer. He could see dirt trails on the white cotton. It shouldn't be like that. As he looked up again, he saw that she was still there, on the path, watching him as he drew nearer. Maybe it was the bottle hanging loosely in his hand that made her stare. He looked up the hill and saw the Gilbert house again, and he heard something, like a soft laugh. He shook his head to get rid of the noise, but it echoed through his brain.

Something wasn't right, he sensed it. The breeze blew the scent of summer towards him, cut grass and flower beds, and he thought of Nancy again. For every day of every year, his life had always been about Nancy. Her cries, the bangs, and the images of her, glimpsed as movement at the edge of his vision.

He took one last deep breath and straightened himself. The woman was getting closer. She was definitely watching him, the sun behind her, her face in shadow. He felt dirty, his clothes wet from perspiration.

Then he stopped; he recognised her. The bottle slipped from his hand and smashed on the floor. She stepped closer, and he felt his chin tremble and beads of sweat burst onto his forehead.

It was her, the policewoman, the one who had warned him. She had waited for him to go to her. He looked down at his hands as he flexed and unflexed his fingers, and he thought they shimmered in the sunshine. When he looked up, he thought the horizon looked indistinct, paler than it had before.

He turned around to see people running towards him from the other end of the park.

He looked back to the policewoman and tried to suck in some air, just to stop the world from shifting under his feet. Then, as a tear rolled down his cheek, he stepped towards her and held out his hands. The cold metal of the handcuffs snapped tightly around his wrist, and he felt his knees give way as he slumped to the floor.

I was taking a break from the story when Harry rang. I was standing at the window, watching the fields acquire orange fringes as the sun slipped lower into the horizon.

'Harry, don't worry, it's all under control,' I said, before he had the chance to say anything.

He started with a cough and then said, 'We've got the front page, with pages four and five on standby, so it better be under control.' His gravelly voice was loud in my ear. 'You haven't got long, Jack. I've got a conference room booked at the Lowry Hotel in Manchester for ten o'clock tomorrow. I'll be on the first train, so don't be late. Bring him in through the kitchens. I'll clear it with the staff tomorrow.'

'No tricks this time,' I said.

Harry chuckled.

'Are you sure you'll be able to cope with the North, Harry?' I asked.

'I'll bring my clogs,' he said, and hung up.

I looked back at my laptop and realised that I had to finish the story, and soon. He would need it before eight, because Harry's job was to fill the paper, and if the story came after the press conference, then it would be old news by the following morning. He wanted the news-stand shock factor, the commuters' double-take.

That wasn't my worry though. I knew the story would be sitting in Harry's inbox within the next thirty minutes. I was onto the fine-tuning stage now, just taking a short coffee stop so that I could go back to it fresh. It was the silence from Claude that was worrying me.

I looked at my phone again, as if that would make it ring. It had been a few hours since I had spoken to Susie, and still Claude hadn't called. I didn't know where he was and if Claude decided to run away again the whole story paled. The rival papers for the next day would be filled with ridicule, and Harry would never forgive me. The scoop of my career could turn me into a laughing stock, and I wasn't ready for that.

Chapter Fifty-Eight

Mike Dobson looked around his cell. There was no natural light, just neon panels fitted into the ceiling spreading a weak light around the white tiles and concrete floor.

He had been there a couple of hours, reflecting on his life, on how it hadn't amounted to much. A sales job and an empty house. There was one way out, the coward's exit, but they had taken his belt and laces and there were no beams or hooks; the cell door swung open on a long metal rod concealed within the door casing, so he couldn't even use his shirt sleeve as a noose.

He couldn't remember much about the arrest. It came back to him in flashes, faded and distant. The cuffs too tight around his wrist, the journey to the station. He knew the streets, had driven round them all his life, but they seemed altered now, as if he knew he was seeing them for the last time. He remembered the feel of the sun on his face as he came out of the van. How long before he would feel that again? And the clang of the doors as he was taken inside. Sounds suddenly seemed to echo and he was no longer in charge of his life. Questions, signatures, and they had only ever talked about Hazel. No one mentioned Nancy Gilbert.

He looked at the wall when he heard the screaming from the next cell start up again. Kicks landed as soft thuds against

351

the cell door. It had been going on since he came in. Someone would walk down the corridor and shout for the occupant to be quiet, but that only made it worse.

Mike put his hands behind his head and lay back on the plastic mattress. It felt cool against the heat coming from his body. He closed his eyes and thought about Hazel. He brought one hand to his face to see if there was anything left of her smell, but there was nothing. He had washed it away, just like he had soaked away the dust and dirt from his suit.

He sat up when he heard the rattle of a key in his cell door. As it swung open, he saw a man there, tall, in a crisp white shirt, with a perma-tan and bright teeth, his boots polished to a gleam and his black trousers pressed razor-sharp. The man came in and closed the door behind him, although he didn't lock it.

'Don't think about running through,' the man said. 'There are people at the custody desk and at least two sets of doors that need keys.'

Mike scuttled back to the wall so that he could feel the coldness of the tiles through the back of his shirt.

'I'm not going to run,' Mike said. 'I've nowhere to go.'

'Do you know why you're here?'

Mike nodded and looked down. 'Hazel, the girl from last night, so I was told.'

'Anyone else?'

Mike looked at his visitor. 'Who do you mean?'

The visitor smiled and sat down on the plastic mattress. 'You know who I mean.'

Mike shook his head.

'Nancy,' the visitor said.

Mike felt the room start to swirl, the tiles fusing into white streaks; when he looked at his hands, they seemed as if they belonged to someone else, detached from him, as if he had become just an observer of his own body. They knew, he realised. They had always known.

'I found her,' the visitor said. 'I was one of the people who dug her up.'

Mike looked at him, trying to focus, but the visitor sounded distant, drowned out by the rush of blood through his head.

'Are you Roach?' Mike asked.

The visitor smiled. 'You know my name.'

'I read about you,' Mike said. 'I followed the story.'

'You had a special interest, Mr Dobson,' Roach said.

Mike nodded and tugged on his lip. 'Tell me something.'

'Go on.'

'How did she look – Nancy, I mean – when you found her?' Mike said.

Roach was silent for a moment, and then he said, 'She looked scared. Dirty and bloodied. Paint and splinters under her nails.'

Mike swallowed. His mouth tasted acidic.

'This is your second chance, Mr Dobson,' Roach said. 'Make it right, for everyone. Tell them what you know.'

Mike didn't say anything for a long time. He didn't notice when Roach left and his cell became empty again. There was just the sound of his breathing and the regular thumps in his head, the drumbeat of Nancy's fists on the wood.

I was running Bobby's bath when I heard Laura come into the house.

The story had gone in and Harry had called to hack and cough his approval, but there was still only silence from Claude. So I was distracted as I knelt on the bathroom floor, bubbles all over my forearms and my trousers wet from the water that had splashed over the side. Bobby was in his room, selecting toys for some water fun.

I looked out of the open window as Bobby climbed into the tub, feeling the last few moments of sun on my face. I heard the heavy clump of Laura's boots as she came upstairs. She hugged Bobby when she saw him, and then she put her arms around me, her mouth against my neck.

'We got him,' she whispered. 'Mike Dobson. He's in the cells. It's nothing to do with Nancy Gilbert yet, but I've tipped the wink to Joe, told him to make sure he is in the interview, just in case Joe can turn it round to Nancy.' She gave me a squeeze. 'Thank you for that.'

I turned around and cupped her face in my hands. 'My good deed for the day. I just hope I can repeat it tomorrow.'

'Why tomorrow?' she asked, but when she saw my raised eyebrows, she nodded in comprehension. 'Claude comes out, doesn't he?'

I nodded. 'Front page in the morning, and then a press conference.'

'Whereabouts?'

'The Lowry, in Manchester.'

Laura laughed. 'That will annoy the brass. A different force might get to the arrest first. No appearance on the lunchtime news for the local boys.'

I smiled. 'I think it's so Harry doesn't have to change trains.'

'Should I do anything?' she said.

I shook my head. 'Just pretend that we haven't had this conversation.'

Then I heard my phone ring downstairs. I peeled away from Laura and ran quickly to answer it. When I jabbed at the answer button, Claude's baritone was loud in my ear.

'You've done well, Mr Garrett.'

'Don't thank me yet,' I said. 'Dobson might be back on the streets by midnight.'

'Maybe so, but at least the jury will be able to wonder about him now.'

'So what about you, Claude? Did you get the message from Susie? You go in the paper tomorrow, and we've got a press conference.'

There was silence for a few seconds, and then he said, 'I suppose now is a good time.'

'Damn right, Claude. If Dobson is charged, then you don't get your say, because we'll have to stay quiet until his trial.'

'Perhaps, Mr Garrett. Perhaps.'

'We need to meet.'

'Midnight,' he said. 'I'll call you later.'

'Why so late?'

He chuckled. 'It's Susie,' he said. 'You know how women are. She wants one last evening. I'll call you.'

And then the phone went silent.

When I turned round, Laura was there. 'Where are you going?' she asked.

'Nowhere yet,' I said. 'I just have to wait here.'

She smiled. 'It doesn't have to be boring.'

Chapter Fifty-Nine

When the cell door opened again, there were two men standing behind the white shirt of the jailer. They were important, Mike Dobson could tell that from their fake smiles of reassurance. He reckoned junior officers would have been more disapproving. These two were fully-fledged, been-around-the-block sort of officers. Mike almost smiled. They had judged him already, he could tell that.

He thought he would feel afraid, but he didn't. You become what you pretend to be, and his life had turned into a lie. Now, he felt relief, not fear; he was almost glad that the hunt was over. He stood up and held out his hands.

'Is it time, gentlemen?' he asked.

They exchanged quick glances before the gaoler said, 'Mr Dobson, come this way please.'

Mike followed them along the corridor until he reached the custody desk. No one spoke to him until the custody sergeant put a clipboard on the desk, and Mike saw where he had signed it when he was first brought in, his signature shaky.

'Are you sure you don't want a solicitor?' one of the suits said, the older one, his Lancashire accent blunt and broad, his moustache neat and trimmed.

Mike shook his head. 'I want to tell my story.'

'This is a serious allegation, Mr Dobson. I really think you ought to have a lawyer with you.'

'I know that,' Mike said, 'but I want to tell you what happened.'

The sergeant looked at the two men and shrugged. 'It's his choice, gentlemen. You need to get him to an interview room.' Mike guessed the subtext: *before he changes his mind.*

Mike was taken to a small room along a different corridor, windowless again, with just enough space for a wooden table and four chairs. There was a machine in the corner with blinking blue lights, and a red plastic strip ran around the room, like the sort he'd seen on buses to tell the driver to stop; a sticker saying 'do not press' indicated that it was a panic alarm.

'This is a digital recorder,' one of the suits explained, the older one, pointing at the machine in the corner. 'We don't use tapes any more.'

Then the younger of the two men introduced himself. Joe Kinsella. He was more casual, with no tie and no shine to his shoes. He seemed gentle, his voice soft. The other man was Alan Nesbitt. There were bold creases ironed into the arms of his shirt that matched the sharp parting in his hair. Call me Alan, he said. Mike smiled. They were being very pleasant to him.

When the recording started, Mike just nodded in the right places, that he understood the caution, that he had waived his right to legal advice, and then he said his name boldly when the time came. They told him it was just a routine interview, to get his story, to check whether they would look further into it.

When they asked him to tell them what he knew about Hazel, Mike looked at Joe Kinsella. 'Have you ever been lonely?' he asked.

Alan started to say that their personal lives weren't relevant, but Joe held out his hand to stop him.

'What do you mean?' Joe said.

'If you've been lonely, you might understand what I'm talking about when I tell you my story,' Mike said. 'And I don't mean just having a few empty hours to kill, but real, never-ending loneliness, where your life stretches ahead of you and you just cannot see it ever getting any better.'

'Did Hazel stop you being lonely?' Joe said.

Mike shook his head. 'No, not Hazel,' he said, and he leant forward, more animated now. 'She was a sweet girl, I enjoyed spending time with her, but she reminded me of someone.'

'Who did she remind you of, Mike?'

Mike looked at the two detectives and listened to their breathing, and knew that he had their attention.

'Hazel reminded me of the woman I killed,' Mike said, and then he sat back, his arms folded.

Mike saw Alan react to that. A widening of the eyes, and then a few fast blinks.

'Who did you kill?' Joe asked. Mike looked at Joe. He had hardly reacted.

'You know who I killed,' Mike said. 'That's why the policewoman spoke to me. That's why the reporter has been looking for me.'

Mike watched as Joe scribbled something in his notebook. Joe was left-handed, he noticed, and he crooked his wrist over so that he could write. Mike tried to read it, but the writing was small and untidy.

'Tell me who,' Joe repeated.

'I'll say the words if you want,' he said, and he put both of his hands on the table. 'It was Nancy Gilbert.'

Even Joe Kinsella reacted to that. His eyes widened with

surprise and, when Joe looked to his colleague, Mike added, 'Claude Gilbert's wife.'

Joe's brow furrowed for a moment, and then he leant across the table, closing the space between them. 'Tell me about it.'

Mike nodded and breathed out slowly, a tear suddenly appearing on his cheek.

'I've been waiting to do this for twenty-two years.'

Chapter Sixty

I was watching television, except that I wasn't really. There was some reality programme on, desperate people hoping for celebrity, but it was just voices and flickering lights to me.

I was sprawled along the sofa, Laura lying next to me, her head on my chest. Bobby had been in bed for a couple of hours and I was watching the clock tick onwards, worried that the midnight meeting would get called off.

Laura looked up at me. 'It will be fine,' she said, and she stroked my chest.

I smiled. 'How did you know what I was thinking?'

'Because you've been twirling my hair around your finger for the past five minutes.' She gave me a playful poke in the ribs.

I laughed and let go of her hair. 'Maybe I just like touching it.'

'I can tell the difference,' she said, and then she straddled me, so that her hair was in my face. She moved her head gently, playfully, her hair tickling my cheeks, and I pulled her towards me until I felt the soft push of her lips.

'I need someone to take my mind off things,' I whispered. 'Can you do that?'

'That'll take care of the first minute,' she said. 'What about the rest of the evening?'

It was my turn to give a playful poke, which turned into a tickle, and then a wrestle, until she stopped and sat up. She looked around, her face serious.

'What is it?' I asked.

'Did you see that?'

'See what?'

'A flash. I'm sure I saw a flash.'

I looked towards the window. 'Maybe there's lightning somewhere,' I said. 'It feels muggy tonight.'

I stood up and went to open the front door, looking up into the sky. It was warm outside, and it seemed like clouds were building up, but it didn't feel quite ready for lightning. I stared around, but there was nothing there but the blackened outlines of the hills around the cottage.

I turned around, saw that Laura was now sitting with her knees drawn up to her chest, her arms folded on top.

'Nothing there,' I said.

Laura shook her head. 'There was something. I'll go outside and check.'

'No, no, I'll do it,' I said, going to get my shoes.

I stepped outside carefully, looking around. I heard Laura draw the curtains in the living room, but that just made things darker. I tried to peer into the shadows.

'Frankie?' I shouted, but there was no response.

I sighed with frustration and went back into the house. Frankie would have to wait until tomorrow.

'So how did you know Nancy?' Joe asked.

Mike didn't say anything at first. He thought back to that time more than twenty years ago, all those spoiled memories.

'We were in love,' he said eventually.

'How did you meet?'

'I sold insurance back then,' Mike said. 'I did house calls to collect the premiums. Nancy was on my books. She was a good client, and she had a lot to insure, so I was friendly and tried to spend time with her.'

'And her being attractive must have helped,' Joe said.

'It wasn't like that,' he said. 'You make it sound cheap, and it was anything but that. She was pretty, but women like her don't look at men like me. She was well spoken, had a rich husband, she lived in a big house. I was an insurance salesman in a cheap suit making out like I was doing well, but I lived in a box of a house and drove a Ford Escort. But then, as we got to know each other, that started to matter less. I realised that for all she had, Nancy felt like she had nothing that really mattered, because she was lonely. Claude was never there for her. He was a womaniser, Nancy knew that, but she dreamed that one day he would settle down. Divorcing Claude wouldn't be easy. She had a lot to give up. A beautiful house, the respect of her friends. And he was a lawyer. What was I? Not much, was how I saw it. Nancy used to say that Claude liked being a lawyer because he could ruin people just because he felt like it.'

'How did that make you feel?' Joe said.

'It didn't make me feel anything. Nancy used to say that it was his way of telling her that he would ruin her if she tried to divorce him, that, as a lawyer, he had the power. So she carried on waiting for Claude to grow up. But men like Claude Gilbert never settle down. Not really. We used to talk when I did my insurance round, and I realised how lonely I'd become. I started to dread going home, and all I could think about was Nancy.'

'What does this have to do with Hazel?' Alan asked, but Joe held out his hand to stall him.

'So how did you become lovers?' Joe said.

Mike bit his lip and wiped a stray tear from his cheek.

'Like most people do,' he said, his voice thick. 'There was just something there. A connection. A bond. You can try and deny it, make out that you're just good friends, but you soon find yourself at a point where something is going to happen, with those looks that we held for too long, things like that.' He gave a small laugh. 'I can't remember now how we crossed the line. One minute we were staring at each other over a coffee, and then we were kissing. The first time, we didn't even get undressed. It was in the kitchen, and it was all too quick. It was just like all the clichés, I suppose. Clothes being torn, fireworks on the floor. Nancy was a different woman, like she had been holding it all in for too long.'

'When was this?' Joe asked.

'It started in the summer before she died. And it wasn't a constant thing. We would have a few weeks when we avoided each other, tried to think of our marriages, but that never lasted. We were always pulled together somehow.' He wiped his eyes. 'I loved her. I started calling round in the afternoon. We went for drives in the country, and long lazy walks, and picnics by the river in an old stone shelter. I took the girl there – you know, Hazel, the dead girl.'

'Why did you take her there?'

'Because it was a special place for me.'

'So how did you end up killing Nancy?' Joe asked.

Mike looked down and took a deep breath. His finger-nails dug into the table, and when he looked up again his vision was blurred by the tears in his eyes.

'By walking away,' he said, and then he licked his lips as the sounds of that night filled his head. 'The baby changed everything. We thought we'd been careful, but when Nancy found out she was pregnant, we guessed it was probably mine, and we didn't know what to do. We thought about coming clean, telling everyone, but Nancy was scared of Claude. She talked about bringing up the child as Claude's. The child would have a good home, everything it needed financially, and maybe it would calm Claude down, stop him gambling or womanising.'

'That can't have been a nice thought, someone else bringing up your child,' Joe said. 'Have you got any children of your own?'

Mike looked at Joe and then shook his head. 'You're hoping I'll say I got angry, or jealous, I can tell. I'm a salesman, I can read people. I have to be able to anticipate their moods, to know what to say to make them buy something they don't want.'

'And you know how to tell a lie to get the sale,' Joe responded.

Mike sat back and folded his arms. He considered Joe, whose stare was measured, calculating.

'No, it didn't make me angry,' Mike said. 'It made me confused, and scared too. I was in a cold marriage, but I didn't want to hurt Mary. I didn't know what the hell to do. A married woman was carrying my child. How the hell do you work yourself out of that one?'

'So you killed her?' Joe said. 'That's an extreme way of solving your problems.'

'It wasn't like that.'

'So tell me, what was it like?'

Mike's fingers started to drum on the table. He took some deep breaths, to keep his control so that he could tell his story.

'We decided to meet up, to sort it out,' Mike said. 'Claude was at the casino, or so we thought, and so I went to her house. It was a rough hour. She was crying. I was crying. I wanted us to be together. Nancy wanted her marriage to work with Claude. And maybe I wasn't a big deal to her. I was just a man in the right place. It was just one big fucking mess, and we were right in the middle of it all, trying to work out how to deal with it.'

'What decision did you reach?'

'We didn't get that far.'

'Why not?'

'Because Claude appeared.'

Chapter Sixty-One

'Claude must have been hiding and listening,' Mike said. 'He just seemed to step out of the shadows. He was holding some kind of cosh, lead piping wrapped in bandage or something, and he swung it hard.'

Mike wiped his hand across his eyes, his teeth clenched, anger in his voice now.

'Poor Nancy didn't even have time to look around,' Mike said. 'It got her right on the back of the head, knocked her face hard into the table. Blood flew over me, went onto the table, everywhere. Nancy just slithered onto the floor. She wasn't moving.'

'I thought you said you killed Nancy,' Joe said, scribbling notes.

Mike looked at Joe and nodded slowly. 'I did, because she wasn't dead then. But I didn't know that.'

'So what did you do?'

Mike looked up as a tear tumbled from his lash. 'I panicked. Claude was waving the cosh around, saying he was going to hit me next, but as Nancy stayed on the floor he started to panic too. I don't know if he meant to hit her that hard. Maybe he was just listening and became angry, couldn't control himself, but as Nancy bled on the floor he became frantic. I became frantic. I wanted to leave, but he said that

367

if anyone found out then everything would come out. Her affair with me, the baby, and so Mary . . .' He stopped and looked at the ceiling. '. . . Mary would find out.'

Joe looked surprised at that. 'Mr Dobson, the woman you claim you loved is lying in a pool of blood on the floor, and you decide to say nothing?'

Mike banged his fist on the table. Alan jumped, but Joe stayed still, his eyes on Mike all the time.

'I know that it sounds like the wrong thing now,' Mike said, his teeth gritted, 'and it *was* the wrong thing, but I wasn't fucking thinking straight. I'd seen what happened to Nancy, but we had spent the night talking about what we were going to do.' He ran his hands over his face. 'I was going to lose her anyway,' he said, more distant now. 'I didn't mean as much to her. I was a stop-gap, a replacement Claude, some below-stairs affair. So why ruin everything for something I couldn't change? I thought she was dead, for Christ's sake. Claude talked me into saying nothing, but that's what he does, isn't it? He's a lawyer. I sell insurance, or double-glazing, or plastic guttering, but Claude sold lies, and sold them well. I was sucked into them. He would live with the guilt, not me. He'd hit her. All I had was the loss.' Mike put his head down and wiped his eyes. 'We decided to bury her.'

'Why bury her in the garden?'

Mike's chin trembled as he looked at the floor, and his hands wiped the tears into grubby streaks across his cheeks before he looked up again.

'Because it meant we didn't have to carry her anywhere.'

'What did you think Gilbert was going to do after that?' Joe asked.

'I don't think he knew,' Mike said. 'It just sort of happened. Maybe he was going to dump her out at sea and forge a suicide letter. Perhaps that's why he put her in a cavity, because he would know the forensic stuff, and so some time away would give him the chance to work something out. Then he would just dig out the soil again, and she would be there, under the boards.'

'Except that she wasn't dead.'

Mike shook his head. 'No, she wasn't dead, but we didn't know that then. She hadn't moved for a while, and there was blood everywhere, and so we dug and then we ripped out the planks from the shed. We carried her out and then took off her clothes so there would be nothing from us on her and just, well, we just dropped her into the hole.'

Joe leant forward and spoke with his voice low. 'So what happened next?'

Mike put his hand over his mouth and sucked in air. He thought he was going to be sick, his stomach turning over fast.

'I heard the banging,' he said. 'It started off light at first, and I thought it was the soil landing on the planks, or maybe it was my pulse – but it got louder.' He had to take a few short breaths and he licked his lips. 'I realised then that she was alive and I wanted to get her out of there, but Claude said that it was too late to go back, that it would be attempted murder and my life would be over anyway, that we would go to prison together, that we had to keep going.' He shook his head, his eyes filled with disbelief. 'We filled that hole and I walked away, so that she would die down there.'

Joe and Alan exchanged glances, both quietened for a moment, before they turned back to Mike as he started to talk again.

'I thought I could still hear the knocks coming from under the soil when I walked out of the garden,' Mike said, his words coming out in a rush, the tears pouring faster now. 'I left Nancy in there to die because I am a coward. I was too scared to do the right thing when Claude hit her, because I was too scared to face Mary, because I didn't want to hurt her if she didn't need to know. And then when I knew Nancy was still alive I became scared for myself, that I would go to prison for the rest of my life. I was naive and cowardly and frightened, thinking that I could go back to my life. But you know what? I couldn't. The knocking stayed with me, that fucking bang-bang-bang, because all the time I could imagine Nancy underground, frightened, panicking, clawing at the wood, carrying my baby, the child I knew I would never have with Mary . . . because, you know, you have to actually get close to have a chance.'

'Some might say that's very convenient for you,' Joe said.

Mike looked surprised and wiped the wetness from his cheeks. 'It doesn't feel convenient,' he said. 'What do you mean?'

'You're a suspect in Hazel's case, and so you know we'll take your DNA. You don't know what evidence we have in Nancy's case, and so you give us an account that blames someone else. But there are problems with your story.'

'It's not a story.'

'The first problem is that Nancy Gilbert's child wasn't yours,' Joe said.

Mike jolted in his chair and he gripped the edge of the table.

'Do you think we hadn't considered a jealous rage, the possibility that she was carrying someone else's child?' Joe said. 'Checks were done, and it was Claude's child.'

The detective's voice seemed to swirl around Mike, as if he was talking from another room, all faint echoes.

'But she told me it was mine,' Mike said, almost to himself.

'She got it wrong then, because it wasn't. Maybe her and Claude got on better than you thought. If you killed her to stop Mary finding out about your child, then you made a mistake. It was Claude's baby.'

Mike shook his head, his eyes scared now. 'No, this isn't right. Nancy told me, she was sure.'

'And there's something else too,' Joe said. When Mike looked at him, confused now, Joe bent down for something that he had stored under the table. It was a large brown paper bag; when Joe put it on the table, it made a loud clunking noise.

Mike looked at the bag, and then back at the detective. 'What's in there?'

Joe reached in and pulled out another bag, this time clear plastic, sealed with a red tie. Joe held it up. Mike could see red smears on the inside of the bag, and there looked to be a piece of metal, heavy and long, with a bandage wrapped around one end.

Mike had seen it before, twenty-two years earlier. His lip started to quiver. What was going on? He didn't understand.

'We found this in your garage,' Joe said.

Mike tried to say something but then he realised that he didn't know what to say.

'It was wrapped up in a towel, covered in blood,' Joe continued. 'Fresh blood. Hazel's, we reckon.'

Mike's hands became clammy.

'Do you want that lawyer now?'

Mike nodded, and then the room seemed to fade out as he slithered slowly to the floor.

Chapter Sixty-Two

The clock had crept just past midnight by the time I got the call from Claude. I was directed to a shale car park fringed by blackberry bushes, next to the canal that runs through Blackley. It was the site of an old textile factory, but was now an employees' car park for a nearby firm of solicitors, one of the new accident-claim factories. It was quiet as I stepped out of the Triumph. I zipped up my jacket to my neck and thrust my hands in my pockets. The only other car there was an old blue Nissan with misted windows, and the slight rock of the suspension told me that it wouldn't pay to walk over that way.

The canal was once a vital trade link, when the cotton came in from Liverpool and was transformed into cloth, the waterway clogged with coal-powered barges and the air heavy with smoke and noise. The canals fell as silent as the mills when the textile trade died, and now just tourist barges patrol them on walking-pace tours of Lancashire, the waterway running through the town via a series of locks and aque-ducts high above the valley floor, the views over Blackley making it a popular overnight mooring spot.

As I looked over at the town, I saw that the full moon was being taken over by clouds, but there was still enough gleam to turn the slate roofs silver and render the disused mill chimneys in silhouette; the skyline of lost industry was replaced by the new Blackley as the crumbling brick fingers were interspersed by sparkling new minarets, the call to prayer taking over from the din of machinery. The circular swirls of orange streetlights marked out the new estates and cul-de-sacs that had sprung up, so different to the regular up and downs of the nearby terraced streets, the traditional mill housing.

I looked both ways when I reached the towpath. Claude's directions had been simple: go onto the path and turn right, but I wanted to check both ways to make sure that there would be no nasty surprises behind me. There was no one there, just the long black ribbon of the canal that curved out of sight a few hundred yards away. No cigarette glow or shifting shadows.

My feet clicked on the cobbled towpath as I started walking. Narrow stone bridges crossed the water every fifty yards or so, making the path curve around the supports and creating patches of dense blackness on my route. Straggly bushes filled the banks and encroached onto the path, and the cobbles were slippery with moss. I could hear the occasional siren in the distance, sometimes the whine of a small car being driven too fast, and there was the pop-pop of a motorbike nearby, but my ears were mainly filled with the sound of my footsteps and the occasional lap of the water against the canal sides.

I thought about turning back. Claude wanted to stage-manage his homecoming, I understood that, and it was good for the story, but he was being too secretive. The flutters in my chest and the way the hairs on my arms prickled against my jacket told me that something wasn't right, but I knew I had to bring him out that night. Harry was going with the story in the morning, and it was too late to turn back. And where was Susie? I'd tried calling her, but all I got was an automated voice telling me that the number was unavailable.

The shadows in the bushes seemed to move as I walked, the soft rustle of the leaves in the breeze making me even more nervous. I tried to peer through them, to see behind them, looking for a threat, maybe the moonlight catching the glint of someone's eyes, but there was nothing. A bridge got closer and I realised that there would be a few yards where I wouldn't be able to see anything at all. I slowed down to listen out, but there was nothing. I ducked down to get under the bridge and felt moisture drip onto my neck from the cold stones. There was little but the black outline of the canal edge to warn me where the path ended and the water began.

I stopped for a moment and looked around. All I could see ahead was darkness as the path got further from the bright lights of Blackley. I couldn't go too much further. The towpath disappeared into the shadows of a wharf building a hundred yards ahead, the wooden canopy stretching across the canal. It had once protected the cotton from the elements as it was loaded and unloaded on huge winches, but now it just created an impenetrable blackness as the path curved round to a series of locks, the huge wooden gates taking the water lower down as the canal headed west.

There was a thrash of branches, and I jumped and gasped, but then a bird sailed over the canal and went towards a five-storey derelict mill on the other side of the canal. I took some deep breaths and then watched as a bat darted across the canal, swooping and then turning. Brambles trailed against my trousers as I set off again.

My phone rang, its electronic chirrup suddenly deafening. I looked at the number and recognised it as Claude's.

'Where the fuck are you?' I asked, my voice low and angry. I was getting tired of the games. 'I'm on the canal path, like you said.'

'Can you see the wharf ahead?' he said.

'Of course I can. Stop playing games.'

'Jack, I've got to take precautions.'

'Where are you?'

'Trust me, Jack,' he replied. 'People know what you are doing. I'm not coming out until I can be sure that no one is following you. I'm protecting you, Jack. And me.'

I looked back and saw just an empty towpath.

'There's no one here,' I said.

'Go into the wharf and wait for me there,' he said, and then his phone switched off.

I sighed and walked onward.

Mike Dobson didn't react when the door to the consultation room opened. A few hours had passed since the last interview, because the doctor had been called to make sure that he was fit to continue.

He had been taken there to wait for his solicitor, but he had spent the time with his hands clamped over his ears, trying to silence the thumping in his head.

'Mr Dobson?'

The voice seemed faint. He looked up. He expected it to be Roach again – he had been waiting outside the interview room – but there was someone else in front of him. A young man in T-shirt and jeans with bleached tips in his hair.

'I'm your legal representative,' he said. 'Craig Selby.'

Mike squinted, tried to focus on him, but it was as if they were in separate rooms; his voice was distant, his movements sluggish, the colours washed out.

'You look surprised, Mr Dobson,' the rep said, and looked

down at himself. 'It's my turn on the night rota. We don't sit in our suits, waiting for the call. I was in bed, and so this was the best I could do. If you want, I'll go home and put on a suit.'

Mike shook his head and held up his hand. 'I'm sorry. I've never been in this situation before.'

'Yes, we need to talk about that,' he said.

Mike sat back and looked at Selby, trying to focus. He took a few deep breaths, narrowed his eyes. The sounds of the room started to rush back in: Selby's breathing, the tap of his pen against the folder he held in one hand.

'I didn't kill her,' Mike said. 'The girl last night, I mean.'

'Hazel?'

Mike nodded. 'She was alive when I left her.'

Selby sat down on the opposite side of the table. 'The police haven't told me much, so right now, stay quiet.'

'But I want to tell you,' Mike said.

Selby shook his head. 'No, you don't. Stay quiet for now. All they've told me is that they've found the murder weapon in your garage.'

'It's a metal pipe,' Mike said.

'Was it in your garage?'

'So they said.'

'It sounds like you're in some deep shit, Mr Dobson, and so trust me on this. We'll work out what to say once we know everything else. That will all come out during the interviews.'

'I don't like this,' Mike said.

'It's not about you liking it. It's about getting you through it.'

'But I thought I had to tell you what happened and you advised me,' Mike said. 'We don't sit around and plan lies.'

Selby threw his folder onto the table. 'You've been arrested

377

for murder, Mr Dobson. This is the real world now, not some fantasy ethical world where everyone follows the rules. You're talking about the rest of your life in a prison cell. If you want that, fine, you go in there and tell them your story, how you were with the dead girl, how that metal pipe was in your garage, and how it's all some almighty coincidence. Go in there and be as lucid as you want and then, when you're looking through the bars of your cell every day until you die, pat yourself on the back and say what a good boy you've been.'

'I just want to tell the truth,' Mike said, perplexed.

'You aren't thinking straight.'

'I'm fine.'

'No, you're not,' Selby said, banging his fist on the table. 'We'll get a doctor to say that, don't worry. And we'll get those interviews excluded so that the jury will never hear them.'

Mike shook his head. 'I'm not hiding any more.'

'It's not about hiding.'

'What is your job?' Mike asked.

The rep looked surprised. 'To advise you, of course.'

'And I can choose not to follow the advice?'

Selby faltered, and then said, 'Yes, I suppose so.'

Mike nodded. 'You don't have to stay.'

'I want to stay.'

'Why?'

'Because it's a murder,' Selby said, 'and you don't walk away from a murder.'

Mike snorted a laugh. 'The pay cheque's bigger, I suppose.' When Selby didn't respond, Mike said, 'So let me tell my story. I'm not running any more.'

Chapter Sixty-Three

I was plunged into darkness as I progressed further into the shadow of the wharf. I could still see the canal stretching ahead, the arms of the locks visible against the metallic sheen of the water, but all else was in blackness and I had to edge forward, my hands outstretched. I heard a fluttering sound, and looked up to see a pigeon in one of the vertical shafts in the sloping canopy, a large metal pulley wheel overhead. My hands found the wall and I started to feel my way along, the large stone blocks rough on my hands. I winced as my fingers found the edge of a broken window.

I sucked on my fingers and tasted blood. I cursed Claude Gilbert and wrapped a handkerchief around the cut before inching forward again. I kicked a beer can, the clatter making me jump, and then used my feet to tap against the wall, looking for a way in. I hit only stone for a few steps, and then the sound changed to a thud that echoed – wood. I had found a door. I stepped forward and gave it a push, but it didn't give. I ran my hands over it, feeling for the point at which it changed to stone again. Instead, I felt it begin to lean inwards. My fingers reached the edge of the door and found that there was a gap between it and the door frame.

I pushed at the wood and inserted my foot into the gap, working to widen it until I was able to squeeze my body through. Once inside, my way forward was illuminated by the glow of the moon through the windows on the other side of the building, though the light served to create more shadows, highlighting more potential threats. I could see the outline of graffiti on the walls and, walking forward, I stumbled on discarded bricks and was almost tripped to the floor by some metal brackets still attached to the ground. Remnants of cables hung from the ceiling like Spanish moss and pieces of broken glass blinked the light back at me as I made my way carefully along.

I reached for my phone and held it out, so that the screen cast some light on the way ahead. There were holes in the concrete in places, where pipes had been ripped up, and it looked like I was one wrong step from a broken ankle.

'Claude?' I shouted, but the word just echoed around the empty space.

I stopped, frustrated. I tried calling him again, but his phone was switched off now. I muttered expletives to myself and again used the light from the screen to help me find my way around.

It took me five minutes to thread my way through, weaving past the huge iron pillars that held up the building. I had to duck to avoid the cogs of some old black machinery bolted to an oak beam that ran across the room, all the time moving towards the silver halo of an open door ahead. I fell to my knees twice; by the time I reached the other side of the building, I was bleeding from a cut to my hand and my right knee was grazed. Then I was outside again, looking out over Blackley once more, and still no sign of Claude.

I sat down. All I could do was wait.

Chapter Sixty-Four

Laura climbed out of bed when she heard the knocking. She checked the clock. Just past one. When she had gone to bed, she had hoped that the next voice she would hear would be the inane chatter of the radio DJ when her alarm sounded.

She peered out of her curtains. There was a Mini there, racing green, and a man at her front door. She didn't recognise him, but she could only see the top of a hat and long hair streaming from it, unkempt and grey.

She looked down at her clothes – loose-fitting pyjamas – and got changed quickly, throwing on some jeans and an old sweatshirt. She didn't know who was there, but it must be urgent if it was this late.

When Laura got downstairs, she shouted through the door, 'Who is it?'

'I'm looking for Jack,' came the reply from the other side of the door. The voice was deep, with a hint of public school in the accent.

Laura looked at the door, unsure what to do. 'Who are you?' she asked.

'I just need to see Jack,' came the voice again.

She opened the door slowly and was faced with a man, scruffy, wearing a long overcoat and a wide-brimmed hat, with flushed cheeks above a grey beard. His hands and coat looked dirty.

'I'm supposed to meet Jack Garrett here,' he said.

'Who are you?'

He smiled. 'Claude Gilbert. I think Jack has been talking about me.'

Laura's hand shot to her mouth. Her mind raced with the descriptions of Claude Gilbert she remembered from the headlines and tried to match it with the person in front of her.

'You're really Claude?'

He looked around, as if someone might be listening, and then he leant forward and raised his finger to his lips. 'Quiet please,' he said, and winked. 'Not everyone knows.'

Laura opened her door. As he walked in, stale whisky drifted past her nose.

'But he's gone to meet you,' she said, closing the door behind him.

He looked surprised. 'He must have got mixed up. I called him back and left him a message, told him that I would come here.'

'Why the change of plan?' Laura asked.

'There were some people there,' he said. 'I became scared. I'm sorry.'

Laura looked towards the stairs and thought of Bobby, unsure what to do. Claude Gilbert was in her house. Jack was out there looking for him, the figure in his big story. But he was a fugitive, a wanted murderer. She couldn't let him walk out.

What would Jack say though? She would ruin his big day, the press conference arranged for the morning.

She closed her eyes for a moment to offer a silent apology to Jack, and then said, 'I can't let you do this.'

'Do what?'

'Be here, in my house,' she said. 'Did Jack tell you what I do for a living?'

Claude sat down on a chair, and groaned as he relaxed. 'He didn't need to. I worked it out.'

She stepped forward. 'I'm sorry, Claude, but it's over.'

'And you're not prepared to wait for the big exclusive?'

Laura shook her head. 'You know what they say, never off duty. I'm going to have to arrest you for the murder of your wife.' She gripped his wrist and reached into her pocket for her phone. 'You have the right to remain silent . . .'

There was a quick movement from Claude and Laura gasped in pain as something hot was sprayed in her face. She stepped away and rubbed her eyes but that made it worse; her eyes were burning, and she stepped away, stumbling slightly.

Then something hit her on the side of the head and she headed towards the floor.

Chapter Sixty-Five

I tried to be as quiet as I could when I went in. I had waited for Claude until it was obvious he wasn't going to show up, and now it was nearly two o'clock and I wasn't in the mood for an argument about noise.

I was surprised to find the door unlocked. I thought I had secured it when I left, but nothing looked untoward as I went inside, although something in the air made my nose itch and my eyes smart.

I sat down with a slump and rubbed my face with my hands. Claude wasn't there, and he wasn't answering his phone. Neither was Susie. The front pages would be filled with my story on Claude, but now there was no Claude. It was too late to do anything about that, and all I could do now was pray that Claude would call me again.

I thought back to when I was in Claude's apartment, when one call would have brought the police running. Instead I got greedy, thought of the bigger payday when I should have thought of the story.

I looked at the ceiling and thought of the warm bed, Laura in there, but I didn't want to go upstairs and wake her, which is what would happen if my phone rang.

I lay back on the sofa and pulled my coat over my body,

my phone next to my head. It was going to be a long night.

Laura was squeezed into the back seat of Claude's Mini, her hands tied behind her back, rope binding her ankles together. The car was old, she could tell that from the vinyl seats and the fusty smell of cigarettes. The fumes from the exhaust seemed to filter into the car, and Claude was driving too fast, every bump in the road jarring her back. It was starting to rain and one of the wiper blades didn't work, so that Claude had to lean forward to get a good view.

She struggled against the ropes, but they were fastened tight, and he had clicked the seatbelt shut. She couldn't get her hands free to undo it.

Laura looked at her lap and concentrated. She had to stay calm. Bobby was on his own in the house. She needed to get back. But it was hard to stay focused with the pain in her cheek from Claude's punch. And her eyes were still smarting from whatever he had sprayed into her eyes. Her face was swelling and her vision was blurred.

Why had it happened? Laura couldn't work it out. And where was Jack? He had gone to the meet. Had something gone wrong there?

Laura looked at Claude in the rearview mirror, and then kicked out at the seat in front, her bound feet having little impact. 'What the fuck are you doing, Claude?' she said. 'You were going to be arrested tomorrow anyway. Dobson is under arrest. He killed that girl last night. It's all working out for you. Why are you doing this?'

'Things have changed,' he said.

'Like what?'

He didn't say anything, and so Laura kicked out at the seat again, angry, frustrated.

'Take me back,' she shouted. She was about to blurt out that she had a son in the house on his own, but then she realised that it might make him go back – but for the wrong reasons. Every mile they drove took them further from Bobby; he was safer that way.

Claude didn't answer and remained silent for a few more miles. Laura tried to get a sense of where they were going, but she was still new to the North and so her knowledge of the area wasn't that good, although she could see that they were heading for the countryside, not the town.

'Where are we going?' she said.

Claude looked at the mirror. 'You do ask a lot of questions.'

'I'm a police officer,' she said. 'That's what I do.'

'Bully for you.'

Laura looked out of the window again and tried to stay calm. She had to work out how to get away from him.

'To meet Susie,' he said eventually. When Laura looked back at him, he said, 'That's where we're going,' and then he reached into his jacket and produced a whisky flask. He raised it to his mouth and then offered it to Laura. There was dirt jammed under his fingernails.

'Do you think you should, when you're driving?'

'Do you think I'm bothered about drink driving tonight?'

'It might make your arrest come around sooner than you'd want,' she said.

He raised the flask in salute and took a drink. 'You better hope for that then.'

'Why? How much worse is it going to get?'

He chuckled to himself. 'Aren't surprises better if they stay that way?'

Laura turned away and tried to get her bearings as they travelled. She had to find her way out of this and to do that she needed to summon help. They had headed out of Turners Fold on one of the back roads that ran behind a golf course, and now they were snaking over one of the hills on an unlit road that would eventually take them into the Ribble Valley, a vast area of rolling green fields and old stone hamlets.

'Where's Susie?' Laura asked.

'Where I'm taking you,' Claude said.

Laura felt a wave of anger. 'Stop fucking around now, Claude,' she said. 'If you're going to run again, just do it, but you've no need to take me with you.'

Claude glanced at her in the mirror. 'It's not about running.'

'What is it about?'

He gripped the wheel and leant forward so that he could see out of the windscreen properly, his concentration on the road, until eventually he said, 'I've been betrayed.'

'By whom?'

'You know by whom,' he said. 'Your Jack, your precious little Jack.'

Laura was confused. 'I don't understand. He did what you wanted.'

Claude laughed, filled with bitterness. 'Did he? What, precisely, did I ask him to do?'

'Write your story, and point the finger towards Mike Dobson.'

'Yes, write the story,' Claude said, and he banged the steering wheel with his hand. 'So why the fuck did he go after Alan Lake?'

'Because he is a good journalist, and so he follows the story.'

'How very noble of him,' Claude said sarcastically. 'But now Dobson is talking, it is royally fucked up, thanks to your boyfriend.'

'I don't understand.'

'Follow the trail,' he said, spitting out the words. 'Roach got Dobson to talk, and it only happened in one of two ways: either you told Roach all about me, or else your Jack got Lake wound up so much that he sent Roach in there, ordered Dobson to spill the beans. Either way, it all comes back to your boyfriend and his fucking big mouth.'

'What do you mean?' Laura said. 'I didn't say anything to Roach about you.'

'*Someone* told him, and there is only Jack and you in the fucking loop, and so it's all gone wrong.'

'But why does Dobson talking affect things?' Laura said. 'If you're innocent, come forward and prove it.'

He pulled into a short dirt track that threw Laura around in her seat. Long grass brushed noisily against the under-side of the car. When Claude came to a halt, Laura saw that they were parked in front of a farm gate.

He stayed in his seat and stared out of the window. 'Sometimes you expect people to protect themselves, but they don't, and it makes me angry.'

'Why? What do you mean?'

Claude turned round to her, his teeth gritted, dirty yellow through his beard. 'Second chances,' he said, his voice angry. 'We all deserve them, no matter what we've done.' He wiped his eyes and tracked dirt across his cheek. 'We do things we regret, in the heat of the moment, and then you get to a point where you can't change things. It's the rat instinct, which is what we are, deep down. We come out fighting when we're cornered, and when the fighting's done, when the danger's gone, you're left with nothing, and so you keep on running, to make sure you don't get cornered again.'

'Who have you been fighting, Claude?'

Claude seemed to slump for a moment. 'Just me,' he said.

'I've spent my whole life fighting myself, my jungle instincts. Then you get a second chance, but your past is always there. You can't reinvent it.'

'So this is it now, it's just about revenge? Taking me, hurting me, just to strike back at Jack, because you blame him for your scheme going wrong?'

'Makes me sound cheap, doesn't it?' he said, and then he climbed out of the car and opened the gate, before he reached back into the car and grabbed Laura's hair. 'We walk from here,' he said, and he dragged her out of the passenger door.

Laura yelped in pain and then fell in a heap as she landed outside, her face into the damp grass. It was cold and she was already shivering as she tried to pull herself to her knees.

He pulled out a knife from his pocket. Laura tried to shuffle away, but he grabbed the rope around her ankles and dragged her along the floor towards him. Laura felt small stones scrape her back and then she saw the flash of the blade.

She screamed out, waiting for the pain, but then she felt her ankles break apart and she realised that he had cut the rope that bound them.

'Don't say that I'm not a gentleman,' he said, and reached for her elbow to help her to her feet.

Laura looked around once she was standing, to work out where they were. The moon blinked through the clouds and threw silver dust over the fields. In the distance she could see the twinkle of water. The air was fresh across her cheeks and she blinked a few times as the breeze cooled her stinging eyes. Spots of rain hit her on the forehead.

'We're going that way,' he said, pointing towards the water ahead. He grabbed her arm and began to push her forward.

'You don't have to do this,' Laura said.

'I don't like being wronged,' Claude said, his smile visible in the darkness. Laura could smell whisky and cigarettes.

'I haven't wronged you,' she pointed out.

'So you say,' he said. 'But if it wasn't you, it must be Jack's fault. All he had to do was raise some doubts, but no, he's a real crusader, isn't he? A real champ.' He stopped and pulled her round, so that she stood in front of him. 'It was a blip, one mistake. Thirty years of a good life, and then Nancy, bang. Everything gone, just like that,' and he clicked his fingers. 'This was the chance to get it back, some of the good life. Maybe another thirty years. Not any more.'

'But you could just leave,' she said. 'I don't understand. Why risk being caught just to hurt Jack?'

'Because they'll be too busy looking for you to go after me, even when my face is on the front pages.'

He set off walking again, pushing Laura ahead of him.

Laura thought fast, tried to work out how she could get away. What did he mean, look for her? She could walk to the nearest village in half an hour, she reckoned, so there would be no search. She would be home before Bobby woke. He might never know.

He meant that something else was going to happen.

She looked round, trying to see where she could run to, but she felt his grip tighten on her arm and then the cold steel of the knife against her back.

They ended up by a bend in the river, the water rippling over stones, no lights visible as far as the eye could see, the surface dappled by raindrops. There was an old tree root in front of her, and the ground dropped away on the other side.

'I can't go down there,' she said, looking down. 'I'll need my hands to support me.'

'No need,' Claude said, and he shoved her hard from behind.

Laura fell, and it felt like slow motion. It was a drop of only a few feet, but she couldn't put her arms out to break the fall, and so all she could do was twist her body and wait for the impact. Her shoulder took the blow and she cried out as a jarring pain shot down her side. Laura stayed down, wheezing with pain, cold shingle against her cheek. When she opened her eyes, she could see the sheen of the river beside her, bubbling gently, broken only by the gentle patter of the rain.

She heard something and she twisted her head to see Claude clambering over the tree root. Laura knew she didn't have long and so she quickly twisted onto her side and hoisted her knees to her chest. She threw her hands down her back and then strained as she tried to fit her arms around her hips. She didn't think she would be able to manage it but, with one last desperate effort, her hips popped free and her hands were in the crook of her knees.

Claude jumped down onto the shingle next to her, but she carried on. She was curled in a ball now, and he would have to carry her or untie the rope to make her secure once more. Laura expected a blow, a kick maybe, but he just watched her, taking sips from the hip flask, as if he was enjoying the struggle.

She pulled her knees as far up as they would go and then dragged her hands downwards, hoping to work them around her ankles. Laura could feel the curve of her spine ache with the pressure, as if it were ready to pop out; she imagined being stuck like that, and the thought made her strain one last time, screeching with effort. Then her wrists were in front of her, her muscles throbbing with the effort.

Claude put his flask away and started to clap. 'Well done,' he said, grinning, and then he reached down and grabbed her arm before pulling her back to her feet, the knife jammed against her neck, just under her ear. He turned her round so that Laura was looking along the river, facing a shadow further down the bank. Laura could see the rough edges of stone cast in shadow.

'Susie's in there,' he said.

'Don't take me there,' Laura said, and she pulled against him. 'Just go, Claude. We're miles from anywhere. I'm tied up, for Christ's sake. You could be wherever you need to be before I get to the nearest town.'

'But you've seen me.'

'So has Susie,' she said. 'Is she going with you?'

He shook his head. 'I had a free life before she came along. I was poor, but no one knew where I was. So no, she is not coming with me.'

Before she could say anything else, he pushed her forward so that she almost stumbled on the river bank. 'Go to it,' he snarled.

She looked up and the knife went to her neck again. Laura thought it best to do as he said. She didn't know what lay ahead, or even what was behind this, but if she swung at him and missed, she might find it too hard to defend herself against his knife.

As they got to the shelter, Laura saw that there was soil piled up near the entrance, the outline detectable in the moonlight. She tried to peer into the interior, but it was too dark, only faint shadows visible.

'Where's Susie?' Laura said, suddenly stopping.

'You'll see soon enough.'

'What have you done with her?'

'The same as I'm doing with you,' Claude said, and then he gave Laura a sharp jab in the back to propel her forward, and she stumbled onto the soil as it rose up.

Then it came to her. The soil, the darkness, no sign of Susie.

Laura turned and got to her knees, to try and move away, get out of the shelter, but she felt a push in her chest. She tumbled backwards over the soft soil, tried to put her arms out to balance herself, but her hands were tied together, so when she felt the ground fall away, she had no choice but to fall with it.

Laura braced herself, waited for the floor, cold soil against her back, but it wasn't there – she kept on falling, a few feet more than she was expecting. Her shoulder took the brunt once more.

Her fall was broken by something soft, but the breath was still punched out of her. She tried to turn over, but her ribs sent jabs of pain through her body. Then she heard movement above her, dragging and grunting. Laura looked up. She could see the edge of what looked like a hole, and above that the moonlight.

Laura tried to roll over to scramble to her knees, but then she heard Claude give a final groan of effort. As she looked up, the moonlight disappeared as something moved across its path. She screamed and something hit her. It was heavy and it slammed down, hit her head hard, knocked her onto her back and then stopped inches above her face, as if it had caught on a ledge. Laura hit out at it. It was a sheet of metal, riveted along a joint in the middle, and it pinned her to the ground. There was more noise from above, like rocks clanging loudly, and then she heard Claude shout, 'Jack didn't have to go that far.'

'Let me out!' she screamed.

'He went too far,' he shouted again. 'He only had to raise the doubt.'

Laura kicked out again, but heard only more bangs in response, like rocks and dirt landing on the metal. She tried to push against it with her bound hands but it was too heavy.

Her head was filled with the noises above, the thuds becoming fainter with each second.

She tried to assess the situation, her heart racing, her mind trying to process what was happening. But it was all going too quickly.

She was on her back, a metal sheet just inches from her nose. It was pitch black, so that she had no sense of the space she was in, except that she couldn't sit up. She felt the panic rise and tried to move herself along, to see where she could go, but her feet hit something – the edge of the hole she thought. She squirmed the other way and her head hit dirt. Six inches spare at either end. There were still noises above, but they were soft and muffled.

Laura closed her eyes. Stay calm, she told herself. She had to work her way out of this. But the terror was surging through her, the confined space, the darkness; her chest was tight, her throat constricted. She wanted to kick and thrash, as if that would somehow get her out, but she fought the impulse, taking deep breaths and letting them out slowly. She had to stay in control.

Laura reached to one side and her bound hands crept slowly across the dirt, fingers feeling in the soil until they hit something soft. It was fabric and, running her hands along it, she could feel that the cloth was coarse. As Laura felt higher, she found a loop, and then she yelped as she felt flesh, cold and soft. She realised that the loop was for a belt. Laura swallowed hard and took some deep breaths. She remembered her landing; something broke her fall. Now she knew why. Someone was in there with her.

She tried to move away but didn't have the room. She counted to ten, tried to calm down, and then she reached out again. She felt the stomach, and then she ran her hand further up. It was a woman, Laura could tell from the rise and fall of her contours, and then her fingers felt the tangle of hair.

Laura knew straight away. It was brittle, like Susie's dyed blonde hair. She moved the hair away and felt something sticky. Blood was her guess. Susie's cheeks were cold, and Laura strained to lift her hands to Susie's mouth to try and feel the warm whisper of her breath. There was nothing.

Laura screamed, the noise loud in her ears, echoing back off the metal lid; but she knew that no one above could hear her. Claude had dug a hole for her and now he had gone on the run. But she screamed just the same, screeching as loud as she could until her throat hurt.

And when she stopped and gasped for breath, she realised that all was silent. No one would ever hear her.

Chapter Sixty-Six

I was jolted awake by the ringing of my phone, loud in my ear. I scrambled around for it, knocking it onto the floor at first, and finally answered in a tired mumble.

'Hello?'

'It's Tony.'

I looked at the clock. It was later than I thought. Nearly eight o'clock. I squinted at the daylight. Rain speckled the windows. So that was the summer. As always, over before the solstice.

'What can I do for you?' I asked.

'I'm just calling to congratulate on the front page,' he said. 'It's good stuff, Jack, with your byline nice and large. You're going to be in demand for a while. This could be award time, finding Claude Gilbert.'

I didn't speak at first. I thought about Claude, I had found him and lost him. And then I thought about Harry. I had let him down.

'Jack?'

'Huh? Sorry, Tony, I'm just tired, that's all.'

'That's okay,' he said, and then, 'but you didn't use any of my stuff.'

'What stuff?'

'The papers I brought round the other night. There was

some good material in there. Perhaps they're saving it for a follow-up?'

I sighed and rubbed my face. 'I'm sorry, Tony. I owe you an apology. Someone went through my papers that night, and we had a police officer on the sofa. Your papers went. I wrote the story from memory.'

'What do you mean, *went*?'

'Just that. The police were here, trying to find out what I knew, getting heavy, but then I went to a murder scene. One of the detectives stayed behind, and the next morning, your papers were gone.'

'The police didn't take your papers,' Tony said.

'Why do you say that?'

'Because Alan Lake would be in custody – and Chief Inspector Roach.'

That woke me up. 'It's too early for puzzles. What do you mean?'

'Did you read what I left?'

'I'm sorry, Tony, but I didn't get round to it.'

'That's a shame,' Tony said. 'I can get it again, if you need it. It will make for a good follow-up.'

'You're being cryptic,' I said. 'What do you mean about Alan Lake and Paul Roach?'

Tony chuckled. 'They were more than just Claude's last client and the cop who dug up Nancy. They were also Claude's landlords.'

Tony's words weren't registering. 'What do you mean?'

'The address on Lower Belgrave Street, where Claude lived, as Josif Petrovic,' he said. 'Alan Lake and Roach own it. Or at least their company does. Northern Works Limited. I wanted to know how Claude could rent somewhere and stay hidden, and so I made some enquiries at the Land Registry, and then at Companies House, like I told you. I called the company secretary, Lake's accountant, told him that I was interested in buying it. He told me that the flat wasn't for sale, that Lake used it as his London crash pad whenever he needed to go down to the capital. He paid rent to the company and then set it off against his personal tax bill. But he never paid enough on it to make it profitable, and so his company didn't pay corporation tax. All the time, the flat increased in value, part-funded by the taxman.'

'Except that Claude was living there,' I said.

'It seems that way,' Tony said. 'I don't know what Claude has on Lake or Roach to make them help him out, but it must be something good, because there's nothing in it for Lake. Even less for Roach. It's career-ending for him.'

I blew out. 'Wow, that is good stuff. Now I know why Lake was getting twitchy.'

I thanked him for the information, and then headed upstairs to wake Laura. It was getting near school time, and I thought she would have been up by now.

I walked into the bedroom and stopped. Laura wasn't there. I remembered the unlocked front door. Where was she?

I heard a noise behind me and turned to see Bobby, his hair ruffled, coming out of his bedroom.

He looked up at me as I stared at him. Something was wrong. Laura would never leave Bobby alone in the house. Not ever.

He must have sensed my thoughts, because he began to look frightened. I went to my knees to reassure him.

'It's okay,' I said. 'We need to go out quickly, Bobby. We're in a rush.'

He looked at me as if he didn't believe me. I took him back into his room to get him ready, the routine stuff, so that he wouldn't guess what was going on. Once he was dressed, I took him outside.

My stomach took a jolt when I saw that Laura's car was still there. And I saw something else. A Vespa, pulled onto its stand. Frankie was sitting on it, his coat pulled over his head to shelter him from the rain, his feet pulled up onto the footboards.

'Bobby, get in the car,' I said. Once he was in there, I walked across to Frankie. 'What the hell are you doing here?'

He pulled his coat down. 'I like watching Laura,' he said, an arrogant smirk on his face. 'She's pretty.'

'Don't push me,' I said, teeth gritted. 'I am really not in the fucking mood.'

He sat upright on the scooter and pulled on the crash helmet, grinning as he fastened the strap. 'I saw her,' he said.

'What do you mean?'

'I saw her last night.'

'Who, Laura?'

'Not just Laura. She was with someone else. An old man.'

A chill rippled through my body. An old man. Claude? Had he been here, with Laura?

'He took her to his car.'

'What do you mean, *took her*?' I said, and gripped his arm.

'I followed them,' Frankie continued, his cheeks flushing slightly, pulling his arm out of my grip. 'I was here, you see, hoping for another picture. The police took my others, and Laura is special. I like her. I wanted some more, but you've started closing your curtains.'

I remembered the flash from the night before.

'You give me what's mine, and I'll tell you more,' he said. 'But not before,' and then he pressed down hard on the kick-start pedal. 'I've seen him before,' he shouted over the engine noise.

I coughed as I was shrouded in two-stroke fumes, and then Frankie clunked his Vespa into first gear before setting off, his tyres sluicing through the water gathering in the road.

I was left alone, rain wetting my clothes, Bobby watching me from the car.

Susie moved. It was a twitch, like a kick of the leg. Her foot banged on the metal sheet. Laura took some deep breaths.

The cold had been tough, and her bare feet were numb. She thought about Bobby. Had Claude gone back for him?

No, don't think about that, she told herself.

Then Susie moved once more.

Laura knew that she was dead; she had heard about this from mortuary assistants, spasms after death, something to do with rigor mortis and the contraction of the muscles. She did her best not to think about the dead body next to her.

Then she heard a light buzz. She thought about that. Susie might have been dead for a couple of hours before she was thrown in here, maybe more, so that Claude would have time to dig the hole. So Susie had been left out in the open, dead, blood on her head. Enough time for the flies to land. And the spasm must have disturbed them.

She blew at the buzzing to get the fly away, but its drone was loud under the metal. Then she heard another.

Laura knew how it would happen. The flies land and lay their eggs. The maggots come out. They turn into flies, and the cycle gets repeated over and over. They will burrow into the body, feed on Susie, break her down into flesh and mush.

Laura gagged, tried to turn over so that she wouldn't choke on her vomit, but her shoulders jammed against the metal. Her mouth filled with the acid taste. How long would it take? Would it happen to Susie as she lay next to her?

She kept her eyes shut, it was the only way she could pretend that she wasn't trapped. She had to remain still, not think about where she was. If she thought about it, she would thrash again, her hands and legs banging uselessly against the metal, unable to sit up or move sideways. That would use up oxygen. There was blood on her toes from where she had kicked out.

Pretend to be in bed, she told herself. Relax. Lie down. No need to sit up. Then Susie groaned, a long drawn-out moan.

Laura grimaced, tried not to think about it, but she felt drawn to reach out, to touch Susie. Maybe Susie was just unconscious, or in a coma?

Laura's bound hands crawled along the small space between them, straining her shoulder until she felt Susie's cold arm. It felt stiff. She pushed against it in the vain hope that she could wake her, but the arm was rigid, tensed.

Laura turned her face away. Susie was dead, she knew that now. Rigor mortis had set in. Claude wasn't going to come back for Susie. For either of them.

Tears of desperation flashed into Laura's eyes, a sob stuck in her throat, and she wished for death. Make it quick. Then she thought of Bobby and realised that she needed to get out, that she couldn't stand the thought of him growing up without her. How long would the oxygen last? Three days without water was a maximum, she had read that somewhere. How airtight was the hole? She would be dead within three days if no one found her. Less, if the air gave out, but Laura knew the soil above was loose and freshly dug. That would let some air through. But if she was going to die in there, make it quick. Don't let her lie next to Susie as she decomposed, unable to move or get away, surrounded by her own piss and shit.

And why would they find her? Only three people had seen Claude, as far as she knew, and two of them were underground, trapped under a sheet of metal and a covering of soil.

Laura thought about what she knew about Nancy. It had been a week before she had been dug out, and she had died in her hole. Claude hadn't come back for her.

Laura opened her eyes. It was a mistake, she knew that straight away. She couldn't see anything in front of her, just darkness, and she felt the surge of panic again. She fought against it, but it was too hard. It wasn't like physical pain, where she could focus on something else. There was no escape. It affected her mind, directed her instincts and she shuffled downwards, used her heels on the floor, wondering whether she could dig her way out. Her feet hit the dirt wall, and she tried to gouge at it with her toes, unable to move her feet much, but it was tightly compacted. She could try her hands. If she could get her fingers around the edge of the metal, then maybe the soil on top would be looser.

But there wasn't much room for Laura to work her arms above her shoulders, her movement restricted by the fact that her wrists were still bound together. She moved to the edge of the hole and slowly worked her arms upwards, her eyes wide with effort, her teeth bared, soft moans escaping. Her fingers snagged on Susie's top, but there wasn't enough room to pull her hands back, and so she kept on pushing upwards, the cloth around her fingertips, her touch revealing more of Susie's cold ribs, until her hands got higher and the cloth slipped away.

Laura stopped to take a few breaths but they came in gulps, her chest hurting. Panic was her enemy but she was losing the battle. She could hear the quiet buzz of insects around her face, but she hoped that it was just her imagination racing in the darkness. It was too early for anything like that. Don't think about what was happening with Susie. Laura knew she would be either found or dead long before Susie's organs spewed into the hole.

Then she stopped. There was something against her foot, cold and wet. Was it just the temperature, her toes losing sensation – but then she felt it against her leg, creeping upwards like icy fingers.

The water was creeping in. Was it raining outside? As the water crawled along the floor of the hole, like icy claws, Laura realised something else too: it was rising.

She started to scrape at the soil again, panting, desperate.

Chapter Sixty-Seven

I drove into the police station car park too fast, almost clipping a tatty black Vauxhall that had been parked badly. I pulled into the first space I saw and headed quickly for the station entrance. I had no plan, nothing worked out, but I knew that Laura wasn't at home, and Frankie had told me that Claude had been to the cottage.

As I ran along the tarmac path that took me to the station, I saw Joe Kinsella emerge from the large double doors. He headed towards a man who was loitering outside, squinting at the rain that was just starting to get heavier, but then Joe saw me and stopped.

'Jack?' he said, his face concerned. 'I thought today was the big day?'

'Claude has gone walkabout,' I said. 'And Laura isn't at home. I don't know where she is.'

'I haven't seen her this morning,' Joe said.

The man stepped forward. 'Are you Joe Kinsella?'

Joe looked at the man, who was holding something in his hand. A disk. Joe nodded.

'A police officer told me to bring this in yesterday,' the man said, and he held out the disk. 'It shows the Mercedes drop the girl off.'

He had Joe's attention now.

'I checked my computer after the officer left,' the man said. 'It looks like I did leave my camera on.'

'What are you talking about?' Joe said.

The man went into his pocket and pulled out a business card. 'DC McGanity,' he said, 'although she was in uniform.'

'Was this yesterday?' I asked.

He nodded, and then he said, 'It's not what you think. It isn't about the sex or anything. I want you to know that.'

'It doesn't matter to me,' Joe said. 'I've been doing this job long enough not to blush any more.'

'No, no, you don't understand,' he said. 'I was setting up a name and shame website. I was going to post the photographs and videos, only those that showed the cars. Who would go down there if they were going to be caught on camera? Explain that to the wife.'

'It's a dangerous game,' Joe said. 'People don't like their income being affected.'

'But you don't know what it's like living round there,' he said. 'Prostitutes and drug dealers everywhere, syringes dropped into your wheelie bin. Can you imagine what it's like to find a used condom on your doorstep most mornings? I thought that if I drove away the prostitutes, everything else would follow.'

I paced impatiently as Joe looked at the man in front of him.

'So what did your camera catch from the night Hazel was killed?' Joe asked.

The man held out the disk again, and Joe took it this time. 'Like she said, I put it onto a DVD. The gold Mercedes comes in at around ten o'clock. I've included the hour before and the hour after, just in case it's important.'

Joe looked at the disk. 'Thank you,' he said. 'What's your name?'

'Kev Smith,' he said. 'I know I want prostitutes away from my house, but I wouldn't want them to be hurt. And I don't want to get in trouble. I'm sorry.'

'Thanks, Kev, I'll take a look at this. Keep the original footage. Someone will be around for it later.'

Kev looked pleased at that, but Joe didn't have time for a long goodbye; he rushed into the station holding the disk, the door slamming back against the wall as he flung it open. I kept close at his shoulder.

'Something has gone wrong,' I said. 'Claude isn't playing ball, and Laura's missing.'

Joe rushed through the atrium, heading for a room on the other side. 'And something else isn't right,' Joe said.

'What do you mean?'

'Mike Dobson. He hasn't really shown up for us before, just some ordinary bloke, and now he's saying that he was there when Nancy Gilbert died. But then, just before Claude is due to come home, Dobson is implicated in a prostitute murder. After twenty-two years of nothing. We're supposed to be picking up Claude today, but now it's getting too complicated. It doesn't feel right.'

We settled down into swivel chairs in front of a television. A fan made notices on the wall flutter, mainly mugshots of Blackley's target criminals, pictures of sullen young men with cropped hair. Joe put the disk into a machine.

'What has Mike Dobson said?' I asked, as we waited for the disk to load.

'About Hazel?' Joe said. 'Last night, he was sticking to the same story, that he was with her, but that she was alive when he dropped her off. A night to stew on it might make him come up with something else.'

'And once you get one lie, more tend to follow,' I said.

Joe nodded. 'The more you get, the easier it is to pick

them apart,' he said, then he pressed play before winding quickly through the footage.

The images were clear and bright, and it seemed that Kev Smith was using a camcorder, not one of the grainy security cameras that disappointed so many searches for evidence. The streetlight outside his house kept the image bright enough for the camera but, as Joe raced through the footage, the parts further away slipped slowly into twilight. Joe tapped the counter in the corner of the screen. 'He said to look at around ten o'clock.'

When the clock got as far as nine fifty-five, Joe pressed play and we settled down to watch.

There were young women in short skirts on street corners, their handbags over their shoulders, but they were mainly in darkness, so that they appeared on the screen like ghostly shadows. Whenever a car went past, they bent down to catch the driver's eye. Some slowed down. Some sped up. I wondered how many pieces of bad luck had taken those women to the street corners of Blackley.

Then we saw it. Mike Dobson's gold Mercedes. It passed right in front of the camera and below the streetlight, although the angle from the bedroom window allowed us to see only the driver. I recognised Dobson from his profile, but it was the other person in the car that interested Joe. The car turned a corner and started to drive away from the camera, towards the waste ground at the top of the street, Hazel's last resting place. There was a shadow in the passenger seat, just a head over the back of the seat, long hair visible.

'He's going to dump her,' Joe said, his finger tapping on his lip with concentration.

Then the car started to brake and it pulled up alongside the kerb. We exchanged looks of surprise when the passenger door opened and someone stepped out.

'Is that Hazel?' I asked.

Joe got closer to the screen so that his face was bathed in blue light. 'It might be.'

We both watched as Hazel tottered along the pavement and straightened the flowery dress she was found in. She was weaving as she walked, drunk maybe, and then Mike Dobson turned back towards the town centre and sped away to his normal life, where no one knew that he patrolled those streets.

Joe straightened and scratched his head. 'So it wasn't him,' he said, almost to himself. 'Dobson was telling the truth.'

'It happens sometimes,' I said.

Joe looked at me, and I could tell there was something on his mind, more than just Hazel.

'What is it?' I said.

'If Dobson's telling the truth about Hazel, maybe he's telling the truth about what happened to Nancy Gilbert,' Joe replied.

'What did he say?' I asked, and I suddenly felt cold, not sure if I was about to hear something that I wouldn't like. My tongue ran over my lips as my mouth went dry.

'He said he was there when Nancy Gilbert was killed,' Joe said. 'Claude hit her, and then persuaded Dobson to help him bury her. Dobson just went along with it, because he was scared.'

'Maybe it's a lie, to cover up what evidence you've got,' I said, although I realised that it didn't sound convincing.

Joe tapped the television screen. 'This tells me that Dobson isn't a liar.'

I felt the blood drain from me. My hand shot to my mouth and I started to pace, looking at Joe and then out of the window, my mind trying to process the threats flashing through my head.

'What's wrong?' Joe asked.

'If Dobson is telling the truth,' I said, 'Claude Gilbert is a heartless murderer.'

'We've always known that,' Joe said. 'Now, we've got a witness.'

Then I saw something on the monitor, like a flash. Then it was there again. Headlights, two quick bursts of light, and then the beams drove slowly towards Hazel.

'What do you think, a Mini?' Joe asked as it drew closer.

I couldn't answer. The car pulled alongside her, and she bent down to talk to the driver, one hand resting on the roof, her chest pushed through the window. Then she walked round to the passenger door and climbed in. The Mini reversed quickly up the street and then performed a U-turn in the road to head away.

As they reached the top of the street, the brake lights came on as the Mini slowed down so that it could drive onto the patch of concrete where she was found.

'Hazel has just climbed in with her murderer,' Joe said.

Chapter Sixty-Eight

Laura thumped the metal sheet, and then kicked it again. Her fingers were raw from scraping at the soil. Dirt was jammed under her fingernails.

She was sweating, despite the water that settled around her. Flies from Susie buzzed in her ear, so that Laura had to blow at them to keep them away from her nose.

There was a moan, Laura jumped, and then Susie's head banged on the metal, as if she had tried to sit up. Except that Laura knew she hadn't, because she couldn't.

Laura tried to scramble away from her, but she couldn't get far, only a foot at the most. She wished for a moment that she smoked, just so that she would have a lighter to see what there was in the hole. Or maybe it was better not to see.

Then she remembered that Susie smoked.

Laura closed her eyes and took deep breaths through her nose to get ready for it. Then she extended her arms.

She recoiled when she felt Susie's body, her arm completely solid now, the muscles tensed by rigor mortis. Laura exhaled to quell the tightness in her chest, and then she reached out once more.

Laura was ready for the feel of Susie this time, and when her fingers brushed her skin, cold like ham, she kept on going, heading for Susie's trousers. Susie's hand was crooked, as if she had been holding something when she died, but Laura could find nothing between the fingers. Laura reached down to the front pocket of Susie's jeans, but when she ran her hands over it, pressing against her hip, there was nothing there.

Laura took another deep breath and reached across Susie's lap to feel for her other pocket, her fingers creeping over the denim and the bump of the zip, trying to keep towards the waist. Laura's body was pressed right up against Susie's now, but she kept her face averted, trying not to get any more of Susie's blood on her, although by now it had dried onto her face.

Laura felt some dampness on the inside of Susie's thighs. It wasn't the water, which was now a couple of inches deep. It was piss, Laura could tell that, with no body heat to dry it out. She had been smelling that acrid stench for a few hours now.

She groped around Susie's lap for a lighter, not breathing, their faces too close, and then she felt the hard plastic in Susie's pocket.

Laura contorted herself to reach into the pocket, and she had to pull Susie closer, so that Susie's dead face rested against hers, cold lips against her cheek. Her fingers closed around it and she felt the lighter wheel. She extracted it slowly, anxious not to drop it. When it was safely out of the pocket and in her grasp, Laura shuffled quickly away.

Laura didn't move for a few seconds. Was she getting out of breath quicker? Was the air getting thinner? There was a film of sweat on her forehead, despite the cold. She had to blink to keep it out of her eyes.

She poised with her finger on the lighter wheel, pointed upwards, clasped between her bound hands, and then she flicked it, expected the flame. But all she got was a puny spark. Her hand was damp with perspiration and she worried about dropping it. She took a tighter grip and tried it again, the wheel rough on her skin, and then, finally, there was a small blue flame.

Laura kept her thumb on the lighter button to keep the butane flowing and began to look around.

She looked down first, saw her bare feet against the mud wall. The light was reflected in the sheen of muddy water that was seeping into the hole, and, looking upwards, her eyes were met by the brown of the rusty metal, a solid ceiling just inches from her nose, no weak points visible except for the line of rivets on a join in the centre. She couldn't turn over, was unable to get into any position where she could use her body effectively.

Susie's legs were lifeless next to her. Laura tracked the lighter up her body, saw the clawed fingers, and then she almost dropped the lighter when she got to the face. Susie's cheek and temple looked sunken, as if she had been struck with something heavy, and blood had collected below her head and was now being rinsed away by the rising water.

Laura turned her face away and let the lighter die out. She knew she would die if she stayed where she was. And so she kicked at the metal, and her hands scraped at the soil, her elbows pushing against Susie to give her some space.

She heard a noise like a scream, and then she realised that it was her own voice, shouting as loud as she could and all the time her fists and feet were hitting out, seized by panic, no longer able to hold it in, trapped. She knew she was going to die.

Chapter Sixty-Nine

I ran up the drive towards Frankie's front door. His Vespa was outside, pulled up onto its stand by the front door. I didn't knock, just twisted on the handle and ran inside.

'Frankie!'

There was silence.

'Frankie?'

I was met by silence again, but then I heard a sound, like the creak of a door. It was coming from upstairs.

I sprinted up the first flight, pausing when I reached the landing. I looked around, tried to work out where the sound had come from. The house seemed still. Maybe it had just been the wind in an old draughty building.

Then I heard it again. Just the creak of a floorboard. Upstairs once more. Frankie's room.

I ran again, two steps at a time, onto the small landing, and then rushed into his room. Frankie was sitting in a chair, looking out of the window. He turned and smiled at me.

'You are in my house,' he said.

'What you said this morning, Frankie, that you had seen Laura with someone,' I gasped, my heart beating fast.

He smirked. 'I'm not sure I remember.'

'Yes, you do, Frankie, and I'm not in the mood for fucking around. Tell me what you saw.'

Frankie glanced at the bare wall. 'I'm not sure I'm allowed. The police took away all my pictures.'

'That's because you look into people's bedrooms,' I said. 'This is different. This is about saving a life.'

Frankie seemed to like that, and he rocked faster, his teeth bared as his smile grew bigger.

'I want my pictures.'

'What kind of man are you?' I said.

'One who knows what he likes,' he snapped. 'And who has got something you want.'

'I could just look at your computer.'

He shrugged. 'Go ahead, but it'll take you some time to get past the passwords.' He watched me, and then smirked again. 'You don't have time, do you? I can tell that, from the way you burst into my home. You're in a panic.'

I paced up and down quickly, losing my temper. 'You said you liked Laura,' I said, turning to him, pointing. 'So help her.'

'Why should I?'

'Because it's the right thing to do.'

Frankie shook his head. 'My pictures first.'

I took a deep breath, and then I reached into my jacket pocket to pull out the envelope containing the photographs.

Frankie snatched them from me and flicked through them, his cheeks flushing red.

'Show me, Frankie,' I said. 'The pictures from last night.'

After a few seconds, Frankie put his photographs down and wheeled towards his computer. He clicked the mouse as the cursor hovered over the 'My Pictures' icon and, as the folder opened, I looked at the screen and saw a collection of images, some showing my house.

'You said there were passwords.'

'Maybe I was wrong,' Frankie replied.

I tried to bite down on my anger. 'Print them off,' I said, and a few seconds later the printer started whirring away under his desk.

When the printer had finished, I snatched up the pictures and studied them. They showed Claude coming out of my house, looking around. It was taken from a distance, but I recognised him.

The other pictures made me sit down, Frankie's bed creaking under me. They showed two people by a Mini, Laura and Claude, the latter with his unkempt beard, his hair hidden under a wide-brimmed hat, more Salvation Army hostel than eighties charmer. In each one, though, there was a good view of his face, and I recognised him. More than that, there was a number plate visible. I would call Joe with that as soon as I got outside. But it was the sight of Laura that shocked me. She was being taken to his car, bound by her wrists and feet, and her face looked swollen and bloodied.

'I'm taking these,' I said to Frankie. 'If you remove them from your computer, I'll burn your house down.'

He smiled, but I could tell from the twitch in the corner of his mouth that he heeded the threat. And right then, I meant it.

'We're even,' he said.

'Not even fucking close,' I snarled, as I slammed the door.

Chapter Seventy

Laura gulped at the air. It was getting harder to breathe. The freezing water had collected as high as her hips and she was shivering.

She tried to stay calm – panic was an enemy – but it was hard. She didn't want this to be the end. Goosebumps flashed across her arms and legs. She didn't know if it was the cold or the thought of what lay ahead.

Laura thought of her parents, made herself think of the happy teenage years she'd had. She had learnt to do things her own way, make her own decisions – the police, the move north – but her parents had always been there for her, supporting, loving. She tried to imagine her mother's voice, soft and warm, and the memory lifted her for a moment.

She turned her face away from Susie. The buzz of insects had grown louder. Or was she imagining it? There was no way of knowing in the darkness. It had got harder to hold the lighter, her fingers now too cold to grip it, and so she had dropped it into the water.

Laura reached up to wipe the sweat from her eyes and she found herself out of breath, her chest moving in hard quick pumps. Her hands shook as she lifted them. Her clothes were getting heavier in the water and she felt tired and cold. Precious sleep would take her away from there.

She shook her head. Don't think like that. Stay alert. Where was Jack? He would know what to do, would have the right words.

She kicked at the metal again, angry now, but her foot moved sluggishly, her jeans heavy with water, her muscles aching. The sound came back as a dull thud followed by a small splash as her foot went back into the water.

Laura hit out again, and then she stopped, panting. She couldn't last much longer, she knew that. The air was getting thin. She was wheezing, her lungs working hard for the oxygen, every deep breath replacing it with carbon dioxide, squeezing out the air that she needed.

Would she be awake when she took that last breath, when there was no more air to be had?

I drove quickly from Frankie's house, my phone wedged between my shoulder and ear. It was against the law, but fuck it, give me the penalty points.

'Joe, it's me, Jack,' I shouted when he answered.

'Where are you?'

'On my way to Alan Lake's house. Meet me there.'

'Why there?' he asked.

'Because he's the link in all of this, and he might know where Claude is,' I said. 'And more than that. I've got pictures of Claude, taken last night, getting into a green Mini, with Laura. He's taken her.'

'What's the registration number?'

I reached across for the photographs and balanced them on the steering wheel, flicking through. I knew I was pushing more than a mobile phone offence now, but that didn't mean I was going to stop.

I barked the registration number at Joe and then threw the photographs back onto the seat.

'If you want a photograph of Claude to circulate, meet me at Alan Lake's house,' I said, and then I clicked off my phone.

I ignored the speed limits all the way there, and there were at least two bright flashes in my rearview mirror as I went over the dashed lines on the road in front of the speed cameras. As I drove towards Alan Lake's house, I saw another car I recognised: a red Jaguar. Chief Inspector Roach. I should have expected it. He was just leaving.

'What brings you here?' he said when he saw me.

'No, Roach, what brings you here?' I said, and then I pointed at the house. 'I'm going to speak with Mr Lake, your business partner. Would you like to join me?'

He paled, and then his brow furrowed. 'Yes, I think I ought to,' he said, and I was aware of him following at my shoulder as I marched towards the big glass door.

Alan Lake looked round as I entered the house, Roach just behind me. He stared at me, his face confused, and then at Roach. I saw Roach shake his head.

'Do you know why I'm here?' I said.

'The same as always,' Lake said. He pointed at Roach. 'Look, you've got the scoop, another player here.'

'Don't be smart,' I said. 'Let me tell you what I know about you both.'

He held out his hands and smiled. 'By all means.'

'Northern Works,' I said, and I saw the smile disappear. Lake looked at Roach. 'It's okay, Paul, I'll handle this.'

I turned round. 'No, stay, I don't mind.'

Lake pursed his lips. 'No, it would be better if he wasn't here,' he said. 'Let's talk.'

Roach looked at me, and then at Alan Lake, before nodding to himself. 'Okay,' he said, and then he turned to me. 'Don't make trouble.'

'Trouble has already arrived, Roach, so go fuck yourself,' I barked.

Roach flushed for a moment, but then he turned and left. I stayed silent until the door had closed, Lake gestured towards a chair. 'Sit down.'

'I haven't got time for pleasantries,' I said. 'Claude has got Laura.'

Alan walked to a cabinet and poured himself a whisky. He raised the bottle to me to see whether I was interested, but I shook my head. He walked to the sofa and sat back, pausing to take a sip, letting out a small sigh of pleasure. My fists clenched and I focused hard on not going for him.

'So, you want to know about Northern Works,' he said. 'Why?'

'No, I want to find Claude,' I said, 'and it seems like you're pretty good at finding him somewhere to hide.'

He raised his glass in salute. 'Congratulations,' he said, although the snipe in his smile was obvious.

'Why did you shield Claude Gilbert?'

'Are you asking as a journalist, as a copper's bed partner, or because you're so damn fucking nosy?'

I sat down on the chair opposite and leant forward. 'I just want to find Laura – and to do that, I need to find Claude,' I said. 'I've got enough to cause you problems, especially if anything happens to Laura, so stop fucking me around and talk. Where's Claude?'

'I don't know where Claude is.'

'I don't believe you.'

'I don't care whether you believe me or not,' he said. 'It's the truth.'

'So what do you know about him?' I said. 'Anything you've got might help.'

He sighed and rubbed his forehead with his fingers.

'I haven't got much,' he said. He looked at me. 'Are you definitely going to print?'

'One hundred per cent. Northern Works is the follow-up story, and finding Laura is the happy ending, so get a move on,' I said. 'Tell me what you know, but if I find out later on that you knew things that could have saved Laura, then I will come after you, and I won't stop.'

He thought for a moment, and then he said, 'Claude came to see me in the cells during my trial. He told me that he was going to run. He didn't tell me the details, just said it was a personal thing, and I didn't ask. You move with crooks and you learn not to ask questions. He needed my help to escape.'

'Why did he ask you?'

Lake fidgeted at that, though I could tell that he had been waiting for the question for twenty-two years.

'Because he thought I had influence.'

'And did you?'

'More than him.'

'But helping him out would keep you in prison for longer,' I said. 'You were halfway through your trial.'

Lake gave me a wry smile. 'But I *was* going to be convicted. The witnesses were good, and Claude, well, he was all over the fucking place. I was glad he was going. Waste of time. I knew it would cost me a few more weeks inside, but I was looking at another couple of years if I lost the trial. Empires crumble in that time, and so it was an easy decision to reach.'

I shook my head. 'I don't accept that. I know how criminal minds work. You think you're going to get away with it every time.'

Lake looked at me, his stare direct. 'I wasn't some grubby little house burglar or drug runner. I knew what I was doing. The little fuckers who can't keep out of prison are the stupid

423

ones, the cannon fodder. The big guys never get caught. Those are the rules.'

'If you're trying to impress me, save your breath.'

Lake sighed and sat back. 'Those days are behind me. And even then I was moving on.'

'By helping your barrister to flee the country?'

'I know how it looks,' he said. He held his glass to his cheek for a moment as he considered me, and then he sighed and looked vulnerable for a moment. I was surprised.

'The girl I glassed,' he said, and then added, '. . . allegedly.' I didn't appreciate his joke. 'She was the girlfriend of someone who did errands for me, but that ended when he went to prison.'

'How come?'

Lake became more reflective, his brow becoming furrowed, an uncertain look in his eyes. 'There was a girl, a kid really. Twelve years old. Innocent, not yet old enough to cause anyone any harm. One day, she was crossing the road, had been to the shops or something, all excited with her bag of sweets.' Lake swirled the drink in his glass and looked down as he spoke. 'She ran in front of my car. It was over so quick. One minute it's a normal drive, and the next she's on the bonnet of my car. She hit the windscreen, smashed it right through with her head. Someone got my number, and so the police came to me and wanted to know who had been driving the car. I told them I didn't know.'

'But you did,' I said.

Lake scowled. 'This runner of mine, he admitted that he was the driver. He went to the police voluntarily, told them how he couldn't remember much about the accident, he was in shock, but he remembered hitting her, and then he panicked when he saw her, and so he left her at the scene.'

'What happened?'

'He got two months in jail for not stopping at the accident, and a ban from driving.'

'Not much for a girl's life.'

Lake nodded, still not looking at me. 'No, it's not, and most people thought the same. The poor fucker was chased off the estate, couldn't go see his parents or anything. You see, it wasn't that he knocked her over, because these things happen, but that she was left to die on her own, in the street, sweets all over the fucking road, no one to hold her, to tell her that she would be all right.'

'And so his girlfriend came to see you, because she was angry with you, because it was your car,' I said. 'So you shoved a glass in her face.'

'It wasn't like that,' he said, looking up at last. 'She came into the pub mouthing off, screaming how she was going to get him to talk, how it was all my fault, that I was nothing but a coward, that I had killed that girl. She just twisted my buttons, and I fucking lost it. I had been drinking, was holding a glass, and I just threw things, my fists, whatever I could get my hands on. I would have fucking killed her if I hadn't been held back.'

As I looked at him, I guessed the truth, and realised that the look in his eyes that I couldn't work out was guilt, and remorse, something that haunted him for more than twenty years.

'You were the one driving the car, weren't you?'

Lake didn't say anything at first, just swirled his drink some more, and then he put his head back on the sofa and took some deep breaths.

'All I saw was her hair,' he said quietly. 'That's what I remember, her fucking hair. I was driving along, a tape in the player, singing along. And why not? Life was fucking good. I was the man, someone people looked up to. The next thing

I know I've got this girl right in front of my car, her face scared, and then it's like slow motion. It was her hair, you see, all blonde and long and sort of frizzy. It was coming towards me, and then it hit the windscreen, the worst sound you could ever hear, like dropping a melon. Fucking blonde hair everywhere, flying through the air, and then stuck into the windscreen, blood dripping through the cracks, and then she slid off.'

'You left her?'

Lake nodded slowly, his lips pursed. 'I can't explain it. But I was untouchable, or so I thought, and there I was, reduced to some fucking clown, with a kid's brains all over my car windscreen. It didn't seem real. So I played the big man for a bit longer. I backed up and turned the car around, left her in the road.'

'And when the police tracked you down, you got one of your runners to take the blame,' I said, failing to hide the disgust in my voice.

Lake nodded. 'I thought I could deal with it, thought that the police would lose interest, and then my life would go back to normal. My runner owed me some money, and so he went to jail, the pay-off, the debt gone, and I carried on as normal. Except that I couldn't carry on. I saw her all the time, the girl, like a flurry of hair coming at me fast. I started to hang around the graveyard, and I would see her parents putting flowers on her grave, sobbing and wailing. I wanted to say something, but there was no point. What could I say? And then that mouthy little bitch came into the club, shouting that I didn't care. But I did care. I had made a mistake, and nothing I could do would make it better, and she just hit the spot.' He sighed. 'That was it for me. I decided when I was inside that I was starting again. I learnt a bit of sculpture, and when I came out I carried it on. It helped me move on, gave me something to think about.'

'And why does this have anything to do with Claude Gilbert?' I asked.

'Because he knew about the girl. Claude didn't tell me how he found out, because he thought it made him powerful, that he knew people who knew things, but it wasn't too hard to work out. The girlfriend told the police, but she didn't put it in writing in case it got her boyfriend in more trouble. If the police knew, they might have mentioned it to the prosecution, and so the prosecuting barrister found out, and you know what barristers are like, most of them working in the same building. It doesn't matter normally, because they play by the rules, but what happens when they don't? So Claude called me, out of the blue. It had been ten fucking years, but he was heading back to England. He told me that he'd seen how well I'd done and that if I didn't help him he would make sure everyone knew about the girl. My dirty little fucking secret.' Lake took another sip of whisky. 'It was just somewhere to live, that's all. He sorted his own cash out, but I let him live in my place. He paid me rent, but it wasn't much. Below the fucking market price, but property was going up and he was keeping it maintained.'

'And that was it?'

Lake nodded.

'So where does Chief Inspector Roach fit into all this?' I asked.

Lake laughed and shook his head. 'Fucking nowhere, at first. He's a hanger-on. Just because he wrote some trashy cash-in book on Claude Gilbert, he thinks he's in with the arty set, so he turns up at my exhibitions, flashing his cheque book. But he buys my pieces, the fucking mug, and so one day we end up talking about Claude Gilbert. Or, rather, he does, because that's his party piece, his attention grabber, that he once dug up a corpse. Not exactly an achievement. What did it take,

427

one spade and thirty minutes? Anyhow, he starts to hint that he knows about Claude living in my flat.'

'How did he know?'

'He was writing a follow-up book, reckoned there was a demand for it, and he was looking at me for the same reason you were,' he said. 'He investigated my assets and found out about the flat, and so he took a trip down there.'

'What made him go to London?'

'Just to be thorough,' he said. 'He was going to paint me as the rich northern wide boy, with properties in Belgravia. He went to the flat, and who should answer the door but fucking Claude Gilbert.'

'So why wasn't he arrested?'

'Because Roach saw the pound signs slipping away. The interest in the Gilbert story was the mystery, not the story. If Gilbert ends up in a cell, people might lose interest, so he called me, told me what he'd seen. He gave me an ultimatum: money or Claude. For me, it was an easy decision. I gave him a hundred grand, a gift, tax free, and a forty per cent share in the company. He thought he was sitting on a gold mine, a Belgravia property.'

'So now Claude wants to come home, Roach is nervous,' I said.

'Very, but then you helped us out.'

'How so?'

'You helped to get Mike Dobson in a cell, so that he could tell his story.'

I was confused now. 'I don't understand.'

'We knew the story, Claude had told me, and we guessed that you had met Claude. Once Dobson was brought in, we knew what Claude was doing.'

'Explain.'

'Dobson was supposed to stay quiet, to protect himself.

Claude thought Dobson was weak and a coward, and so he wouldn't say anything about what happened to Nancy, because if he stayed silent, there would be no evidence against him. Dobson was a red herring, nothing more, his silence just more proof that he must be the real killer, letting Claude off the hook. But Claude's gamble on Dobson's silence failed, because Dobson talked, and that was down to Roach tweaking his conscience. So Claude has got to run again, and for as long as he keeps running, our dirty little secrets stay that way, as secrets. Except that you've done his dirty work for him, because you're going to write about us anyway.'

'But Claude took his gamble a step further,' I said. 'He killed a woman to blame Dobson.'

Lake shook his head. 'That's his problem: he's over-elaborate.'

'So where is Claude now?'

'I don't know,' Lake said. 'I know he's left London, because he turned up here, demanding to be accommodated. He told me that he won't be going back.'

'And did he stay here?'

'Do you think I'm stupid?' Lake said. 'Claude Gilbert in my spare room would be hard to hide.'

'How do I know you aren't lying?' I said. 'You don't want Claude found.'

Lake pointed at me. 'You're the reason.' When I looked confused, he said, 'My secret is out now. I've nothing to gain any more.'

'Does Northern Works own any other buildings he might be able to use?' I said.

Lake raised his glass to me. 'You know the answer to that.'

'What do you mean?'

'The company search you did, left on your table, next to your computer.'

I took a deep breath, my anger building now. 'You went into my house.'

'I had to know how much you'd found out,' he said.

I looked towards the high windows, at the rain running down the panes. 'You're just full of grubby little secrets, aren't you, Lake?' I said. 'Dead girls, fugitive murderers, bent coppers. You never really moved on.'

'I don't need your approval,' he said. 'Look at yourself, at how you were taken in by a conman, too greedy for the big story. The big question was not why he came forward, but why now, and if you had worked that out earlier, you wouldn't be in this mess, trying to find your missing girlfriend.'

'What do you mean?' I said.

'The inheritance,' he said. 'Claude's father on his deathbed and his sisters trying to get a declaration of death, so that Claude's share goes to them. Like you, he's greedy, just after the money, gambling on Dobson's silence so that he can grab his share of the estate.'

I sat back and ran my fingers through my hair, frustrated. I knew more now, but I was no nearer to finding Laura.

'Why would Claude take Laura?' I said.

'Greedy people don't like losing out, and so it's just plain old revenge,' Lake said. 'I've spoiled his great plan, and so he's lashing out, like he lashed out at Nancy when he found out she had been sleeping around.' He sat forward. 'You need to find Laura quickly though, because if you think of what happened to Nancy, you know just how nasty he gets when he strikes back.'

I closed my eyes, knowing just how true that sounded.

Chapter Seventy-One

I was back outside Susie's house, with Joe this time, who was waiting for me outside, trying to shelter from the rain under a shop awning.

'This is a shitty part of town to end up in,' Joe said.

'I've been here before,' I said, and looked along the street. There was no sign of a green Mini, and the house was quiet.

Joe went into the shop next door as I pressed my face up against Susie's window. The curtains were drawn so it was impossible to see inside, and I couldn't hear any movement.

Joe came out of the shop. 'Claude's been here for a couple of days,' he said. 'The shopkeeper recognised the description. He hasn't seen him today though, or Susie. She wasn't here last night either.'

'How does he know?'

'Because she plays her music too loud when she gets drunk, and he didn't hear it last night. She bought some booze yesterday, and so he expected a noisy night, but he doesn't complain. She's good for trade.'

I pushed open the communal front door and rapped hard on Susie's door. No answer. I knocked again. Still no reply. Then I heard a door open on the landing above and a face appeared over the rail.

'Are you the police?' It was a man in his thirties, with long dark hair trailing over the railing, the words coming out in a drawl. The sickly scent of cannabis wafted down the stairs.

Joe looked up. 'Yes. We're looking for Susie Bingham. Have you seen her?'

He shook his head in response, his hair swaying from side to side. Joe turned away, but then the man said, 'I heard her though.'

Joe looked up again. 'What did you hear?'

'Just like a row, man. Shouting, and something got broken, and then it went quiet, like eerie.'

'When?'

'Last night.'

Joe went upstairs and showed him Frankie's photograph of Claude, his hand over Laura. 'Do you recognise him?'

The man pulled his hair to one side and then nodded. 'He stays here sometimes. Funny dude. Doesn't speak. Keeps out of the way. She's sweet though.'

'Do you and Susie talk much?' Joe said.

'Yeah, like all the time, man,' he said. 'She comes up for a smoke sometimes.'

'Does she talk about her love life?'

'Sometimes. She told me that she was all loved up, that she would go for drives with a man, that kind of thing.'

'Did she say where?'

He shook his head. 'Just in the country somewhere. Said it was their special place.'

Joe came back down the stairs and aimed a kick at the door. It took three sharp kicks to the lock area to splinter the wood, and then a fourth to make the door swing open.

Joe and I exchanged glances and then entered. The flat was empty and even messier than when I had been in before. Papers were scattered on the floor and a bottle had been knocked over. Then I saw a dark patch by the fire.

432

'Is that blood?'

Joe got to his knees to look closer. 'That would be my guess,' he said, and pointed me towards the bedroom. 'Find some clue about her life with Claude. We need to know more.'

I went through the archway, pulled aside the old blue curtain, the one concession to privacy. I hadn't got a good look before, and so I was surprised by how different the bedroom was to the rest of the flat. It was chintzy and bright, with a white silky four-poster and pink heart-shaped cushions, clean and tidy. There was a white dresser, with a mirror surrounded by lights, like something from an end-of-pier dressing room, and the curtains were shiny and pink, to match the cushions. The bedroom seemed like a haven, somewhere for Susie to escape the failures elsewhere in her life, and there was a doorway to a bathroom.

'What do you think about this?' Joe said, passing me a framed photograph through the curtain. It showed Susie and Claude relaxing together by a river. It was recent, showing Claude's full beard and straggly hair; there was a bit of stone in the foreground suggesting that the pictures were taken using a self-timer. Claude was smiling into the camera but Susie was staring up at him, a look of devotion on her face. 'Their special place?'

'Maybe,' I said, going to the dresser. The top drawer was chaotic. Knickers and socks almost jumped out when I opened it, and I scrambled through, throwing them onto the floor before moving on to the other drawers. There was nothing of interest, just T-shirts and jeans thrown in, nothing that would help in the search for Claude Gilbert. And, more importantly, for Laura.

The wardrobe was much the same, with white chipboard doors that didn't match up well, filled with short skirts and lacy blouses and a shelf at the top, with boxes and old shoes. I pulled the largest box down and, opening it, I felt a burst of sadness. There was a christening outfit, billowing cream silk, perfectly folded and packed under soft tissue. I looked quickly around the room. There were a couple of photographs of a little girl, but no recent ones. It seemed as if her motherly bond had ended when the girl had grown up. Where were the more recent photographs, of the teenage girl, or graduation photographs?

I went to the next box, and when I opened the lid, I shouted, 'Joe!'

He put his head around the curtain. I held up a pile of photographs. 'More pictures of the happy couple.'

Joe came into the room and flicked through them. I scoured through the rest of the box. There were mostly pictures of Susie, flirty and happy, laughing at the camera, blowing kisses or posing in mockingly provocative poses. Then there were some of Claude Gilbert, but he looked more serene, smiles of contentment behind the beard. There were others taken on a self-timer, with Susie draped over Claude, and I could see a blush behind the broken veins in Claude's cheeks. They looked like they had been taken during winter, with Claude and Susie holding up hip flasks against an ice-blue sky, and there was a snow-coated river bank in some.

'These photographs are mostly taken in the same place,' I said. 'Look at the views,' and I pointed at the trees in the background. 'The trees all follow the same line. It looks like they found a little hideaway. What's so special about that place?'

'We need to find out where it is first,' Joe said. Then he thought of something. 'Mike Dobson.'

'What about him?'

'He used to go for drives to the country with Nancy,' he said. 'Maybe the special place for Nancy was the same for Claude, so Claude took Susie there?'

'Tenuous,' I said.

'Got any better ideas?'

I shook my head.

'Let's go then,' he said, and he ran for the door. I was right behind him.

Chapter Seventy-Two

Joe rushed into the station with me in his wake. He fumbled with his swipe card and then headed towards a door at the end of a corridor, past lockers that lined the wall and towards a bright light that shone through a glass panel in a door.

'Do you really think it will be the same place?' I said.

'I don't know,' Joe said. 'But it's the only quick option we have right now. You heard what was said, that Susie called it their special place. There's a river, and in the photographs the water just bubbles over the pebbles on the river bed. That's how Dobson described where he took Hazel, the dead girl, because it was a special place for him and Nancy. It sounds like Nancy might be speaking from the grave here, because I reckon it's where Claude and Nancy went when they were young and in love. And then Nancy took Mike Dobson, for the same reason, because it was quiet and secluded, or maybe because she had good memories from when her husband loved her. And, because it reminded him of Nancy, Dobson took Hazel there.'

'And Claude took Susie.'

'Something like that,' Joe said. 'It's the one place that repeats itself.'

We crashed through into the custody area. The custody sergeant seemed initially reluctant to let us through into the

437

cell; Mike Dobson had legal representation now. But there was something in Joe's eyes that made him hand over the key.

When we opened the door, Mike Dobson was lying on his bed, his hands behind his head. He looked up calmly as we entered.

'The best night's sleep I've had in a long time,' he said.

Joe was surprised.

'I can never get absolution, I know that,' Mike said. 'I helped someone die, but I can stop keeping it a secret.'

'Tell us this then,' Joe said. 'Did Nancy have a special place?'

Mike sat up. 'For us? Down by the river, like I told you, where I took Hazel.'

'Where is it?'

'It's an old fishing shelter by the Ribble. It's on private land, used to be owned by Claude's family, so not many people know it's there, but the owner never goes to it, and so we would always have it to ourselves.'

Joe passed him one of the photographs of Susie. 'Is that it?'

He paused as he looked at the picture, taking in the background. But then he scowled as a spark of recognition ignited him.

'That's Claude, isn't it?' he said.

'We'll talk about that later,' Joe said. 'Just tell me if that's the same place you took Hazel.'

Mike looked at the photograph for a few seconds more, the picture twitching as his hands shook, and then he looked at Joe and nodded.

'I need directions,' Joe said. 'If you tell me exactly where it is, you might just take some weight from your conscience.'

And so Mike did.

* * *

The water was now over Laura's shoulders, her head raised to keep it out of her ears. Her forehead pressed against the metal, her breasts and knees like islands, but it was hard to keep it there. Laura shivered violently. Her bones ached, her skin was numb, her teeth chattered. Each breath seemed laboured, the air squeezed out by the water, and she was starting to gulp. If help was on its way, it had to come soon.

She closed her eyes and fought the urge to lie back, to let the water take her over, an end to the pain.

She shook her head. She couldn't think like that. She had to have hope until there was no hope left.

Laura tried to shuffle sideways, just to shift her position, but it was hard to move through the water. She tried to use her hands against the metal sheet, but she couldn't make her arms work. They were sluggish, powerless, like dead weights.

Her head dipped back, she couldn't stop it, and the cold water filled her ears, so that all she could hear was the rush of blood through her head. Her face was numb, but she felt the water lap against her cheeks, like soft slaps, inches from her mouth. If she left her head there, the water would rise up and gather around her lips, held back for a few seconds by the skin and tiny hairs, and then they would give way and the water would tumble over, filling her throat, her lungs, and release her from the hole.

She lifted her head quickly. Don't think like that. Fight it, for Bobby's sake. He needs a mother.

The breaths came quick and fast as she wondered how soon the end would come, when all she would see would be the film of water over her eyes as her body tried to take a breath without air. Would it hurt, or would it be blessed relief?

Chapter Seventy-Three

We were silent as we drove for the shelter by the Ribble, away from the shadows of Blackley and into countryside, through rolling lanes and hedgerows. I couldn't enjoy the views though. The rain was falling harder against the windscreen, it had been going all morning, the wipers finally getting rid of the midges that had died there in the days before. I clenched and unclenched my fists.

'Are we nearly there?' I asked.

'Not much further,' Joe said, but I noticed that he sped up, and the hawthorn turned into a blur through the side windows. Then the glint of the Ribble appeared ahead, just a grey shimmer against the green of the backdrop, the colour broken by the black and white of cows. I scanned the landscape, looking for a sign that we had reached the right place.

Then I saw it. 'There,' I said.

Joe slowed down quickly. 'What is it?'

'We just passed a track,' I said. 'There was a Mini parked by a gate. A green one.'

Joe slammed his car into reverse and backed up at top speed to a gnarled old five-bar propped between stone gateposts.

I climbed quickly out of Joe's car. 'He's still here.'

'And our time is running out,' Joe said, and joined me as I scrambled over the gate.

I ran with Joe, my fear growing. I had seen one dead body – Hazel, Claude's work. What would I find down there? But I couldn't think of that. I had to keep going.

The ripple of the river got louder as we got closer, the rain drumming on the surface and the wet grass squeaked underfoot as I ran. My trousers became wet and slapped hard against my shins. The thin strip of grey turned into a wider stretch of water, but then the river bank came to me abruptly after I jumped over an old tree root. I dropped down a few feet and landed heavily on shingle, the water just a few inches from my toes. Joe landed next to me and we both looked around and tried to get our bearings. Mike Dobson had said that the fisherman's shelter was where the river trickled over the low bed on the shallow part of the bend, but the rain had made the river rise, and so there were only slight ripples to give the site away. I looked along the bank, left and right, and then I saw it.

'There it is,' I said, pointing to a small, open-fronted stone structure in the shadow of the trees that hung over the water.

We raced quickly towards it, our feet crunching loud on the shingle that bordered the river. As we got closer, the place looked empty, and I thought we'd guessed wrong. I was expecting three people to be in there. The front was open to the elements, and there were small windows at the side, like an ornate stone bus stop. Then I saw some feet sticking out, battered old suede shoes, brown and muddy, and light-coloured trousers. My heartbeat quickened. As he came fully into view, I saw it was Claude, fat and drunk, a bottle of supermarket whisky in his lap.

'Claude,' I said. 'Where is she? Where's Laura?'

He looked up, and then waved the bottle of whisky at me.

442

'Miss McGanity?' he said, his voice slurring. 'Susie told me that she was a real lovely. She was right.'

'Where is Susie?'

He laughed and shook his head, and then wagged his finger at me. 'You don't care about Susie,' he said. 'It's Laura you want.'

'So where is she?'

Claude sniggered to himself. 'She's having a lie down,' he said, and then he looked up at me. 'More of a long sleep.'

My stomach turned over and my lip trembled. I tried to stay calm, but I wanted to run forward and grip him, shake the truth out of him.

'This was your last gamble, wasn't it, Claude?' I said.

'Go on, superstar, what do you mean?'

'Just that. You're a gambler, have been all of your life. Cards. Casinos. But sometimes you get to the shit or bust play, don't you, Claude, when all of your chips are down, and it's this play or no play?'

Claude shook his head. 'I'm still not with you.'

'Mike Dobson,' I said.

Claude looked at Joe Kinsella, and then back to me, before he paid attention to his whisky and then took a deep breath.

'Coward to the end,' Claude said.

'What do you mean, coward?' Joe said.

Claude jammed the bottle into the ground and then tried to stand up, but he stumbled drunkenly in the soft soil and sat back down again.

'Dobson was supposed to keep his mouth shut,' I said, looking at Joe. 'Claude knew he would be arrested, and he would have his trial, and he was going to give the jurors the chance to play detective, twelve little Miss Marples, all wondering whether there was a different theory, and Claude would give it to them. Michael Dobson, spurned

443

lover, couldn't stand the thought of Nancy staying in her marriage.'

Joe looked at Claude. 'Good plan, Claude. Dobson could never give evidence, because it would mean implicating himself, and no one could force him, because witnesses aren't obliged to incriminate themselves. If you're helping out the court, the system will stop you saying anything to put yourself in the shit.'

Claude laughed. 'Good old British justice. It still has a sense of fair play.'

'And you had him sunk twice over, didn't you?' I said. 'Because what if he tried to bluff his way out of it and deny any knowledge of Nancy? That's where Hazel would sink him, isn't it, Claude?'

'Hazel?'

'The young woman you killed the other night, just to make it worse for Dobson.'

'Hazel?' he said, and then smiled. 'I didn't know her name.' He waved his hand dismissively. 'She's been rescued from her life.'

'That wasn't your choice to make, Claude,' Joe said.

'Oh, do be quiet, both of you,' Claude said, his voice getting angrier. 'Don't you get it? You should be happy now. You've got the big man, the feather in your cap,' and he banged his hand against his chest before he jammed his bottle into the soil. 'Doesn't anyone give decent legal advice any more?'

'What do you mean?' I asked, kneeling down to his level.

He crooked his finger towards me. 'Because, hotshot,' he whispered at me, 'the first rule in the police station is that you don't admit to anything.'

'Maybe some people can't live with the guilt,' I said. 'Leaving a woman to stew in her own blood and piss, trapped underground. That doesn't sit easy with some people.'

444

Claude looked away.

'And how did you know Dobson had talked?' Joe asked.

I turned to Joe. 'Alan Lake,' I said. 'Chief Inspector Roach got Dobson to talk and let Lake know. Alan Lake made sure that Claude knew all about it, because he needed Claude to run again.'

Joe looked confused. 'Why?'

'Alan Lake and Roach are Claude's landlords. They helped him because Claude knew Lake's worst secret, and Roach was just cashing in. If Claude came out of hiding, they were both in trouble, so they made sure that Claude knew Dobson was talking, that his gamble had failed, to make him go on the run again.'

Joe looked surprised, his eyes wide.

'Have I got it right so far, Claude?' I asked.

He waved me away and took a sip of his whisky.

'So you gambled on Dobson's silence, the perfect red herring,' Joe said, 'because you took Dobson for some local small-fry who would be scared of the consequences.' Joe stepped closer to Claude. 'But Dobson has something you don't have, and that's balls, Claude, and a conscience. What he let you do has haunted him for over twenty years. He couldn't stay quiet once he got the chance to talk.'

Claude started a sarcastic hand clap, but stopped when Joe looked down at him and said, 'What were you hoping for? To come home and stake a claim in your inheritance, your father on his deathbed, happy at the return of his innocent son?'

Claude twitched slightly, and then he shrugged and took another pull out of the bottle. 'How did you know about the inheritance?' he said eventually.

I watched Claude, remembering what Lake had said.

'If they can get you declared dead,' Joe said, 'your share would go to them.' Joe smiled. 'They sound as greedy as you.'

'Father believed in the law,' Claude said. 'You would have to convict me to convince him of anything.'

Joe knelt down, so that he was next to me, his breaths hot in my ear.

'It was a plant,' Joe said, every word uttered slowly.

Claude looked confused for a moment. 'What do you mean, a plant?'

'The story about your father,' Joe said. 'He is ill, that's all true, but he isn't in dispute with your sisters. He contacted the police. He did it quietly, so no one would know. A word in the Chief Constable's ear, and so it gets delegated to me. But your father knows you, Claude. He knows what a shallow little man you really are, how only money would bring you out of hiding. He knows that his death could make you rich, if you got a share of the pot, and so he agreed that the press could publish his illness, padded with the news that your sisters were trying to get you declared dead so that they could take your slice.'

Claude's cheeks had gone pale behind the beard.

'It was all bullshit,' Joe said. 'You're already written out of your father's will. He knows you killed Nancy, and you are an ulcer on the family name. Your sisters were dragged down by you – they were only ever *your* sisters, not people in their own right. Bad news, Claude, you were never going to get anything, though you didn't know that.' Joe straightened. 'So this is it, Claude. You should have stuck with the cards you had, because the house didn't even have a hand. You couldn't resist though, and I knew that. Once a gambler, always a gambler. That's how it works. You couldn't resist one final turn of the cards, and you came up with twenty-two.'

'You're lying,' Claude said.

Joe smiled. 'Am I? Secrets had been kept for more than twenty years. Mike Dobson wasn't going to say anything

446

about Nancy until you forced him. Nancy hadn't told anyone else about the affair. We looked at her private life and we came up with virtually nothing. Mike Dobson was nothing to her. He was a stop-gap, a time-filler and, worse than that, Claude, Nancy was carrying your child.'

Claude took a deep breath and wiped his hand across his forehead. He looked down. 'My child?'

Joe nodded. 'You heard it right, Claude. Nancy was carrying your child, not his. All you had to do back then was work it out together. You were sleeping around. Nancy was sleeping around. You took the wrong choice. One whack across the back of her head and you ended her life, and ruined yours. And Dobson's, and all those people who loved Nancy.'

A tear left Claude's eye and tracked through the mud to rest on his beard.

'Tell me this,' Joe said. 'Why couldn't you resist? You could have kept on running. Why wait until money came into the picture?'

Claude looked at Joe, and then across to me. He wiped his eye and his shoulders slumped. 'I am sick of running,' he said quietly, and then tugged at his coat, threadbare around the elbows. 'Sick of living like this. We can all have regrets.'

'You've got self-pity, Claude,' Joe said. 'There is a difference. If you had regrets, you would say you were sorry.'

'How did you know I was alive?' Claude said.

'We didn't,' Joe said. 'It was a bluff. And you bought it.'

'So where is Laura?' I said.

Claude looked at me for a few seconds, and then looked down. 'I said it before, that silence should be observed when under interrogation.'

'Claude! *Tell me*. Save another life.'

Claude sighed. 'Too late,' he said, and took a swig from his whisky bottle.

I stepped forward and gripped his collar. 'What do you mean, too late?'

Claude didn't respond.

'Tell me!'

Claude shook his head and then held out his hands. 'Cuff me.'

I looked at Joe. I could taste bile, my stomach churning as my mind filled with images of Laura, of where she might be.

'Claude, please, tell me where Laura is,' I pleaded.

Claude lowered his hands, and then he smiled. 'Maybe there is time for one more turn of the cards,' he said.

'What do you mean?' Joe said.

'I go to my car. You give me your radios, your car keys, and your phone,' and he pointed at Joe. 'You let me drive away. I might even go in your car. I'll call Jack and tell him where he can find Laura and Susie.' He waved his phone. 'But I ring just the once. If the phone is engaged because you're calling your station, you'll miss the call.'

'That's ridiculous,' Joe said. 'We can't just let you go again.'

'Then it's your gamble that you'll find them in time,' Claude said.

'What do you mean *in time*?' I asked.

'Like it sounds,' Claude replied. 'Think about a life,' he said to Joe, 'not the feather in your cap.'

'It's not about my ego,' Joe said.

'So let me go.'

Joe looked at me, and I looked back at Claude. Joe held out his phone to Claude.

'You will ring us?' Joe said.

'My word is my bond,' Claude said, and reached out with his hand to take the phone from Joe, but then Joe grabbed his wrist and threw him to the floor. He dragged him out of the shelter and pulled him towards the river.

448

'Deal's off,' Joe said.

'Joe!' I shouted. 'What are you doing?'

'Sit there,' Joe said to Claude, and then he turned back to me. 'Dig.'

'What do you mean?'

'Where Claude was sitting,' Joe said. 'The soil was too soft after days of sunshine. And his hands when he reached out for my phone were black with dirt, ingrained into the skin.' Joe turned back towards Claude. 'If he wanted to run, he'd have done so before we came here. He hasn't run because he doesn't know where to go. This was his old courting stop, this fishing shelter.'

Claude hung his head.

I went to my knees and began to scrabble at the soil. It was loose in my hands. There were tears streaming down my face, my lips in a grimace. 'Don't be in there, Laura,' I said, and then I thrust my hands deeper into the dirt, throwing it back like a dog digging out a bone.

The shivering had stopped, but that didn't register. The water had got higher, so that there were only a few inches between the water and the metal. Laura's head was as far up as it would go, sucking at the little air that was left, the water cold, making her skin shrink tight against her skull. The rusty metal was rough against her nose. She couldn't feel her hands any more.

She flung her hands towards Susie, for a hand to hold, but she couldn't even feel her own hands any more. Laura pushed at Susie, but she was just a heavy bundle of wet clothes.

Laura couldn't cry. This was it. The end. Bobby left behind.

For a moment, she forgot where she was. She was floating upwards, away from the water, dry and warm, a dream of summer, soft licks of sunshine. But, when she relaxed, she was woken up with a cough as the dirty water seeped over her lips and into her throat.

She thrust her head upwards but it was met by metal, and she coughed some more, but this time she couldn't spit out the water. And more came in, a gritty silt creeping over her lips and tickling her nostrils. She tried to inhale but it made her choke as she took in more water. Her chest was starting to hurt as she strained for a breath, as her body coughed and racked, but she couldn't find the air – every deep breath just sucked in more water.

Her hands pushed against the metal, but it was futile. She tried to say goodbye. To her mother. Her father. To Bobby and to Jack. It wasn't meant to end like this. She still had living to do, but it had been stolen from her.

Laura sank back into the water, knew that the space had filled. There was nothing else to fight. She had lost. The game had ended. She smiled, let the water roar in. Her chest bucked towards the metal. This was it. She saw the light. It was above her. A growing light that spread across the water.

My hands were black with mud and I was on my knees, scraping it back, throwing it out of the hole. I was two feet down, wet, dirty. I looked back at Claude. He was watching us dig, and I thought I detected a slight smile, as if he was waiting for us to realise we were in the wrong place.

Joe was next to me, digging too, his clothes filthy.

'She's not here,' I cried out, as I clawed at the ground desperately.

'Keep going,' Joe yelled.

So I did, my hands starting to bleed, driving through the soil, water seeping through my fingers.

Then my hands hit something hard. I looked at Joe, who

had seen how my fingers had jarred, and he moved nearer to me. He burrowed quickly, uncovering a patch of metal, brown and old.

'Under here,' he said.

I closed my eyes for a moment. I hoped not. Water covered the surface and, even as Joe swept his hand over it, moving more soil, water quickly submerged it again.

'Jack, dig!' he shouted.

I started again, working across now, getting all the dirt from the metal, desperately hurling wet soil over my shoulder.

It took us a few minutes to expose it, a wide piece of iron, riveted down the middle, covered in water that bubbled around the edges.

'Lift it,' Joe said, and I threw myself to the floor, my fingers clawing at the edge of the metal. It was heavy and it was hard to get in a good position to lift it. We had to get out of the hole and lie on our stomachs, our fingers wedged under the edges. I could feel the water inside, freezing cold against my fingers. Joe counted down so that we could lift together.

It took a few seconds for it to budge, but then we managed it, both us roaring with effort as we strained, the metal sheet moving slowly upwards.

I saw her toes first, bobbing in the water as we disturbed the surface. I slid forward through a small gap to get in the hole, scrambling over the mud piled up at the side, the metal sheet above me, Joe holding it in place. My face hit the water and I almost gasped with the cold, but I wasn't going to stop.

There wasn't much room to move in there, but I found the ground and kept on pushing forward until I was squeezed in between Susie and Laura. I could hear Joe straining to hold on to the metal sheet, but I had found some inner strength, was determined to move it.

I scrambled to my knees and tried to take the weight of the metal sheet with my hands, my head out of the water now, and I shouted with exertion as I pushed upwards. My feet slipped on the floor but I wasn't going to stop, and I heaved the metal higher until it was upright, jammed into the mud. I was in water up to my knees and I could feel Laura and Susie banging against my shins, both of them lifeless.

I pushed at the metal. It stayed vertical for a few seconds, wedged into the ground, and then it started to topple, moving slowly backwards towards the wall behind, landing with a loud bang that echoed around the stone walls.

I looked down and saw Laura's face in the water next to Susie's. Laura was bobbing, her wrists bound.

I reached down, grabbed at the rope between her wrists and pulled hard.

Laura's arms came up, but she was heavy, and so I had to get my head under her wrists so that I could use my shoulders. I looked down and saw that her eyes were closed, her mouth slightly open. I started to lift her, straining, shouting, until her head emerged from the water, her hair hanging down, her skin shiny and wet, but she was a dead weight, her clothes sodden, her skin cold. I reached down and wedged my arms under hers. It felt like our last embrace, her hands behind my neck, my face next to hers as I pulled her up, her cheeks icy. I was screaming her name, terrified, and then her body cleared the water and she was in my arms.

I turned her around and put her against the mud, face down, and I held her, to say goodbye, hot, angry tears streaming down my face, through the mud and the cold water.

Then Joe grabbed Laura and pulled her away from me, so that she slithered away from the hole and onto the mud outside the shelter.

I went to her, to make sure I was with her to the end, while Joe slid into the hole to pull at Susie.

I held Laura in my arms, tears streaming down my face, my mind filled with what this would do to Bobby. I saw that Joe had pulled Susie out, and he was looking at her head, laying her down. I saw the deep gash on her temple, and how rigid and pale she looked.

But Laura wasn't like that. She was flaccid and cold, her lips blue, her skin pale.

Claude stood up and began to step backwards, away from the scene.

'Stay there!' Joe shouted.

'Ignore him,' I pleaded to Joe. 'Help me, with Laura.'

Joe looked at me, and then down at Laura.

'I don't know what to do,' I said. I felt powerless, Laura limp in my arms.

Claude moved further away, out of the shadow of the stone shelter now and heading along the river bank.

'Claude, stay there,' Joe said again.

'Leave him!' I shouted. 'Save Laura. He's not important.'

Joe faltered, wanting to go after Claude, but then he looked at Laura and he scrambled over to me. He pushed Laura onto her front and began to push hard on her back. Water spewed out of her mouth.

Claude walked away quickly. Joe threw Laura onto her back, and then pinched her nostrils as he tilted her head backwards before blowing two quick breaths into her. The kiss of life.

Laura's feet looked wrinkled and blue from the water and I held her hand as Claude scuttled along the shingle by the river, heading for his car. Laura remained lifeless, but I was jolted by Joe as he put his hand onto her chest and pressed hard, like rapid pumps. Then he went to blow more air into her mouth . . . but it felt more pointless with each passing second. We didn't know how long Laura had been submerged. I thought of Bobby again, blissfully happy at school, not knowing what was happening to his mother, or how his life would change when he came home. And what about me? What would I do now? I had lost too many people close to me. I didn't think I could take another loss.

I raised my eyes to the sky, let the raindrops hit me like pinpricks, the clouds a blanket of grey as I looked up.

I heard Claude's Mini turn over and then grumble into life. Joe shot me a glance as it was put into gear and reversed back onto the road.

Then I heard something else. A cough, like a rattle in Laura's chest. Joe heard it too, because he looked at me, his eyes wide, and then bent down again, renewing his efforts.

There was another cough, and I saw Laura's chest take a big heave as she sucked on the air.

I put my hands to my face and felt my tears soak my fingers.

Chapter Seventy-Four

I was looking out of the bedroom window, at the dark hills that surrounded our house. I had my face pressed close to the glass, trying to see past the reflections caused by the bedroom light. It was always on now. Laura couldn't sleep in the dark, not without bringing nightmares, and I wanted her to take as long as she needed to get things right again.

It had been over a month since I had pulled her out of the hole dug by Claude Gilbert, but I still did this every night, looked out of the window, checking for Claude Gilbert, wondering whether his thirst for revenge would bring a visit. He was out there somewhere, I knew that.

And it wasn't just Claude, because I had made some powerful enemies. Roach had been suspended from his duties as the police waited for DNA tests to be done in Claude's Belgravia pad. If any came back that matched Claude's DNA, then he was looking at a spell in prison for assisting an offender. But people like Roach made friends in the force, and those who didn't know the full story thought I had wrecked a good man's career. My car was stopped for a routine check whenever I went out, and so I had started to use Laura's more and more. I worried about how it would be for Laura though when she went back. She had helped to bring down one of her own.

Alan Lake's status took a dive as well, no longer the poster boy of the northern art set. He had once been a dangerous man. I wondered whether he might pay me a visit, now that he was looking at another spell in prison for perverting the course of justice – his one-time fall guy happy to come forward to clear his own name – but my guess was that he would just try and sit it out, perhaps hoping that his notoriety might improve his sales once things calmed down.

The press had gone wild though, even with Claude gone. Harry English played his part, adapting my article and syndicating it worldwide, but none of that seemed to matter any more. I hadn't written a word since Claude had vanished.

It had seemed more like relief at first, that I could spend some precious time with Laura, but then I realised something else: I didn't want to work. As Laura rested, and I insisted that she did a lot of that, I tried to start my novel again, but whenever I was in front of a keyboard, my fingers froze, unable to make the words jump onto the screen. My last story had ended with Laura spluttering for air on a wet Lancashire river bank as I sobbed into her neck, my northern reserve gone, no longer the tough guy. The paramedics had taken over. Oxygen. Blankets. A breakneck rush through the countryside to get her to hospital, but that was all a blur. I just remembered Laura's hand in mine, the twitch in her fingers telling me that she was alive, and so I gripped them hard and kissed them, just grateful for the second chance.

Laura told me to go back to work, to give it time, but I knew I didn't want to write any more. I had no stomach left for the chase, and I wanted to settle for my life.

Laura, of course, wanted to go back to work, to take the sergeant's exam, but her bosses were strict about it. Stay away. Get better. They didn't want her to get delayed shock and bear the cost of her disintegration.

But I knew Laura. There would be no disintegration. She was strong, much tougher than me, and she was going to get better for Bobby, so that the mother he had wasn't just some empty shell, but was the mother he'd always known. Fun. Loving.

I looked back at Laura. Her dark hair was splayed across the pillow, her arm draped over my side of the bed, where I should be, instead of staring out over pitch-black Lancashire hillsides.

I wanted to whisper that I loved her, but I didn't. I still held back my feelings, but I had resolved to open up more. Anyway, I wanted Laura to sleep. Someone had to, because I didn't sleep as much as I used to. Most nights were spent like this, watching Laura sleep, her breathing gentle, her face bathed in the yellow glow of the lightbulb.

I reached into my pocket and pulled out a small red box. I opened it and looked at the ring, one diamond set in platinum. I did that a lot, just looking at the ring, waiting for the right time to ask, but there never seemed to be one. I had almost lost her, and I didn't want that to happen again.

I turned back to the window, one hand cupped around my face; all I could see were the dark outlines of night, a whole world beyond my little cottage in the hills.

But I knew that somewhere out there was Claude Gilbert, the man who had killed his wife and lied about it as if it had never really mattered. The man who had run away again to leave Mike Dobson to face the court on his own, charged with murder, his confessions to Joe Kinsella cleansing his conscience but ending his life as he knew it.

More importantly, Claude had tried to kill the woman I loved and, for as long as there was still life in my body, I wanted to know where he was, just so that I could hunt him down one more time and give him a taste of the hurt he put me through.

I heard Laura move, and as I looked round, I realised that the ring box was still open. Her eyes were open, and I saw that she was looking at the box. I looked down, and then back at Laura. I didn't know what to say, feeling caught out, worried that I had spoiled a moment, but then she smiled, and I knew then that everything was going to be all right.

Read on for an exclusive extract from Neil White's new novel, to be published by AVON in 2011.

Chapter One

Rupert Barker nodded to sleep in the semi-darkness, the light coming from the glow of the coal fire, as orange flickers bounced off the Christmas decorations draped over the tree. His favourite armchair did its work, as always, high-backed leather, and he had drifted in and out of a doze for most of the afternoon.

Then he heard a noise.

He sat up quickly and looked around. The newspaper slid from his knee to the floor. He couldn't hear anything else, apart from the crackle of the fire. Perhaps it had been in his dream. Then he heard it again.

His eyes shot to the window. It sounded like someone was at the fence that ran along the garden at the back of his house, climbing over maybe, the noise like heavy feet kicking against the wooden panels, the fence the only thing that separated him from the darkness of the church yard.

He pulled himself to his feet and groaned as his knees froze for a few seconds, age catching up with him, sixty-six the following month. He shuffled towards the window, but he felt scared, exposed. He was in a room at the back of the house, the curtains open, and he knew that whoever was out there would be able to see in. When he reached the window, he pressed his face against the glass to blot out the glare from the fire and tried to see into the garden. He could see only shadows and the silhouette of the church tower, a square Norman block with the iron finger of the weather vane creaking in the breeze, a dark outline against the clear sky, the stars emerging as dots in the blanket.

He cupped his hands around his eyes. There wasn't much to the garden, just a square patch of grass surrounded by plants and trees, a bird-feeder hanging from a branch. A laurel bush in one corner took all the water from the ground, so that the grass was threadbare underneath, and some bamboos he had planted a couple of years earlier swayed in front of the fence. But there was no one there.

He stepped away from the window, told himself that it must have been a cat, or maybe kids playing in the church yard. But then he thought he saw some movement from the side of the laurel bush, something large and fast. He went to the window again. There was something there, and he shouted out when he saw it turn and rush at the glass.

Rupert stepped back, scared, and tumbled over the chair he had been sitting in. He was falling, flailing at the air, the flicker of the hearth turning sideways as he headed to the ground.

He landed heavily, searing pain coming from his wrist, but then he heard the back door open and heavy footsteps came into the house.

Rupert looked up and saw the outline of a man, tall and broad, his clothes dark, black trousers tucked into his boots and with a woollen hat hiding his hair. A hand was outstretched.

'Are you all right?' the voice said.

Rupert looked up and then shuffled quickly along the floor, moving away from the intruder until he felt his back hit the wall. 'Who are you, and why are you in my house?'

'I'm sorry, Doctor Barker, I didn't mean to scare you, but I had to come and see you,' the voice said. He sounded scared, the words coming out with a tremble. 'You're the only one who can help me.'

Rupert felt his stomach turn over. *Doctor Barker*. It was a patient, it had to be, thirty years as a child psychologist giving him a hit-list of the frightened and vulnerable across Lancashire, helping children who showed worrying signs that they were heading the wrong way.

'I can't help you,' Rupert said. 'I'm retired. Look at me. I'm just an old man now.'

The man stepped closer to Rupert, and his face came within the light of the fire. The flames danced around his features, so that his eyes seemed to glimmer menacingly. Rupert smelled stale beer and cigarettes and sweat. Then Rupert recognised something, just in the way that he tilted his head as he took in what Rupert had said.

'No, no, it's you I need,' the intruder said, his voice breaking. 'It's happening again.'

'What's happening again?' Rupert said.

'The need,' the intruder said.

'What need?'

'Don't talk like you don't know, doctor,' the intruder said, his voice breaking. 'We talked about it, you taught me how to control it, but I can't do that any more.'

Rupert closed his eyes for a moment and tried to remember where he had seen that stare before. The tilted head, the wide eyes. But the man in front of him looked nearly forty, and so it meant going back too many years.

'When does it come, this need?' Rupert said.

'All the time now,' the man said. 'Before, it would come mainly at night, when I was alone, feeling, you know, wound up, but now it's there when I wake up, like an itch, an urge.' He paused, and Rupert thought he was trying not to cry. 'It's all I think about, Doctor Barker. I want to hurt someone.'

Rupert closed his eyes for a moment.

'I follow people,' the man continued.

'What do you mean?' Rupert said, his eyes open, alarmed.

'Just that,' was the reply. 'I see someone, and I start to imagine what they would be like naked, and then I think of how they would be if I was hurting them, how scared they would be.'

'Have you hurt anyone yet?'

The man shook his head.

'You need help,' Rupert said quietly. 'It can't come from me. I'm too old now, retired, out of touch. But you must get help. Speak to your doctor. Trust them like you trusted me.'

The intruder paused, and then he said, 'You said you would be there for me, and now I need you, you're sending me away.'

'No,' Rupert said, his voice steady now, trying to keep the intruder calm. 'I'm telling you where to get help. Speak to your doctor. Please. It's for the best.' Rupert sat up. 'I don't remember you. What's your name?'

The intruder shook his head. 'I thought I mattered. I see people all the time, you see. On the street, in their homes, and I want them, and I know that I will take it. I want to stop myself, but it never ceases. All day. All night. You have to stop it, Doctor Barker.'

Rupert shook his head. 'No, *you* have to stop it,' he said. 'Don't make it my fault. You have the power now.'

The intruder took a deep breath and put his head back. Rupert closed his eyes and waited for the blow, for his life to be squeezed away, but there was nothing. He opened his eyes slowly, and he saw that he was alone again, just the orange flickers around the walls, the back door swinging open, letting the heat out from the fire.

Chapter Two

Laura McGanity looked around the scene in front of her and tried not to smile. She had earned her sergeant stripes, nine months in uniform, working in the community, but now she was back where she wanted to be, on the murder squad. And even though this was a tragedy, someone's death, she felt that familiar flutter of excitement as she took in the blue and white police tape stretched tight around the trees and the huddle of police in boiler suits holding sticks, ready for the slow crawl through the undergrowth, looking for scraps of evidence. A footprint, a dropped piece of paper, maybe a snag of cloth on the thorns and branches. This was it, the start of the investigation, the human drama yet to unfold.

She had pulled on her paper coveralls, put paper bootees over her shoes, and now her breaths were hot against her cheeks behind the face mask. But Laura knew the excitement wouldn't last long, because in a moment she would face the dead, the lifeless body lying in a small copse of trees behind the new brick of a housing estate, just visible as a flash of pink in the green. Then the tragedy would hit her, the life snuffed out, but for now, all that held her attention was fascination.

Joe Kinsella came up behind her, poised and still, his face hidden, the hood pulled over his hair. His eyes flickered a smile, soft brown, and then he said, 'C'mon, detective sergeant,' his voice muffled. 'Let's see what there is.'

Laura smiled back, invisible behind the mask. The title still felt new, but as Joe set off walking she realised that the back-patting had to go on hold for the moment.

The ground sloped down to a small ribbon of dirty brown water that ran into underground pipes that carried it under the nearby estate, birch and willow filling the scene with shadows. Ivy trailed across the floor like tripwire, but Joe strode quickly through it, the crunch underfoot in contrast to the soft rustles of Laura's suit as she trotted to catch up. Laura was grateful that it had been dry, spring starting with sunshine, or else she imagined she would have found herself skidding towards the small patch of pink by the edge of the stream.

The body had been found by teenagers looking for somewhere to do whatever teenagers get up to in the woods, and since then the area had swarmed with police and crime scene investigators, the ghoulish and idly curious hovering on the street. There was a policeman in plain clothes mingling with those craning their necks to get a view, posing as a journalist, snapping pictures of the onlookers, hoping that the killer had come back to revel at his work. That had been Joe's idea.

As Laura reached the body, she saw that her inspector was there, Karl Carson, large and bombastic, shiny bald, no eyebrows, so that his forensic hood highlighted a band of scrubbed pink and glaring blue eyes.

'Looks like we've got another one, McGanity,' he said, his eyes watching her, waiting for her opening remark.

Laura sighed. That word, *another*. It made everything harder, reduced the chances of it being a family thing, or maybe a violent boyfriend faking it as a stranger attack.

Laura watched as Joe walked closer to the body and knelt

down. She knew that he wasn't looking for forensic evidence, but for other things, those little signs, hidden clues that reveal motivation. Joe was the squad star at that. Laura was still new to the team, but she had worked with him before, and so he had eased her into the murder squad. It was good to be back doing the serious stuff. She had moved north a few years earlier, away from her detective role in the London Met, and had done the rounds of routine case mop-ups and a short spell in uniform, learning the community role to help grease the push for promotion, but this was where she felt most at home.

Laura knelt down alongside Joe, and as she looked, she saw that Karl Carson was right, that it confirmed everyone's worst fear, that the murder a month earlier wasn't a one-off. There were two now.

The victim was a young woman, Laura guessed in her early twenties, more there than the skinny hips and ribs of a teenager but with none of the sag of the later years. The body had been hidden under bark ripped from a nearby tree, and when it had been disturbed, the kids who found her had been swamped by bluebottles. Laure gritted her teeth at the smell. Even outdoors, with her nose shielded by a mask, the smells made it through. A mix of vomit and off-meat, it made the air around the body busy with flies. As she looked at the floor, she could see the shifting blanket of woodlice and maggots spilling onto the ivy leaves, disturbed by the movement of the bark, their work interrupted, of turning the corpse into mush and then bones. The body's stomach was distended by the gases brewing inside, and Laura knew that she didn't want to be around when it was rolled onto plastic sheeting to be taken from the scene, because whatever was inside her stomach was going to come spewing out of her mouth.

Laura peered closer to try and see the face, so that she could see more of the person and less of the corpse, but it was dirty and distorted, and so they wouldn't get a better idea until the post mortem clean-up later. Laura tried to be scientific and dispassionate, but she knew that the sight of a healthy young woman mutilated by a stream was something that would come back to her in quieter moments.

Laura took a deep breath, more heat through the mask, and tried to take in what she could.

The woman was naked, the clothes taken away, no sign of them torn up and thrown to one side. Just like with the other one. There were bruises on her body, grazes and scrapes that might have come from a struggle, but it wasn't those that drew her eye. It was her mouth, stretched, soil and leaves jammed in so that it looked like the dead woman had gorged herself on the ground, the cheeks puffed out. There were bruises around the neck, so Laura guessed that it was another strangulation case, just like the other girl. Laura looked down towards the woman's hips, and she didn't need to have a close examination in order to see the dirt trails and scratches where soil and leaves had been jammed in between her thighs.

It was the tears that made her angry though. The woman's face was dirty, but there were streaks, where her tears had run through the dirt as she choked on the leaves and looked up at the man who ended her life.

'What do you think?' Carson said.

Laura saw that his eyes were fixed on her, and she knew that it was a test, Carson checking whether Joe had been right to ask for her to be on the team.

She took a deep breath and had another look along the body.

'She was alive when all of that was jammed in there,' Laura said, and pointed to the woman's genitals.

468

'Why do you say that?'

'Those scratches and scrapes along the woman's legs have drawn blood,' she said, and pointed towards trails of ragged skin that had since dried brown. 'They will have been caused when he jammed the leaves and dirt up there, inside her, and so it must have happened when the woman was alive. The dead don't bleed.'

Carson gave a nod and a flick of what should have been eyebrows. 'Why is that important?'

'It makes it more likely that she was killed here rather than just dumped,' she said. 'And we might get some of his DNA from her thighs or face.'

'Provided he wasn't wearing gloves.'

Laura smiled behind her mask. 'That goes without saying.'

Carson nodded. 'What about the clothes?' he said. 'She didn't walk down here naked.'

'He's got some forensic awareness,' Laura said, 'because his DNA will be all over her, and so he took them away to stop him being identified, which makes it more likely that he wore gloves. And he's cool.'

'What do you mean?' Carson asked.

'Look around,' Laura said, and she pointed towards the houses that overlooked the scene. 'All it would take is for someone to look out of their bedroom window, or even hear the struggle, and we would be down here. An eyewitness is the best we can hope for right now, unless he's slipped up.'

'Anything else?'

Laura looked at the body, and as she felt Carson's stare bore into her, she tried to think of something she might have missed. Or maybe he was just trying to make her spout wild guesses, to use against her later. She wasn't the only woman on the team, but she still felt like she had to prove herself for spoiling the macho party, and she'd heard the little digs that she was Joe's new favourite.

Then it struck her.

'If she was alive when he was filling her with soil, it meant that she wasn't being raped when she died,' Laura said. 'If all of that was in there, he wasn't, and so if he raped her, whatever he did afterwards was just to degrade her.'

Carson titled his head and Laura saw the skin around his eyes crinkle. It looked like there was a smile there. Test passed.

Laura looked at Joe, and she saw that he was still staring intently at the corpse.

'What is it, Joe?' Carson asked.

Joe didn't respond at first, it was just his way, quiet, contemplative, but then he rose to his feet, his knees crackling, and looked down.

'This isn't going to end,' he said, his voice quiet.

'Why do you say that?' Laura said.

'Because he has attacked before, and once you start, you don't stop,' he said.

'We know he's done this before,' Carson said, his brow furrowed. 'A month ago.'

'No, even before then,' Joe said, and gestured towards the body with a nod of his head. 'The signature is so fixed. The debris and soil in the vagina, the mouth, the anus. Too much like the last one. But why does he do it? No one just chances on that, the perfect method. Signatures grow and develop. This one? It's replicated on its first repeat.'

'But we haven't got any unsolved deaths like this,' Carson said.

'Maybe they aren't deaths,' Joe said. 'We need to look for cases where the victim has fought back and won.'

Carson sighed behind his mask. 'This is sounding like a long haul,' he said, almost to himself.

Joe shot worried glances between Laura and Carson. 'We haven't got the time for that,' he said. 'We need to catch him quickly, because the gap will shorten.'

'Are you sure about that?'

Joe nodded. 'It is bound to. These murders are a month apart, but identical methods were used. He's found his style and likes it.'

'Why is all that dirt in there?' Laura asked.

Joe looked down at the body, and then he looked at Carson, and then Laura.

'I don't know,' he said slowly. 'And we might need to know the answer to that to catch whoever did this, but I do know one thing: he's going to want to do it again.'

Chapter Three

I turned away from the crime scene and put my camera away.

I had managed some shots of the white suits as they were bent over the body, and I knew one was Laura. I knew she wouldn't tell me anything. Having a reporter as her squeeze had caused her enough trouble, and so far we had been able to rebuff any suggestions that we were swapping secrets over the pillow, but it would only take one lazy article by me, where I forgot what was official and what was secret, and she would struggle to keep herself in her job.

The crowd around the police tape had grown during the morning, from the simply curious passing on their way to work to the unemployed looking for a way to fill the day. Teenagers rode in tight circles on bikes, all in black, hoods drawn around their faces in spite of the warmth, laughing and talking too loudly. Young mothers smoked and gossiped, and two men at the end were drinking from a can of Tennents, which was passed between them as they watched the police activity.

I had taken some pictures of the crowd, wondering whether it would make a *community in shock* story, and then I checked my watch. I knew that no information would be released for a few hours, and even when it was, I knew the internet would provide all the news people wanted.

I checked my phone. Another text from Harry English, my former editor at the *London Star*, where I had worked when I first tried to escape from my small Lancashire town. I hadn't lasted long, but Harry regarded me now as his northern correspondent.

As I guessed, the text was about *Night Wire*, an anonymous police blogger who had gained a public following, his posts an angry rant, much different from the weary moans of most secret bloggers. Harry wanted to unmask him, and he had this theory that Night Wire was from Lancashire. I had told him that I wasn't interested. Whoever he was, discovery could cost him his job, and I wasn't going to have that on my conscience for the sake of a sidebar story.

I put my phone back in my pocket and looked at my watch. It was time to go to court, the crime reporter's fall-back option, low-life tales of shame from the grim streets of Blackley, a weather-beaten Lancashire town built on seven hills that had once hummed with the sound of the cotton mills, the valleys shrouded in smoke and once green fields changed into grids of terraced streets. All that industry was gone now, just the shadows left, although traces of Blackley's former wealth could still be seen in the Victorian town centre, where three-storey fume-blackened shop buildings, filled with small town jewellers and century-old outfitters, compete with the glass and steel frames of everyday High Street. The wide stone steps and Roman portico of the town hall that overlooked the main shopping street carried echoes of men in long waistcoats and extravagant sideburns twirling gold watches from their pockets.

The town has changed since those times though. The Asian influx in the sixties added an ethnic buzz, when textile workers from Pakistan headed to England to do the shifts the local population wouldn't do, and so mosques and minarets were sprinkled amongst the warehouses and wharf buildings now, the call to prayer the new church bells.

The court building had survived redevelopment though, four storeys of millstone with tall windows and deep sills, decorative pillars built into the walls on the upper floors. The police station had once been next door, the way into court through a heavy metal door at the end of the cell corridor and then up the stairs, but the move to an office complex by the motorway meant the prisoners now get to court in a van and in chains. The court carried on though, dispensing justice from draughty courtrooms with bad acoustics and plaster crumbling from the walls.

The drive into town from the murder scene was pleasant though, with the wind in my hair, the roof down on my 1973 Triumph Stag in Calypso Red, my father's pride and joy, and as I walked quickly up the court steps, I had a bounce in my stride. So I didn't notice at first how quiet it was, my usual guard of honour up the court steps, of tobacco haze and glazed looks, not there, no throng of unwashed tracksuits and last night's booze. All I had was the echo of my feet as I walked into the waiting area, really just a long tiled corridor cast in yellow lighting with interview rooms to one side. Then I noticed that it was nearly deserted, just three people waiting, all of them staring into space. I glanced at the clock. Eleven thirty. It seemed too early to have cleared the morning list.

The duty solicitor room was busy, but the small square room designed for client interviews was filled with bored lawyers moaning about how they couldn't make a fortune any more.

I put my head in to ask if anyone had a case worth free publicity. There was a general shake of the head and then it went quiet. I wasn't part of the club, and so they waited for me to pull my head out again before the mutter of conversation restarted.

I sighed. A quiet court meant nothing to report. Then I heard a noise from the corridor that led from one of the back courts. It was the sound of footsteps, bold clicks on the tiles, and I guessed the owner before I saw him: David Hoyle.

Most of the lawyers in Blackley were sons of old names, the firms passed through the generations, sometimes split up and married off to other firms, but the lineage of most Blackley lawyers was based on history rather than ability. They moaned because the good lives their fathers had enjoyed had been snipped and cut back. But David Hoyle was different from the rest. He was sent to Blackley to head up the new branch of Freshwaters, a Manchester firm trying to establish a foothold away from the big city. No one had expected it, and Hoyle just arrived at court one day, in a suit with broad pinstripes and a swagger that no one seemed to think he had earned.

The other lawyers didn't like him. Client loyalty was generational in Blackley, where the children of criminals become the clients of lawyers' children, and David Hoyle upset that arrangement, because he made bold promises that made clients shift loyalties. Low level crooks, usually just people who had acquired a habit of making bad life choices, want nothing more than someone to shout on their behalf, and David Hoyle did that. The prosecution liked him even less, because he upset the give and take, where a weakness shouldn't be probed too deeply, except for those special clients, the high-rolling money spinners, because one day the favour might have to be repaid.

David Hoyle didn't play that game. He didn't care who he upset, because he accepted that losing was part of the game, except that he didn't lose that often. And he didn't work out of an office. Freshwaters had premises, but it was really just somewhere for Hoyle to park his Mercedes. He ran his files from home and visited his clients in theirs.

His client trotted behind him, a red-faced man in a grey suit, his stomach pushing out the buttons, his shoes shiny underneath the pressed hems of his trousers. He wasn't the usual court customer. Hoyle turned to smile and shake hands with his client, but from the look of regret Hoyle gave, I guessed that things hadn't gone his way.

I checked my pocket for my camera, get the picture first, the story later, because the shame sells better if there's a face a neighbour might recognise, and headed after them as they made their way to the steps outside. As I put my hand in my pocket, I felt my phone buzz against my fingers.

When I saw the number on the screen, I thought about letting it go to voicemail, but I knew that he would not give in. He had a newspaper to fill.

'Morning, Harry,' I said. 'Let me guess: Night Wire.'

I heard a chuckle and then a cough. Harry's new-found health drive was trying to repair too many years of abuse.

Harry had lived the newspaper life, with decades spent in the smoke and alehouses of Fleet Street, the deadline an excuse to go drinking. Things were different now, the news industry worked around the clock, with websites to be updated, the online adverts as important as the space in the paper the next day.

'Night Wire is still posting and winding up your people,' he said, his voice hoarse from the cough.

'They're not my people,' I said.

'They're Laura's people.'

'So that's her business.'

Harry didn't say anything for a while, and so I let the silence gather momentum, hoping that it might let the call end. But Harry had other ideas.

'You need to get back on the horse,' he said. 'Write some decent stuff.'

'I've told you,' I said. 'I'm having some time out. The court stuff pays the bills, that's all.'

'But if you take too much time away, you can never get back in. Things are changing, Jack. I haven't got long left now. I'm retiring in two months, and so once I'm gone, you've got little sway at this place. They'll take whoever feeds them the story, and you'll spend your life as a small town hack.'

'I know you, Harry,' I said. 'You're a newsdesk editor. You don't care about me. I don't do the big scoops any more, Harry, you know that.'

'What, because it got dangerous once or twice?'

I sighed and looked around. I saw the lawyers watching me from the duty solicitor room. The mention of Night Wire must have grabbed their attention.

'You know he's going to get an award, don't you, Jack?' Harry said.

'Who, Night Wire?'

'Some civil liberties group wants to laud him for speaking the truth, for giving ordinary people a voice.'

I gave a small laugh. 'Being an anonymous police blogger will make the acceptance speech tricky,' I said.

'And so you can help him out,' he said. 'Let him have his day in the spotlight.'

I sighed. I could feel that tickle of interest, and so I fought against it, tried not to think about Night Wire.

'What do you see from your window, Harry?' I said.

He grunted. 'You know what I see: Canary Wharf. Glass, metal, and egos. What's that got to do with anything?'

'Because I work from home, and all I have are hills and sky, and I'm starting to like it that way.'

'Okay Jack, I get the message. If you hear anything though, let me know.'

I smiled. 'No problems, Harry,' I said. 'Stay well,' and then I hung up.

The court corridor was silent again, just the occasional shuffle of someone's foot as they waited to go into court and the mumbles of the watching lawyers. I glanced at the security guards by the entrance, old men in crisp white shirts, security wands in their hands. They were already counting the minutes until lunch. So this was it? Jack Garrett, hotshot reporter, my career dwindling away to nothing.

I tapped my lip with my phone. Night Wire.

Then I put my phone away and went after David Hoyle. Harry was sucking me in, and I knew I wanted to fight it.

Chapter Four

Laura leaned against her car and peeled off her forensic suit. The hood had made a mess of her hair, and so she used the car wing mirror to tease it back to life and then wiped the perspiration from her eyes.

The body had been taken away, rolled onto plastic sheeting and then wrapped up in a bag, and was now heading to the lab. Now it was time for the fingertip search of the undergrowth, and she could see the cluster of police in blue boiler suits waiting to crawl their way through the small patch of woodland. Joe was looking back towards where the body had been found, his hood pulled from his head. Carson was in his car, talking into his phone.

'What is it, Joe?' Laura said, reaching into her car for her suit jacket.

He didn't answer at first, his gaze trained on where the stream headed under the estate. Then he turned round, chewing his lip.

'Something about this isn't right,' he said.

'What do you mean?' Laura said.

'The location. It doesn't make any sense. Why here?'

Laura looked around and saw the housing estate that backed onto the crime scene, a line of wooden panel fences forming the boundary on both sides.

'The seclusion?' she guessed. 'Only overlooked by the backs of the houses.'

'But it isn't secluded,' Joe said. 'One scream from her and all of those lights are going to flicker on, and what escape route is there? There is only one way to the street, because the other way is down that path, into the woods, but he couldn't get a car down there. So if he drove to the location, he would have to leave his car on the street, and so he would be blocked in and easy to catch.'

'Perhaps she was just walking past?' Laura said. 'You know, the wrong place at the wrong time, and he was hiding in there, waiting to pull someone in.'

Joe shook his head. 'Same thing applies. Too many houses. What if she fights back? If she runs or screams, there is a whole community to wake. And you saw how the body was concealed, just left on the ground and covered in leaves and bark. She was always going to be discovered.' He sighed. 'It just doesn't feel right.'

'You're giving the killer too much credit,' Laura said. 'How many people do we catch because they do dumb things?' She checked her hair in the wing mirror again, and then pulled away when the sun glinted off some grey strands, her fortieth birthday getting too close. 'So what do *you* think?'

Joe looked around and chewed on his lip. 'I just don't know,' he said.

They both turned as they heard a noise behind them, and they saw it was Carson, grunting as he climbed out of his car.

'We've got a possible name for her,' Carson said. 'Jane Roberts.'

'Don't know it,' Laura said.

'No, me neither,' Carson responded. 'But I know her father. Don Roberts.'

Laura shrugged, the name didn't mean anything to her, but she saw the look of surprise on Joe's face.

'*The* Don Roberts?' Joe said.

Carson nodded. 'It was called in two days ago, when she didn't return home at the weekend.'

'Why would he leave it so long?' Laura asked.

Joe turned to her. 'Because it involves calling us,' he said. 'Don Roberts will not want us snooping around his life. He's a drug dealer, but high up the chain. You won't see him hanging around phone boxes with dirt under his nails, and you won't find any drugs in his house, but he avoids us, because if we had the chance to scour his phone records and computers, we might find something we weren't supposed to see.'

'And he put that before his daughter?' Laura said, incredulous.

'Don Roberts is business first,' Carson said. 'What if he had invited us in and then it turned out that she'd taken off for a wild weekend with her friends? No, he wouldn't do that, but I can tell you one thing: we've got trouble now.'

'What do you mean?' Laura said.

'Because this is one of two things: turf war or bad luck. We need to look into the last murder again, see if there is any link with drugs, and if it is, we can expect the revenge killings.'

'And if it isn't a turf war?' Laura asked.

Carson almost smiled at that. 'The killer just has to hope that we catch him first, because if Roberts gets to him, he will die, but it won't be quick and it won't be pleasant.'

I skipped down the court stairs towards David Hoyle, who was straightening his tie and his hair, using the glass panel in a door as a mirror, a freshly-lit cigarette in his mouth.

'I'm too good for this place,' he said to his reflection, and then turned round and blew smoke towards me. 'Mr Journo, you're looking twitchy.'

'Has your client gone?' I said.

He took another long pull on his cigarette. 'Now, what do you want with that poor man?' he said, wagging a finger at me.

'There isn't much going on, and so I have to chase what I can,' I said.

'Didn't you have bigger ambition than that when you first started out?' he said. 'Dreams of travel, interviewing presidents, uncovering conspiracies?'

'What do you mean?'

He grinned, smoke seeping out between his teeth. 'This?' he said, and he pointed up the stairs. 'Was this your plan when you left reporting school, or wherever you people graduate from, trying to shame people for stepping on the wrong side of the line sometimes?'

'It's not like that,' I said, bristling defensively.

'So what is it like?'

'It's the freedom of the press,' I said. 'It's about letting the wider community know what is going on around them, where the threats lie. Over the years, it paints the town's history.'

Hoyle raised his eyebrows.

'And you planned this too?' I said. 'Did you always dream of giving speeches to a bench of bored greengrocers in a backwater Lancashire town? What about the big city, uncovering rough justice?'

'I can change lives,' he said, stepping closer. 'You just tell other people about the things I do, a gossip, tales over the garden fence, pandering to everyone's instinct, revelling in someone else's downfall. God help us if the world is ever as bad as the papers make out.'

'I can't believe I'm having a debate about morals with a lawyer,' I said.

He checked his watch and then winked at me. 'You're not,' he said, as he flicked his cigarette onto the pavement outside. 'You've been delayed. My client should be in his car by now, and well away from your camera lens.'

I sighed. Doesn't Hoyle ever stop playing the game?

'You need to stop wasting your time in there,' he said, pointing back up the court steps. 'Go after Night Wire.' When I looked confused, he added, 'I heard you mention him when you were on the phone before.'

'Okay,' I said, wearily. 'Let's do it your way. Why should I go after Night Wire?'

'Because he lets out too much,' he said. 'I know a lot of the rank and file love him, I've heard them talk about the blogs. I suppose he speaks their language, with his bile, his prejudices, but he's breaking the rules.'

'Why does that bother you,' I said.

'Why do you say that, because I'm a defence lawyer?' he said. 'Being a lawyer is about working within the rules.'

'No, being a lawyer is about trying to weasel your way around the rules,' I said.

He smiled at that. 'Still all about rules though,' he said. 'Night Wire is ignoring them, and he's skewing the game.' He patted me on the shoulder. 'Next time, ask my client the questions, not me, because I'll just protect my client every time,' and then he set off walking away from the court, a brown leather bag thrown over his shoulder.

I leant against the doorframe and watched him go. Night Wire again. I had two people telling me to go after better stories. And I knew they were right. I *did* need to kickstart my life again, instead of trying to get by on inquests and court stories.

485

My life as a reporter seemed like past tense though. I hadn't written anything worth reading for nearly a year now, and I softened the blow by pretending that I had taken some time out to write a book. But it felt like a lie. I had written some scenes, a searing satire on modern living, or so I thought, but I spent most days surfing the internet and rewriting scenes that didn't say much to start off with. I couldn't do it, I realised that now. Every time I went to the keyboard, my fingers hovered over the letters and waited for the stream of consciousness to transfer to the screen, but they didn't, and so I spent another aimless day wondering where the rest of my life was going to take me.

I knew what the problem was though: it had become too dangerous too often. Criminals are bad people, it comes with the job description, but reporters don't come with the protection that police or lawyers enjoy, because we are not players in the game. We're on the sidelines, observing, annoying, interfering. I had gotten sick of the risk, had been hurt a couple of times.

I laughed at myself. I knew what Harry English was doing. He was trying to tweak my curiosity, knowing that it's what drives me, why I became a reporter, because I wanted to know what was happening out there, the stories going on behind the suburban curtains.

Night Wire? What was different about him? Police bloggers were nothing new, they have been around for as long as the internet, jaded and weary cops having an anonymous rant at the system.

But Night Wire *was* different, because he screamed that little bit louder, was strident and angry, more than some weary beat bobby moaning about paperwork and protocols.

The blog was tolerated at first, like most of them, just a chance for the rank and file to vent some steam, but there was something about Night Wire that struck a chord. The police liked him, of course, because he was their voice, and some posted messages of support, but then it started to ripple outwards, into the general public, and that's when the force got twitchy. His supporters jammed the site, and the police hierarchy in Lancashire got a little angrier whenever he posted a new blog, their attempts at community relations hampered by the loose words of Night Wire. There were posters around the station, Laura had told me that, warning disciplinary action for anyone proved to be blogging police secrets, but that didn't seem to stop him.

I smiled and almost gave him a mock salute, and then I realised that I had to think of something else to do, because I was thinking of logging on, just to read the latest.

What's next?

Tell us the name of an author you love

| Neil White | Go ▶ |

and we'll find your next great book.